HISPANIC CLASSICS
Golden-Age Drama

Tirso de Molina
DAMNED FOR DESPAIR

(El condenado por desconfiado)

Edited and Translated with an Introduction & Commentary

by

Nicholas G. Round

ARIS & PHILLIPS

WARMINSTER

ISBN (cloth)   0 85668 329 9
    (iimp)   0 85668 330 2

Printed and published in England by ARIS & PHILLIPS Ltd, Teddington House Warminster, Wiltshire.

0156775
6.4.87

CONTENTS

For Gráinne

ERRATUM

p.89   3 lines of translation have been omitted.
Line 1295 onwards should read...

           Octavio enters.

Octavio   I've just met Albano
           alive and well.

Enrico   I know it.

Octavio   You, sir, gave me your word. . . *etc.*

PREFACE

In the last six decades there have appeared some fifty
editions of El condenado por desconfiado; why one more? Such
a history itself confirms that, for those who know something
of the Spanish theatre in its classic period, this is an
important play. It is also seventeenth-century Spanish
theatre at its most uncompromising: a bleak and violent
evocation of human worldliness under divine judgment. Other
readers, who begin their explorations into the comedia here,
will not be reassured so much as challenged by what they find.

It is in its capacity for challenging a readership so far
removed from its own time that the importance of El condenado
very largely consists. Its extremes of character and action
test to the limit the assumptions on which it rests, and
invite us, in our turn, to subject our own beliefs about
human nature to a parallel testing. Moreover, all this is
achieved dramatically; El condenado por desconfiado is,
before all else, a powerful fiction. If it has not achieved
the same mythic status as its companion-play El burlador de
Sevilla, that may actually be the result of its still greater
substance: intellectual substance in the intense dilemma
which it poses; human substance in its two protagonists, each
in his way as extraordinary as Don Juan himself.

The play also raises unanswered, and perhaps unanswerable
questions of a factual sort. Was its author Tirso de Molina,
who is also thought – though this too is disputed – to have
written El burlador de Sevilla? If not, who did write it?
When was it written, and with what ascertainable purposes? An
editor can do little more than sketch out the state of these
arguments, adding, for whatever it may or may not be worth, a
personal view of them. Much the more important task will be
to convince readers that, for all the apparent strangeness of
its concerns, such a play can be of concern to them. That,
when a substantial new group of readers is in question, seems
well worth doing.

The readers addressed for the first time by this
bilingual edition are English-speakers lacking Spanish, or
insufficiently secure in their command of it to tackle a text
of this sort unaided. The motive for so addressing them is the
claim which the play itself establishes to make itself heard
across the boundaries of language which, in this case as in
so many, have isolated speakers of English from a major piece

vii

of Spanish writing. I have not seen the translations made in the 1950s by Angela Martínez in the USA, and in Britain by the late John Boorman, though I have heard the latter highly praised. But it is a sadly typical footnote to that more general history of cultural limitation that neither of these has circulated at all widely. It is a matter purely of my own good fortune that the present translation should be the one to find its way into print. For that I have to thank the editors and directors of the Aris & Phillips series, and in particular Mrs Lucinda Phillips for encouraging the preparation of this book. For help with its actual production I must also thank Dr David Bickerton and his colleagues, who have generously made available the technical resources of the Glasgow University Hetherington Language Centre.

I have been heartened, too, by the generosity shown by my *Tirsista* colleagues towards a non-specialist's perhaps foolhardy venture into their field. Dr Daniel Rogers in particular unselfishly allowed me to use the text of his Pergamon Press edition as the basis for my own (for which privilege I also have to thank his publishers), and to work from his own photostat copies of the 1635 *Segunda parte*. Professor Henry Sullivan found time to discuss my drafted Introduction at length. Miss Ivy McClelland not only read the translation and commented on it kindly – she does everything kindly – but was warm in her encouragement at every stage. Dr Ann MacKenzie made the initial contact with my publishers. Dr P.J.Donnelly has offered me a great deal of shrewd and constructive discussion. My wife Ann has sustained me in this work as in everything that I undertake, and has taken a major part in preparing the book for print.

'Nobody', wrote an early twentieth-century commentator on *El condenado*'s doctrine of grace, 'is damned except by his own fault, and nobody is saved except by divine mercy'. If I have managed to do this fine play justice, it is through the help of all those I have named; if not, the blame must be mine.

Milngavie, October 1985.   NICHOLAS G. ROUND.

ABBREVIATIONS

AmH	American Hispanist.
AUA	Annales de l'Université d'Abidjan.
BC	Bulletin of the 'Comediantes'.
BH	Bulletin Hispanique.
BHS	Bulletin of Hispanic Studies.
BRAE	Boletín de la Real Academia Española.
BUSC	Boletín de la Universidad de Santiago de Compostela.
DHR	Duquesne Hispanic Review.
FMLS	Forum for Modern Language Studies.
HBalt	Hispania (Baltimore, etc).
HR	Hispanic Review.
KRQ	Kentucky Romance Quarterly.
LetD	Letras de Deusto.
MAe	Medium Aevum.
NCMH	New Cambridge Modern History.
PQ	Philological Quarterly.
RF	Romanische Forschungen.
RoN	Romance Notes.
RUNC	Revista de la Universidad Nacional de Córdoba.
RyF	Razón y Fe.
TRI	Theatre Research International.

BIBLIOGRAPHY

This is a working bibliography of the items consulted in preparing the present edition and referred to in its notes. For the overall bibliography of Tirso de Molina see items by Williamsen (1979), Placer, and Darst, listed below; for editions of El condenado por desconfiado see Reynolds (1980).

A. Editions of works by Tirso de Molina and his contemporaries:

Tirso de Molina, Cigarrales de Toledo (Madrid, 1942).
Tirso de Molina, El condenado por desconfiado, ed. G.M. Bertini (Turin 1938).
Tirso de Molina, El condenado por desconfiado, ed. D. Rogers (Oxford 1974).
Tirso de Molina, El condenado por desconfiado in Teatro español del siglo de oro, ed. B.W. Wardropper (New York, 1970).
Tirso de Molina, Historia general de la Orden de Nuestra Señora de la Merced, ed. M. Penedo (Madrid, 1973-4).
Tirso de Molina, Obras dramáticas completas, ed. B. de los Ríos (Madrid, 1946-58).
Tirso de Molina, Poesía lírica: Deleytar aprovechando, ed. Lois Vázquez (Madrid, 1981).
Tirso de Molina, Segunda parte de las comedias del Maestro Tirso de Molina recogidas por su sobrino don Francisco Lucas de Avila (Madrid, 1635).
Tirso de Molina, El vergonzoso en palacio; El condenado por desconfiado, ed. A. Prieto (Barcelona, 1982).
Luis de Góngora y Argote, Obras completas, ed. J. and I. Mille y Giménez (Madrid 1943).
Lope de Vega, La fianza satisfecha, ed. W.M. Whitby and R.R. Anderson (Cambridge, 1971).

B. Studies of 'El condenado por desconfiado', of Tirso, and of the 'comedia':

F. Abrams, 'Catalinón in the Burlador de Sevilla: is he Tirso de Molina?', HBalt, 50 (1967), 472-7.
F. Abrams, 'Una nueva teoría sobre el origen del seudónimo Tirso de Molina', DHR, 6 (1967), 21-9.
C.V. Aubrun, 'La comedia doctrinale et ses histoires de brigands: El condenado por desconfiado', BH, 59 (1957), 137-51.

xi

C.V. Aubrun, La comédie espagnole 1600–1680
(Paris, 1966).

G.M. Bertini, see above, Tirso de Molina, El condenado
por desconfiado (Turin 1938).

C. Bruerton, review of I.L. McClelland, Tirso de Molina,
HR, 17 (1949), 343–7.

A. Cioranescu, 'La biographie de Tirso de Molina: points
de repère et points de vue', BH, 64 (1962), 178–84.

E. Cotarelo y Mori, 'Tirso de Molina: investigaciones
bio-bibliográficas (Madrid, 1893).

D.H. Darst, 'Bibliografía general de Tirso de Molina,
1975–1980', Estudios, 38 (1982), 63–74.

M. Delgado, 'El condenado por desconfiado como tragedia'
in Homenaje a Tirso (Madrid 1981), 425–32.

J.M. Delgado Varela, 'Psicología y teología de la
conversión en Tirso' in Tirso de Molina. Ensayos (Madrid,
1949), 341–77.

D. Devoto, 'La materia tradicional en Don Juan Manuel.
II: Don Juan Manuel y El condenado por desconfiado', BH, 68
(1966), 195–202.

D. Dougherty, 'El legado vanguardista de Tirso de
Molina', in V jornadas de teatro clásico español (Almagro,
1982), II, 11–28.

M.A. Ferreyra Liendo, 'El condenado por desconfiado de
Tirso de Molina: Análisis teológico y literario del drama',
RUNC, 10 (1969), 923–46.

M.L. Freund, 'Una nota a la interpretación de La fianza
satisfecha de Lope de Vega, Hispanófila, 25 (1965), 17–19.

E. Gijón Zapata, El humor en Tirso de Molina
(Madrid, 1959).

E. Glaser, 'Pugnare necesse est: a Beast Simile a lo
divino in La ninfa del cielo' in Homenaje a William L. Fichter
(Madrid, 1971), 241–8.

A. González Palencia, 'Quevedo, Tirso, y las comedias
ante la Junta de Reformación', BRAE, 25 (1946), 43–84.

Homenaje a Guillermo Guastavino (Madrid, 1974).

Homenaje a Tirso (Madrid, 1981).

R.M. de Hornedo, 'La tesis escolástico-teológico de El
condenado por desconfiado', RyF, 138 (1948), 633–46.

C.A. Jones, 'Tirso de Molina and Country Life', PQ, 51
(1972), 197–204.

H.G. Jones, 'Una posible fuente para El burlador de
Sevilla y El condenado por desconfiado', Estudios, 32 (1976),
89–96.

R.L. Kennedy, 'Attacks on Lope and his Theater' in

Hispanic Studies in Honor of Nicholson B. Adams (Chapel Hill, 1966), 57-76.

  R.L. Kennedy, 'Did Tirso Send to Press a Primera parte of Madrid (1626) which Contained El condenado por desconfiado?', HR, 41 (1973), 261-74.

  R.L. Kennedy, 'El condenado por desconfiado: its Ambient and its Date of Composition' in Homenaje a Guillermo Guastavino (Madrid, 1974), 213-52.

  R.L. Kennedy,'El condenado por desconfiado: Various Reasons for Questioning its Authenticity in Tirso's Theatre', KRQ, 23 (1976), 129-48.

  R.L. Kennedy, 'El condenado por desconfiado: Yet Further Reasons for Questioning its Authenticity in Tirso's Theatre', KRQ, 23 (1976), 335-56.

  R.L. Kennedy, Studies in Tirso, I: The Dramatist and his Competitors, 1620-26 (Chapel Hill, 1974).

  J. Konan, 'L'aspect divin ou surnaturel du Condenado por desconfiado', AUA, 7 (1974), 151-67.

  J. Konan, 'La foi comme phénomène psychologique dans El condenado por desconfiado', AUA, 7 (1974), 141-7.

  A.D. Kossoff and J. Amor y Vázquez, eds, Homenaje a William L. Fichter (Madrid, 1971).

  F. Lázaro Carreter, 'Cristo, pastor robado (las escenas sacras de La buena guarda)' in Homenaje a William L. Fichter (Madrid, 1971), 413-27.

  I.L. McClelland, Tirso de Molina: Studies in Dramatic Realism (Liverpool, 1948).

  G. Mancini, 'Caratteri e problemi del teatro di Tirso' in Studi Tirsiani (Milan, 1958), 11-89.

  B. Marcos, 'Motivaciones de la actitud condenatoria y salvífica en sendos dramas de Tirso de Molina y Calderón de la Barca', LetD, 15 (1978), 5-43.

  A. Marni, 'Did Tirso Employ Counterpassion in his Burlador de Sevilla?', HR, 20 (1962), 123-33.

  S. Maurel. 'La risa y su efecto de distanciamiento en El condenado por desconfiado' in Homenaje a Tirso (Madrid, 1981), 433-8.

  S. Maurel, L'univers dramatique de Tirso de Molina (Poitiers, 1971).

  T.E. May, 'El condenado por desconfiado', BHS, 35 (1958), 138-56.

  M. Menéndez Pelayo, 'Tirso de Molina: investigaciones biográficas y bibliográficas' in Estudios y discursos de crítica histórica y literaria, III (Santander, 1941), 47-81. Originally 1893.

R. Menéndez Pidal, 'El condenado por desconfiado de Tirso de Molina' in Estudios literarios (Buenos Aires, 1948). Originally 1906.

J.C.J. Metford, 'The Enemies of the Theatre in the Golden Age', BHS, 28 (1951), 76-92.

J.C.J. Metford, 'Tirso de Molina and the Conde-Duque de Olivares', BHS, 36 (1959), 15-27.

D. Moir, 'The Classical Tradition in Spanish Dramatic Theory and Practice in the Seventeenth Century' in Classical Drama and its Influence: Essays Presented to H.D.F. Kitto, ed. M.J. Anderson (London, 1965).

D. Moir (with E.M. Wilson), A Literary History of Spain: The Golden Age: Drama 1492-1700 (London, 1971).

J. Moll, 'El problema bibliográfico de la Primera parte de comedias de Tirso de Molina' in Homenaje a Guillermo Guastavino (Madrid, 1974), 85-94.

A. Nogué, L'oeuvre en prose de Tirso de Molina (Paris, 1962).

R.J. Oakley, 'Time and Space in El condenado por desconfiado', FMLS, 21 (1985), 257-72.

M. Ortúzar, 'El condenado por desconfiado depende teológicamente de Zumel' in Tirso de Molina. Ensayos (Madrid, 1949), 321-6.

A.A. Parker, The Approach to the Spanish Drama of the Golden Age (London, 1957).

A.A. Parker, 'The Devil in the Drama of Calderón' in Critical Essays on the Theatre of Calderón, ed. B.W. Wardropper (New York, 1965), 3-23.

A.A. Parker, 'Santos y bandoleros en el teatro español del siglo de oro', Arbor, 13 (1949), 395-416.

A.K.G. Paterson, 'Tirso de Molina: Two Bibliographical Studies', HR, 35 (1967), 43-68.

M. Penedo, see above, Tirso de Molina, Historia de la Orden (Madrid, 1973-4).

C.A. Pérez, 'Verosimilitud psicológica de El condenado por desconfiado', Hispanófila, 27 (1966), 1-21.

G. Placer, 'Bibliografía de Fray Gabriel Téllez (Tirso de Molina)' in Homenaje a Tirso (Madrid, 1981), 623-731.

A. Prieto, see above, Tirso de Molina, El vergonzoso...; El condenado... (Barcelona, 1982).

J.J. Reynolds, 'An Anecdote in El condenado por desconfiado', BC, 8, 1 (1956), 13-14.

J.J. Reynolds, '"Como un padre": a Note on El condenado por desconfiado', RoN, 16 (1975), 505-8.

J.J. Reynolds, 'El condenado por desconfiado. Tres

siglos y media de ediciones' in Homenaje a Tirso (Madrid, 1981), 733-52.

B. de los Ríos, see Tirso de Molina, Obras dramáticas (Madrid, 1946-58).

D. Rogers, Tirso de Molina: El burlador de Sevilla (London, 1977).

D. Rogers, see Tirso de Molina, El condenado por desconfiado (Oxford, 1974).

D. Rogers, 'El manuscrito de El condenado por desconfiado de la Biblioteca Municipal de Madrid' in Homenaje a William L. Fichter (Madrid, 1971), 659-71.

F. Sánchez Escribano and A.Porqueras Mayo, Preceptiva dramática española (Madrid, 1972).

N.D. Shergold, A History of the Spanish Stage from Medieval Times until the End of the Seventeenth Century (Oxford, 1967).

Studi Tirsiani (Milan, 1958).

H.T. Sturcken, 'El condenado por desconfiado: a Literary Debate in Retrospect', Symposium, 12 (1958), 189-95.

H.W. Sullivan, Tirso de Molina, and the Drama of the Counter-Reformation (Amsterdam, 1976).

H.W. Sullivan, 'Tirso de Molina, the Arias Dávila Family and other Curiosities', BC, 28 (1976), 1-11.

Tirso de Molina, Ensayos sobre la biografía y la obra del Padre Maestro Fray Gabriel Téllez (Madrid, 1949).

E. Tourón del Pie, 'Aproximación a las fuentes e interpretación de El condenado por desconfiado' in Homenaje a Tirso (Madrid, 1981), 407-24.

B. Varela Jácome,'Antecedentes medievales de El condenado por desconfiado', BUSC, 61-2 (1953-4), 127-42.

J.E. Varey,'La campagne dans le théâtre espagnol au XVII siècle' in Dramaturgie et société. Rapports entre l'oeuvre théâtrale, son interprétation et son publique aux XVI et XVII siècles, ed. J. Jacquot (Paris, 1968).

J.E. Varey, 'Social criticism in El burlador de Sevilla', TRI, New series, 2 (1977), 197-221.

J.E. Varey, 'The Staging of Night Scenes in the comedia', AmH, 2, 15 (1977), 14-16.

Lois Vázquez, see Tirso de Molina, Poesía lírica (Madrid, 1981).

Luis Vázquez, 'Gabriel Téllez nació en 1579', in Homenaje a Tirso (Madrid, 1981), 19-36.

K. Vossler, Lecciones sobre Tirso de Molina (Madrid, 1965). Originally 1938.

G.E. Wade, 'Tirso de Molina', HBalt, 32 (1949), 131-40.

B.W. Wardropper, ed., Teatro español del siglo de oro (New York, 1970).

B.W. Wardropper, 'The Implicit Craft of the Spanish Comedia' in Studies in Spanish Literature of the Golden Age presented to Edward M. Wilson, ed. R.O. Jones (London, 1973).

W.M. Whitby and R.R. Anderson, see Lope de Vega, La fianza satisfecha (Cambridge, 1971).

V.G. Williamsen and W. Poesse, An Annotated, Analytical Bibliography of Tirso de Molina Studies 1627-1977 (London, 1979).

V.G. Williamsen, 'Some Odd quintillas and a Question of Authenticity in Tirso's Theatre', RF, 82 (1970), 488-513.

M. Wilson, Spanish Drama of the Golden Age (Oxford, 1969).

M. Wilson, Tirso de Molina (New York, 1977).

F. Zamora Lucas, 'Elogios literarios, dedicatorias y aprobaciones de libros de Tirso de Molina y de sus amigos y admiradores' in Homenaje a Guillermo Guastavino (Madrid, 1974), 375-401.

C. Other works consulted:

G. Bleiberg, Diccionario de historia de España (Madrid, 1979).

F. Braudel, The Mediterranean and the Mediterranean World in the Age of Philip II (London, 1972-3).

J. Caro Baroja, Las formas complejas de la vida religiosa. Religión, sociedad y carácter en la España de los siglos XVI y XVII (Madrid, 1978).

J. Corominas, Breve diccionario etimológico de la lengua castellana (Madrid, 1961).

G. Correas, Vocabulario de refranes y frases proverbiales (1627), ed. L. Combet (Bordeaux, 1967)

R.T. Davies, Medieval English Lyrics (London, 1963).

S. Mary Clemente Davlin, O.P., 'Kynde knowyng as a Middle English Equivalent for "Wisdom" in Piers Plowman B', MAe, 50 (1981), 5-17.

A. Durán, ed., Romancero general (Madrid, 1849-51).

J.H. Elliott, The Revolt of the Catalans (Cambridge, 1963).

E.G. Friedman, Spanish Captives in North Africa in the Early Modern Age (Madison, 1983).

J. Lynch, Spain Under the Habsburgs, vol.II, Spain and America, 1598-1700 (Oxford, 1969).

New Cambridge Modern History, vol. IV, The Decline of

<u>Spain and the Thirty Years War. 1609-48/59</u> (Cambridge, 1971).

    G. Parker, <u>The Army of Flanders and the Spanish Road</u> (Cambridge, 1972).

    E. Partridge, <u>A Dictionary of Slang and Unconventional English</u>, 8th.edn, ed. P. Beale (London, 1984).

    D.H. Pennington, <u>Seventeenth-Century Europe</u> (London, 1970).

    R. Stradling, <u>Europe and the Decline of Spain</u> (London, 1981).

    F. Yates, <u>The Art of Memory</u> (London, 1966).

New portrait of Tirso de Molina by Anthony Stones.

INTRODUCTION

I

El condenado por desconfiado and its author

It is a matter of some significance for any attempt at an understanding of the seventeenth-century Spanish theatre that each of its three greatest exponents ended his days in holy orders. Lope de Vega and Calderón both entered the priesthood in their early fifties, though both continued to write secular plays long after this. Tirso de Molina was a Mercedarian friar for the whole of his adult life. This common factor reminds us of the everyday interpenetration of secular and religious concerns which was so much a fact of Spanish – as indeed of European - life in that period. But there is also an instructive contrast between Tirso and the other two. It helps to account for an approach to religious themes in Tirso's comedia which is markedly different from theirs. The difference is not a matter of sincerity; all three were Catholic believers, writing for a public which shared those beliefs and expected them to be given expression. They also expected – and this is of particular relevance for a play like El condenado por desconfiado – that any attempt to explore human experience at a certain level of seriousness would find its natural expression in religious terms. What marks Tirso off from the others is the distinctive experience of religious commitment on which that expression draws.

Lope de Vega, despite the notorious chaos of his private life, shared with his audiences a fervent popular piety, as he shared so much else that was theirs, by a kind of instant empathy. There was nothing naive about this; Lope was a man of sharp and well-informed intellect. But first and foremost he was a professional entertainer for whom theatrical ripeness was all. In the presentation of religious themes on stage this meant plangent poetry and striking action, miraculous incident and straightforward doctrine. All these are to be found, for example, in La fianza satisfecha, whose criminal hero, saved at the last, has features in common with both Enrico and Paulo here.[1] But he lacks the depth of either; still less does Lope convey that sense of dizzying paradox

which comes from the presence of both their problematic
destinies within the one play. Lope sought no such effects;
it was not his business to make sacred subjects difficult,
either for himself or for other people. By contrast, the
Jesuit-educated Calderón knew his religion by the book and
wrote accordingly. His version of Catholicism, though no
less thoroughly or sincerely adhered to, communicates itself
as a prescriptive, propositional, intellectual construction.
His rational understanding of his themes, and his powerful
poetic imagination worked together to demonstrate a close and
necessary integration between the providence of God, the
harmony of nature, and the order of society as he knew it.
It would be very unfair to paraphrase the characteristic line
of argument in Calderón as 'This is what God does, and I
think he's right because it's what the king does, and anyway
St Thomas Aquinas says so'. But it would not be so unfair as
to be unrecognizable. Only when he invents a dramatic dilemma
which all his scholastic reasoning cannot quite resolve does
he avoid this type of model altogether.

Lope's immersion in the more theatrically viable elements
of his religion stands in evident contrast to Calderón's
fascination with its possibilities as a total intellectual
system. Yet both seem recognizably the responses of men
initially aware of the religious dimension as something apart
from the immediate business of their lives. Tirso de Molina
is different again. As Brother Gabriel Téllez he had lived
his religion more directly and more continuously than either
of his great contemporaries was able to do. That alone, of
course, was no guarantee that he would be able to think about
it more intelligently, or to write about it better. But it
did make it likely that he would write about Christian themes
in a rather different perspective. So it turns out - notably
in El condenado por desconfiado. There religion is made
present, not primarily as Lopean folk-belief nor yet as
Calderonian intellectual theory (though elements akin to both
are used in the drama), but as lived experience. What
happens to Paulo and to Enrico is, above all, spiritual
biography. And this has a perhaps unexpected consequence. A
twentieth-century audience may well find itself at some
remove from that common ground on religious matters which
Lope and his public shared, or from the conceptual framework
which Calderón's theology could take for granted. Not all of
us now hold these beliefs, and many who do will hold them in
rather different ways. As a result, some quite complex
adjustments of perspective are in order before we can relate

to Lope's or to Calderón's writing on religious themes. By contrast, we can still meet the anxieties of Paulo and the aggression of Enrico in the place where they are represented as happening first - on the shifting, yet still recognizable ground of the human self.[2]Paradoxically, it is the most unworldly and remote of seventeenth-century Spain's three great playwrights, Brother Gabriel the friar, who addresses himself most directly to us in our world. Nowhere does he do so more effectively than in this play.

There is, even so, some controversy as to whether Brother Gabriel, under his habitual pseudonym of Tirso, really was the author of this piece. A good deal of mystification surrounds the volume in which it first appears, the Second Part of Tirso's Comedias, published in Madrid in 1635.[3]Its title-page declares that the texts have been collected by the playwright's nephew, Don Francisco Lucas de Avila, a young man of whom nothing else is known, and who may well be merely a second pseudonym for Brother Gabriel himself. The author's own dedication, to the guild of booksellers in Madrid, disowns authorship of the greater part of the volume:

I dedicate, of these twelve plays, four which are
mine in my own name, and in the name of those who
own the others, eight (for, by I know not what
misfortune of theirs, being the offspring of such
eminent parents, they have laid them at my door)
which remain...

What he nowhere does, however is to name the four plays acknowledged as his own. This may be because the entire statement is an oblique attack on adaptors or plagiarists or both. Tirso may, in fact, be the author of considerably more of the volume than he admits. Indeed, it seems a thoroughly unsatisfactory nephew who can identify his uncle's work with only a one-in-three chance of accuracy, and the problem is merely compounded should Francisco Lucas turn out to be Tirso himself in disguise. Yet some of the plays in the Segunda parte have been identified beyond doubt as non-Tirsian. There is no way of knowing whether, or to what extent, Tirso is here telling the truth, much less whether El condenado ought, on this evidence, to rank among the rejected plays. It has been shown, however, that its versification is not typical of Tirso's normal output.[4]Only in the very general sense that it is not, as poetry, particularly impressive except at high dramatic moments, can the poetry of this play be assimilated

xxi

to the rest of his work. There has been an attempt to prove that El condenado por desconfiado had figured at some stage in the actual or projected contents of Tirso's Primera parte, but was omitted when that volume finally appeared, after many delays, in 1627.[5]But even this would provide at best a conjectural proof of authorship. On balance, then, the weight of the bibliographical and technical evidence falls rather against Tirso's authorship than for it. Yet the weight of the literary and critical arguments must be heavily on his side.[6]The play seems unmistakably a product of the same mind which conceived El burlador de Sevilla. There is even a thematic connection: the Don Juan of the latter play is, in a sense, el condenado por confiado – damned for exactly the opposite fault to Paulo. If Tirso is not the author, then we have another great seventeenth-century dramatist on our hands, of comparable and closely-related genius, yet entirely anonymous. If he is the author, then we have to accept that, for a work that is in other respects sui generis, he adopted an untypical pattern of versification, and that at a later date he made a minor editorial mystery of this play among others. It is the second of these alternatives which seems to strain credulity less.

It by no means disposes of those other extrinsic problems which attach to El condenado, much less those which relate to Tirso de Molina himself. The career of Brother Gabriel Téllez bristles with enigmas at every point. The first such mystery concerns his birth.[7] His age when he died in 1648 is recorded on a portrait which once hung in the provincial friary where several of his last years were spent; it implies that he was born in 1571. The same inscription, however, states that the date was 1572. Other documentary evidence conflicts with this. In 1616 he and a party of other friars took ship for Santo Domingo. Their official passport survives; it lists Fray Gabriel Téllez as being thirty-three years of age (and having a black beard). The effect is to focus attention on 1583. But a statement made by Tirso himself in January 1638 gives his age as fifty-seven, implying that he was born in 1580 or 1581.

We know, both on the evidence of the portrait and on that of his writings, that his birthplace was Madrid, and Gabriel – always assuming that he did not adopt it when he became a friar – is not the commonest of Christian names. Evidence from baptismal registers, however, only multiplies the contradictions. On the tenuous authority of a heavily-erased marginal note, 'Gabriel, son of Gracia Juliana and of an unknown father', registered in the Madrid parish of San Ginés in 1584, has been identified as a son of the Duke of Osuna, head of the aristocratic Téllez Girón family, and as the future Tirso de Molina. At that time, however, and for two years previously, this great personage was living in Naples, where he was Viceroy. It does not seem likely that Gracia Juliana's bastard can have been his son, or our playwright. A better case can be made for identifying Tirso with the 'Grabiel Josepe', son of Andrés López and Juana Téllez, whose birth was registered in San Sebastián parish in March 1579. This would fit several of the known facts - though not, as it happens, any of the datings cited above. Even so, it seems sensible to think of Tirso as being born within a year or so of 1580, and to abandon the notion - so dear to his biographer and editor Doña Blanca de los Ríos - that he might have been the unacknowledged by-blow of a great noble lineage.

Yet there is something about Tirso - it is perhaps the justification for dwelling on so peripheral a matter - which strongly suggests that, in some indefinable way, he did not entirely fit the accepted categories of his world. His cast of mind seems unexpectedly, not to say tactlessly, vigorous and robust. He did not suffer fools gladly, nor did he run for cover in time of controversy. Nobody who habitually did either of these things, it might be added, was likely to have written El condenado por desconfiado. Fray Gabriel, moreover, regarded himself as being somehow hard done by; he tells us that he had a sister, 'his equal in talent and in misfortune'. He does not specify what their shared or several misfortunes were. It is possible that bastardy might have been one of them. Many of Tirso's plays are about natural sons who make good in the end, but so are a great many plays by other authors. About the circumstances of his birth we still know nothing at all for certain.[8]

We do know that he entered the Order of Friars of Nuestra Señora de la Merced in 1600, and made his full vows a year later.[9] The Mercedarian Order had been founded in the early thirteenth century under the auspices of King Jaime I of Aragon; it may be relevant to Gabriel Téllez's choice of Order that he appears to have had some family connection with Catalonia. The Order had a practical purpose: to raise money with which to ransom Christian prisoners out of the hands of the Moslems. By 1600 there were no Moslems left in the Iberian Peninsula, but there were plenty of pirates along the Barbary coast, and the work of ransom still occupied the Mercedarians. They had, however, also developed a strong intellectual tradition as a teaching Order. It is clear from Tirso's writings that he was a man of wide culture, and if, as seems most likely, he had joined the Mercedarians before he was twenty, he must have acquired much of it from them. Certainly he spent some of the following decade in the University cities of Salamanca and Alcalá de Henares. We know, too, that he spent a tour of duty in Santo Domingo from 1616 to 1618 as a teacher of theology. It appears to have been well before that journey that he first began, while he was living in the Mercedarian house at Toledo, to write for the theatre.

No doubt a diversion at first, and the source of a purely local celebrity, his dramatic output as 'Tirso de Molina' soon came to be more than a sideline, as his plays began to attract attention in Madrid. By 1621 he could claim to be the author of some three hundred pieces. The claim may well be a gross exaggeration; even so, the fact that it could be made at all suggests at least a respectable output. In 1621 too he came to reside permanently in the capital, marking his début there by sending to press his critical miscellany, Cigarrales de Toledo.[10]Cigarrales were the country retreats on the far side of the Tagus, to which the Toledan aristocracy used to retire for relaxation and entertainment. In such a setting, Brother Gabriel offers both a sample of his own work - the fine comedy of love and intrigue, El vergonzoso en palacio was first printed as part of Cigarrales - and a critical defence of the kind of dramatic writing which he favours. He also provides a self-portrait, under his chosen pseudonym, projecting himself as a simple, but still highly literary 'shepherd of the River Manzanares'. It is very much the image which the name Tirso de Molina would lead us to expect. Tirso was the Spanish word for the thyrsus - the ceremonial staff carried by the votaries of Bacchus. It was exotic and classical, and perhaps a shade risqué; Molina as a surname was homely and Castilian. A similar mixture of qualities can be observed in the rustic clowns named 'Tirso' or 'Tarso' who appear with some frequency in his plays, and often turn out not to be such fools as they look. There is in all this a pattern of interlocking ironies, strongly characteristic of our author: the highly educated friar assumes the role of a country bumpkin, but the bumpkin is wittier than his supposed betters, and the friar has a far shrewder knowledge of the world than some of the worldly-wise. To compound the irony yet further, the title-pages of the plays often style their author 'El Maestro Tirso de Molina'. If anyone was entitled to the academic dignity of 'Master', it was the learned Mercedarian, Friar Gabriel Téllez, not the rustic Tirso; yet might not the latter claim to be a master in the craft that concerned him most? Certainly over the next four years Brother Gabriel, under his by now wholly transparent assumed name, was a figure to be reckoned with at the heart of the Spanish literary world.

That world was even then at the height of one of its most tumultuously creative periods. The story is inseparable from the politics of the time: seventeenth-century Madrid was _la villa y corte_ - cultural capital and king's residence.[11]In that same year of 1621 there was a change of king. Philip III, the son of the Philip who had sent out the great Armada, died in his middle age at the end of March. He had not been a king on the pattern of his mighty father. An amiable, lazy, transparently decent man, he had left most of the business of government to his chief minister the Duke of Lerma. The Lerma regime had one sensible thing at least to its credit - in 1609 it had made peace for twelve years with the Dutch. But Spain had let that relief from the running sore of a long, quasi-colonial war slip away, with no other significant action to remedy the state of her decaying economy and institutions. A reforming Cortes (the assembly of the estates of the realm) was finally summoned in 1617; one of the first things to happen after that was that Lerna fell from favour. But the Cortes, though it sat for three years, never carried its projects for reform past the stage of pure theory, and Philip died as he had lived, a pleasant, ineffectual king. Yet, however damaging this inertia might prove in the longer term, one could, in the shorter, live under many worse styles of monarchy. Tirso, for one, recalled him kindly:

> ... a king
> whose preternatural meekness
> enables Spain to enjoy
> her wealth, her peace, her laws
> free from all shocks, all fears.

Spain in the old king's reign, he went on, had been a land flowing with milk and honey. It had not, of course; the praise is overdone. But Tirso was under no obligation, the man once dead, to praise him at all unless he had wanted to. Certainly, by comparison with the beloved Philip III, more strenuous times were on their way with his successor. Philip IV, a boy of sixteen, was already under the sway of the man who was to be the real ruler of Spain for the next two decades - Gaspar de Guzmán, soon to be known as the Count-Duke of Olivares.

Olivares' government was characterized by a commitment to action both at home and abroad.[12]The truce with the Dutch was wound up, though its renewal was within Spain's grasp. An extravagant diplomatic initiative was launched to outflank the French by getting the young Prince Charles of England married to a Spanish princess. The project came to nothing, but the festivities for the prince's visit to Madrid in 1623 were particularly splendid. Olivares also adopted a boldly aggressive policy against French interests in Italy, which led to war there in 1625. All these great undertakings cost money, and to secure a reliable flow of money meant reforms at home. But it was not Olivares' way to seek such changes through the established and leisurely channels of the Cortes and the official Councils of State. Instead, he preferred to set up his own ad hoc committees, directly empowered to take executive decisions, and a Reforms Committee, the Junta de Reformación duly made its appearance. As for the young king, Olivares encouraged him to do what many, perhaps most boys of sixteen would do, on suddenly finding themselves invested with supreme power and apparently limitless wealth. In sharp contrast to the flow of demands for austerity issuing from the Junta de Reformación, in yet more marked contrast to the pious seemliness of his late father's domesticity, Philip IV flung himself into a life of pleasure as a free-spending patron of the arts and lover of women. For the latter aspect, Brother Gabriel Téllez could scarcely be expected to feel much sympathy; his plays offer plenty of examples of very young rulers who, influenced by ruthless favourites, give themselves over to private pleasure, betraying the prudence of their parents. But the new king's enthusiasm for the arts was a different matter. Every poet, every playwright in the country saw his opportunity there. The great Lope, not long priested, but still hale, productive, and unreliable as ever; Calderón, at this stage a clever, quarrelsome young aristocrat rather than the Catholic sage of later years; the sharp, sardonic Mexican, Ruiz de Alarcón; Luis de Góngora, the Andalusian canon, with his extraordinary new style in verse, as wrought and complex as Latin itself; the ever-formidable Quevedo; these and dozens more, less well-known, were all in Madrid in these years, and all active. It was a notable company in which Tirso had to hold his own.

Doing so was rendered somewhat more difficult by the fact

that his relations with Olivares were never of the best. The new royal favourite had well-defined literary preferences: for fellow-Andalusians like Góngora; for courtier-poets like Antonio Hurtado de Mendoza, to whom Tirso for some reason took a particular dislike; for anyone who would flatter him, which Tirso was unwilling to do. Apart from such political hazards, life for a Madrid playwright in those days was further complicated by a number of purely literary quarrels. Some of these involved rival poetic schools. On the one hand, for example, there was Góngora, whose marvellously inventive verse might be seen either as the growing-point of a new kind of poetry or as an artistic blind alley, but was, in either case, just the opposite of the public poetry of the popular comedia. At the other extreme were the flimsy improvisations of the poetas repentinos - palace poets like Mendoza, who could turn a neat verse as part of their art of conversation. Tirso's treatment of Celia's poem-factory in Act I of El condenado por desconfiado (ll. 399–402; 460–77) shows clearly enough what he thought of that sort of thing.

Other controversies were more directly concerned with the drama itself.[13]Literary theorists who knew their Aristotle were well aware that the comedia as practised by Lope de Vega broke all the rules; Lope himself had compounded the offence by cheerfully admitting that this was quite deliberate. Such critics saw the popular theatre as a vulgar genre, and one which failed to observe the proper disciplines. These charges ceased to be merely academic and became actively dangerous when, as occasionally happened, they coincided with demands from other quarters for social and moral reformation. A well-regarded line of thinking in official circles, for example, ran as follows: if people spent less time at plays and more time at work, they would produce more goods; if they produced more goods, prices would go down; if prices went down, more people would be put out of work, and the king would have more men to fight in his armies, which would be a great benefit to the state. Aristotelian objections to the most successful examples of the comedia chimed alarmingly well with this early specimen of a style of economic thinking still not quite extinct today. They could combine even more threateningly with the voices of extreme puritanical moralists - many of them clerics and popular preachers. Such people, sometimes referred to by Tirso as 'the Catos', regarded Lope as a lobo - a wolf, preying on the innocent public; they denounced the theatre as a school of the most lamentable vice. Nor were these marginal voices; they carried real

weight and authority in the Madrid of the 1620s. When Tirso
arrived in the capital – an established dramatist in the
popular manner, who was also a member of the regular clergy,
a trained theologian, and well-informed about Aristotle into
the bargain – Lope, who had been somewhat beleaguered of
late, must have thought the news too good to be true.

For the new arrival, whether or not, as seems to be just
possible, they had met already in Toledo, was wholeheartedly
on Lope's side.[14]His praise of Lope, and his admiration for
Lope's way of writing comedias found expression in Cigarrales
de Toledo, and in his own dramatic output. Lope, for the
moment, responded in kind, dedicating one of his plays, Lo
fingido verdadero to the younger writer 'in gratitude for the
lesson he teaches us all'. Was it a sign that he was also a
little irked by Tirso's successes and wished to set a frontier
to them that he should have singled out the Mercedarian's
works on religious themes for particularly fulsome praise?
With Lope such things are hard to tell. Certainly he was
also busy at this time making himself agreeable to Olivares
and his circle, in ways which Tirso was unlikely to approve.
And when, a few years later, Tirso found himself in trouble,
he does seem to have regarded Lope as one of the 'envious'
who were to blame for it. Their later relations were correct
but wary; compliments were exchanged, but no longer with the
old warmth, and Tirso conspicuously failed to write anything
for the memorial miscellany published after Lope's death.

If Lope in fact sought to distance himself from this most
brilliant but most idiosyncratic of his literary disciples,
one reason may have been that he sensed the enigmatic nature
of Tirso's literary commitment. For it is often not at all
easy to grasp what Tirso is driving at; his drama persistently
throws out hints of unexpected depths and subtleties, going
far beyond the well-tried Lopean formulae. Much of Tirso's
work, it is true, consists of hastily-written pieces, light
comedies of love and social folly, flimsily held together by
ingenious plotting, wild farce, and occasional low buffoonery.
The classic example – though it happens to date from before
Tirso's Madrid period[15]– is Don Gil de las calzas verdes,
in whose climactic scene four characters (one of them female)
parade across the stage, all wearing green breeches, and all
pretending, for various complex reasons, to be a wholly
non-existent young man called Don Gil. Yet even in plays
like this there may be something more going on than meets the
eye. One feels that Tirso is, at some level, satirizing
those same public expectations which he purports to fulfil

- trying, perhaps, to see how absurd he can make his play and still have it qualify as a well-made entertainment. But other pieces of his are altogether weightier. Those with historical themes often embody a surprisingly shrewd and active political intelligence. His plays on Biblical subjects are no stained-glass moralities, but are rich in feeling and atmosphere; La venganza de Tamar, for instance, explores with much compassion the human meaning of a story which could all too easily have lent itself to a merely chilling exemplarity and exoticism. And time after time, in plays of the most diverse kinds, Tirso presents some character - interestingly, it is very often a female character - with a depth of insight which seems quite untypical of the Spanish theatre of his age.

It is, above all, an insight into the unpredictability of these characters: the product, as it seems, of an almost Shakespearian brooding on the possibilities present in this or that fragment of conventional dramatic or human material. Both Lope and Calderón, for slightly different reasons in each case, tend to see their personages in terms of a fixed range of conventionalized types. They may be given certain individuating touches; they may even undergo processes of sudden change or conversion. But they remain in character as Rash Young Man, Jealous Husband, Girl Made Ingenious by Love, Innocent Victim, and the like. Even repentance registers as a transformation of conduct, rather than a development of personality. Tirso's characters are different: what they are about to do, and what they are about to become, remains subject to a real uncertainty. On that uncertainty as it applies to Paulo and Enrico the whole development of El condenado por desconfiado depends. But who would ever have guessed, in addition, that the gibbering, hunger-obsessed Pedrisco would become the reliable witness to Enrico's death, and the last source of human comfort for the doomed Paulo. Of such unexpectedness is Tirso's drama at its greatest made. And of course, the play which above all others has brought him fame is one whose protagonist astonishes us, not by what he does, but by what in defiance of expectation he declines to do. The Don Juan Tenorio of El burlador de Sevilla is a character whose conventional function ought to be to repent; Tirso being Tirso, and Don Juan being Don Juan, he does not.

What one registers in Tirso de Molina at his best, then, is an intelligence which seems to run beyond the theatrical idiom which he is content to practice. This might be seen in various ways - as a challenge to more straightforward dramatic practitioners, as food for thought on the part of audiences, as a source of problems, or as something at least potentially subversive. Perhaps it was this last possibility that the Junta de Reformación had in mind when it issued, in March 1625, the decree which brought Tirso's Madrid career to an abrupt end:

Master Téllez, otherwise known as Tirso, writer of plays. The Committee discussed the scandal caused by a Mercedarian called Master Téllez, otherwise known as Tirso, by his writing of profane comedies which incite to ill conduct and give bad examples. Since the case is common knowledge, it was agreed to advise His Majesty that his Confessor ought to tell the Papal Legate to order him to be expelled from Madrid and sent to one of the remoter houses of his Order and bind him over under pain of major excommunication to write no more comedies or other forms of profane verse. And let this be done at once.[16]

Certainly Tirso was being singled out for special attention, and for reasons other than the reasons stated. The examples of evil conduct in his plays appear neither more prominent nor more insidiously attractive than those furnished by other writers. It was, of course, a bad moment for playwrights in general. In the year and a half since the Prince of Wales went home official Madrid had become acutely conscious of the need for economies. The Junta had several times adopted a threatening attitude towards the theatre generally, and had shown particular hostility towards clerics who wrote for the stage. But Lope, though a priest, continued to write plays unmolested. That Tirso's position should be undermined while his own remained intact was a development calculated to give much satisfaction to Lope. It is at least possible that he had helped, in some way, to bring it about. Equally the causes may have been political, rooted in Tirso's history of estrangement from Olivares. The precise circumstances of his removal from the Madrid scene remain, like so much else in Tirso's life, mysterious.

One further element in this mystery is the decidedly cool way in which the authorities of the Mercedarian Order took all this. They did get Tirso away to a provincial convent, but they also took the opportunity to make some markedly assertive statements about their right to discipline their own members in their own way. Tirso himself did make a rather general declaration of contrition (in verse) in 1630, and he more or less observed the ten-year ban against his publishing or writing plays. In fact, he wrote very little more for the theatre after this date and he postponed most – though not quite all – of the collected volumes of his work until after 1635. But he went on, without much obstruction, to enjoy a long and distinguished career in the Order, becoming one of its senior functionaries in Castile, and its official historian. No doubt these were the achievements which, as his death in 1648 approached, seemed central to his life; to have imagined, twenty years before, words which an actor might speak for an afternoon on a Madrid stage to keep an audience awed or amused or guessing would rank as a small enough matter. Yet if we in our own day are in any sense able to know how Brother Gabriel Téllez and his audience experienced the world and their place within it, the words which he imagined for Don Juan and for King David, for the hermit Paulo and the bandit Enrico have a unique authority among our evidences.

II

Dating; sources; doctrine

Our most immediate evidence for the date of El condenado por desconfiado comes from the Segunda parte de las comedias del Maestro Tirso de Molina, in which the text of the play first appears.[17] The official note of Aprobación, granting permission for the volume to be printed, was signed in Madrid on 20 November 1634. Its author, Doctor Andrés de Espino, must have read the entire text by then; his description of the book as 'a piece of recreation for the studious, a source of instructive example for the young to avoid moral dangers, and a credit to its author's wit' suggests that he read Tirso more intelligently than the Junta de Reformación had read him, nine years earlier. The end of 1634, then, supplies a terminal date; a note on the title-page of El condenado itself, stating that it was acted by Figueroa, helps to establish an early limit. Roque de Figueroa was in the process of forming his own theatrical company in the early months of 1624. The list of plays in his possession in March of that year includes several items associated with Tirso, but not this one. We cannot be sure, of course, that he had mounted no production before this date, or that Tirso's play was newly-composed when the Figueroa company first presented it. Nevertheless, there are other indications which converge on a date in the mid 1620s, at the height of Tirso's brief but intense literary glory in Madrid. No text of El condenado occurs in the first published collection of his plays, the Primera parte which appeared in Seville in 1627. But that volume itself has a curious history.[18] It was announced as being in the press as early as 1624; there is some evidence that it may actually have appeared in a Madrid edition in 1626, but that it was withdrawn almost at once, because Tirso was still under a cloud. Since these early states of the text are wholly conjectural, we cannot tell what plays the volume then contained. But a handwritten list of titles, dated in the early 1630s by its discoverer Alan Paterson, and headed 'Primera de Tirso', does include an item clearly recognizable as El condenado por desconfiado. If, as seems possible, the list reflects the contents of a lost Primera parte, the play must have been ready for the press in 1624 or very shortly thereafter.

Much of our other information points to the same date.[19] In 1620 Lope de Vega had published a play, El remedio en la desdicha, from which Anareto's advice on marriage in Act II here (ll. 1186-9; 1191-4) would appear to have been quite shamelessly lifted – a practice not too ill-regarded among the writers of the comedia. There is some more respectable imitation in the Pastorcillo episodes. Here again, the source would seem to be Lope this time his La buena guarda of 1621. Unless we suppose the indebtedness to be on Lope's side – which, of course, remains a possibility – these parallels would imply a terminus a quo in the early 1620s. This is precisely the period for the fashions affected by the two fops who visit Celia in Act I; they were all the rage in 1622, and probably on the wane by the middle of the decade. The title El condenado por dudar in a producer's list of plays, compiled in 1627, makes it seem almost certain that El condenado por desconfiado had been in circulation for some time by that date. The variant title suggests that it may even have existed for long enough to attract a remodelling by some other hand, though, equally, it may be a mere error of notation. Also from 1627 comes a much more startling piece of evidence. It is an item in a Madrid newsletter, printed in March of that year:

> On the 6th of this month news came that a Mercedarian friar called Brother Maldonado had shot a carrier on the road between Yébenes and Orgaz with intent to rob

him.   The Holy Brotherhood [the rural police force]
arrested him and took him in irons to Orgaz, where he
was handed over to his Order at their urgent request.
He had been on the run for three years, robbing and
murdering under arms, and on horseback.[20]

Brother Maldonado, on this evidence, had begun his life of
crime in March 1624. That would give Tirso time enough to
absorb the startling news that one of his brethren in the
Order had turned bandit, and to have his play ready for
inclusion in a lost Primera parte, compiled in that same
year, and perhaps published a couple of years later. At all
events, it makes 1624 overwhelmingly the likeliest date for
El condenado. It cannot be much later (on the evidence of
the fashions, and of the producer's list); if it is earlier,
we have to consider which of several alternative views we
should take regarding the bandit-friar's delinquency. It may
have been wholly coincidental, and Brother Maldonado may
never even have known of Brother Gabriel Téllez's play.   On
the whole, given that they were in the same Order, and given
Tirso's celebrity, this appears unlikely. This leaves the
possibility that Brother Maldonado knew the play, and had
taken to crime in imitation of Paulo. It seems a curiously
obtuse reaction to El condenado. Enigmatic that text may be,
but there are limits to its ambivalence. It makes better
sense altogether to regard 1624 (just possibly 1625) as the
date of the play, and the Brother Maldonado incident as its
most likely immediate catalyst.
    If that incident was, in itself, startling enough to have
set Tirso's imagination working, there was an earlier, more
edifying link between the Mercedarian Order and banditry, of
which he was quite certainly aware.[21]There is the rather
important distinction to be made that this link concerned a
bandit turned religious, rather than the reverse, but the
whole Order was extremely proud of the one-time Catalan
bandit who had ended his days as San Pedro Armengol. Tirso
himself wrote and published a short life of this notable
example of repentance, as part of his miscellany Deleitar
aprovechando. Bandits were also familiar enough figures on
the seventeenth-century stage, where they provided a somewhat
glamourized image of spectacular wickedness, especially
appropriate where this was to be followed by spectacular
repentance.[22]City crime as the theatregoing public knew it
from first-hand experience was less likely to prove an object
of fascination.   Even so, Enrico's long autobiographical

speech in Act I of El condenado offers a fair panorama of it, and his retinue provides other living examples. Enrico, on this evidence, is not a bandit at all, though at the end of Act II he appears to contemplate joining Paulo in that role. Rather, he is a rufián – an urban figure of generally more sordid characteristics. He lives by gambling, blackmail, contract killings, and the immoral earnings of his mistress Celia. It is perhaps apt that his henchman Galván, when he tries to soften Pedrisco by appealing to a professional solidarity among thieves, receives a very dusty answer (ll. 1756-61). Certainly Enrico, as he first appears to the appalled Paulo and to the audience, represents a moral and social type which the latter could identify as both familiar and distinctively low. There was a sense in which bandits were neither.

Yet bandits were undeniably wicked, and they were, albeit at some remove from the cities, as much a part of contemporary reality as the rufianes. It was the unusual background of Brother Maldonado which earned him his mention in the news; his way of life was a commonplace in many parts of Spain. Catalonia, for example, was classic bandit territory; the seventeenth-century stereotype of the Catalan was not the paunchy and industrious small manufacturer of nineteenth-century lore, but Roque Guinart, armed to the teeth. Some areas of Italy were, if anything, even worse infested – not least the hinterland of Naples, where El condenado is set. Tirso's choice of that setting may have had more specific intentions behind it. El burlador de Sevilla, it might be noted, also begins in Naples, though it does not linger there for long. The city and its surrounding countryside offered a useful location for any play presenting a spectacle of major delinquency which in a Spanish context might have seemed subversive. Enrico is subversive to the extent of killing the Governor of Naples; it would be hard to imagine the author of an equivalent misdeed in a Spanish setting being represented on stage as forgiven by God. Indeed, Tirso in one respect masks the quality of the act even here. The actual ruler of Naples in the seventeenth century was not a Governor but a Viceroy, who was the direct representative of the Spanish king. It was safer to have Enrico kill a mere Governor, and a certain vagueness as to the period of the action makes this plausible. But Tirso's presentation of Naples clearly corresponds in its broad outlines to the awareness of that turbulent dependency which his Madrid public might be expected to have. It is a hotbed of ruffians and assassins, an exotic, cosmopolitan city where one might come across 'Germans, English, Magyars, Armenians, Indians'. And to this list of Celia's admirers, Tirso adds the Spaniard, an object of hate among the people of Naples (ll. 363-5). Hated the Spaniards certainly were, as the quasi-colonial power there, but the matter-of-fact wryness with which that hatred is noted is Tirsian enough.[23]

In matters of more detail, however, social observation in El condenado por desconfiado is not about Naples, in which the audience were interested only as an exotic point of departure for dramatic invention but about Madrid, in which they were absorbingly interested for most of their waking hours.[24] There were ready laughs to be got from Celia's instant verse-factory with its output of repentista poetry, and from the identifiable social type of the high-class literary prostitute herself – for that, plainly, is what she is. Contemporary fashions also invited satirical asides: the yards of padding extruded from the young fop's jerkin when Galván knifes him (ll. 539-40) or the ringlets and moustaches of the marquesotes (ll. 547-9) are recurring topics from play to play; in this, as in much else, the dramatists of Lope's school drew on a common stock. Inevitably, they often drew on the old master himself. We have already had occasion to note the borrowings of Anareto's advice on marriage from El remedio en la desdicha and of portions of the Pastorcillo speeches from La buena guarda. There is another allegorical shepherd in Lope's La fianza satisfecha, though the character whom he recalls to virtue – successfully, as it happens – is much more like Enrico than Paulo. Indeed, the man of sin and violence who is redeemed in the end is essentially a stock motif - the most central of several which Tirso uses in this play and, it must be said, substantially transforms.[25]

Along with the theme of the 'converted villain', we might include under this head the supernatural agents – the Pastorcillo and the Devil – as well as certain effects, used mainly in contexts associated with those agents: music, heard off stage at certain key moments of the characters' inner life; the vision of Enrico saved, and that of Paulo 'wreathed in flames'.[26] Neither the otherworldly personages nor the spectacular tramoyas could have offered any very convincing or sustained illusion of literal marvels, especially as plays of this period were performed in broad daylight. But they were elements in a theatrical language which audiences of the seventeenth century were used to decoding; moreover, such audiences could and did take pleasure in them for their own sake, as in swordplay or disguise, regarding them simply as sources of excitement. Tirso, however, leaves none - or almost none - of these familiar dramatic resources where they were.[27]The little Shepherd is neither a fixed allegorical counter nor a mere lyric voice; as we shall see, he shifts subtly and without incongruity from one identity to another. The Devil operates in similarly adaptable fashion, according to the needs of the characters' inner drama. To the anxious and spiritually overwrought Paulo of Act I he is a powerful, if misconstrued, visual presence; to Enrico in his dark cell he is a more mysterious, less tangible, much more immediately dangerous phenomenon. Tirso exercises an equally specific control over the non-supernatural elements of stock theatrical entertainment. Although Enrico is a man of violence, Tirso does not allow him to become bogged down in merely spectacular fights; what swordplay there is whets, but does not sate, the appetite for action. The use of disguise and blindfolds in the latter part of Act II enables Tirso to stage what is perhaps the most remarkable scene of the whole play. He shows a similar originality of touch with stock characters. Most theatrical companies had a specialist comedian for the gracioso role; most also ran to a barba, whose particular aptitude was for the portrayal of old men.[28]Anareto at times (for example in the lines plagiarized from Lope) talks as if he were just such another routine ancient. In fact, he is anything but that, just as Pedrisco, by the end of the play, has grown to be very much more than just another gracioso.

For all these items Tirso could draw on a recent and flourishing theatrical tradition. His basic plot is itself traditional, but in another mode, and in a very much longer perspective.[29]From its beginnings in the ancient Hindu scriptures, through Moslem and Jewish moralistic writings, there had come down to the medieval West an exemplary story of a good man obliged to learn the nature of good from someone who was, by any obvious standard, his moral inferior. In its earliest form the tale was about a Brahmin, told to seek for the pattern of true virtue in a hunter and butcher - in terms of the Hindu caste system the lowest of the low. The butcher, it turns out, accepts his divinely appointed lot with true humility, and (this is perhaps the crucial point) pays special honour to his father and mother. The Brahmin accepts that this is a level of virtue he has yet to attain. In Jewish versions the protagonists are a Rabbi and a butcher; in Arabic the Rabbi is replaced by Moses. One new note in these stories is that the good man is made to enquire of God 'who will be his companion in Paradise?' The answer that it is going to be a butcher disturbs him, but he ends by recognizing the butcher's merits and thanking God for his mercy. The tale had already entered Christian tradition in an older form when stories of the Desert Fathers were being collected to make up the Vitae Patrum. In one of these versions, St Anthony hears a voice from Heaven, telling him that he has not yet equalled the righteousness of a certain tanner of Alexandria. He goes to see him, and finds him a man of the utmost humility . Of more interest in the present context is another fourth-century Christian variant in which the holy hermit Paphnutius asks God to show him which of the saints he will resemble. He is given the name of a certain musician, whom he finds to be a drunken, disreputable thief. This unprepossessing character has, however, performed one or two outstandingly charitable actions in his time (they involve novelesque episodes of aid given to ladies in distress). Learning of these, the saint expresses his wonder at God's design. When the musician hears the full story, he goes off to join the hermits, and puts his talents to good use singing psalms. On his death, Paphnutius is given a vision of him in glory, and draws the moral that nobody, however low – 'whether a thief or an actor or a ploughman or a merchant or a married man' ought to be despised, for there are elect souls, known to God, among them all. We have come some considerable way towards the moral framework of Tirso's drama.

The Desert tradition in its many variants establishes the 'good' man of the tale as a hermit; this version of it intensifies the central paradox by making the companion of his spiritual destiny not merely of low status, but a morally disgusting human being. These are still the key elements in the best-known medieval Spanish version of the tale, that supplied in the fourteenth century by Juan Manuel in his Conde Lucanor. There, a certain hermit, told that King Richard of England will be his companion in Paradise, objects strongly because of the king's well-known violence and sinfulness. He is sternly informed that Richard, 'in a leap which he leapt' at the siege of Acre, has earned more merit than he (the hermit) has acquired in the course of his whole life. The hermit quietens down at that, as well he might. Among the earlier versions of the legend this is one of those which Tirso is likeliest to have read.[30] Yet two major discrepancies should prevent us from identifying it as his source. In the first place, neither Juan Manuel nor any of the written Christian variants of the story preserves a detail common in the non-Christian versions, and centrally important to El condenado. This is the fact that the chief merit of the apparently evil character is his filial piety towards his parents. It seems that Tirso either 'reinvented' this detail in a quite fortuitous way or, more probably, came across it in some lost – and perhaps orally transmitted – version. The second discrepancy is still more crucial: in Tirso, uniquely, the 'good' protagonist does not acknowledge the mystery of good in the apparent sinner; instead, Paulo revolts, and loses his own salvation.

What Tirso has done, as Menéndez Pidal's classic study demonstrates, is to weld together two separate legends: the story of the hermit whose salvation is linked to that of a thief, and the story of the hermit who renegues on his faith because a thief is saved. In the latter, a thief begs a hermit to receive him as a brother in penitence; the request is rejected, but shortly afterwards, when the thief dies, the hermit has a vision of him being received into Heaven. In disgust that this evil liver should attain such a reward, while he with all his long history of self-denial may not, the hermit becomes a robber himself, is killed by the forces of the law, and goes to Hell. By comparison with the other story, this one seems altogether less remarkable. It is cruder, less profound – not an intimation of the mysterious nature of holiness and the redemptive potential present in every human destiny, but a mere illustration of a 'thou shalt not'. The other legend draws on a centuries-old tradition of meditative wisdom; this one seems to belong to the more simplistic world of the popular sermon.[31] Yet it does have ingredients calculated to make it memorable in that context, and to commend it as the basis for the plot of a comedia: powerful contrast, unexpected reversal, a violent climax. By marrying the dramatic substance of this tale to the thematic substance of the older legend, Tirso created a framework strong enough to become that of a very remarkable play indeed.

Characteristically, he gives us few clues as to the immediate sources on which he has drawn, and those which he does give seem to be misleading. It is all there, says Pedrisco in the closing lines of the play, in the Vitae Patrum and in Cardinal Robert Bellarmine. In fact it is not all there. The Vitae Patrum do contain a version of the 'linked salvation' legend whose form is not too distant from Tirso. But in this – the Paphnutius story – the hermit is not damned; he takes the point and repents. As for Cardinal

Bellarmine, his works contain stories of holy men tempted to despair, but none which precisely matches El condenado.[32] His principal relevance would appear to be that he had views of interest to Tirso on the theological point at issue. That point was the question of human freewill and divine grace – a matter of the liveliest controversy in the sixteenth and seventeenth centuries, and one whose relevance to El condenado por desconfiado seems inescapable.

This need not raise insuperable problems for modern readers or audiences. For Tirso and his contemporaries, the language and the conceptual patterns of theology were the indispensable idiom for exploring the contradictory depths of human nature; to be serious at all about these matters was to be theological. In our age that idiom has, to a considerable degree, been displaced, yet the human agenda to which it is addressed remains. The concepts through which Tirso confronts and orders his human material are theological. But he conveys the resulting awareness of that material through images which are, first and foremost, fictional and dramatic. It is his success on this imaginative plane which can still convince us that he has important truths to tell. In this regard we are not too far removed from his original public. Most of them were not trained theologians either; it was Tirso's dramatic substance which gave meaning to his theology for them – though they acknowledged the latter in principle as an authoritative system of belief. Many twentieth-century audiences would make no such acknowledgment. Yet for them too, Tirso's dramatic imagination can guarantee the seriousness of what he has to say, in theological terms, about what it is to be human. The need for any detailed knowledge of particular doctrinal disputes hardly arises; what the play itself tells us is enough.[33]

Yet the disputes over freewill had been so intense and so public that few members of Tirso's original audience could have remained unaware of them. Some understanding of these controversies, therefore, and of where Tirso's play stands in relation to them, can help to clarify the original intention and possible impact of El condenado por desconfiado.[34]

Bitterly fought though they were, these debates had their origin in a set of propositions to which virtually everyone involved gave assent: that God is omnipotent and knows everything; that some people are saved, and that others are damned. It can be argued, then that from the beginning God, who knows all things, knew which people would be saved and which damned, and even (since he is an all-powerful God) ordained that these things should be so. But in that case, what happens to human freewill? The answer given by Martin Luther, at the start of a century of uniquely embittered theological disputes, was that mankind has no freewill. Or rather, if it exists at all, it is so vitiated by sin that salvation can only come about by the special favour of God – that is, by grace. This grace promotes a faith (in some) which justifies the sinner. The others – those who are not in this sense chosen or 'elect' – are thus 'reprobate', damned from the outset. The religious life is the pursuit of the saving faith that marks out God's elect. This view of predestined salvation was narrowed yet further by John Calvin. Catholic theology, reacting against it at the Council of Trent, laid it down firmly that nobody can have any natural certainty that he is saved or damned. To that extent, <u>El condenado</u>, in which Paulo's very first fault is to have asked for just such a certainty, is distinctively a Catholic play, and critical of Protestant thinking.[35]

Yet there was also controversy among Catholics as to precisely how much or how little scope divine foreknowledge did leave to human freewill. The Dominican friars were foremost among those who believed that this scope was very limited indeed. They argued that God, by an efficacious grace, caused the human will to assent to its own salvation; where that assent was lacking, the sinner was a reprobate, in receipt only of so-called 'sufficient' grace. Sufficient grace meant that a potential for salvation existed, but this could not become actual without efficacious grace: the sinner <u>could</u> be saved, but as it happened, was not. Against all this, the theologians of the Society of Jesus contended that God's involvement in the salvation of his elect was an essentially collaborative affair, not a predetermining one. As soon as human will assented, sufficient grace <u>became</u> efficacious. As for sinful acts, God permitted these only after the will had consented to them; he certainly did not will in advance that the sin should go unprevented. In the larger perspective, God's foreknowledge of salvation and damnation was a knowledge not of what must occur, but of what was capable of occurring – of <u>futurabilia</u>.

Between the promoters of these two sharply contrasted doctrines, it is not too much to say that all Hell broke loose in the later sixteenth century. The Dominicans said that the Jesuits were lax and permissive heretics, probably Pelagians – and nobody had had a good word for the Pelagians since the fourth century. The Jesuits replied that the

Dominicans were, as near as made no matter, Protestants. The dispute reached such a pitch in the 1590s that Pope Clement VIII set up a special Commission and ordered the contestants to cease arguing. They went on arguing in the Commission instead. The Dominicans set up a Commission of their own and told the Pope to condemn the Jesuits. Pope Clement died, while chairing his own Commission. In 1607 that body made its report to the new Pope, Paul V, who declared the whole affair a drawn battle. Both opinions could be defended, he ruled, but nobody was to accuse anybody else of heresy, or to write any more on the subject without Papal permission. The Jesuits decided to treat this outcome as a victory, and threw public parties all over Spain. The argument rumbled on.

Two aspects of all this seem particularly relevant to Tirso. The major protagonist on the Jesuit side was a professor of theology from Coimbra, Luis de Molina. In the light of this, and of his own well-attested interest in things Portuguese, Brother Gabriel Téllez's choice of pen-name might be seen as reflecting a particular attitude towards the freewill controversy.[36]That possibility, though it would accord well with his regard for the Jesuit Bellarmine, is rendered somewhat less likely by the involvement in the debate of Tirso's own Mercedarian order. This took the form of a contribution by one Francisco Zumel, whom Tirso admired greatly, as his History of the Order makes clear.[37]And Zumel, on balance, is regarded as having favoured not the Jesuit-Molinist position, but the opposite view adopted by the Dominicans. This was certainly the case as far as the positive operation of grace was concerned: for Zumel salvation was a mysterious work of God, in advance of any act of the human will. But on the negative side he took an independent stance. He rejected any notion of negative antecedent predestination. That is to say, he insisted that God's grace in all its forms was always available to all men and women. If they then rejected that grace, or failed to persevere in good living, it was because they were using their freewill to do so. They were not predestined to fail. In a word, it is God who saves those who are saved; those who are damned are damned through the choices which they make themselves.

In some ways El condenado por desconfiado is quite clearly a Zumelian work. It presents both Enrico and Paulo as being offered salvation at every stage; only as Paulo's will hardens against the offer does the possibility recede from him. Paulo, moreover, is at fault in assuming that Enrico – and therefore he himself too – must be reprobate of

God – predestined to damnation. That is not, in Zumelian doctrine, an assumption which can ever legitimately be made. It is less clear whether, as the controversy itself receded in time, Tirso was prepared to allow more scope to Molinism than his regard for Zumel might suggest, and to make the response of the human will an active component in the process of salvation.[38] But if El condenado never clearly commits itself to this sort of doctrinal openness, it is orientated dramatically towards an openness of a different though still related kind.[39]

The starting-point of the drama is Paulo's perverse search for a closed certainty regarding his salvation; the play as a whole demonstrates how wrong he is in this. But it would hardly be a sufficient demonstration to show that, having fallen into this error, Paulo is inescapably and justly damned. That would be to provide a certainty parallel in form, if opposite in content, to the one he seeks – which, of course, is precisely what the Devil does provide. Tirso has to do more: he has to show that it is still possible for Paulo to be saved, and indeed that God wills him to be saved. But this also involves making his audience feel that this is an outcome to be desired – that Paulo is worth saving. The ending, in which he is not saved, must be experienced not merely as something exemplary, but as a tragedy.[40]

The key to this achievement is implicit in the work's title: El condenado por desconfiado. Paulo is damned for his desconfianza, for despair in the sense of lack of trust – lack of hope, perhaps, more precisely than lack of faith.[41] Insofar as this outlook is the voluntary product of Paulo's intellect, in command of its own choices, he is, of course, to blame. But despair could also be an involuntary emotional reaction. There were stories circulating in Madrid in the early 1620s that King Philip III had suffered from bouts of despair as he lay dying – not despair over the prospects of his kingdom, but an agonized doubt about his own salvation. For this – for desconfianza as feeling – Tirso clearly had much sympathy.[42] It is the tension between that sympathy and the clear condemnation of Paulo's unreasonable thought which gives the ex-hermit his status as a genuinely tragic figure. He is, in the literal sense of that potentially awesome cliché, 'a good man gone wrong'.

It may have taken a good man tempted by wrong to see how this was possible. A final possibility among all those diverse elements which may have made their contribution to the play returns our attention once more to Tirso's situation as a writer. As a possibly relevant background to the creation of El condenado that situation has its points of interest. A devout and serious friar with a talent for dramatic poetry comes to Madrid to experience life as a writer in the place where most writers are, just then, most active. His own temperament and talents lead him to identify with - perhaps even to hero-worship at a distance - the greatest playwright of his age. But when he comes closer, he finds that this great man to whom he has yoked his own star is everything he despises: a womanizer on a gargantuan scale; an intriguer and a flatterer of great personages; envious by nature; notoriously ungrateful; an ill-living priest. And yet to this man, more than to any other in Spain, Providence has given the divine grace of poetry. What is the friar to make of that? How is he to come to terms with his confused and tangled feelings? El condenado por desconfiado cannot, of course, have been wholly about this. But it may well have been in some part Tirso's attempt to make sense, in terms of his own faith and the other's art, of his relations with Lope de Vega, and of the curious destiny which, for a few years, threw them so incongruously together.[43]

This survey of the various elements which could have contributed to the composition of El condenado cannot, of its nature, be definitive. Some of the items discussed may be of marginal relevance, or even of none at all, and there will certainly have been other inputs now unknown to us.[44]Even so, the present listing provides some basis for a tentative account of how such a play as this may have come into being. The basis of personal experience which demanded to be transformed into drama could well have been furnished by Tirso's uneasy relationship with Lope. The more immediate pretext for writing the play was perhaps the Brother Maldonado incident - all the more striking for Tirso because of the prestigious counter-example of San Pedro Armengol. To compel these fragments, each with its puzzling juxtaposition of positive and negative moral factors, into some coherence, Tirso would have needed to relate them to a framework of thought. This was where the theology of grace and redemption would have come to the fore - Zumelian theology, no doubt, as befitted a member of the same Order, but with a strong underlying 'openness', which puts our author on the more liberal fringe of that tendency. Hence his choice of a more specific narrative model: the ancient legend of the hermit whose salvation is linked to that of a thief. What mattered to Tirso in the Vitae Patrum or Conde Lucanor version - to

name the two which he is likeliest to have known - was very
evidently its theme - a theme which he was to take as that of
his own play: that the judgments of God are both inscrutable
and merciful. But it would also have put him in mind - if he
had not thought about it already - of another story: the tale
of the Renegade Hermit. And with the sense of aesthetic
balance so typical of his period, he would have seen the
possibility of linking that with the well-tried theatrical
and sacred motif of the Repentant Bandit. These stories, of
course, correspond in their general terms to the Maldonado
and Armengol episodes. But each of them exists primarily as
a distinctively outlined plot, and it was the conjuction of
these plots which gave Tirso the structure of El condenado.
They also supplied the bare indications, very much elaborated
in the eventual text, of the play's two chief characters.
Into its texture went all the various stock theatrical
devices, special effects, surprises, topical references and
borrowings, including, no doubt, a very large number of items
not identified here. It could well be the case that the
play's first audiences - of whose reactions, by the way, we
have virtually no record - valued it chiefly for these more
incidental elements. Its longer-term critical reputation
rests, rather, on certain aspects of its wholeness. But we
have to assume that Tirso was fully in charge at either
level. El condenado por desconfiado is both the carrier of a
unique imaginative vision and the product of a pre-existing
theatrical tradition.

III

The making of *El condenado*: themes, form and characters.

It is possible to list the ingredients that go into El
condenado por desconfiado with reasonable thoroughness, if
never quite completely. It is possible, too, to delineate
the functions of these disparate elements, and to state how
they are ordered in relation to one another. One may do all
this and still miss the essential creativity of Tirso's
imagination, through which the play becomes more than the
mere aggregate of its parts, so that these come to carry
meanings which they could not have borne outside that setting.
That creativity is capable of transforming even quite minor
and tangential scraps of dramatic matter.
    The point is well illustrated by a couple of merely
local instances. The first is supplied by that moment in Act

xliv

III when, to the sound of music, two angels are seen por una apariencia, bearing the soul of Enrico up to Heaven. This tableau bodies forth an important aspect of the play's doctrine, and the tramoya through which it is effected is the most spectacular of its staging devices. Yet the techniques employed were probably basic enough - a painted scroll, no doubt controlled by some arrangement involving ropes and pulleys.[45] And the verses in which Paulo describes it are scarcely less conventional:

> And through these cloudy canopies,
> to live in glory in the skies,
> the soul triumphant takes its rise. (ll. 2782-4)

For the modern spectator a scene like this is liable to carry the same risks of triviality as do the court pageants and heraldic set-pieces of Shakespeare's history plays. Either the effect is elaborated - in which case attention drifts from the theme to the effect - or it remains embarrassingly cursory. Moreover, the function of the effect as a sign of something else - the soul with angels illustrating salvation; pageantry signifying kingship - may itself seem unacceptably trite. This is the more likely to happen if, as is probable too, notions of salvation or kingship mean something different to the twentieth-century spectator, or perhaps mean nothing at all. Such moments, instead of being dramatic climaxes, can be the high-water-marks of detachment between the modern audience and the seventeenth-century playwright. Yet if the latter is fully in charge of his medium, he will have pre-empted that detachment by building the particular effect into the wider system of meanings that is the language of his drama. And so it is with the spectacle of the redeemed Enrico. In dramatic terms the overwhelmingly important fact is that this is indeed Enrico's soul and no other. Presumably the audience are meant to recognize it as such. But Paulo, for his part, fails to do anything of the kind; he merely sees an anonymous soul on its way to glory - more fuel for his despair. That at once returns us directly to the play's central concern. What seemed a rather fatuous and distracting piece of theatrical "business" turns out to be a powerful and precise index of Paulo's spiritual state.

An episode in the gaol scene furnishes us with our second instance. It is, indeed, a passage which requires some attention to its textual problems before it can be read in the sense proposed here.[46] But the changes involved serve to bring the whole episode into focus as a notable example of Tirso's capacity for endowing even minor characters and incidents with an unusual depth of purely human substance. Enrico, savaged by the Prison Governor for his murder of the guard Fidelio, returns that savagery in a speech of horrific violence. The Governor, quite unmoved, has him loaded down with chains and taken off to a dungeon. Enrico's reaction is of a piece with that delicate charting of a psychology in crisis which Ivy McClelland has shown to be such a feature of the whole prison sequence.[47] Instead of a fresh outburst there is a collapse into fatalistic passivity which makes him, for the spectator and for Pedrisco, a figure of perhaps unexpected pathos: 'Poor fellow! Poor Enrico!' (1. 2212). But the surviving gaoler will have none of that. In the classic reproach of any champion of law and order, he tells Pedrisco to start feeling sorry for Enrico's latest victim (who, as it happens, is still lying there with his brains all over the cell floor). Tirso rejects any easy sentimentalism; God's mercy for Enrico is to be mercy for the man who has just done that. But there is more still to this remarkable little scene. The Governor and the gaoler have no more lines. Presumably, though the placing of the stage-direction is one of the matters which require editorial attention here, they leave the stage, taking the corpse with them. Left alone, Pedrisco turns his thoughts to another topic of grave concern to him – his dinner. And a cry runs through the gaol that a meal is on its way. Life – life in Pedrisco's very basic, minimal sense – goes on through all these moral complexities.

This human density in Tirso is often identifiably related to the theological perspective in which his characters are seen. But in examples like this it has more to do with the sense – also, in the last analysis, a religious sense – that human beings are at once deeply unsatisfactory and endlessly fascinating creatures. Whatever we may make of Tirso's beliefs about the next world, his presentation of this world is, in this important regard, one which we can recognize. That recognition can lead spectators not otherwise committed to Tirso's beliefs to take them seriously in the human context of his play. No doubt it achieved the same result with the more wordly-minded of his original audience.

Yet there was something much more elementary which Tirso had first to achieve if El condenado was to convey any message at all. He had to make his disparate original materials into a play – an object capable of standing up to the potentially rough handling of that robust tribunal, the Madrid public. To this end he had to sustain a flow of elements which that audience could recognize and applaud as good theatre. Besides finding words to express those meanings which mattered to him most, he had to give them dramatic and non-verbal shapes. And he needed to link all this together in a clear and consequential theatrical design. The flow of gratifying effects is certainly there – suspense, violence, pathos, tender lyricism here and there, ultimate issues of Heaven and Hell. Above all, there are the extreme contrasts so relished by the seventeenth-century comedia audience: roistering disreputability and ecstatic prayer, high tragedy and low comedy.[48] Dramatic irony is present, not as an incidental feature but as something profoundly embedded in the play's whole structure; at its heart is the confrontation in the woods of the bandit-hermit Paulo and his prisoner Enrico – a magnificently imagined scene of disguise and cross-purposes. There are half a dozen supernatural manifestations; there are nine violent deaths, either witnessed or described. It is true that the play is short on women's roles, but the cameo of Celia offers a distinctive female lead for the right kind of actress: waspish and self-possessed, and embodying a recognizable social type. All this was surely enough to hold the attention of the most demanding spectators.

But the greater part of this often well-tried theatrical matter also embodies identifiable aspects of Tirso's major thematic concerns. This comes increasingly to be the case as the play advances. At the outset it is a story in which literally anything might happen, or so it appears as we shift from the forest hermitage to immersion in the low life of Naples. By Act III it is clear that whatever happens has to concern the salvation or damnation of the two protagonists. There is, in effect, a shift from randomness to relevance, which affirms the rule over all that is presented of a providential design. In this regard, El condenado is a particularly striking example of a process which occurs in many of the most achieved products of the seventeenth-century Spanish theatre: the sound structural craftsmanship commended and exemplified by Lope becomes the vehicle of an immanent poetic justice. The importance of this latter element in the comedia generally has been definitively asserted in the criticism of A.A. Parker.[49] The pattern is reinforced in El condenado by a strongly symmetrical construction, at once knitting the whole piece together and helping to define its sense of thematic direction.[50]

Act I falls fairly obviously into three sections, one

presenting Paulo in the wilderness and the other two Enrico
in Naples; the last section in fact brings the two men
together, although Enrico remains unaware of this, and they
do not at this stage speak to one another. Nevertheless, the
crucial event with which the Act ends is Paulo's overreaction
to their encounter. Act II is bipartite: first Enrico in
Naples, then Paulo in the woods. It too culminates in a
meeting between them; this time indeed there is communication,
though its outcome remains open and problematic. Act III
begins with two sequences involving Enrico in Naples: first
we see him in the common gaol, and then in the isolated
confinement of his dungeon. For its conclusion the Act
returns to Paulo in the forest. Here he is brought into
contact - through his vision; through Pedrisco's narrative -
with Enrico's exemplary end. Again, his reaction is a
disastrously wrong one, but this time he under-reacts. His
perverse decision at the end of Act I, despite the moment of
openness and implied potential for grace in Act II, has
finally established itself as a perverse disposition. To an
extent, this structure makes the process look like something
foredoomed - by tragic fate, predestination, or psychological
determinism. There is a symmetrical circularity about Acts I
and III: Paulo / Enrico / Enrico: Enrico / Enrico / Paulo.
This suggests the predetermined course, the serpent with its
tail in its mouth. And we may well recall that in Paulo's
renunciation of his hermit's role in Act II - thematically
speaking, the centre of the play - the image of the snake is
present:

> How clumsily
> my hands move to their work,
> as a snake shuffles off its skin!
> Yet snakes at least
> change worse for better.
> I slough off goodness; wear my sin (ll. 1882-6).

Like all the other signs that Paulo fails to read, this one
depends on how it is read.[51] The snake's shedding of its
skin is potentially a figure of good action; moreover, the
association of the serpent with the cross - also mentioned in
this speech, and visible to the audience as part of Paulo's
rejected regalia - has a scriptural background in the use of
the serpent uplifted by Moses as a figure of Christ's Passion.
Yet the creature's primary associations are of evil: the
serpent is the tempter of the Genesis story who, through the

desire of knowledge, traps mankind into the determinism of original sin. In an early scene of this play the Devil puts off his garment to assume a better appearance for no good purpose – to accomplish, in fact, the parallel temptation of Paulo himself.

The associations of the serpent image, then, reinforce the circularity of the play's first and last Acts, to imply a pattern of predestination. We have to be brought by such means to take such a pattern seriously; otherwise we shall hardly understand the tragedy of Paulo's story. At the same time it is a pattern which we are invited to reject. That rejection in its turn is underwritten by the very different structure of the intervening Act II. That structure is linear, sequential, narrative, purposive. We are in the domain here of lived biography, the theatre of human freewill, in which right or wrong choices can be made. In Act II as elsewhere, such choices confront both protagonists; some of them are concerned with what they are going to do about the ultimate matters of sin and repentance, faith and despair. But a high proportion of the choices which are to the fore in this particular Act have to do with what the characters are going to do next. In the play as a whole, this kind of choice and this kind of biography belong, characteristically, not to Paulo but to Enrico. He gives his life-story at an early stage; we have to piece together similar information about Paulo. Enrico, importantly, has a father; he also has what Paulo will not allow himself to have – a future. He does not think of it prudentially, as Anareto with his plans for a marriage tries to make him do; indeed at the end of Act II, when he actually tries to sketch out a future for Paulo and himself, it is a flawed and muddled plan which emerges. But it seems preferable to Paulo's obsessive sense of a life that has stopped already. Enrico is fully inserted into a human existence that is subject to time, sin, and appetite, yet also the object of divine redemption. In this regard he can be seen as living more wisely than the otherworldly Paulo, desperate to make his escape into a purely mechanical, predestined security. Complex though all this is when stated in abstract and theoretical terms, it is made present in its essentials through El condenado's strong and simple underlying design.[52]

As a piece of writing, El condenado is at first sight more vulnerable to criticism. It has sometimes been regarded as hasty and undistinguished in its verbal texture. When all due allowance is made for the hazardous processes by which the text of a seventeenth-century <u>comedia</u> found its way into print, there might still seem to be some warrant for this.[53] There are obvious lacunae and defects of metre in the text as it now survives. When these are set aside, what we have seems workmanlike enough. Yet considered as poetry it is unremarkable. Paulo's opening praise of nature, for example, seems low pressure, conventional stuff:

> Now dawn
> whitens the grass with shining dew,
> now greets the early sun,
> as he comes riding out through briars
> and with her bright hand lays
> the shades of night aside. (ll. 7-12)

That version itself, it might be added, already simplifies a rather overblown original. The little Shepherd has some delicate and tender lines, especially in Act III, but most of what he says in Act II is rather disconcertingly cast in the form of a sermon on repentance and grace.[54] It is a disagreeable fact about this play that those speeches which are most striking imaginatively tend to be the most violent: Paulo's dream of damnation, his threat to festoon the forest with human corpses, Enrico raging at the Prison Governor. But this should perhaps be our first clue to how Tirso's language actually does work: it is the intensity of the dramatic situation, not the wording itself, which enforces point and emotion. A minor example will illustrate this. Albano, the old man whom Enrico declines to murder in Act II, has just four lines:

> The sun is almost set
> - and my day too is nearly over
> my wife will be wondering
> where I can be... (ll. 1245-8)

In themselves they do not amount to much; in context they are everything. Albano's age and apparent innocence - and his seeming ignorance of what Enrico stands poised to do - remind us powerfully of Anareto whom we left a moment before. His worried domesticity even recalls the other old man's closing homily on marriage. All this, of course, will be registered by the audience for its effect on Enrico, especially if, as Daniel Rogers surmises, there was a way of having both parts played by the same actor.[55] But there is still more. 'The

1

sun is almost set...' casts over the whole violent, worldly scene of the early part of Act II an aura of weariness and decline to which Enrico's impatient spirit has already begun to respond in other ways. The speech is effective because it is right - in terms of character, of drama, and of theme. The same is true of much more major and central instances, like Paulo's speech in Act II, as he renounces his religion for the last time:

> Give me my sword and dagger now,
> and take this cross.
> The holy blood shed here is powerless.
> I have forgotten how
> to reach it, and all hope is loss. (ll. 1897–1901)

Relatively undistinguished language is raised in the original to a major creative level because of its aptness to the dramatic work it has to do.[56]

That said, other imputations of hasty writing remain possible. What, for example, should we make of the play's opening scenes: four long speeches, each a soliloquy by a different actor: Paulo, Pedrisco, Paulo again, and then the Devil? It looks the sort of opening which might have been thought up by someone who had never actually seen a play before. Only the contrasting assurance and mobility of all that follows can prevent this from counting as powerful presumptive evidence against Tirso's authorship. We have to accept, if we accept the case for that as made, that Tirso had his reasons for beginning his play in this extraordinary fashion, but it might well have caused a few sleepless nights for Roque de Figueroa, who had to produce it. Yet it does, after all, work.[57]The four speeches, shrewdly contrasted in style, content, and metre, also interact dramatically. The comically hungry Pedrisco parodies his master's more serious spiritual wrestlings. Paulo, hagridden by his nightmare of damnation, prompts an ironic reassessment of his earlier, rather smug piety. The Devil in his turn is swift to exploit that irony. Once he steps down from his crag, the flood of action sweeps away any qualms which might remain about the rather static prologue.

Yet here too there may be signs of hasty composition in the sheer breakneck pace of events. Paulo disappears to the woods after Act I; by the middle of Act II, he has his own gang of bandits. His former life, says Pedrisco, was only 'yesterday' (l. 1391). Enrico, having promised in Act I to do a killing, defaults on that promise in Act II, then plunges into the sea; he emerges somewhere near Paulo's part of the forest to find the latter in full cry as a bandit chief. At one moment in Act III Paulo sees Enrico's soul ascending; minutes later Pedrisco, an eyewitness to the latter's death, turns up in the woods. Besides this unnatural swiftness of events, there is the problem of how Enrico, after diving into the sea at Naples, can possibly come up again on the coasts of Paulo's bandit territory, two hours' hard ride away. It is possible to get round some of these dilemmas. Pedrisco's 'yesterday' is merely a figure of speech: it seems like yesterday. The murder for which Enrico is paid in Act I need not be that of Albano; one killing, one broken promise in Enrico's world is much like another. The vision of Enrico's end need not coincide with his execution; the fate of the soul belongs to eternity, not to time. More generally, this hectic, kaleidoscopic sequence of actions was part of the theatrical idiom of the comedia, closer in this respect to film than to some modern expectations of what ought to be possible on stage. We simply have to learn to read that idiom and its conventions as they are given to us. It is as convention, certainly, that we are obliged to take the matter of Enrico's extended swim. Literally it could not have happened. But such transitions were accepted for dramatic purposes. In Tirso's usage this particular example may have had a symbolic purpose too.[58] In his fine but neglected play La república al revés a fugitive Byzantine princess makes a similar escape by water. These are characters who trust themselves in moments of crisis to the unknown, to the winds and waves of God. Only Don Juan, whose response to being rescued from the waters is to seduce and betray his rescuer, perversely abuses that trust with his 'plenty of time to pay that debt'. Not all the anomalies in El condenado can be explained like this. For example, how does Galván, at the end, come to know that Enrico 'is with God' (1. 2927)? He may, of course, be merely chancing a lucky guess – which, when one comes to think of it, would be very like Galván. But it is much more probable in this case that Tirso was simply in a hurry to finish the play. Some discontinuities in the work's imaginative fabric are likely to remain, even though the majority may lend themselves to explanations of one kind or another.

Yet the principal and central elements of El condenado por desconfiado seem to respond in remarkably specific ways to the author's shaping intention. This is especially true of the characters. A great deal of what we learn about them appears random and casual; much of it, too, is unexpected. Yet the greater part of this information is built into a conscious and coherent bodying-forth of Tirso's central spiritual concerns. Again, this process can be traced at the level of the play's broad structure. From the sheer length of time - with brief and functional exceptions, the entire drama - for which one or the other of them is on stage, it is clear that _El condenado_ is, above all else, about Paulo and Enrico. From its even division between them, we may conclude that it is about them both equally - 'glory and punishment exchanged' in the words of what may have been the original subtitle (1. 3005). From the rare and equivocal occasions on which they appear before us together - only one of which, at the end of Act II, is an actual meeting, and that strangely at cross-purposes - it can be deduced, again correctly, that it is about both their togetherness and their separateness.

The point about their equality of status might be seen as the most controversial of these assertions.[59] In Ivy McClelland's view, for example, Tirso 'did not... pursue the character of Paulo as far as he did that of Enrico'. Margaret Wilson, by contrast, holds that 'Of the main elements in the play, the character of Enrico is the one that seems most contrived.' Plainly, both these views cannot be right. Yet one part of the problem which they present is that most readers or spectators will feel temperamentally inclined to take sides one way or the other - with Paulo, the tormented intellectual, or with the swaggering, instinctual Enrico. It takes a large sympathy indeed - a Tirsian or a Shakespearian sympathy - to accommodate them both. The play itself, one feels, can only just do it. Yet accommodate them it does. The two actions which begin so far apart, in the hermit's cell and the ruffians' Alsatia, and then are drawn so fatally together, are not, like the double actions of many other Tirsian plays, plot and subplot. They involve issues of precisely equal weight: one man saved; another damned. And the drama moves, as Margaret Wilson herself notes, with memorable symmetry. The protagonists converge towards their central meeting, then go their separate but opposite ways, both literally and spiritually. Enrico's possibilities of redemption come to the fore as Paulo sinks deeper into guilt. At the moment of their meeting they are close indeed. They are mutually dependent: Enrico's life is at Paulo's mercy; Paulo is desperate for an assurance which only Enrico can give him. Both men are great sinners - dangerous criminals, in fact - yet capable at that moment of going towards either a good or an evil end. The outcome is ambiguous for them both: neither the sort of good for which Paulo implausibly hopes, nor yet the sort of evil which we might have come to expect from Enrico. The scene is, as Margaret Wilson finely puts it, 'the crux of the play'. It lies at the heart of a design which we may call, with her, 'X-shaped', or, using Aristotelian terms with Duncan Moir, 'a double tragedy'.[60] One man's rise counterweights another's fall.

What gives the play its life, however, is the way in which that is shown to us in terms of character. In Paulo, the extreme complexities involved are evident from the start. Long before the action begins he has adopted a peculiarly searching and challenging form of religious vocation: the life, not of a member of a religious Order, but of a hermit, a solitary, living a regime of personal penance and devotion, and aspiring to become a saint.[61] Initially he seems to thrive on this: his hermitage is a 'safe refuge' or 'happy shelter' and he thanks God for it humbly enough. Yet we might well wonder why he chooses to praise the place precisely as a shelter, a refuge. Why does he say (ll. 39-40) that his chosen path is bound (es fuerza) to lead to a vision of God? Why is he so insistent - it is a thought which evidently troubles him - that he wants to see what Heaven holds in store? It is the desire to be secure, to know, to possess his own salvation, which opens the way for Paulo to be tempted.[62]

The Devil, for his part, says that Paulo's trouble is pride. There is something in this: certainly, there is an odd discrepancy between what Paulo's life is shown as being and what he himself makes of it. He is, for example, naively self-important in his assurance that his way of life as a hermit must entitle him to some special consideration from God. His attitude is similarly flawed when he tries to evaluate a particularly strange and equivocal piece of his own experience: his dream of judgment. Disturbing though this vision undoubtedly is - the more so for a man who clearly has a literal belief in the pains of Hell - it is far from clear why he should come to regard it so unreservedly as a spiritually significant experience. As a Christian he must know that there is something very wrong with a vision of God in terms exclusively of a 'pitiless' face (l. 163), and with a vision of judgment in which his own guilt is measured only against his own good works, with no mention of the redemptive role of Jesus Christ. The dream is, naturally, a frightening experience, but Paulo's very natural fear and depression cannot in themselves account for the curious bargain which he attempts to strike: if he promises to remain a hermit all his life, will he be saved? That can only be explained in the light of his restless appetite for certainties, and of the fact that – at least partly through pride – he is already in a state of very considerable confusion. Out of that confusion comes his major error: the demand for a certain knowledge of his spiritual destination. That gives the Devil his chance.

Modern spectators may well find the incursion of the Devil (here in angelic disguise) disconcerting. Audiences in the seventeenth century probably did so too for, away from the stage, he was not in the habit of appearing to them either.[63] They, like ourselves, would have had the advantage over Paulo of having heard the Devil's opening soliloquy. Like us too, they would have been prepared, by the hermit's confused reaction to one misleading vision, for him now to botch his response to another. But they would also have had some notion of what to expect from the Devil, and this in turn would have thrown more light on precisely where Paulo goes wrong. The Devil was a liar, and could be expected to imitate a divine message deceitfuly. But his power was limited by God; he was not allowed to deceive anyone in such a way that the deceit could not be overcome. Thus he was likelier to tell an equivocal form of the truth than to lie outright. On the other hand, he remained a deceiver by nature, doomed by his own perversity to lie even when lying was no part of his plan. And so here his message offers enough anomalies to put anyone – anyone but Paulo, that is – on his guard.[64]

His very first instruction is that Paulo should go to Naples, thereby breaking both his rule as a hermit and the promise which he has just made to adhere to that rule for life. He further instructs him to pay close attention to Enrico, whom he describes in terms that have a decidedly worldly ring: tall, handsome, a <u>gentilhombre</u> (ll. 268-9). He makes it clear that the encounter with Enrico will be crucial for what Paulo wants to know. But he has, for the moment, no licence to go further; 'I shall say no more', he declares (l. 270). Let us suppose, then, that Paulo goes to Naples on the basis of this information alone, and finds Enrico as odious as he afterwards turns out to be. What, in that case, are Paulo's options? He could take flight and head for the wilderness once more. Or he could stay on in Naples and try to convert Enrico. Either course might lead to salvation.

An even better prospect, of course, given the already suspect character of the Devil's message, would be for Paulo to take no notice of it and to remain where he is. What he actually does, however, is the worst of all choices: he follows his obsession and asks, not once but twice, for more definite information. Only on the second of these occasions does the Devil come out with his major equivocation:

> the end which that man comes to
> will be your end also. (ll. 283-4)

It is, precisely, an equivocation and not a lie because they will share the same end in that both die at the hands of the law. They could, indeed, share the same fate after death too if Paulo reacted aright. But from the outset he reacts in the wrong way:

> He must certainly be a saint
> How could he be anything else? (1.289-90)

Paulo is a natural doubter; there is no great harm in that. The harm arises because he doubts the wrong things - the religion whose beliefs he is supposed to know; the mercy of the God he worships - and fails to doubt the right ones - his own dream-experiences; the conclusions to which his spiritual pride jumps in wholesale default of evidence.

These intellectual confusions are compounded when he sees and hears Enrico. Just as he has already rushed to the conclusion that his dream is a threat to his salvation, so he now careers through a whole sequence of defective arguments to reach a wholly fallacious inference.[65] He reasons along the following lines:

(a) <u>I can be quite certain that Enrico will never be saved</u>. But this first premise is unsound: nobody is entitled to write off anyone else as reprobate of God.

(b) <u>God's angel told me that I would share Enrico's end</u>. But Paulo has now heard from Enrico's own mouth that he is not, as the disguised Devil had asserted, of noble family. So either it was a somewhat unreliable angel or the message was not from God at all. Either way, the

(c) <u>Therefore I must be damned</u>.

second premise collapses. Paulo, however, presses on regardless to arrive at his false conclusion.

This ill-founded <u>desconfianza</u> now becomes the first premise of a new argument, directed against the justice of God:

(a) <u>I am damned already</u>.

Untrue for the reasons given already.

(b) <u>But I have earned the right to be saved by my years as a hermit</u>.

Paulo should know, if he has any theology at all, that salvation does not work like this.

(c) <u>Therefore God is unjust</u>.

The most serious error yet.

On this ramshackle basis in logic, Paulo decides to go off and live a life of crime.

Being Paulo, however, he does so for reasons that are dauntingly complex, and only partly logical in their nature. On one level he wants to 'take revenge on God'; the reaction is one of sheer rage. That rage is compounded of a desperate violence (of which the play offers a number of other examples) and an equally desperate self-assertion. 'I will <u>show</u> them', he declares; 'I shall destroy them all' (1. 996). These factors seem more important than the pragmatic explanation which he also offers: that there is no point in making himself uncomfortable with penances if he is to get the same reward as Enrico, who lives in comfort in the city. With this simple cost-benefit analysis, Pedrisco, as we might expect, fully concurs. Yet how much can it really mean to Paulo? If what is sought is a comfortable life, being a bandit is by no means an obvious choice. And although bandits may be assumed to pick up the odd luxury as they go along, Paulo, when he gets to the forest, seems less interested in these things than in violence for the sake of violence, and in his own reputation.[66]

An altogether more disturbing explanation for his conduct is prompted by the fact that he more than once asks God to pardon his decision. The appeal is no more that residual; Paulo is now without hope in God. Yet he remains, in a sense, a deeply religious man – but now he believes in a God who has damned him. He can only justify the ways of such a God by behaving as damnably as possible, and at a deeper level it is perhaps this that he is trying to do. It is a religious commitment, but no longer a Christian one; with his loss of hope, Paulo's Christianity has collapsed into a monstruous self-parody. More than that, his very personality has collapsed into another identity. And the name which he gives to that indentity is 'Enrico'. The note is insistent: 'let me share his way of life' (ll. 969, 979-80). 'I want / to live like Enrico', he says in Act II (l. 1464), and in the last Act, 'In cruelty I am Enrico' (l. 2821). But Enrico, by now, has become something else.

To understand fully how Paulo arrives at this point we have to consider not just his intellectual but his emotional life. His nightmare of judgment is one clue to this; so is his overreaction to Pedrisco's fairly harmless reminiscence of a striking Neapolitan blonde, when he urges his companion to trample the lust out of him. Like Enrico, Paulo - an ex-soldier, as we shall discover towards the end of the play - is a man with much violence in him.[67] Internally directed now, it will, with the collapse of his selfhood, be projected outwards to others, like the unfortunate captives in the wood. For the rest of the play Paulo will oscillate between such obsessive cruelty and a kind of weary tenderness, in a classic manic-depressive pattern.

But he is not damned for being a manic-depressive any more than he is damned for being a temperamental doubter. His fault is, rather, that he fails to use any of the means that are available to him for coping with these aspects of his condition. He does not use his intelligence or his religion, both of which are real enough. He does not use his human contacts - Enrico in Act II - or his apprehensions of the divine in the person of the Shepherd. His approach to the captive Enrico, for example, is no fresh initiative; it is merely a renewal of his old pursuit of definitive knowledge ('trying / to find what's in his mind'). Even if he did learn from such an exercise that Enrico was penitent, it would do Paulo no good. His hopes would still be based on the quasi-magical significance which he assigns to that possibility, rather than being grounded in his own relation with God. Nor would this be the only problem if Enrico were to make his confession to Paulo. The latter at this moment is neither a true priest nor a true Christian; any value which the confession would have as a sacrament would obtain because divine grace has the power to manifest itself despite the unworthiness of its human vehicle. In the traditional phrase, 'The water of life is the water of life though it flows through the jaws of a dead dog.' But this is what

Paulo refuses to accept with regard to Enrico. He has been told that Enrico is relevant to his salvation; thus far the Devil told him no lie. But finding that Enrico is a man of wicked life, Paulo has concluded that both of them must be damned. It does not seem to occur to him that, in the mercy of God, Enrico might possibly be a means to his salvation. Yet Tirso, in the last and strangest of the many reversals which mark their confrontation, appears to hint at just that possibility. The spurious hope of extracting a confession out of Enrico has failed at last; Paulo has made his moving renunciation of the habits he wore and the beliefs that once sustained him as a hermit. It is in this last extremity, though, that he is able to offer Enrico something wholly genuine for a change. It is the one thing which he can in fact offer – the truth about his own despair – and it evokes a very different response from Enrico from any which we have witnessed hitherto. That response is still a long way from being morally or spiritually adequate. But it involves a decent compassion, a puzzled but hopeful simplicity in matters of religious belief, and a worldly comradeship, all of which are worth something. They are worth something even to Paulo, who finds himself a little comforted. If there is any basis at all for his potential recovery, it is here at the end of Act II that we are allowed a glimpse of it.

The appearances of the little Shepherd, it might be argued, are a more explicit witness to the possibilities which divine grace holds out to Paulo. Yet their function in the play seems slightly different, in ways that are highly characteristic of Tirso's handling of religious themes. The Shepherd is a supernatural figure (or partly so at least) and Paulo recognizes him as such; his desconfianza has never taken the form of an inability to recognize the supernatural. His problem lies with what he does about it. The Shepherd, on his first appearance, tells him what to do – tells him indeed what he already knows from Christian teaching. Paulo is moved by the sermon, and promptly rationalizes its message into the fatuous project of testing Enrico to see whether he is repentant. Only from Enrico's disruptive refusal to play this strange game by Paulo's rules does the possibility arise of a contact between the two men which might bring Paulo to take a less mechanistic view of whether they are to be saved or damned. Supernatural promptings point the way for man, but his spiritual destiny is worked out, for good or ill, in his human living.

In Paulo's case, the working-out is for ill rather than

good because of the way in which he remains locked in his despair. 'I despair of trust in anything', he tells Enrico; it is, for him, a fact about his own nature (l. 2043). The final index of his failure to progress is the fact that he reacts no more positively to the second appearance of the Shepherd than to the first. He makes no reference to the whole extraordinary scene of his meeting with Enrico. That scene will have made its mark on any audience, but for Paulo it might just as well never have happened. He is not even perturbed by Enrico's failure to return from Naples as he had promised. His whole concern is with his old pain and the end which it foretells for him. All his responses now fall within the mental set which that concern determines.

Thus, while he again recognizes that the Shepherd is more than a mortal figure, his reactions in ll. 2762-4 to the latter's tale of the Lost Sheep are cold and abstract. ('His words must carry in them / some deep and complex mystery'.) The vision of a saved soul prompts confused thoughts of luck (ventura) and of deserving, but none of repentance or grace. At the end he simply cannot take in the news of Enrico's death, much less what it means. Even his acceptance on the factual level that Enrico has been saved leaves him clinging to the cold comfort of the supposed promise that he will go Enrico's way:

> God gave me that promise:
> if Enrico was saved,
> I will be saved; I've a right to expect it.
> (ll. 2903-5)

And that, without actual repentance, remains the sheerest superstition.[68]Paulo has surrendered the faith in which a desconfiado might yet live for the vain pursuit of religious belief as a 'magic amulet', a charm against desconfianza. That error has eaten away all his capacity for feeling or for thought, and all his rich complexity as a person. Tirso has made his audience witnesses to that collapse, in both its literal and its doctrinal meaning. Indeed, the two meanings can hardly be separated; the 'truth' of this aspect of the play is, irreducibly, our experience of Paulo's loss.

Enrico, by contrast, grows on us as the play advances. At first he appears a simple, not to say simplistic, character - a roaring boy with the street glamour which can fascinate a Lidora or even a Celia. Demonstrative in his vices, he tells his tale of crime with real gusto. Yet his drowning of the beggar, horrific as it is, suggests motives of a less obvious

sort: 'He stank of poverty; I couldn't face it! (l. 662).
The poverty hurts Enrico, who does not like being hurt; he
therefore kills the source of the hurt.[69]Paulo in his
opening scenes reacted in a very complex way to motives which
his self-awareness made very explicit. Enrico reacts in a
brutally simple fashion to motives which remain obscure - for
he is not self-aware at all. Similar difficulties in forming
an adequate view of Enrico's inner life attach to his long
autobiographical speech. It is essentially about the external
facts of his existence as a criminal. The recital of evil
deeds and blasphemies is comprehensive enough; Tirso is
concerned to rule out any easy option of viewing Enrico as a
'pious thief'. But it is not his record alone which makes
Enrico sound like a criminal; the tone of what he says is
just as important. 'I was born wicked...'; 'gambling -
that's the start / of all the crime there is' (ll. 722;
743-4) - the News of the World itself was never more banal in
its sensationalist whine. Or we might take another effect:
having just assured his hearers that he never told a lie in
his life, Enrico now says 'I've often perjured myself... /
just for the hell of it' (ll. 826-7). The unreliability like
the banality, like the joke in doubtful taste about his being
lucky to find six virgins nowadays, makes its contribution to
a criminal style. And at this stage, Enrico is identified
with this style and with very little else. Even so, and in
this very speech, though characteristically unremarked by the
listening Paulo, there is already the small matter of Enrico's
relationship with his father Anareto.

As it turns out in Act II, this half-hidden virtue of
Enrico's is not such a small matter in its implications. Yet
even there it remains contaminated by the kind of man that he
still is.[70]There is something distinctly less than
impressive in the fact that he keeps back one per cent of his
gaming stakes to buy his father food; the use for the same
purpose of a rake-off from Celia's immoral earnings seems
even less reputable. And who is it that Enrico is trying to
fool when he says that he has never in his life offended his
father? We can remember, if he cannot, the speech he made to
his gang: 'I took the old man's money...' (l. 738) The
curious thing is that when he makes his later claim Enrico is
alone on stage. This suggests that he may be trying to fool
himself - which would immediately make him more interesting
as a character. Even worse problems attach to his assertion
that Anareto knows nothing of his life of crime. As Terence
May observes, it is far likelier that Anareto does know - how

could he not? – but that he chooses to conceal it for love of
his son, and in the faint hope that the boy may repent. It
would also add a special pathos, as father and son offer one
another a sort of primary kindness, laced with more or less
loving deception on either side. Yet Enrico's respect for
his father is still real enough to inhibit him from attacking
Albano, and almost – but not quite – enough to turn him back
when fleeing for his life. At this stage, then, we have a
violent, impulsive, self-dramatizing criminal, with a certain
obscurely-defined potential for becoming something better,
and a close, if flawed relationship with his father.

Later in Act II, when Enrico is brought face to face
with Paulo, his devotion to Anareto is not much in evidence.
Certainly it cannot yet be said to function straightforwardly
as a 'redeeming' feature. It is the mixture of qualities in
Enrico which is more important at this stage. He can shrug
off calls to repentance as readily as ever, but the strange
nature of Paulo's subsequent conduct evokes quite another
reaction. Both responses, however, are recognizably those of
the same personality. Enrico's refusal to confess was marked
by violent obstinacy, but also by a certain crude integrity
of feeling – 'I should repent. / I want to but I can't' (ll.
1776-7) [1] – and by pride in being true to himself – 'What
I've never done / I'll not do now' (ll. 1828-9). Confronted
with Paulo's despair, he has no difficulty in recognizing the
element of aggression in the other man's outlook – 'a sort of
revenge / for the message you had from God' (ll. 1970-1).
But his answer is worked out with the same clumsy directness
that has characterized his earlier, negative replies:

> Paulo, my friend, if God
> sent anyone word by an angel,
> wouldn't the words be the kind
> to carry some hidden meaning
> that men alone couldn't reach?
> I wouldn't have left the life
> you were living... (ll. 1961-6)

And he goes on to insist that Paulo too should have stuck to
his original commitment.

In addition, Enrico voices something which is new in
him, yet quite coherent with what we already know about him:
an instinctive trust in God's mercy, which seems very much
akin to his trust in his own luck. The latter, as earlier
episodes in this Act have made clear, has its limitations,

and Enrico plainly has much work still to do before he becomes capable of disentangling the two attitudes.[72]With only a shade more cynicism, his 'I do still have hope / that I will be saved' (ll. 1994-5) would sound very much like the 'plenty of time for me to pay that debt' of the all too confiado Don Juan Tenorio. In effect, Enrico is in the position, though distinctive in personality and outlook, of Don Juan while the latter still has a chance to repent. But at least he still has that chance, and has not renounced it; Paulo has.

That state of affairs, however, would not be radically altered by the suggestion which Enrico now puts to him. He regards Paulo's stance as a desatino, a 'damn fool thing' to do (l. 2002). But Enrico himself has done a great many things which would merit just this description, and it is not his way to regard them as matters about which anything can or should be done afterwards. And so it is with this one: he does not urge Paulo to repentance or amendment of life, but to a joint 'good time' (l. 2005) in the woods - presumably as bandits operating in collaboration. Even the residual human solidarity implied by this would be of some potential use to Paulo, but it is hard to see how Enrico might learn anything from such an experience. In the event, though, something draws him back from this unprofitable course. It is, as might have been anticipated, the memory of Anareto. That recollection is not yet associated with any thoughts of repentance; all that Enrico wants to do is to bring the old man out of Naples so that he can look after him. Like much of his thinking about his father to date, the notion is not very realistic. It is not clear that the forest is the best place for a bedridden invalid to receive the care he needs, or how Enrico proposes, while living the life of a bandit, to preserve Anareto's sedulously fostered illusion of his son's moral worth. The best that can be said is that this concern for Anareto is a decent impulse, and one on which providence might yet build to bring about Enrico's redemption. And so it proves, even though its first result is to land him, unpromisingly if also predictably, in the town gaol of Naples.

The prison scenes with which Act III opens culminate in Enrico's conversion. But if that had been all that they were meant to do, the whole sequence could have been a great deal shorter. Their actual elaboration achieves something else: it makes Enrico as thoroughly known to us as Paulo already is. The rudimentary state of Enrico's own self-knowledge means that he cannot be made to tell us what we need to know in this regard; we have to be shown it. The showing, finely analysed in its psychological aspect by Ivy McClelland, reveals two governing patterns.[73]One is the recapitulation of all that Enrico has been so far; the other is a set of parallels and contrasts with Paulo. The latter on its own would have given his repentance a purely doctrinal context of meanings; the former supplies its human and biographical substance. The most important fact about Tirso's presentation is that he offers us both.

Thus to remind us of Enrico's life as it has been and is we have the stubborn trust in gambler's luck, the passage with Celia, and following Celia's refusal to help him, an outburst of the old rage, culminating in the murder of the guard. But these things are also reminders about Paulo. Like Paulo hanging corpses from every tree, Enrico carries his surrender to passion to a pitch of anti-natural violence in his threat to eat the prison Governor a piece at a time. Like Paulo again, he collapses thereafter into apathetic self-reproach. He too exhibits a perfect manic-depressive pattern. The difference in Enrico's case is that he does not fortify it with the intellectual conviction that this is the only way to live. Rather, once in his solitary cell, he falls back on his old values of honour and public reputation. It is by no means the best of preparations for the test which now faces him as, like Paulo in Act I, he has to discriminate between angelic and demonic promptings. Yet it is not the worst either: at least Enrico comes to the test free of Paulo's preconceptions about what God owes to him, and with a directness of human reaction which the latter's obsessive state could not match.[74]Believing the Devil to be another prisoner, he feels an immediate pity for him; seriously tempted by the promise that he will make his name famous, he candidly admits his inhibiting fears. But above all he has the wit - or, in another perspective, the simplicity - to ask the question which Paulo ought to have asked but did not: 'Who are you?' (1. 2275). The Devil's necessary evasion on that point creates just enough uncertainty for Enrico to hesitate about accepting his promise of freedom; in that moment of uncertainty he hears the angelic voices promising life, and it is their promise which he prefers to trust.

To the play's early audiences this conflict of impulses might well have seemed as dark in its implications as it does to Enrico. They would have seen a figure on stage, probably cloaked, certainly meant to be only partially visible to Enrico himself, as the words of the scene would have told them. They would have heard the singers off stage.[75]But in a play which turns so largely on illusions, they could not have been sure as yet which of the two phenomena was intended to be illusory. There are, as we have observed, certain clues; the manner of the production could have supplied more – or fewer. However that might be, the audience were being challenged to do what both Paulo and Enrico were challenged to do: to exercise their judgment aright. The enigma and the challenge remain the same if we take the vision and the voice – as a modern audience may perfectly well want to take them – to represent what is going on at this moment within Enrico's mind. He still has something to get right, in contrast to the way in which he has lived up to now. The decision which he now has to take is still of relevance to that process, though we cannot yet be certain just how it is relevant. What is very clear, on every possible reading of the scene, is that the actual decision is a close-run business. That is clear enough to Enrico too, as he settles down, rather grimly, to await 'the worst that's coming to me' (l. 2327).

Nor does he have to wait very long, for the next thing he hears is the Prison Governor pronouncing his sentence of death. It can scarcely come as a surprise to someone with a proven record of multiple murder – the last instance not ten minutes past. But Enrico resents it bitterly as a denial of what the voices promised him. He resents even more the suggestion that he should now make his peace with God, and the two modes of resentment alternate in the series of short scenes which follow. The most interesting aspect of Enrico's obduracy is the range of its motivation. To the gaoler he turns his public front of pagan, self-sufficient swagger: 'I'll face my punishment / without help from anyone' (ll. 2385-6). To himself he admits a deeper hesitancy – how is he to face God? how can he even remember all his sins? – together with a touch of his old, superstitious over-confidence that it can all be left to God's mercy. This is at once truer than ever – it will indeed prove vital to Enrico that he does believe this – and more perilous than ever, because the time for his own essential act of co-operation with that mercy is now running out. More than anything else, though, as he makes clear to Pedrisco, Enrico is simply irritated by all this talk of repenting. Nor is this irritation, in one sense, entirely unreasonable: the threat of imminent death is a poor sort of reason for making your peace with God. Enrico is going to need, and be offered, a better one: his father's love.

But before he comes to that he has yet to reach his very

lowest point. In a last soliloquy he actually undoes the act
of faltering good judgment by which he has just discriminated
the angelic voice from that of the Devil, and begs the latter
to come back. It is at this precise point that Anareto, of
all people, enters the cell. His arrival, therefore, cannot
be taken as the recognition of any actual spiritual growth in
Enrico at all. For the latter is on the verge of getting it
all wrong once more, despite the sporadic points of potential
growth which have made their fitful presence felt throughout.
Instead, Anareto's coming is a free gift, an act of
grace.[76] And Enrico responds to it as such – just because
Anareto is who he is, loves him as he loves him, and suffers
for him as he has made him suffer:

> My soul has been more touched
> (as God is my witness)
> by the sorrows you feel
> than by all my fears
> of the death which awaits me. (ll. 2508–11)

To have made clear at once the freely given nature of Enrico's
salvation and its consequentiality in terms of his flawed but
redeemable character was an achievement on Tirso's part no
less rich psychologically than the portrait of Paulo himself.
    There are no other characters in the play like the two
principals; there would scarcely be room for them. But there
is, among its minor personages, an interesting deployment of
two sets of roles. The first of these is the pair constituted
by Pedrisco and Galván. Pedrisco, in particular, begins as
an absolutely conventional stage funny-man, a _gracioso_ role,
not importantly different from hundreds of others, and
included merely because theatre companies and their audiences
were agreed that every play should have one.[77]His initial
motivation seems to be limited to food – always worth a laugh
in the Spanish seventeenth century, when there was not often
an abundance of it around, and an apt enough concern in his
particular situation as a hermit's apprentice.   This apart,
he seems totally tied to the personality and motives of
Paulo. When Paulo says 'be a hermit', he is a hermit; when
Paulo says 'go to town', he goes; when Paulo tells him 'take
up banditry', he does that too. Occasionally a sounding-board
for his master's opinions, this _gracioso_, like so many of his
kind, seems little more as yet than a piece of stage
furniture. But even in his early scenes there are hints of
something more.   There are independent memories of a past

among the bars of Naples. And, as with Don Juan's abject body-servant Catalinón, there is a flow of ironic comment on his master's grand gestures. This tends to promote a certain solidarity with the audience, most of whom – most, that is to say, of us – are much more like Pedrisco that we are like Paulo.[78] 'Feel no pain for me', Paulo tells him in the trampling scene. 'Don't worry', says Pedrisco, 'I'm not the one who's likely to' (11. 649-50). He goes off to the hills again, drawn by Paulo's perversely inflamed will, but with the wry remark that he is likely to find himself dragged down to hell as mere baggage.

In Act II he is capable of a similar irony when he comments on Paulo's career as a bandit: 'Nothing surprises me now' (1. 1390). Yet he fits in with it fatalistically, and even seems to enjoy the life. 'He's a brave fellow', says Paulo, packing him off to Naples (1. 2027). There are obvious parallels drawn, too, between Pedrisco and Galván, Enrico's dense, slyly cowardly henchman, though Pedrisco's residual respectability makes him object to taking the blame for the other's criminal record. Again, in the gaol scene, he feels it an affront as well as a source of danger that he should be blamed by association for the crimes of Enrico. Here too his comic hunger reappears as a motif, skilfully integrated, as we have seen, with the human depth of the prison episode. Indeed, the figure of Pedrisco is itself undergoing a similar integration with the play's profounder themes. Because Tirso uses him as a source of comment on Enrico, he becomes a focus both of normative commonsense – the kind of thing a not very bright member of the audience might be expected to think and feel[79] – and of sympathetic concern for Enrico's fate. Later, when he encounters the dying Paulo, he supplies the same basic human comfort, together with a last, desperate attempt to wean him from his despair. By this time Pedrisco has become a character of oblique but real importance. When Paulo welcomes him we welcome him too – after a scene or two in Paulo's company a little normality is a refreshing change. When Pedrisco struggles to make Paulo comprehend the fact of Enrico's salvation – 'Oh, dear God! / Convince him, quickly' (11. 2891-2) – we both share his urgency and register that, for a moment, the fool is wiser than the man of wisdom. And Pedrisco's final concern (1. 2912) for the 'poor body' – not his own belly this time, but the corpse of his tormented friend – has a minimal decency that is a value in itself.[80]

It is perhaps only a limited value. Pedrisco and Galván and their like do not live on the heights of embattled passion, ultimate questioning, proud, wild destinies that Paulo and Enrico inhabit. Their nervous dialogue at the very end, after the vision of Paulo has faded with the scent of brimstone, suggests that their kind of life will shuffle on a little better - though perhaps not a whole lot better - as a result of that shattering experience. But this was what Tirso, essentially a realist in spiritual matters, knew that he could expect of them, of most people, of his audience, of us. Pedrisco is of interest because he is a _gracioso_ who becomes an Everyman. In speaking the last lines of the play, he also assumes another identity. One can hardly suppose that the original Pedrisco would have been well up in the study of Cardinal Bellarmine and the _Vitae Patrum_; no more would most of the play's spectators. But Pedrisco here speaks for the one man concerned who certainly was, and the learned theologian, Master Gabriel Téllez, once disguised as Tirso the Shepherd, here assumes the second disguise of a poor, down-to-earth fool like the rest of us. Most plays of the period ended with a request to the audience to pardon the faults of the author. Here we have something which looks very like genuine, rather than merely conventional, authorial humility.

The other pair of characters with a particular claim on our attention are Anareto and the Shepherd. As Terence May has demonstrated, Anareto can only be played coherently as someone who, from the outset, knows far more about the kind of person Enrico is than either man admits.[81] This would make him a much more complex character than the tender-hearted old invalid with whom we are, on a surface level, presented; he would also be a far more striking example of forbearing, self-denying paternal love. But as such he is not simply, in May's terms, one of the 'fools of love'; he must also be, given all that we know about Tirso's theological frame of reference, a direct figuration of the love of God the Father.[82] Indeed, the course of his relation with Enrico seems to enact the parable of the Prodigal Son. It is not a case of a the direct re-enactment of the story, as in Tirso's own parable-play on the Dives and Lazarus theme, _Tanto es lo de más como lo de menos_. We are not even dealing with allegory in the sense made familiar to seventeenth-century playgoers by the _autos sacramentales_. Rather, the figure of Anareto is made to stand at one and the same time for the man himself and for more than himself. This double identity is very evident in his final scene with Enrico. Much of what he says identifies him firmly as Enrico's earthly father. He has risen from his sickbed to come to the prison; he gives concerned, chiding advice: 'A fine kind of Christianity!' (l. 2479). Yet he also speaks with a special authority in terms of the story as a whole. He identifies Enrico's impenitence as 'taking revenge on God' (ll. 2482-3), thereby establishing its kinship with Paulo's lethal despair. He talks of 'putting this off too long' (l. 2486) in terms which render inescapable the connection of this play with Don Juan's 'plenty of time to pay that debt'. In effect, a great measure of Tirso's authority as the creator of the play passes into Anareto at this moment. And when he says 'You are no longer my son / if you do not keep my law', (ll. 2470-1), he speaks not only with his own voice but with that of a creator in a more absolute sense – as the God of the scriptures. Enrico for his part appears to respond to both these identities; for him in his repentance, Anareto is both the 'dear father' of his human affections (l. 2507) and the representative of a divine fatherhood. The moment when Anareto moves back into focus as a vulnerable human individual – from the divine serenity of 'Then you are once again my son' (l. 2529) to the wholly mortal grief of 'It breaks my heart to lose you' (l. 2532) – is among the most moving of the whole piece.

El condenado por desconfiado, for all its supernatural elements, is not a play about the supernatural; it is a play about the encounters between the life of man and what lies beyond it. The shifting identity of Anareto helps Tirso to chart those encounters; the little Shepherd belongs more obviously to the supernatural domain. Yet even he makes his first appearance as a boy singing above the wood, and a simple, devout religious believer – 'with all my heart' (l. 1505) – who has been taught his doctrine by the church. He also claims in the same breath to have been instructed by God too, and it becomes clear as he preaches his sermon that his formation is not that of any ordinary shepherd.[83] His use of the parable of the Lost Sheep, with its evident application to Paulo, like the latter's impotence to detain him, confirms that there is something otherworldly about him. But the Pastorcillo too has no single identity. Most obviously he appears to be a minister of God, perhaps Paulo's guardian angel with a special responsibility for this one soul. Yet his second appearance suggests something else:

> The soles of my feet
> are all bloodied and broken
> with the print of the barbs

and the thorns that I trod. (ll. 2716-19)

Both the fact and the detail of the Pastorcillo's suffering
for the lost soul - bleeding feet and sharp thorns, at least
by association, recall the Passion - strongly imply that the
Shepherd is Christ himself.[84] If that is the case, then his
last lines of all come to bear an unexpected meaning:

> Alas! what shall I answer?
> There is nothing to answer,
> unless my tears are the answer. (ll. 2755-7)

Before we draw back, in a characteristically twentieth-
century reaction from El condenado, and criticize it for its
acquiescence in the cruel damnation of Paulo, we would be
well-advised to ponder these lines. If the divine Shepherd's
tears are potentially 'the answer' to Paulo's damnation, then
it may be that Tirso is allowing for the possibility that, in
the mercy of God, he himself may have the matter wrong.

Logically, indeed, he must allow for this. For the
purpose with which he has written El condenado por desconfiado
is to show the nature of divine justice. And what he has to
say of it amounts to this: 'Divine justice can be quite
unlike what we, with our human awareness, understand by
justice; yet we must understand it as just.' That, of
course, can scarcely be shown on the stage at all in any
direct fashion. For let us suppose that Tirso sets up one
scheme of justice - the obvious, humanly intelligible scheme,
in which holy hermits like Paulo go to Heaven and villains
like Enrico go to Hell. And then let us suppose that he
supplants this with an alternative scheme, in which it is
possible for hermits like Paulo to go to Hell, and villains
like Enrico to Heaven, for this and that and the other
identifiable reason. If we are convinced by these reasons,
they will fall within the scope of human justice anyway; if
they fail to convince us, the second scheme will not, after
all, seem just.[85] If this were all that El condenado had to
offer, then the play would be a failure, masked perhaps in
its own day by the orthodoxy of its teaching, but patently
inadequate in ours. What Tirso needed to suggest, therefore,
was not that his second scheme of justice was a reliable
image of how divine justice worked. It might be so, of
course; it could well represent what many theologians would
want to say about these matters. But even theologians were
human and fallible, and it made sense that the work should

offer some caveat to the effect that its last word might not be the very last word. The demonstration which he did have to make, however, was this: that the difference between human and divine justice was like the difference between his first scheme and his second. In other words, he had to make his drama not only out of things which we know or can be made to know, but also out of things which we do not, and perhaps cannot know. That is to say, he had to make it like life which, whether or not we understand it in terms of Tirso's religion, irreducibly contains these unknowns. Paulo's thirst for a mode of knowledge that will put him firmly and totally in control of his own existence, and Enrico's spontaneous defiance of rule are not characteristics which our own world can either securely explain or safely ignore. Nor have we come much closer, if at all, since Tirso's time to a rational way of doing justice between them. Tirso's imaginative justice – expressed as much through the way in which the two men are seen as through the way in which their story ends – still has its relevance, and its revelations for us.

IV

The poetry of *El condenado por desconfiado*; the translation

Paradoxically, given this immense richness of theme, the purely linguistic achievement of El condenado por desconfiado remains a relatively modest one. Tirso - beyond all question a great dramatic poet – is not, in the absolute sense in which we might apply the term to either Lope or Calderón, a great poet. We have already observed where the chief strength of his language lies: in its remarkabaly close integration with the dramatic situations in which it is uttered.[86] The most obvious instances of this are those single lines and phrases by which his major characters define themselves, in terms quite startlingly well-adapted to their personalities and circumstances. Don Juan's self-identification as 'a man who's nameless', and in this play Enrico's 'I am the Devil' (ll. 495-6) are effects of this kind. The same contextual rightness can also extend to whole speeches: Paulo's outbursts of cruelty or rage, Enrico's criminal autobiography, the maundering benevolence of Anareto in Act II. In this last example, however, much of the text is actually cribbed from Lope de Vega – and that surely underlines the point which needs to be made. Tirso's genius is for the contextualization of language, not for its invention.

This is equally the case with his imagery. Deployed with much skill, it is in itself unremarkable. Enrico, for example, describes the stab-wounds in the breast of one of his female victims as, in literal terms, 'gates of rubies / in fields of crystal'. (ll. 822-3) It is a tired, artificial figure - even, to a degree, a confused one. What still renders it striking is its incongruity in this brutal context, and the strange mixture of qualities which that incongruity reveals in Enrico himself.[87] He is clearly in some measure sadistic; if not, why would he talk like this? Yet there is an element of naivety here too. A sadist who was describing the situation with a fully conscious relish would, one feels, describe it with rather greater skill. Tirso's threadbare linguistic means, then, accomplish quite a complex effect in this case. More generally within the play, patterns of imagery, especially those connected with its range of Biblical references, help to sustain the imaginative coherence of the whole. Even images that are wholly conventional at first sight can carry important dramatic and thematic patterns. Death in Paulo's first vision hunts him down with the bow (l. 153) precisely as the peasant vigilantes will hunt him down in Act III. The many passages of what appears to be merely decorative, low-pressure description of nature are more than verbal embellishments - necessary though such embellishment was in a theatre which lacked material scenery. They also illuminate the precise character of Paulo's error. It is true that he falls from grace and not from nature, and that nature, viewed in a theological perspective, is fallen already. Yet nature remains accessible to grace. Paulo, however, cuts himself off from grace, by refusing to live according to nature.[88] Instead he opts to follow rules of his own intellectual devising. At times, as in his barbarous treatment of prisoners, this leads him into perverse acts of violence. He implements his own 'law', defying both the jus gentium and natural justice, and profaning the natural order of the forest by making the trees bear a crop of corpses (ll. 1436-40). But on other occasions, when nature offers him a still recognizable reminder of the good he has lost, his alienation from it emerges as tragic rather than horrific. The 'safe refuge' of his hermitage was a reassurance of providential order; the pleasant place by the fountain in Act III can do no more than distract him for a moment from his underlying despair (ll. 2614-5). Yet the elements of either picture are the same, and they are predictable enough: singing birds, green grass, running water. Their very conventionality for the audience, however, underlines how tragically their meaning for Paulo has been altered and reduced.

It is scarcely ever possible to say how far such effects were consciously intended. But all that we know of Tirso's dramatic verse tends to confirm that the limitations of his language were involuntary and natural to him. He observes the good manners of poetic composition, as these conventions were understood in his day, but he does not transcend them. Though it can frequently enhance our awareness of dramatic substance or our understanding of themes, his language is rarely charged with the specifically poetic excitments of Lope or Calderón. It is sustained, rather, by its easy adherence to the basic poetic decorum of seventeenth-century Spanish verse-drama. To convey something of the quality of that poetic idiom to readers with no knowledge of Spanish is perhaps the most difficult single task which presents itself to the translator of Tirso's work. The example of Elizabethan and Jacobean theatre, so potent in the minds of most English-speakers, is particularly unhelpful here. The habitual diction and dramatic poetry of the Spanish comedia are wholly distinctive, because their metrical basis is different.

Unlike the English drama of the time, which is bound almost exclusively to the unrhymed iambic pentameter, the comedia is not tied to any single metre. Strictly speaking, indeed, the pentameter could have no equivalent in Spanish, whose metres are based on syllable-count, with stress-patterns playing a subordinate role, and subject to much variation. For practical purposes, even so, Spanish does have its equivalent: a standard long line for educated verse. This is the hendecasyllable, imitated from Italian poetry from the early sixteenth century onwards. These eleven-syllable lines are by no means rare in the comedia, where they are often combined in various stanzaic forms with lines of seven syllables - also of educated and Italianate origins. But the commonest metre by far in the seventeenth-century theatre was the eight-syllable line, belonging - as did the much rarer six-syllable form - to native Spanish tradition. Rhyme, a sporadic embellishment in most Elizabethan and Jacobean plays, is predominant, though not quite universal, in the verse-forms of the comedia. Unrhymed hendecasyllables do occur - there are a couple of brief passages of this sort in El condenado - but they are not common. More usually, such lines are grouped in rhyming stanzas - octavas, as in Paulo's dream, or tercets, or even sonnets - or combined with lines of seven syllables in the stanzaic _lira_, or the freer but still rhyming _silva_. The native metres habitually rhymed. Five-lined _quintillas_ and _décimas_ of twice that length offered a variety of possible schemes. _Redondillas_ (quatrains rhyming ABBA/CDDC/...) were another very common form, though less prominent in this particular play. The most important of all the eight-syllable metres was something of an exception. The _romance_ - the classic form of Spanish balladry - offered no full rhymes, but every second line was marked by an assonance (vowel-rhyme). Taken together, these octosyllabic forms, with their well-defined recurrences of sound, dominate this play, as they do most others of the time. They furnish the _comedia_ in general with a very great deal of its essential character. That character is further defined by the many shifts of pace and density which the polymetric convention makes possible.

That is one reason - there are, naturally, others - why the Spanish theatre of this period can seem a faster-moving, more kaleidoscopic, in some senses more superficial, in others more authentically theatrical genre that its English counterpart. This kind of drama - in all senses a 'theatre of movement' - was what the Spanish public demanded, and the most immediate function of the metrical structure described here was to give it to them. A second, equally practical purpose was mnemonic. Given the rate of replacement of plays in performance which audiences, again, demanded, there was a premium on writing which actors could learn easily. Rhymed texts, for the most part in simple metres, met the need. It is much harder to pin down the expressive functions of Spanish polymetry. Lope de Vega tried to do so in his _Arte nuevo de hacer comedias_, assigning to each verse-form its own specific area of expression, but this was largely a matter of rationalization after the event.[89] Any accomplished playwright, of course, used the various metres and the shifts between them to shape the movement of each play. This might even include some observance of the rules of thumb formulated by Lope: sonnets for soliloquies, _romance_ for narratives, and so on. But the metres and their changes did not underwrite the play's content in any fixed or predictable way. They were part of the work's musicality rather than part of its semantics - though it also has to be said that the two aspects often worked together to common expressive ends.

In the present version, this free-flowing metrical variety, and the still greater variety of mood and tone which Tirso's language encompasses, have prompted a strategy of

translation which avoids rigid formal patterning. The point
of departure for this strategy has been the predominance of
octosyllabic forms among Tirso's metres. This is reflected
not in a parallel attachment to eight-syllable lines in
English, but in a consciously similar rhythmic habit. The
Spanish octosyllable normally carries three main stresses –
occasionally two or four – with scope for variation as to
their actual placing within the line. It is the permanent
interplay between these rhythmic patterns and the rhythms of
normal speech which makes the language of the comedia at once
speakable as discourse and recognizable as verse. The present
translation offers a similar rhythmic range: three-stress
lines, varied with examples of two stresses and of four.
However, no fixed line-length has been adhered to; typically,
lines are of between six and nine syllables, but there are
occasional departures from this in either direction. The
result is a verse idiom flexible enough, it is hoped, to
render both Tirso's habitual eight-syllable metres and his
more sporadic use of other forms. No attempt has been made,
however, to match metre for metre, or even to mark each
metrical change by some parallel change. Rather the aim has
been to recreate in English the tone and movement of each
successive passage; a coincidence of metres may sometimes be
the means to this end, but it has not been pursued at all
systematically. Pentameters, in particular, have been
avoided on the whole, even where the original lines are
hendecasyllables, since their presence tends to carry an
unfortunate air of sub-Shakespearian pastiche.
  Within this general approach it has proved possible to
mark Tirso's more strongly-characterized passages in a variety
of ways: rhyme, assonance (either of vowels or of consonants),
stanzaic patterns, alliteration, the use of longer lines as a
norm, or the heightening of rhythmic regularities. Echoes of
Biblical, liturgical, and literary language are deployed to
enhance the texture here, as they are in Tirso's original.
His more rhetorical passages, being far less tied to specific
verbal formations than is the case with a poet-dramatist like
Calderón, will lend themselves readily enough to such flexible
treatment. By contrast, the relatively unmarked portions of
his text can prove much harder to handle. Here, without
pursuing any special poetic effect, or even being particularly
elegant, Tirso's language remains sinewy and functional.
Something can be done to sustain the right level here by the
incidental use of minor regularities like alliteration, or
even of rhyme. But the translator's only reliable hope of

picking out a path between a prosaic loss of energy and a
rhetorical loss of credibility lies in paying the closest
attention to the functional quality of Tirso's writing.

This is a point which deserves some further comment,
since it bears importantly on the controversial question of
how literal the translation of a work like this ought to be.
Attentiveness to what is said is, of course, the primary
discipline of all translation, since that activity involves
first the receipt and then the transmission of a message.
Translating a play entails giving atttention to all that
happens verbally between the characters and on the stage.
That will quite certainly involve more than the unglossed
meaning of the words used; the translator will need to be
responsive to the rhythms, pauses, and silences, to the
coherence of speech-acts with speakers and hearers, and to
the many sub-texts of irony and implication which pass between
the characters, or between them and their audience. At any
given point it will simply be inadequate to say that one is
translating linguistic categories of any kind; one translates,
rather, a set of dramatic functions. It is, of course, the
language of the original which gives us access to these
functions; when we describe Tirso's language as contextually
'right', we mean that it defines them fully and clearly. But
it is the functions themselves, not the language as such,
which ought to control the translator's choices. In a sense,
then, theatrical translation is not even from language to
language; it cannot usefully be word-for-word. Hence the
rather ample degree of freedom assumed by the present
version. As between plain sense and embellishment, literal
rendering and adaptation, seventeenth-century reference and
twentieth-century usage, it opts for those alternatives which
seem to do the dramatic work predicated by Tirso's original.
Its aim is not to say exactly what the text of El condenado
says, but to do as much as possible of what it does.

It will not have succeeded, of course. Many of the
notes appended to the text will be there because of the need
to bring to the reader's attention things which the original
text does, but which the translation leaves undone. There
are many more occasions on which something of the sort could
have been said. There are more still, no doubt, when it
ought to have been said, if only this editor had been aware
of it. For in Tirso de Molina we have to do with a dramatic
poet of the first rank, the fulness of whose meanings no
single reader or critic - and certainly no translator - is
going to encompass.

NOTES TO THE INTRODUCTION

The detailed references in these notes (and in the notes to the text) are to works listed in the Bibliography, where full titles will be found. Reference here is normally by author's name and page-number only, with such additional information as is needed to avoid ambiguity.

1. In Lope's play, best known in English by way of John Osborne's adaptation _A Bond Honoured_, Leonido's wickedness reaches monstruous extremes, emphasizing the miracle of his conversion. See Freund, 18; also the edition by Whitby and Anderson, 41-8.
2. Cf. Marcos, 5-43; also Kennedy (1974: _Guastavino_), 247: 'a work that must be interpreted anew in terms of the generation that is reading it.'
3. On bibliographical problems of the _Segunda parte_ see Wilson (1969), 114-5; (1977), 115-6; Rogers (1974), 15-16; Kennedy (1976), 131; Cioranescu, 178-84.
4. Bruerton, 346; Williamsen (1970), 488-513 – both drawing in part on S.G. Morley (_BH_, 7 (1905), 387-408 and 16 (1914), 177-208).
5. Paterson, 53-68; counter-arguments in Kennedy (1973), 261-74 and Moll, 85-94.
6. There are important dissentient voices, however; see Sturcken, 190 and especially Kennedy (1974: _Studies_), 298n; (1976), 129-48, 335-56. The attribution to Tirso of _El burlador de Sevilla_ is itself open to question; see Rogers (1977), 15-16. For thematic links between the two plays see Wilson (1969), 116-7; Wardropper (1970), 369. Among alternative authors proposed, the most credible is Mira de Amescua, but in his case too there are problems over versification; see Kennedy (1974: _Guastavino_), 251.
7. On possible birth-dates see Wilson (1977), 13-20; Luis Vázquez, 19-36 proposes 1579; contrast los Ríos, I, 83-4.
8. For some inferences drawn from his supposed illegitimacy see Wade, 138n; Abrams (_DHR_), 21-9. Sullivan (_BC_), 1-11 deduces from the Téllez Girón connection a link with the formerly Jewish family of Arias de Avila – incongruous if true, given Tirso's regrettable endorsement of contemporary caste-prejudice in plays like _La gallega Mari-Hernández_.
9. Biographical summary in Wilson (1977), 11, 17-29; on the Mercedarian Order see Bleiberg, II, 1020-2; Friedman, 106-7 and passim.
10. Permission to print obtained in 1621, but not finally published until March 1624 (Paterson 43-53). See _Cigarrales_, 13, 116-7 for details cited here. There is a full-length study of the work in Nogué.

11. On Philip III see Lynch, 14-39; for Tirso's admiration and praise of him, Kennedy (1974: <u>Studies</u>), 59-61. Tirso's political judgment is not necessarily invalidated by the fact that Lerma may have been his patron; see Wilson (1977), 22.
12. On Olivares see Lynch, 62 ff. and latterly Stradling, 85-8; his relations with Tirso: Metford (1959), 15-27; Kennedy (1974: <u>Studies</u>), passim; ibid., 37-8 on the array of talents in Madrid; 77-150 on Tirso and Mendoza.
13. Wilson (1977), 32-4; Kennedy (1966), 57-76; (1974: <u>Studies</u>), 35-6, 41-54. Also Moir (1965), 197-200 (the Aristotelians); Metford (1951), 76-92 (the moralists). I am indebted to Ms Lesley Miller for bringing to my notice the economic case against playgoing contained in sumptuary legislation of the period.
14. Both were in Toledo in 1604-7 and in 1615 (los Ríos, I, 98-9) but there is no evidence that they ever met there; see Kennedy (1974: <u>Studies</u>), 152. Tirso's eulogy of Lope in <u>Cigarrales</u>, 143-7 does not present him as a Toledan figure; references in Lope's letters of 1615-6 to <u>el Mercedario</u> and <u>Don Molina</u> suggest no great closeness (Kennedy, ibid., 157-8; Wilson (1977), 22). On their relations in the 1620s and thereafter see Kennedy, ibid., 151-87; Zamora Lucas, 388-94.
15. It was already being performed in 1615; see Kennedy (1974: <u>Studies</u>), 157.
16. Text and circumstances in González Palencia, 83, 77-84 passim; also Kennedy (1974: <u>Studies</u>), 85-8; Wilson (1969), 91-2. For Lope's possible involvement see Kennedy, ibid., 184; for political motives, Metford (1959), 15. On Tirso's compliance see Kennedy (1973), 272; (1976), 131; on his 'act of contrition', Wilson (1977), 27.
17. See above, n. 3. On Figueroa see Cotarelo y Mori, 203-6; Rogers (1974), 16 and 44n; also Kennedy (1974: <u>Studies</u>), 337. The same company had presented the first performances of <u>El burlador de Sevilla</u> and of Lope de Vega's <u>Fuenteovejuna</u>; see Aubrun (1966), 39.
18. Discussed in detail by Paterson; also Kennedy (1973), and Moll (above, n. 5). The date of Paterson's list has been shown to be 1638, not 1632 - see Kennedy (1973), 268 - but it could still have the status which he claims for it.
19. See Kennedy (1974: <u>Guastavino</u>), 216-24, 228-32; also Cotarelo, 103 (on <u>El remedio en la desdicha</u>); Lázaro Carreter, 413-27 (on <u>La buena guarda</u>). A further reason for thinking that Tirso had the latter play in mind is his use at ll. 1411-13, just before the Shepherd's first appearance, of the jest-book of Juan de Arguijo, the Sevillan magistrate to whom <u>La buena guarda</u> is dedicated; see Reynolds (1956), 13-14.
20. Kennedy (1974: <u>Studies</u>), 87-8; (1974: <u>Guastavino</u>), 216-7;

Rogers (1974), 25.

21. On San Pedro Armengol see Nogué, 274-81; Vossler, 85-6; Wardropper (1970), 369; Kennedy (1974: Guastavino), 249.

22. For bandits on stage see Parker (1949), 395-416; Aubrun (1957), 137-51; in real life, Braudel, II, 734-54; Elliott, 51-2, 63-5; Rogers (1974), 24-5.

23. On Spanish rule in Naples see NCMH, IV, 276; also Pennington, 39: 'an incompetent absolutism in face of endless, sporadic rebellion'.

24. Kennedy (1974: Guastavino), 224-32.

25. Cf Ludovico in Calderón's Purgatorio de San Patricio (see McClelland, 131-64); Eusebio in his Devoción de la Cruz and Gil in the Esclavo del demonio of Mira de Amescua (Sullivan (Tirso), 66-7), and Luis in Part III of Tirso's La Santa Juana (May, 155); also two female examples: a bandit-heroine in Vélez de Guevara, La ninfa del cielo (Vossler, 67-87; Williamsen (1970), 503), and the promiscuous Margarita of Tirso's Quien no cae no se levanta (Delgado Varela, 341-77; Maurel (1971), 133-5).

26. See Rogers (1974), 2-4; Shergold, 213-32 (on the theatrical background). Cf. also the 1824 revival, advertised as a 'spectacular comedy... with music, flyings, trapdoors, transformations' (Rogers (1971), 662).

27. On his deployment of the play's supernatural characters see Mancini, 79.

28. In Figueroa's company these were respectively Manuel Coca de los Reyes and Luis de Cisneros.

29. On the traditions underlying Tirso's plot see Menéndez Pidal, 13-85 (originally the author's inaugural lecture (1902) to the Royal Spanish Academy).

30. Devoto, 202 admits the possibility but thinks oral tradition a likelier source; similarly cautious about this and other medieval precedents (Berceo; Cancionero de Baena) is Valera Jácome, 127-42.

31. It occurs, for example, in the devotional manual of Gerónimo de Alcalá, Verdades para la vida christiana (Valladolid, 1632); see Tourón del Pie, 419-20.

32. De Arte Bene Moriendi, II, x, identified by Bertini (see Rogers (1974), 18; Wardropper (1970), 493; Caro Baroja, 235n), concerns a desert monk, tempted to despair by thoughts of past sins. Tourón del Pie, 417 cites De Doctrina Christiana: a young monk, dying, rejects the diabolically-inspired claim that he has no hope of salvation; he will still love God. Tirso had a wider interest in Bellarmine's work: in 1624 he wrote a verse commendation for the Spanish version of the Cardinal's Officium Principis Christiani; see Zamora Lucas, 383.

33. Even so, the theological dimension has sometimes made the play seem less acceptable - for example, to the 19th-century Protestant Ticknor, or the 20th-century ex-Jesuit Cejador (Sturcken, 192), and perhaps also to Madrid audiences of the Machado brothers' short-lived revival in 1924; see Rogers (1971), 664; Dougherty, 22.

34. History of the controversies in Sullivan (Tirso), 28-34; Caro Baroja, 228-35; Rogers (1974), 19-21; theological readings of the play to 1958 summarized in Sturcken, 192-3; Rogers (1974), 28-31.

35. This aspect, important to some 19th-century critics, is dismissed by Menéndez Pidal, 59-62; contrast Tourón del Pie, 410.

36. Vossler, 78, sc. following Menéndez Pidal, 56-9; latterly Konan, 151-67. The Molinist reading, however, is generally rejected, e.g. by Delgado Varela, 363; Sullivan (Tirso), 34.

37. See Sullivan, ibid., 36. Zumelian accounts of the play in Ortúzar, 321-36; Delgado Varela, 341-77.

38. Cf. Caro Baroja, 227, 234-5: the play, though not Molinist, leaves 'a notable margin' to freewill.

39. It has been widely argued, both by Tirso's theological commentators (Hornedo; Ferreyra Liendo; Marcos) and by his literary critics (Mancini, 74; May, 146, 148; Pérez, 19), that Tirso advances no specific doctrinal case, but explores human and dramatic problems. If so, theological sources may have mattered less to him than devotional writers like Ludovicus Blosius (los Ríos, II, 425-7; Maurel (1971), 517-21), or perhaps Rodrigo de Valdepeñas, author of a poetic warning to those who put off conversion (H.G. Jones, 89-96).

40. On El condenado as tragedy see Moir (1965), 208; also Delgado, 425-32.

41. Parker (1949), 411 sees fear as the major factor in Paulo's character (cf. also Delgado Varela, 363); Rogers (1974), 23-4 argues that the vice of acedia has a part in his fall; the text itself stresses pride (ll. 217-8).

42. Cf. Rogers (1974), 36; Kennedy (1974: Guastavino), 248. On Philip III's death, ibid., 239-45, 250; rumours of his distress were spread by the Olivares faction, whom Tirso opposed; see Kennedy (1973), 273n.

43. Lope's ingratiating verse-epistle to Hurtado de Mendoza would have become known to Tirso early in 1624, causing him to feel 'rage and contempt'; see Kennedy (1974: Studies), 193. March 1624 is the probable date of Fray Maldonado's defection from the Mercedarians (above, n. 20). The coincidence of dates is of some interest. I have developed its implications further in an unpublished paper on 'The Politics of El condenado por desconfiado', read to the 1986 conference of the Association of

Hispanists of Great Britain and Ireland. In this I argue that the play's author is Tirso, its date late March or April 1624, and its immediate public context the collapse of the previous year's negotiations for an Anglo-Spanish royal marriage.

44. Penedo, I, cxxxi–cxlii relates the play to an internal quarrel in the Mercedarian Order, and sees it as an attack on a Mercedarian friar – a _converso_ by descent and a relative of Olivares – who was later arraigned for unorthodoxy on the issue of predestination; see also Tourón del Pie, 422-3. But it is difficult to think of Paulo as embodying Tirso's 'attack' on any such opponent. The tragic aspect of his case – the theme, as Parker (1949), 400 expresses it, of _corruptio optimi pessima_ – is too poignantly expressed.

45. Shergold, 229 refers without explanation to 'machines'. Rogers (1974), 164 thinks that the 'soul' was only represented in some symbolic fashion, but the _Segunda parte_, fol. 200r is quite explicit: _suben... al alma de Enrico_.

46. See note to ll. 2211-18. Only the _Segunda parte_ gives the complete passage, and the present edition follows Hartzenbusch and Castro in regarding the text which survives there as corrupt.

47. McClelland, 59-61, 154-63.

48. Aubrun (1957), 147 and Kennedy (1976), 135-6 find the play's extremes of contrast disconcerting, and argue that they are potentially a fault.

49. Parker (1957) passim. Aubrun (1957), 145-6 sees this type of play as structured to reaffirm established _social_ values. Tirso's scepticism, here and in the _Burlador de Sevilla_, about human justice leaves this contention in some doubt; see notes to ll. 2097, 2331-3, and cf. also Varey (1977: _TRI_), 208-9.

50. It has not been universally admired. Where Kennedy (1976), 135 finds a 'Calderonian' economy of structure, untypical of Tirso, Sturcken, 190 sees the play as 'poorly put together'. Maurel (1971), 528 draws a distinction based on the French terms _intrigue_ (here, he argues, ineptly handled) and _action_ (which he sees as well-integrated). The present analysis owes much to Maurel's résumé of the latter element (ibid., 545n), but presses beyond it to identify other patterns.

51. Cf. John 3: 14; Numbers 21: 9; Genesis 3: 1-15. See also Rogers (1974), 3 on the visual effect of the scene. Both Glaser, 242 and Oakley, 267-8 comment (the latter in Jungian terms) on a similar image used in _La ninfa del cielo_ – a play of related theme (above, n. 25).

52. Simplicity on this level, of course, does not preclude the elaboration of the play's themes through other patterns present within it: the crossed destinies of the two protagonists; their parallel but opposite relation to self-knowledge, as Oakley,

257–72 traces it; the sequence of biblical allusions; the various series of linked images.

53. Cf. Menéndez Pelayo, 73: 'only moderately written'; also Vossler, 76; Sturcken, 190; Kennedy (1976), 137. Certainly Lois Vázquez, 11–13, 39–40 would find little in this play – or, it must be said, in some others, less debatably attributed to Tirso – to support her ambitious revaluation of him as a lyric poet. For textual corruptions in the Segunda parte see Rogers (1974), 37–8.

54. Pérez, 4 misses this point, merely finding the first of these interventions 'incredibly pedestrian'.

55. Rogers (1974), 2–3: at l. 1234 Galván draws the curtain across the recess or 'inner stage' where Anareto lies sleeping; the actor then reappears as Albano via another entrance.

56. Cf the fine analysis of ll. 902–57 in Rogers (1974), 7–8.

57. It might have worked more readily with audiences used to the modes of presentation of the auto sacramental, where such tableaux were commoner. (I owe this suggestion to Dr P.J. Donnelly.)

58. Oakley, 262–3 and 269 interprets this passage on broadly similar lines, though without baptismal overtones.

59. McClelland, 135 (also 32, 149); Wilson (1969), 120. Pérez, 5 inclines to the former view. Among earlier critics Manuel de la Revilla and Menéndez Pidal were similarly opposed; see Maurel (1971), 556n. In the 1824 production the leading actor opted to play Enrico rather than Paulo; see Rogers (1971), 663. By contrast with all these, Moir (1971), 92, 93–4 forcefully affirms the equal standing of both protagonists.

60. Wilson (1969), 123; Moir (1965), 226. For an alternative view see Oakley, 257–72. For Pérez, 3 the similarities between Paulo and Enrico invalidate the notion of the play's 'double construction'.

61. Aubrun (1957), 139; (1966), 66 suggests that Tirso, a member of a regular Order, would have disapproved of such freelance holiness. C.A. Jones, 201 notes that 'Paulo's love of solitude is... a snare.' Yet Tirso nowhere implies that he was wrong to make the attempt at this form of holy living.

62. Cf. Aubrun (1966), 66; Maurel (1971), 528–9; Sullivan (Tirso), 38.

63. See, however, Caro Baroja, 66–74 passim for accounts of such apparitions. On some of the risks and rules involved in representing the Devil on stage see May, 145; Parker (1965), 4–5; also Rogers (1974), 2.

64. See May, 139–43, 147.

65. Cf. Aubrun (1957), 142 for Paulo as 'un arbitrista du salut', a far-fetched theorist of his own salvation; also Delgado, 431: 'When Paulo tries to reason he fails calamitously.'

66. A point also made by Oakley, 264, arguing that Paulo returns to the woods as to a Hell he cannot escape. It does seem to be the case that he now inhabits such a Hell. But the idea of 'damnation in life', canvassed by Marni, 125–33 in relation to Enrico here, and to the Don Juan of *El burlador de Sevilla*, would tilt the play's fine balance too far away from freewill.

67. There is also a link with the fear which is so large a part of Paulo's problem; cf. Tirso's view in *Cigarrales*, I, 11–12: 'all self-abasement which is not undertaken for God's sake is pusillanimity.'

68. Cf. May, 148: 'Actually, it is the Devil's word he is trusting, but this would not matter if he repented.'

69. The text of this scene as it stands requires some adjustment; cf. note to ll. 663–4.

70. Cf. May, 149–55 for the view of the Anareto–Enrico relationship adopted here.

71. It is not necessary to follow Ortúzar, 331–2 in seeing these lines as an allusion to notions of 'sufficient' grace and 'efficacious' grace; cf. Maurel (1971), 543–4. They can be explained just as well in terms of a refusal to admit to the fear of death (Parker (1949), 413–4), or a simple lack of familiarity with what repentance is.

72. Cf May, 145: 'If Enrico blindly trusts in God, he has blindly trusted in all kinds of other things, most of them evil, all his life'; also Pérez, 13–14.

73. McClelland, 130: 'He manages to link up the thought behind Enrico's conversion with human processes of thinking'; ibid., 59–61, 154–63 for what follows here.

74. Maurel (1971), 549 claims that Enrico has 'deserved' a better chance to choose aright. This seems doubtful; he chooses, rather, 'in all naivety' (May, 146), 'without knowing how' (McClelland, 157).

75. Enrico is in a dark cell but the audience, who watched the play in daylight, could see what he could not; see Varey (1977: *AmH*), 14.

76. Cf. Sullivan (*Tirso*), 37. This must cast doubt on the claim by McClelland, 161 that Enrico is already converted. Equally, one has to question the assertion of Ortúzar, 328 ('Enrico has only defects.'), and that of Delgado Varela, 363 (Enrico has 'no other preparation than an endless series of crimes and sins'). Clearly his growing-points are real, though incomplete without Anareto's paternal love.

77. Rogers (1974), 11; see also above, n. 28. Gijón Zapata, in a sensible general treatment of the *gracioso* figure in Tirso's theatre, finds little to say of Pedrisco.

78. Maurel (1981), 433–8 sees Pedrisco as distinctively an observer, even in Acts I and II. For Catalinón see Rogers

(1977), 53; Abrams (<u>HBalt</u>), 473.

79. Cf. Aubrun (1957), 143: 'un homme qui se dit quelconque, et se fait l'interprète du <u>senado</u>'.

80. Vossler, 79–80 notes Pedrisco's rise from a mere clown to Paulo's companion in this final scene, and registers his 'simple, Aesopian wisdom – to bend, rather than to break'.

81. May, 149–50; his developed view of Anareto (149–55) is rejected by Kennedy (1976), 337. For Maurel (1971), 551 the implausibility inherent in Anareto's not knowing of his son's wickedness is a sign that he is meant to stand apart from the human world altogether.

82. Cf McClelland, 148: 'He is not meant to display the more earthly aspects of fatherhood'; Rogers (1974), 10–11 is doubtful of the link made by Parker between Anareto's moral authority and the social order – rightly so, since the latter is represented in Act III not by Anareto but by the Governor of the gaol. See also May, 155.

83. He is something more, too, than 'the Church' (Wardropper (1970), 478. The analogies with the Shepherd–Christ of <u>La fianza satisfecha</u> (above, n. 1) and <u>La buena guarda</u> (Lázaro Carreter, 413–27) are important here.

84. Wardropper (1970), 491–2 recognizes this aspect of the Shepherd's second appearance. Cf. Sullivan (<u>Tirso</u>), 38–9, who takes the Shepherd's melancholy as proof that 'divine will has no part in the cause of Paulo's reprobate end'.

85. Wilson (1969), 122 finds Paulo's damnation 'in human terms an injustice'. This would create a conflict with the admiration which she plainly feels for the play. She resolves the dilemma by identifying Tirso himself with this sense of injustice: the play is 'a cry of unavailing protest' (123). It is, perhaps, not quite that: Tirso's theology would, in any case, have baulked at the 'unavailing'. But if the present phase of our argument is valid, he did anticipate something of this modern reader's dilemma.

86. Above, pp.

87. Cf. Maurel (1971), 533: 'Cette poésie de sang... est au service d'une volonté sacrilège.'

88. Again (cf. above, n. 76) one has to question the too absolute assertion of Delgado Varela, 363: 'In [these] characters, the fruit of nature is only sins and crimes.' Aubrun (1966), 148 is nearer to Tirso in distinguishing a divinely ordained <u>natura naturata</u> from the demonic <u>natura naturans</u> of Paulo's own will.

89. Sánchez Escribano and Porqueras Mayo, 162.

DAMNED FOR DESPAIR
El condenado por desconfiado

INTRODUCTORY NOTE

There is far more to be said about <u>El condenado por desconfiado</u> than can be said in any commentary of acceptable length. I have tried to give some coverage to questions of six kinds: matters relating to text, translation, staging, allusions, poetic texture, and theme.

    (a) <u>Text</u>. Notes on the Spanish text are addressed to those readers who know that language, and who need to know what text is being presented, and what its major problems are. On all such matters this edition is massively indebted to that of Rogers (1974), itself based on the <u>Segunda parte</u> of 1635. The text printed here is substantially Rogers' text, reproduced by kind permission of the editor and of Pergamon Press. Virtually all the information given on other readings comes from the same source.

    Sometimes – either to complete the sense of inherently defective passages, or because my own interpretation followed other lines – I have translated from readings not accepted by Rogers. On these occasions the text appearing here is the text as translated.

    The notes record, and attempt to justify, all these departures from Rogers. They also document his own departures from the <u>Segunda parte</u>, and – where these seem relevant – alternative readings discussed by him. Some minor items have as a rule been left out: Rogers' or my own adjustments to stage-directions (though these are marked in the text with square brackets); his indications of missing lines (again, clearly shown as lacunae); instances of defective rhyme and metre.

    Reynolds (1981), 734–6 lists six uncollected early editions or <u>sueltas</u>; textual information here is limited to the sources used by Rogers. I have modified some of his abbreviations to give the following series:

P: <u>Segunda parte de las comedias del Maestro Tirso de Molina</u> (Madrid, 1635).

K: <u>suelta</u>, mid 17th-century, bound with other plays in vol. II of <u>Collectio dramaticorum hispanicorum</u>, in Copenhagen, Royal Library; also in Freiburg University Library.

S: <u>suelta</u>, late 17th-century; printed by Francisco Sanz (sc. in Madrid).

D: <u>suelta</u>, mid 18th-century; identified by serial number 232; in British Library (11728 d. 57) as '?Seville, c.1740'.

T: MS prompt-copies from Teatro de la Cruz, Madrid (1824); in Madrid, Biblioteca Municipal (1–203–9 and 2–203–9).

H: Hartzenbusch (1839–42).

C: Castro (1919).

R: Rogers (1974).

I have scarcely begun to survey the fifty or more editions which Reynolds lists as appearing since Castro, though I have sometimes consulted Wardropper (1970) or Prieto (1982).

(b) <u>Translation</u>. Notes on the translation aim to bring readers without Spanish closer to the text than a readable literary version will of itself allow. They have, after all, a right to know what they are getting, and what they are missing.

I have therefore covered fairly generously - though by no means exhaustively - the literal sense of passages where the translation follows a non-literal course. I have given particular attention to passages of three kinds: those which are especially radical in their divergence from literal meaning; those where the English version sacrifices important effects of phrasing or style; those which illustrate some general problem or principle of the translation process. For more general comment on this translation see Introduction, p. lxxiii-lxxvi.

(c) <u>Staging</u>. I have made some effort (very largely informed by Rogers' work) to show how the play might have been presented on the stage of a seventeenth-century <u>corral de comedias</u>. These notes, however, are in no sense a sufficient guide for the producer. Other modes of staging will undoubtedly suggest themselves, and in one respect - its division into scenes at major breaks in the action -- the English text lends itself to these.

(d) <u>Allusions</u>. Every literary text assumes certain areas of shared knowledge between author and public. These assumptions do not always hold good across boundaries of place, time, and social formation. If modern readers are to understand what Tirso is doing, his references to mythology, balladry, religious teaching, contemporary literature, and social life will sometimes need to be explained. <u>El condenado</u> is not, from this point of view, an especially demanding play. Even so, the reader or spectator who can cope with allusions to fashionable long hair, or to Aeneas rescuing his father may well have more trouble with Phaethon or Amalthea, or with the names of poetic forms improvised by Celia. Some items of the latter sort, therefore, have been sacrificed or remodelled in translation. The notes, where necessary, explain this too.

(e) <u>Poetic texture</u>. This play, like others of its genre, is poetic drama not merely because it is written in verse, but because of the way in which it has been imagined and organized. What Wardropper (1973), 356 has called the 'poetic coherence' of the Spanish <u>comedia</u> involves the complex overlapping of imaginative patterns at many levels. In general, the broader structural and thematic shapes lend themselves to discussion at length, and this is attempted in the Introduction here. By contrast, the details of imagery and verbal organization are better reflected in more

2

piecemeal commentary; many of the notes which follow are designed to show how Tirso's imagination worked in these matters.

The notes also register, with occasional interpretative comment, the play's various changes of metre.

(f) Theme. The division just suggested cannot be an absolute one; the two aspects belong together in our understanding as in the original. Some discussion of language and imagery, as these things affect the wholeness of the text, found its proper place in the Introduction. In the same way, there are aspects of the detailed working-out of themes — especially as these are revealed through character — which emerge most readily through the ongoing series of notes. I have supplied cross-references as necessary, and have tried not to repeat the same material in both places.

The line-numbers to which all notes are cued are those of the corresponding passages of Spanish text. In the English version (which is not line-for-line) the line-number cues for all notes except those concerned with questions of text or metre are inserted in the right-hand margins of the passages to which they refer.

EL CONDENADO POR DESCONFIADO
comedia famosa por

EL MAESTRO TIRSO DE MOLINA
Representóla Figueroa

Hablan en ella las personas siguientes:

Paulo, de ermitaño.
Pedrisco, gracioso.
El Demonio.
Octavio y Lisandro.
Celia y Lidora, su criada.
Enrico.
Galván y Escalante.
Roldán.
Cherinos.
Anareto, padre de Enrico.
Albano, viejo.
Un pastor.
Un gobernador.
Un alcaide.
Un portero.
Un juez.
Un músico.
Algunos villanos.

TITLE. a famous play. Cf. Margaret Wilson (1969), 39: 'comedia is the Spanish for "play", without any distinction between comedy and tragedy.'

CHARACTERS. Cherinos. Corominas, 191 states that this name comes from the French epic (as does Roldán; the Arthurian 'Galván' adds to the note of chivalresque parody). It was a conventional 16th-17th century nickname for bandits and ruffians - a usage of which Pedrisco (1. 704) seems to be aware. His comment - literally 'a small thing' - is linked by R with the Mexican chiringo, meaning 'a trifling amount'. With this and Cherinos' criminal modus operandi in mind, 'Fingers' seemed a defensible version.

Bandits... I have added to the list in P those characters not included there who also appear in the play.

4

DAMNED FOR DESPAIR
A famous play by
MASTER TIRSO DE MOLINA
Acted by Figueroa

CHARACTERS

Paulo	a hermit.
Pedrisco	his servant.
The Devil.	
Lisandro and Octavio	two gentlemen of Naples.
Celia	Enrico's mistress.
Enrico	a criminal.
Galván	⎫ four of
Escalante	⎬ Enrico's
Roldán	⎬ criminal
Cherinos ("Fingers")	⎭ associates.
Anareto	Enrico's father.
Albano	an old man.
The Governor of Naples.	
Bandits.	
Three Prisoners.	
A Shepherd.	
Prison Guards.	
Prison Governor.	
A Judge.	
Peasants.	
Musicians (off stage).	

Scene: Naples and the surrounding countryside.
Time: The seventeenth century or earlier.

SCENE. Scenery in the corral de comedias, with its projecting stage, its gallery and pillars, and its curtained recess, was minimal. One result of this is that indications in P as to the place of action are only rudimentary. For the sake of coherence I have rationalized these to some extent but I have not amplified them very much. In general, the spoken text carries the essential cues and clues; we have to learn to respond to these as early audiences did. It was the spectators' imagination which supplied the forest and the city, the hermit's cell, the outlaws' camp, the gaol. The comedia's swiftness of action owed much to this.

TIME. The action of El condenado is not assigned to any particular epoch. Its general ambience is that of Tirso's own time; the reference at the end to the fourth-century subject-matter of the Vitae Patrum is, from this point of view, disconcerting.

5

Sale Paulo de ermitaño.

Paulo   ¡Dichoso albergue mío!
        ¡Soledad apacible y deleitosa,
          que al calor y al frío
        me dais posada en esta selva umbrosa,
          donde el huésped se llama   5
        o verde yerba o pálida retama!
          Agora, cuando el alba
        cubre las esmeraldas de cristales,
          haciendo al sol la salva,
        que de su coche sale por jarales,   10
          con manos de luz pura
        quitando sombras de la noche obscura,
          salgo de aquesta cueva
        que en pirámides altos de estas peñas
          naturaleza eleva,   15
        y a las errantes nubes hace señas
          para que noche y día,
        ya que no hay otra, le hagan compañía.
          Salgo a ver este cielo,
        alfombra azul de aquellos pies hermosos.   20
          ¿Quién, ¡oh celestes cielos!,
        aquesos tafetanes luminosos
          rasgar pudiera un poco
        para ver...? ¡Ay de mí! Vuélvome loco.
          Mas ya que es imposible,   25
        y sé cierto, Señor, que me estáis viendo

1-76. Metre: a stanzaic *lira*: six lines, alternately of seven and eleven syllables, rhyming ABABCC. Diction and imagery are characteristic of the elevated poetic usage of the time - well enough handled by Tirso, despite minor anomalies of rhyme and syntax. Though appropriate to the sentiments here, this *culto* vein also highlights a certain rhetorical self-consciousness in Paulo's piety.

1. 'Safe refuge'. The literal meaning is 'Happy shelter of mine!' See Introduction, p. xliv.

3. P: *el calor*, unintelligible; KR: *al calor*.

8. *esmeraldas... cristales*. Literally 'emeralds... crystals' - heavily conventional elements in *culto* usage for green grass and

6

ACT ONE

SCENE ONE

A wild mountain valley. Paulo enters, dressed as a hermit.

Paulo   Safe refuge here for me!   1
                To lodge untroubled and alone,
                come sun, come storm,
                safe in the shadow of the wood
                with grass or yellow broom for company.
                Now dawn
                whitens the grass with shining dew,   8
                now greets the early sun,
                as he comes riding out through briars,
                and with her bright hand lays
                the shades of night aside.
                Time, then, to leave my cave
                among these pinnacles of stone   14
                that beckon dusk or day
                down from the shifting clouds
                to come where no-one comes but they.
                Time to look up
                at the blue firmament, beyond which walk
                the saved souls of men...   20
                                Heaven!
                If I could make one little tear
                in your bright veils, and peep within, and see,
                and see... But this will drive me mad.
                I know, dear Lord, it is impossible.
                I know that you look down

---

transparent dewdrops. Other consciously artificial images follow: the sun's coach (ll. 9-10); the 'blue carpet' and 'taffeta veils' of Heaven (ll. 20-2).

14-18. The Spanish syntax is complex and ambiguous. Nature 'raises up' the cave among the crags; nature (or perhaps the cave itself) calls down night and day (or possibly the clouds) as company in an otherwise lonely spot. I have simplified this a good deal in translation.

18. P etc.: haga; R: hagan, helping the sense a little.

20. 'saved souls'. The original phrase ('those beautiful feet') could refer either to the saved in Heaven or to Christ himself.

                desde ese inaccesible
        trono de luz hermoso, a quien sirviendo
            están ángeles bellos,
        más que la luz del sol hermosos ellos,   30
            mil glorias quiero daros
        por las mercedes que me estáis haciendo,
            sin saber obligaros.
        ¿Cuándo yo merecí que del estruendo
            me sacarais del mundo,   35
        que es umbral de las puertas del profundo?
            ¿Cuándo, Señor divino,
        podrá mi indignidad agradeceros
            el volverme al camino,
        que si yo lo conozco, es fuerza el veros,   40
            y tras esta victoria,
        darme en aquestas selvas tanta gloria?
            Aquí los pajarillos,
        amorosas canciones repitiendo,
            por juncos y tomillos,   45
        de vos me acuerdan, y yo estoy diciendo:
            si esta gloria da el suelo,
        ¿qué gloria será aquélla que da el cielo?
            Aquí estos arroyuelos,
        girones de cristal en campo verde,   50
            me quitan mis desvelos
        y son causa a que de vos me acuerde,
            tal es el gran contento
        que infunde al alma su sonoro acento.
            Aquí silvestres flores   55
        el fugitivo tiempo aromatizan,
            y de varios colores
        aquesta vega humilde fertilizan.
            Su belleza me asombra:
        calle el tapete y berberisca alfombra.   60
            Pues con estos regalos,
        con aquestos contentos y alegrías,

---

40. PK: <u>no</u>, unintelligible; CR: <u>lo</u>.
51-2. 'awake me now...' Literally 'take away my sleeplessness
and cause me to remember you.' <u>Acordarse</u> in its other meaning of
'to awaken' implies a contrast which is made more explicit in
translation.
56. P: <u>tiempo</u>; H: <u>viento</u>. Taken together with <u>fugitivo</u>, either
meaning suggests 'the air; the breeze'.

on me from your inaccessible bright throne,
adored by angels fairer than the sun,
and therefore I will glorify your name
for all the goodness you have shown me
- goodness I cannot ever merit.
For when did I deserve
that you should rescue me
out of a world that slopes to the abyss?
I, the unworthy, how should I ever thank you,
who brought me back to the way
which, if I learn it well, must lead to you,
and, having overcome in this,
gave me the glory of this wilderness
to be my home?
For here the small birds, singing of their loves
in reeds and scented herbs, tell me of you,
and I take up their tale:
given such glories here below,
what of the glories Heaven gives?
These crystal streams across the grass,
that lulled me in my bed
awake me now to thoughts of you   51
- such joy of soul their music brings.
Here wildflowers scent the air;
here vallies rich with colour   57
outshine in subtle splendour
the pomp of tapestries.
For all this wealth, these joys,   61
in everlasting thanks to thee,
my voice, my God, I'll daily raise,

57-60. 'here vallies... tapestries'. Once more the translation
abridges a largely decorative passage. Though 'fertilize this
humble valley with variegated colours' is no great loss, the 'Berber
carpet' of l. 60 perhaps is.

61-76. Paulo's prayer is much remodelled in translation, assuming
a deliberately stanzaic form which may perhaps compensate for the
loss of repetitive force ('Here I mean to follow you... Here I mean
to serve you...') in ll. 65-7.

9

. . . .
. . . .
¡bendito seas mil veces,
inmenso Dios que tanto bien me ofreces!
   Aquí pienso seguirte   65
ya que el mundo dejé para bien mío.
   Aquí pienso servirte,
sin que jamás humano desvarío,
  por más que abre la puerta
el mundo a sus engaños, me divierta.   70
   Quiero, Señor divino,
pediros de rodillas humilmente
  que en aqueste camino
siempre me conservéis piadosamente.
   Ved que el hombre se hizo   75
de barro, y de barro quebradizo.

Sale Pedrisco con un haz de hierba. Pónese Paulo de rodillas
y elévase.

Pedr.   Como si fuera borrico
       vengo de yerba cargado,
       de quien el monte está rico.
       Si esto cómo, desdichado,   80
       triste fin me pronostico.
         ¿Que he de comer hierba yo,
       manjar que el cielo crió
       para brutos animales?
       Déme el cielo en tantos males   85
       paciencia. Cuando me echó
         mi madre al mundo, decía:
       "Mis ojos santo te vean,
       Pedrisco del alma mía."
       Si esto las madres desean,   90
       una suegra y una tía
         ¿qué desearán? Que aunque el ser
       santo un hombre es gran ventura,
       es desdicha el no comer.

---

  72. P: humildemente – an extra syllable; R: humilmente.
  76-7. Stage-direction. Paulo may well have knelt to pray
already. The Spanish instruction elévase could mean that he is
rapt in ecstasy or – disconcertingly – that he gets up and walks
off. Variants at l. 139 will match any of these possibilities.
  77-136. Metre: quintillas: octosyllabic stanzas, rhyming either
ABABA or AABBA. Pedrisco's opening rhyme assonates with Paulo's
last couplet; his address to God travesties Paulo's prayer.

who wrought these benefits for me.
And having left the world behind ⎱ *Reason for*
to seek my greater good,   ⎰ *being Here*
may no temptation turn my mind
from love and service of my God.
The doors of pleasure open wide;
the world's deceits lie rich within;
humbly I seek your mercy, Lord;
suffer me not to sin,
but keep me steadfast in your way,
for man is base and brittle clay.   76

As Paulo, kneeling, is borne up out of sight, Pedrisco
    enters, carrying a large bundle of grass.

Pedr.   Way hey!
Here come I carrying grass
- for all the world like an ass.
It's not in short supply   79
(it's the only thing that's not
hereabouts) but if I don't get
something better to eat, I'll die.
Think of it! Living off food
that's only fit for brutes!
God give me patience! What I have to suffer!
When I think my dear old mother
when I was a baby used to say:
"Pedrisco, son, I hope you'll be a saint one day"!
If that was what my mother wanted,   90
I'm glad they never asked my auntie
or the wife's mother - that'd be worse still!
This sainthood lark's all very well   92
but, if it means not eating, you can go to -

79-81. 'not in short supply'. The bureaucratic cliché replaces
Pedrisco's fortune-telling cliché: 'I foretell a sad end for
myself.'

90-2. More literally 'If mothers want this, what will an aunt or
a mother-in-law want?' (with no suggestion that Pedrisco himself
has ever been married). But the stand-up comedian's phrase is in
line with the *gracioso*'s function.

92-4. There is nothing very alarming about Pedrisco's remark in
the original ('though being a saint is great good luck, not eating
is bad luck'), or about the very minor blasphemy which he courts in
the English version. But both have to be measured against the
discipline required of a hermit's assistant.

11

Perdonad esta locura 95
y este loco proceder,
   mi Dios, y, pues conocida
ya mi condición tenéis,
no os enojéis porque os pida
que la hambre me quitéis, 100
o no sea santo en mi vida.
   Y si puede ser, Señor,
pues que vuestro inmenso amor
todo lo imposible doma,
que sea santo y que coma, 105
mi Dios, mejor que mejor.
   De mi tierra me sacó
Paulo, diez años habrá,
y a aqueste monte apartó;
él en una cueva está, 110
y en otra cueva estoy yo.
   Aquí penitencia hacemos,
y sólo yerbas comemos,
y a veces nos acordamos
de lo mucho que dejamos 115
por lo poco que tenemos.
   Aquí al sonoro raudal
de un despeñado cristal,
digo a estos olmos sombríos:
"¿Dónde estáis, jamones míos, 120
que no os doléis de mi mal?
   Cuando yo solía cursar
la ciudad y no las peñas
(¡memorias me hacen llorar!),
de las hambres más pequeñas 125
gran pesar solíais tomar.

---

106. 'Amen' parallels the heavy bathos of mejor que mejor.
   107-16. The gracioso's comic flatness of diction is conveyed in
English through rhyme, and through some extensive remodelling of
sentences (e.g. the use here of direct speech).
   109. P: y aqueste; KR: y a aqueste.
   117-19. Here, by contrast, Pedrisco deploys the same culto
register as his master: 'by the sounding torrent of crystal pouring
down, I say to the shady elms...' The intention is clearly parodic:
'I talk to the trees' is preposterous in the right way.
   117 P: el; KR: al.
   120-1 and 130-1. These lines parody the ballad '¿Dónde estás,
señora mía?' (Durán, II. 486, no. 1545), a forsaken lover's
lament. Interestingly enough, it contains the lines 'River, flow

God forgive me! What am I saying?
God forgive me, and hear me praying:
Oh Lord, you know the way I feel;
would you mind if I proposed a deal?
You want me for a saint - alright?
Then take away my appetite!
Or grant me this, since power you've got
to make it possible (which it's not)
- to be a saint and eat my fill.
Oh Lord, that would be better still.
                                    Amen!   106
                                                             107
It must be ten years now
since Paulo comes and says
"Say goodbye to your land and your home
and live in the wilderness."
And here we live, in caves
- that's his, and this one's mine.
"Come and do penance with me," says he,
and so we do, and we pine
for all that we left behind
compared with what we've got
- which, with nothing but grass to eat,
certainly isn't a lot.
I tell you, I talk to the trees   117
here by the waterfall.
"Ham and eggs, where are you?" I cry,   120
but they never answer at all.
When I was back in town
and not out here on the rocks
- those were the days! - I was never short
of a plate of ham and eggs.

---

backwards / since faith turns back on itself'. Still more
interestingly, the speaker of the whole poem is named as 'Tirsi'.
    120. 'Ham and eggs'. Ham as an object of comic hunger   defined
the speaker - otherwise devoid of any claim to status - as an Old
Christian, without Jewish ancestry. Tirso refers explictly to this
racial-religious litmus test in La gallega Mari-Hernández. Here it
is merely an underlying cliché. 'Ham and eggs', a more reputable
cliché, also has the advantage for the translator of being, like
jamones, plural.
    125-31 The translation, remodelling extensively, loses the
contrast between las hambres más pequeñas and las mortales: 'You
took great pity on my least hunger. You were loyal, ham... though
now you take no pity on my mortal hunger.' It still conveys,
however, the pseudo-personal relationship with the well-loved food.

Erais jamones leales,
bien os puedo así llamar,
pues merecéis nombres tales,
aunque ya de las mortales   130
no tengáis ningún pesar."
   Más ya está todo perdido;
yerbas comeré afligido,
aunque llegue a presumir
que algún mayo he de parir,   135
por las flores que he comido.
   Mas Paulo sale de la cueva obscura:
entrar quiero en la mía tenebrosa
y comerlas allí.

Vase y sale Paulo.

Paulo   ¡Qué desventura!
Y ¡qué desgracia cierta, lastimosa!   140
El sueño me venció, viva figura
(por lo menos imagen temerosa)
de la muerte crüel; y al fin rendido,
la devota oración puse en olvido.
   Siguióse luego al sueño otro, de suerte   145
sin duda, que a mi Dios tengo enojado,
si no es que acaso el enemigo fuerte
haya aquesta ilusión representado.
Siguióse al fin, ¡ay Dios!, el ver la muerte.
¡Qué espantosa figura! ¡Ay, desdichado!   150
Si el verla en sueños causa tal quimera,
el que vivo la ve, ¿qué es lo que espera?
   Tiróme el golpe con el brazo diestro,
no cortó la guadaña. El arco toma:
la flecha en el derecho, y el siniestro   155
el arco mismo que altiveces doma;

135-6. Literally 'I shall give birth some May, because of all
the flowers I've eaten.' Almost certainly proverbial; clearly
inappropriate in biological terms; probably intended to be broadly
vulgar.

137-200. Metre: <u>octavas</u>: eleven-syllable lines, in stanzas
rhyming ABABABCC. A portentous metre to match the elevated diction
and solemn subject-matter of Paulo's vision. The translation seeks
to register his mental state rather than his precise conceptual
meanings; hence much abridgment.

139. SD: <u>Vuelve en sí Paulo</u> ('Paulo recovers consciousness') ,
cf. above, note on ll. 76-7.

139-40. The literal sense carries a still clearer notion of

```
                 I didn't have to be starving;                    125
                 I thought of them; there they were!
                 Ham and eggs were good friends to me then,
                 but now they just don't care.                     130
                 They're gone for good; it's over;
                 it's grass or nothing at all;
                 but if I have to munch much more,
                 I reckon I'm going to foal!                       135
                 Here's Paulo coming out again;
                 well, I'll go in and feed as best I can.
        Pedrisco retires into his cave, as Paulo comes out
                              from his.
Paulo                  I am full of dread.                         139
                 I have seen such sights... such warnings...
                 Sleep is like death, they say; can it be
                 death's true shadow?  Sleep unmanned me,
                 and sleeping I forgot my prayer.
                 I must have angered God; he sent me such a dream
                 - unless the Devil sent it.
                 I saw death, hideous as death is
                 - so much a horror, yet only a dream,
                 that when death comes to me truly, in life,
                 what can I feel but despair?
                 This was not Death the Reaper                     153
                 but death like an archer, hunting me down.
                 It fitted the arrow to its string;
                 the bow that tames proud spirits sang,            156
```

---

fatality: 'What ill-fortune! and what a sure and pitiful calamity!'

149. K: de; SDR: el.

153. P: fuerte, disrupting the rhyme-scheme; KR: diestro.

153-4. An ambiguous passage, depending on how the central phrase
no cortó la guadaña ('the scythe did not cut') is turned. We might
think of Death first failing to wound Paulo with this traditional
weapon of mortality, and only then taking up the bow. But it
creates a clearer picture to translate: 'Death loosed its shaft at
me with practised arm; it was not the scythe which dealt the wound.'

156. Paulo, as the Devil later explains (ll. 217-18), is himself
proud. Tirso may have had in mind here the similar shapes of bow
and yoke.

        tiróme al corazón: yo que me muestro
        al golpe herido, porque al cuerpo coma
        la madre tierra, como a su despojo,
        desencarcelo el alma, el cuerpo arrojo.   160
            Salió el alma en un vuelo, en un instante
        vi de Dios la presencia. ¡Quién pudiera
        no verle entonces! ¡Qué cruel semblante!
        ¡resplandeciente espada y justiciera
        en la derecha mano! Y arrogante   165
        (como ya por derecho suyo era)
        el fiscal de las almas miré a un lado
        que aun en ser victorioso estaba airado.
            Leyó mis culpas, y mi guarda santa
        leyó mis buenas obras, y el Justicia   170
        Mayor del cielo, que es aquél que espanta
        de la infernal morada la malicia,
        las puso en dos balanzas; mas levanta
        el peso de mi culpa y mi justicia
        mis obras buenas tanto, que el Juez santo   175
        me condena a los reinos del espanto.
            Con aquella fatiga y aquel miedo
        desperté, aunque temblando, y no vi nada
        si no es mi culpa, y tan confuso quedo,
        que si no es a mi suerte desdichada,   180
        o traza del contrario, ardid o enredo,
        que vibra contra mí su ardiente espada,
        no sé a qué lo atribuya. Vos, Dios santo,
        me declarad la causa de este espanto.
            ¿Heme de condenar, mi Dios divino,   185
        como este sueño dice, o he de verme
        en el sagrado alcázar cristalino?
        Aqueste bien, Señor, habéis de hacerme:

    157-60. Much abbreviated in translation: 'I, proving to be
wounded by the blow, so that mother earth might consume my body as
her spoil, freed my soul from its prison and cast aside my body.'
    163-5. P has commas after both semblante and mano, making it
possible to allocate the sword to God and the description arrogante
to the 'Prosecutor of souls' or Recording Angel. Contrast the
reading in KR: semblante! / Resplandeciente... mano, y arrogante,
which would assign the sword too to the latter. Though 17th-century
punctuation is notoriously arbitrary, P's version seems more in
accord with Paulo's distorted vision of God.
    170-2. Justicia Mayor. Unless this 'Chief Justice of Heaven' is
subordinate to the Juez santo of l. 175, he must surely be

and I was shot through the heart. Ah! the pain   157
as earth took my body to feed on it,
and my soul flew up to God!
Yes, I saw God. Oh!
not to have seen him then!
His face was pitiless; he held a shining sword   163
like Justice itself. And the Recording Angel
stood there at his side, waiting, knowing
that I was in his power;
still angry, though he had me helpless.
He read the record of my sins;
my Guardian Angel read the good I'd done.
And then the Judge, the Christ who harrowed Hell 170
weighed them both in the balance
and found me wanting. I was damned.   173
Trembling and sweating, I woke up.
All I could feel was guilt, and more guilt.
What am I to think?
Was it only an unlucky dream?
Was it some trick of the Devil,
a weapon of his against me?   181
Oh God! tell me why!
Was my dream true?
Shall I be damned? Shall I come safe to Heaven? 187
Lord, you must grant me this at least: 188

---

identified with Jesus Christ, who is the ultimate judge of souls.
(R, however, suggests St Michael, traditionally represented both as
fighting demons and as weighing souls in the balance.)

173. P: los; KR: las (agreeing with culpas... obras).

174 P etc.: justicia; HR: injusticia, but the earlier reading,
construed as 'my just deserts', seems a credible expression of
Paulo's despair.

173-5. More literally 'But the weight of my guilt and of my just
deserts raises my good deeds so high'. This is how scale-balances
work, but the version given seems a little clearer.

181-2. Literally 'or a device, deceit, or intrigue of the enemy,
brandishing his burning sword against me.' Paulo is quite right,
momentarily, in supposing that the Devil is at work in this. The
reference to the sword (omitted in the translation) is confusing
after ll. 164-5.

187. Literally 'the sacred crystal castle' – a very culto Heaven.
But Tirso was evidently attached to the term alcázar in this context
(cf. below, ll. 1545, 2533).

188 'you must'. A hazardous way of addressing God - as is the
assertion of a claim in ll. 189-90, and the proposal of a bargain
in ll. 193-7. None of this will help Paulo.

<pre>
            ¿Qué fin he de tener? Pues un camino
            sigo tan bueno, no queráis tenerme   190
            en esta confusión, Señor eterno.
            ¿He de ir a vuestro cielo o al infierno?
              Treinta años de edad tengo, Señor mío,
            y los diez he gastado en el desierto,
            y si viviera un siglo, un siglo fío   195
            que lo mismo ha de ser; esto os advierto.
            Si esto cumplo, Señor, con fuerza y brío,
            ¿qué fin he de tener? (Lágrimas vierto.)
            Respondedme, Señor, Señor eterno,
            ¿He de ir a vuestro cielo, o al infierno?   200
                Aparece el Demonio en lo alto.
Demon.   Diez años ha que persigo
            a este monje en el desierto,
            recordándole memorias
            y pasados pensamientos;
            y siempre le he hallado firme   205
            como un gran peñasco opuesto.
            Hoy duda en su fe, que es duda
            de la fe lo que hoy ha hecho,
            porque es la fe en el cristiano
            que sirviendo a Dios y haciendo   210
            buenas obras, ha de ir
            a gozar de él en muriendo.
            Este, aunque ha sido tan santo,
            duda de la fe, pues vemos
            que quiere del mismo Dios,   215
            estando en duda, saberlo.
            En la soberbia también
            ha pecado, caso es cierto.
            Nadie como yo lo sabe,
            pues por soberbio padezco.   220
            Y con la desconfianza
</pre>

---

198 P: yierto; KR: vierto.
  200-1.   Stage direction. The literal meaning of en lo alto is
simply 'up above', i.e. in the gallery of the corral stage. It is
an important and disturbing visual effect that the Devil makes his
speech while Paulo prays, all unknowing, on the main stage below.
  201-48 Metre: romance assonating in E-O.
  202.   monje is literally 'monk' - possibly a sign that Tirso was
writing with the Vitae Patrum in mind; monachus for 'hermit' is
common usage in the literature of the Desert Fathers.

```
             to know what my end will be.
             I have walked in the paths of righteousness.
             Oh Lord, take away my doubt.
             Heaven? or Hell?
             I am thirty years of age.
             Ten of those years I have spent
             in penance in this place,
             and if I live to be a hundred,
             I will spend a hundred here; I promise you that.
             And if I keep my promise, if I am steadfast,
             Lord, what will become of me in the end?
             Take pity on my tears.
             Dear God, answer my prayer; tell me the truth.      200
             Heaven? or Hell?
                 The Devil appears on the top of a crag.
Devil        Ten years in the wild
             I have tempted this hermit                           202
             with echoes of pleasures
             and thoughts of his past.
             Ten years he resisted,
             unyielding as granite.
             Today he has doubted;                                207
             I have him at last!
             A faithful believer
             should trust that, performing
             good works in God's service,
             he'll live when he dies.
             This penitent liver
             now asks God to prove it,
             because he has doubted;
             his faith he denies.
             His pride has betrayed him
             – that's certain; I know it,
             none better, for pride
             was my downfall too.
             And doubting God's promise,                          221
```

207-10. More literally 'Today he doubts in a matter of faith,
for what he has done today is a doubt as to faith, for it is the
faith of the Christian that...' The Devil makes his doctrinal
point very explicit indeed, for the instruction of the audience.

221-8. Further heavily explicit instruction, again abridged in
the English version: 'And with despair he has offended him, for it
is certain that he who does not give credence to God despairs of
God. A dream was the cause, and who can doubt that to rank a dream
above God's faith is manifest sin?'

le ha ofendido, pues es cierto
que desconfía de Dios
el que a su fe no da crédito.
Un sueño la causa ha sido;   225
y el anteponer un sueño
a la fe de Dios, ¿quién duda
que es pecado manifiesto?
Y así me ha dado licencia
el juez más supremo y recto   230
para que con más engaños
le incite agora de nuevo.
Sepa resistir valiente
los combates que le ofrezco,
pues supo desconfiar   235
y ser como yo soberbio.
Su mal ha de restaurar
de la pregunta que ha hecho
a Dios, pues a su pregunta
mi nuevo engaño prevengo.   240
De ángel tomaré la forma,
y responderé a su intento
cosas que le han de costar
su condenación, si puedo.

Quítase el Demonio la túnica y queda de ángel.

Paulo   Dios mío, aquesto suplico: 245
¿Salvaréme, Dios inmenso?
¿Iré a gozar vuestra gloria?
Que me respondáis espero.

Demon.   Dios, Paulo, te ha escuchado,
y tus lágrimas ha visto.   250

Paulo   [*Aparte*] ¡Qué mal el temor resisto!
Ciego en mirarlo he quedado.

Demon.   Me ha mandado que te saque
de esa ciega confusión,
porque esa vana ilusión   255
de tu contrario se aplaque.
Ve a Nápoles, y a la puerta
que llaman allá del Mar,
que es por donde tú has de entrar

---

230. Literally 'the sovereign and righteous judge'. The Devil,
in spite of himself, is compelled to describe God as God is. This
becomes the basis of a famous scene in Calderón's El mágico
prodigioso, and it seemed worthwhile to stress the point in the
translation here.

he ranks as despairing.
God's faith he has doubted;
his dream he thinks true.
So God allows me now
(I can't deny his justice)   230
to tempt this Paulo
with new deceits.
Let him try to resist them
– he knows how to doubt,
and he has it in him
to match me, pride for pride.
Let him undo the harm
that his question has done.
He asked God a question
– that's the root of his trouble –
and there I come in.
He asked God a question;
very well, I'll answer it
disguised as an angel,
and damn him if I can.

The Devil casts off his tunic and appears disguised
as an angel.

Paulo   Oh God! hear my prayer.
Shall I find salvation?
Shall I taste of your glory?
Lord, I beseech you, answer my prayer.

Devil   Paulo, God has heard you.
He has regarded your tears...

Paulo   [Aside] An angel! The sight of him blinds me   251
and I am afraid.

Devil   ...and I am commanded to say this,   253
to end your confusion
and stop your enemy's deceits:
"Go to the city of Naples
and there, by the Harbour Gate,
as you enter the town, you will see a man

249-328. Metre: redondillas, for the first of the play's dialogue
passages.
    251-2. Blindness is a relevant notion, and fear a relevant
reaction when the Devil manifests himself. Paulo, ironically,
misses the relevance of both.
    253. God has given no such command, yet Paulo could overcome his
confusion by reacting aright to this approach. The Devil, though
he equivocates, does not lie outright.

	a ver tu ventura cierta	260
	o tu desdicha; verás	
	cerca de allá (estáme atento)	
	un hombre...	
Paulo	¡Qué gran contento	
	con tus razones me das!	
Demon.	...que Enrico tiene por nombre,	265
	hijo del noble Anareto;	
	conocerásle, en efeto,	
	por señas, que es gentil hombre,	
	alto de cuerpo y gallardo.	
	No quiero decirte más,	270
	porque apenas llegarás	
	cuando le veas.	
Paulo	Aguardo	
	lo que le he de preguntar	
	cuando yo le llegue a ver.	
Demon.	Sólo una cosa has de hacer.	275
Paulo	¿Qué he de hacer?	
Demon.	Verle y callar,	
	contemplando sus acciones,	
	sus obras y sus palabras.	
Paulo	En mi pecho ciego labras	
	quimeras y confusiones.	280
	¿Sólo eso tengo de hacer?	
Demon.	Dios que en él repares quiere,	
	porque el fin que aquél tuviere,	
	ese fin has de tener.	
	<u>Desaparece</u>.	
Paulo	¡Oh misterio soberano!	285
	¿Quién este Enrico será?	
	Por verle me muero ya.	
	¡Qué contento estoy, qué ufano!	
	Algún divino varón	
	debe de ser. ¿Quién lo duda?	290
	<u>Sale Pedrisco</u>.	
Pedr.	Siempre la fortuna ayuda	
	al más flaco corazón.	

---

266. 'the noble Anareto'. More equivocation: Anareto is morally noble, but Enrico specifically denies his social nobility (ll. 729-30).

268-9. Equivocal still: <u>gentil hombre</u>, unlike <u>caballero</u>, could refer to a man's person and lifestyle, without necessarily

	who holds the clue to your fate."
Paulo	How it comforts me to hear your message!
Devil	The man's name is Enrico;
	the noble Anareto is his father. 266
	You will know him; every inch a gentleman, 268
	handsome and tall.
	I shall say no more.
	As soon as you get there you will see him.
Paulo	But what am I to ask him?
Devil	Nothing; you are to do one thing.
Paulo	And what is that?
Devil	See him; say nothing;
	only watch how he acts and speaks.
Paulo	You throw me into new confusion...
	I do not understand.
	Can this be all I have to do? 281
Devil	It is God's will that you should watch him closely
	because the end which that man comes to
	will be your end also. 284

The Devil vanishes.

Paulo	The strangest vision!
	Who can he be, this Enrico?
	I must see him without delay.
	But oh! what relief! what joy!
	- he must certainly be a saint.
	How could he be anything else? 290

Enter Pedrisco.

Pedr.	[Aside] Fortune helps those 291
	who help themselves; I've helped myself

---

involving his ancestry or social status. See also Introduction, p. lv.

274. P: cuando; KR: cuando yo, giving the line its proper length.

281. Only in response to Paulo's insistent questioning does the Devil provide the information which will really mislead him; cf. Introduction, p. lvi.

284. 'your end also'. Again, what the Devil says is at once true and not true; see Introduction, p. lvi.

290. Literally 'Who doubts it?', redoubling the ironies: Paulo doubts so much that he ought not to doubt.

291-2. Literally 'Fortune always helps the weakest heart.' Fortune, proverbially, might favour the brave or even the early riser but scarcely the faint-hearted. The translation attempts to convey Pedrisco's confusion through the pun on 'help themselves'.

	Lindamente he manducado:	
	satisfecho quedo ya.	
Paulo	Pedrisco.	
Pedr.	A esos pies está	295
	mi boca.	
Paulo	A tiempo ha llegado;	
	los dos habemos de hacer	
	una jornada al momento.	
Pedr.	Brinco y salto de contento.	
	Mas, ¿dónde, Paulo, ha de ser?	300
Paulo	A Nápoles.	
Pedr.	¿Qué me dices?	
	Y ¿a qué, padre?	
Paulo	En el camino	
	sabrá un paso peregrino.	
	(¡Plegue a Dios que sea felice!)	
Pedr.	¿Si seremos conocidos	305
	de los amigos de allá?	
Paulo	Nadie nos conocerá,	
	que vamos desconocidos	
	en el traje y en la edad.	
Pedr.	Diez años ha que faltamos;	310
	seguros pienso que vamos;	
	que es tal la seguridad	
	de este tiempo que en una hora	
	se desconoce el amigo.	
Paulo	Vamos.	
Pedr.	Vaya Dios conmigo.	315
Paulo	De contento el alma llora.	
	A obedeceros me aplico,	
	mi Dios; nada me desmaya,	
	pues vos me mandáis que vaya	
	a ver al dichoso Enrico.	320
	¡Gran santo debe de ser!	
	Lleno de contento estoy.	
Pedr.	Y yo, pues contigo voy.	
	(No puedo dejar de ver,	
	pues que mi bien es tan cierto,	325
	con tan alta maravilla,	
	el bodegón de Juanilla	
	y la taberna del tuerto.)	

<u>Vanse y sale el Demonio.</u>

295-6 and 299. The literal meanings here ('My mouth is at your

24

	to a double helping of breakfast,	
	and it's helped.	
Paulo	Pedrisco!	
Pedr.	Father Paulo! I'm all yours.	295
Paulo	Just as you're wanted, you're here.	
	We two must go together	
	today on a journey.	
Pedr.	Hurray!	299
	But where are we going?	
Paulo	To Naples.	
Pedr.	To Naples, Father? But why	
	on earth...?	
Paulo	On the way	
	I'll explain it all. It's a strange mission	
	– please God, a happy one!	
Pedr.	And our friends	
	there – will they know us?	
Paulo	No; our clothes will be different	
	and we shall look older.	
Pedr.	We've been away ten years	
	– that should be safe enough;	
	it only takes an hour	
	these days to forget a friend.	
Paulo	We start at once.	
Pedr.	I'll be ready, God help me!	
Paulo	Lord, I could weep for joy!	
	I hasten to obey,	
	for who shall stand against me?	
	I go by your command	
	to see Enrico the blessed	
	– how holy he must be!	
	Ah! happy errand!	
Pedr.	I'm with you, Father, [Aside] and,	
	seeing my luck's turned	
	so unexpectedly,	
	I think I'll go and see	
	Juanilla's bar again	
	and one-eyed Pietro's tavern.	

Paulo and Pedrisco leave the stage, and the Devil
                        reappears.

---

feet' – in a gesture of homage   and 'I leap and jump for joy')
give the actor playing Pedrisco his cues for stage business.

```
Demon.      Bien mi engaño va trazado:
            hoy verá el desconfiado                          330
            de Dios y de su poder
            el fin que viene a tener,
            pues él propio lo ha buscado.
                  Vase y salen Octavio y Lisandro.


Lisand.     La fama de esta mujer
            sólo a verla me ha traído.                       335
Octavio  ¿De qué es la fama?
Lisand.                        La fama
            que de ella, Octavio, he tenido,
            es de que es la más discreta
            mujer que en aqueste siglo
            ha visto el napolitano                           340
            reino.
Octavio           Verdad os han dicho:
            pero aquesa discreción
            es el cebo de sus vicios;
            con ésa engaña a los necios,
            con ésa estafa a los lindos;                     345
            con una octava o soneto
            que con picaresco estilo
            suele hacer de cuando en cuando,
            trae a mil hombres perdidos,
            y por parecer discretos                          350
            alaban el artificio,
            el lenguaje y los concetos.
```

329-33. Metre: a single quintilla (AABBA). The Devil speaks
this stanza from the upper gallery; immediately afterwards, on the
lower level, from which Paulo and Pedrisco have just made their
exit, the entry of the two fops plunges us into the very different
world of disreputable Naples.

334-477. Metre: romance assonating in I-O.

335. sólo can be taken either with a verla ('I came only to see
her') or, as here, with la fama (Celia's reputation).

339. en aqueste siglo, taken here as 'in the whole history of
this world', can also mean 'in this century'.

341-52. A number of women in Madrid at this time combined
literary brilliance with equivocal reputation, as Celia does here.
See Kennedy (1974: Guastavino), 224-8.

346-7. English-speaking audiences are unlikely to recognize the
octava; hence 'couplet' in this translation. A 'picaresque' style

Devil	My plan's well found.	329
	Since he's despaired	
	of God and of God's power,	
	he'll find today the end	
	that he himself has made.	

Exit the Devil

SCENE TWO

Naples. The street before Celia's house; later within the
courtyard. Enter Octavio and Lisandro.

Lisand.	Merely because I'd heard so much about her,	335
	I came to see her for myself.	
Octavio	What had you heard?	
Lisand.	That Celia is wiser	
	and wittier, Octavio,	
	than any other woman	
	Naples has ever seen.	339
Octavio	Yes, but her wit and wisdom	341
	are sprats to catch mackerel,	
	bait to tickle fools' fancies,	
	lures for men of fashion.	
	She'll dash off a sonnet	
	or turn a neat couplet	
	full of double meaning,	346
	and men by the hundred	
	lose their heads over her,	
	all of them exclaiming	
	– just to seem cultured –	350
	"How stylish! how clever!	
	What exquisite imagery!"	

---

in a woman poet would be markedly indecorous; 'double meaning'
brings out this aspect more clearly.

   350-2. discretos... concetos. The 'conceit' – in its most
general sense the bringing together of two or more seemingly
disparate elements in a single figure of speech – was highly prized
as a literary phenomenon in 17th-century Spain. Quevedo was perhaps
its most brilliant exponent, and Gracián its outstanding theorist.
In the latter's view, which on this point was widely shared, the
conceit was a mark of intellectual distinction, and of that
cultivated wit which went by the name of discreción. Tirso here is
satirizing not so much the serious application of this vocabulary
as its adoption in the world of shallow literary fashion;
'cultured', 'stylish', and 'imagery' seemed appropriate parallels
in English usage.

```
Lisand.    Notables cosas me han dicho
           de esta mujer.
Octavio                    Está bien.
           ¿No os dijo el que aqueso os dijo,            355
           que es de esta mujer la casa
           un depósito de vivos,
           y que nunca está cerrada
           al napolitano rico
           ni al alemán, ni al inglés,                   360
           ni al húngaro, armenio o indio,
           ni aun al español tampoco,
           con ser tan aborrecido
           en Nápoles?
Lisand.                    ¿Eso pasa?
Octavio    La verdad es lo que digo,                     365
           como es verdad que venís
           de ella enamorado.
Lisand.                    Afirmo
           que me enamoró su fama.
Octavio    Pues más hay.
Lisand.                    Sois fiel amigo.
Octavio    Que tiene cierto mancebo                      370
           por galán, que no ha nacido
           hombre tan mal inclinado
           en Nápoles.
Lisand.                    Será Enrico,
           hijo de Anareto el viejo,
           que pienso que ha cuatro o cinco              375
           años que está en una cama
           el pobre viejo tullido.
Octavio    El mismo.
Lisand.                    Noticia tengo
           de ese mancebo.
Octavio                    Os afirmo,
           Lisandro, que es el peor hombre               380
           que en Nápoles ha nacido.
           Aquesta mujer le da
           cuanto puede, y cuando el vicio
```

---

357. _depósito de vivos_. R contrasts _depósito de muertos_
('mortuary'); _vivos_, in the widely-current sense of 'rakes', would
be deposited in a brothel. 'Open house' conveys the right innuendo.
  359. PK: _Enrico_; DT: _al Cimbrio_; HR: _rico_, sensibly.
  363-5. Spaniards were not, in fact, well-liked in Naples; see

28

```
Lisand.   I've certainly been told
          remarkable things about her.
Octavio   They're all true,
          but did they also tell you
          she keeps open house                              357
          for a regiment of rakehells
          - rich Neapolitans,
          Germans, English,
          Magyars, Armenians,
          Indians, come to that?
          And even Spaniards!                               363
          - you know what they think of Spaniards
          here in Naples!
Lisand.                    I can't believe it!
Octavio   All true, I assure you,
          just as it's true
          that you've fallen in love with her.
Lisand.   I admit I find her reputation
          irresistible.
Octavio                    That's not all.
Lisand.   You're my friend; I'm sure you're telling me      369
          for my own good.
Octavio   Her current fancy-man
          is the quickest-tempered villain
          in the whole of Naples.
Lisand.   That must be Enrico, then,                         373
          son of Anareto.
          His poor old father, I hear,
          has been crippled and bedridden
          these four or five years.
Octavio   The very same.
Lisand.   I've heard a great deal about Enrico.
Octavio   Lisandro, I can tell you
          he's the worst man ever born
          in Naples.  This woman gives him
          everything she earns,
          and when the gambling fever's on him
```

Introduction, p. xxxv.

369. The translation expands the meaning: 'You are a faithful
friend.'

373-4. Mention of Enrico establishes the link with the play's
opening sequence - all the more startlingly because Lisandro takes
his reputation so much for granted.

	de juego suele apretalle,	
	se viene a su casa él mismo	385
	y le quita a bofetadas	
	las cadenas, los anillos.	
Lisand.	¡Pobre mujer!	
Octavio	También ella	
	suele hacer sus ciertos tiros,	
	quitando la hacienda a muchos	390
	que son en su amor novicios,	
	con esta falsa poesía.	
Lisand.	Pues ya que estoy advertido	
	de amigo tan buen maestro,	
	allí veréis si yo os sirvo.	395
Octavio	Yo entraré con vos también;	
	mas ojo al dinero, amigo.	
Lisand.	Con invención entraremos.	
Octavio	Diréisle que habéis sabido	
	que hace versos elegantes,	400
	y que a precio de un anillo	
	unos versos os escriba	
	a una dama.	
Lisand.	¡Buen adbitrio!	
Octavio	Y yo, pues entro con vos,	
	le diré también lo mismo.	405
	Esta es la casa.	
Lisand.	Y aun pienso	
	que está en el patio.	
Octavio	Si Enrico	
	nos coge dentro, por Dios,	
	que recelo algún peligro.	
Lisand.	¿No es un hombre solo?	
Octavio	Sí.	410
Lisand.	Ni le temo, ni le estimo.	

Salen Celia leyendo un papel y Lidora con recado de escribir.

Celia	Bien escrito está el papel.
Lidora	Es discreto Severino.

394-5. 'thanks for the warning'. Like many of Tirso's more worldly characters, Lisandro recognizes good advice when he hears it, and then proceeds to ignore it. Octavio, however, may be less of an authority than we now suppose; see below, note to l. 1041.

400. 'an accomplished poet'. For Tirso's very jaundiced view of the repentistas - virtuoso authors of impromptu verse - see Kennedy

```
                he comes in here and beats her
                until she hands over
                necklaces, rings, the lot.
Lisand.                              Poor Celia!
Octavio    She's every bit as bad.
                With her... "poetic" arts
                she wheedles the last penny
                out of her gullible lovers.
Lisand.    Well, my prudent friend,
                thanks for the warning.                    394
                Perhaps I can help you too, sometime.
Octavio    We'll both go in together,
                but keep a tight hold on your money.
Lisand.    We'll need some story ready.
Octavio    Tell her... tell her you've heard
                she's an accomplished poet                400
                and you would like her to write
                some verses for your mistress
                -- you might offer her a ring as a reward.
Lisand.    Splendid!
Octavio                        And I'll spin her
                much the same kind of story.
                This is the house.                        406
Lisand.    Look, she's come down
                into the courtyard.
Octavio                        If Enrico
                should find us here, my God!
                we'd be in trouble.
Lisand.                        Enrico?
                There's only one of him, I take it?
Octavio    Only the one.
Lisand.                        Then why be afraid?
                Think nothing of him!
    Enter Celia reading a paper and Lidora with a writing-case.
Celia      Ha! he writes well...
Lidora     Yes, Severino is intelligent.
```

(1974: Studies), 285-7.

406-7. The two men approach Celia's door (one of the exits),
glimpsing her in the courtyard within. But once she and Lidora
have entered (1. 412), the audience are meant to understand that
the action has passed through the door and is taking place in the
inner court (cf. 1. 480).

Celia	Pues no se le echa de ver	
	notablemente.	
Lidora	¿No has dicho	415
	que escribe bien?	
Celia	Sí, por cierto.	415a
	La letra es buena; esto digo.	416
Lidora	Ya entiendo. La mano y pluma	417
	son de maestro de niños.	417a
Celia	Las razones de ignorante.	
Octavio	Llega, Lisandro atrevido.	
Lisand.	Hermosa es, por vida mía.	420
	Muy pocas veces se ha visto	
	belleza y entendimiento	
	tanto en un sujeto mismo.	
Lidora	Dos caballeros, si ya	
	se juzgan por el vestido,	425
	han entrado.	
Celia	¿Qué querrán?	
Lidora	Lo ordinario.	
Octavio	Ya te ha visto.	
Celia	¿Qué mandan vuesas mercedes?	
Lisand.	Hemos llegado atrevidos,	
	porque en casas de poetas	430
	y de señores, no ha sido	
	vedada la entrada a nadie.	
Lidora	(Gran sufrimiento ha tenido,	
	pues la llamaron poeta,	
	y ha callado.)	
Lisand.	Yo he sabido	435
	que sois discreta en extremo,	
	y que de Homero y de Ovidio	
	excedéis la misma fama;	
	y así yo y aqueste amigo	
	que vuestro ingenio me alaba,	440
	en competencia venimos	
	de que para cierta dama	
	que mi amor puso en olvido	
	y se casó a su disgusto,	
	le hagáis algo; que yo afirmo	445
	el premio a vuestra hermosura,	

414-18. P: <u>Celia. Pues no... ver?</u> / <u>Lid. Notablemente.</u> / <u>Cel. La</u>
<u>letra es buena.</u> / <u>Lido. Ya entiendo.</u> / <u>Celia. Las razones de</u>
<u>ignorante.</u> KSDT all omit the passage; R follows P but notes its
defective state. The text here is as restored by H; its point is

32

Celia	I can't say he shows it in this farrago.
Lidora	Didn't you say he writes well?
Celia	Just that. His writing's <u>very</u> good.
Lidora	Of course! – like a schoolmaster's.
Celia	But he thinks like a dunce.
Octavio	Forward, Lisandro! Now's your chance.
Lisand.	Such beauty and such a mind together!
Lidora	Madam, those two gentlemen (at least they look the part) are coming to visit you.
Celia	What can they want?
Lidora	The usual.
Octavio	She's seen you now!
Celia	Good morning. Your business, gentlemen?
Lisand.	Our business makes us bold, knowing that poet's houses like the mansions of the great stand open to the world.
Lidora	[Aside] They called her a poet and she's said nothing – she's playing patience with them.
Lisand.	I had heard, of course, of your unique talents and established reputation – greater than Homer, or Ovid, even. My friend here, too, told me so much about you. So I have come with this small request: could you, I wonder, compose some trifling thing for a lady who has rejected my love and married a man I know she dislikes? [Offering her a ring] Your beauty entitles you

433

---

the ambiguity of <u>Bien escrito está</u>: fine handwriting can coexist with foolish substance.

433. <u>sufrimiento</u> is literally 'forbearance'. It is not clear, unless Tirso is making a joke at his own expense, why being described as a poet should call for this quality.

	si es, señora, premio digno	
	el daros mi corazón.	
Lidora	[Aparte a Celia]	
	(Por Belerma te ha tenido.)	
Octavio	Yo vine también, señora,	450
	pues vuestro ingenio divino	
	obliga a los que se precian	
	de discretos, a lo mismo.	
Celia	¿Sobre quién tiene de ser?	
Octavio	Una mujer que me quiso	455
	cuando tuvo qué quitarme,	
	y ya que pobre me ha visto,	
	se recogió a buen vivir.	
Lidora	[Aparte] Muy como discreta hizo.	
Celia	A buen tiempo habéis llegado;	460
	que a un papel que me han escrito	
	querría responder ahora;	
	y pues decís que de Ovidio	
	excedo la antigua fama,	
	haré ahora más que él hizo:	465
	a un tiempo se han de escribir	
	vuestros papeles y el mío.	
	[A Lidora] Da a todos tinta y papel.	
Lisand.	¡Bravo ingenio!	
Octavio	Peregrino.	
Lidora	Aquí está tinta y papel.	470
Celia	Escribid, pues.	
Lisand.	Ya escribimos.	
Celia	¿Tú dices que a una mujer	
	que se casó?	
Lisand.	Aqueso digo.	
Celia	¿Y tú a la que te dejó	
	después que no fuiste rico?	475
Octavio	Así es verdad.	

---

449. Belerma. In Spanish balladry (Durán, I, 260, no. 387) Belerma was loved by the knight Durandarte. Dying at Roncesvalles, he ordered that his heart should be taken out and given to her. The allusion would have been instantly familiar in the 17th century – see Don Quijote, Part II, Ch. 23 and Góngora's wicked travesty of the theme (Obras, 14-18) – but it would be lost on modern audiences. Accordingly, the translation reshapes the passage, linking it more directly with the gifts of the ring and the chain, which must be handed over at about this point.

	to ask for any reward,	
	and with it my unworthy heart.	
Lidora	[Aside to Celia] He obviously thinks	
	you collect them – hearts, I mean.	449
Octavio	[Offering a gold chain] I too, madam,	
	come seeking a similar favour,	
	so strong is the fascination	
	your genius exerts	
	over all men of taste.	
Lidora	What's the subject this time?	
Octavio	A woman, once my mistress	
	– while my fortune lasted –	
	but now that I'm penniless,	
	she has become a nun.	
Lidora	[Aside] Most sensible thing she could do.	
Celia	You've come in the nick of time.	
	Now here I have a poem	
	requiring an answer	
	(Severino sent it).	
	You compared me, to my advantage,	
	with Ovid; very well,	
	I'll attempt an exercise	
	that Ovid never tried.	
	I shall now compose	
	all three poems at once.	
	Paper and ink for everyone, Lidora!	
Lisand.	What virtuosity!	
Octavio	Amazing!	
Lidora	Paper for you, sir... Ink for you...	470
Celia	Are you both ready?	
Lisand.	Quite.	
Celia	You want to write	
	to a lady who has married...	
Lisand.	Yes, indeed.	
Celia	And yours is for the girl who left you	
	when you lost your money.	
Octavio	Correct.	

---

455. P etc. give the speaker's name as <u>Lisandro</u>; clearly an error.

461. P: <u>ha</u>; KR: <u>han</u>. P is factually if not grammatically correct: the paper has one author (Severino).

470-1. Literally 'Here is ink and paper... Write then... We are already writing' - a clear instance of the need to translate dramatic functions, rather than linguistic categories; see Introduction, p. lxxvi.

Celia	Y yo aquí

le respondo a Severino.

Escriban, y salen Galván y Enrico con espada y broquel.

Enrico   ¿Qué se busca en esta casa,
            hidalgos?
Lisand.   Nada buscamos;
            estaba abierta y entramos.   480
Enrico   ¿Conóceme?
Lisand.   Aquesto pasa.
Enrico   Pues váyanse noramala,
            que, voto a Dios, si me enojo...
            no me haga, Celia del ojo.
Octavio   ¿Qué locura a aquesta iguala?   485
Enrico   Que los arroje en el mar,
            aunque está lejos de aquí.
Celia   [Aparte a Enrico]
            Mi bien, por amor de mí.
Enrico   ¿Tú te atreves a llegar?
            Apártate, ¡voto a Dios!,   490
            que te dé una bofetada.
Octavio   Si el estar aquí os enfada,
            ya nos iremos los dos.
Lisand.   ¿Sois pariente, o sois hermano
            de aquesta señora?
Enrico   Soy   495
            el diablo.
Galván   Ya yo estoy
            con la hojarasca en la mano.
            Sacúdelos.
Octavio   Deteneos.
Celia   Mi bien por amor de Dios.
Octavio   Aquí venimos los dos,   500
            no con lascivos deseos,
            sino a que nos escribiese
            unos papeles.
Enrico   Pues ellos,
            que se precian de tan bellos,
            ¿no saben escribir?

478-621. Metre: redondillas.
    481. Aquesto pasa is printed as a question ('Can this be happening?') by PKR; as a statement by SD. The latter seems more apt: Lisandro at this point is mulish rather than enraged.
    487. 'if I have to carry them...' Literally 'even though it's a

36

Celia	All of which leaves me	
	with Severino's answer...	
	As they begin to write, Galván and Enrico enter	
	with swords and bucklers.	
Enrico	You, sir,	
	and you! What do you mean,	
	coming in here like this?	
Lisand.	Mean? Why, nothing.	
	The place was open, so in we came.	
Enrico	Do you know who I am?	
Lisand.	Such things do happen, you know.	481
Enrico	Well, the pair of you	
	can go to Hell, do you hear?	
	By Christ! if I lose my temper...	
	[To Celia] What is it? Out with it, woman!	
Octavio	This fellow's mad, quite mad!	
Enrico	I'll throw them both in the harbour	
	if I have to carry them there on my back!	487
Celia	[Aside] Enrico, my love, please...	
Enrico	Damn you! Keep out of this	
	or you'll feel my fist!	
Octavio	You are, I take it, this lady's brother	
	or some other relative?	
Enrico	I am the Devil!	
Galván	And here's my shiv	497
	at the ready – let's be at them!	
Octavio	I can explain.	
	We had nothing improper in mind.	
	Our sole intention	
	was to ask this lady to write	
	certain papers for us...	
Enrico	Well, well!	
	Dressed up to kill,	
	and neither of them can write.	504

---

long way off'; ll. 486-7 anticipate the murder of the beggar at the
Puerta del Mar (ll. 653 ff.), previously translated (ll. 257-8) as
'the Harbour Gate'; hence 'harbour' rather than 'sea' for mar here.

497. hojarasca. Criminal slang (via hoja, 'blade') for a sword
or dagger. The translation uses a term from a similar background
(Partridge, 1055).

504. More literally 'They pride themselves so on their
appearance', but bellos is close in meaning to lindos, 'men of
fashion' (cf. above, l. 345).

37

| Octavio | Cese | 505 |

      vuestro enojo.

Enrico   ¿Qué es cesar?
¿Qué es de lo escrito?

Octavio   Esto es.

                   Rasga los papeles.

Enrico   Vuelvan por ellos después,
porque ahora no hay lugar.

Celia   ¿Los rompiste?

| Enrico | Claro está, | 510 |

y si me enojo...

Celia   ¡Mi bien!

Enrico   ...haré lo mismo también
de sus caras.

Lisand.   Basta ya.

| Enrico | Mi gusto tengo de hacer | |
| en todo cuanto quisiere; | | 515 |

y si voarcé lo quiere,
sor hidalgo, defender,
    cuéntese sin piernas ya,
porque yo nunca temí
hombres como ellos.

| Lisand. | ¿Qué ansí | 520 |

      nos trate un hombre?

Octavio   ¡Calla!

Enrico   Ellos se precian de hombres,
siendo de mujer las almas;
si pretenden llevar palmas

| y ganar honrosos nombres | | 525 |

    defiéndanse de esta espada.

                   Acuchíllelos.

Celia   ¡Mi bien!

Enrico   Aparta.

Celia   Detente.

Enrico   No
me detendrá el mismo infierno.

516-7. <u>voarcé</u>... <u>sor</u>. Contracted vulgarisms for the politer
modes of address <u>vuestra merced</u> and <u>señor</u> (cf. below, ll. 676, 680
for <u>seor</u>, <u>voarcedes</u> in the conversation of Enrico's gang).
    518. Literally 'regard yourself as legless'; sc. 'because I will
cut you down.'
    519-22. Enrico is so caught up in his own image as a man of
violence and so contemptuous of the intruders that he speaks of
them in the third person, as if they were not there. The

Octavio	So if you could perhaps restrain...
Enrico	Restrain, is it?
	Show me the papers.
Octavio	Here they are.

<u>Enrico tears them up</u>.

Enrico	You can come back for these later on.
	Not today, thank you.
Celia	You've torn their poems to shreds.
Enrico	I did, and if the mood
	takes me, I'll do the same
	for their faces...
Celia	Enrico, no!
Lisand.	I'm not going to stand for this...
Enrico	You will, because I
	do what I want
	as and when I want it,
	and if you, little man, try to argue,	516
	it won't be good for your health.	518
	Did you think you were the man	519
	to frighten me?
Lisand.	How dare you...?
Octavio	Don't answer back, you fool!
Enrico	Your sort have plenty of swagger
	(you strut about like men)
	but you've no more guts than women.
	I know you: you enjoy	524
	the applause for being hard men,
	but when it comes to swords...

<u>He attacks them</u>.

Celia	Enrico!
Enrico	Out of my way!
Celia	Stop, stop!
Enrico	Don't try to stop me; I'll not be stopped
	by Hell itself!

---

translation aims at a parallel effect through the heavily stressed
antithesis between 'you' and 'me'.
  521. P: <u>Calla</u>; KR: <u>Callá</u>, making good the rhyme.
  524-6. More literally 'if you [possibly still 'they'] want to
carry off palms [trophies for bravery], and win honourable names,
defend yourselves against this sword.' The translation adapts
Enrico's 'palms' and 'honour' in terms more familiar to our own
century.
  527-8. P etc.: <u>No / ...infierno</u>, making nine syllables in 1.527,
but anticipating with unconscious irony Enrico's eventual avoidance
of Hell.

Celia	¿Qué es aquesto? ¡Ay desdichada!
Lidora	Huyendo van, que es belleza.
Galván	¡Qué cuchillada le di!
Enrico	Viles gallinas, ¿Ansí
	afrentáis vuestra destreza?
Celia	Mi bien, ¿qué has hecho?
Enrico	Nonada.
	¡Gallardamente le di
	a aquel más alto! Le abrí
	un jeme de cuchillada.
Lidora	¡Bien el que entra a verte gana!
Galván	Una punta le tiré
	a aquel más bajo, y le eché
	fuera una arroba de lana.
	¡Terrible peto traía!
Enrico	¿Siempre, Celia, me has de dar
	disgusto?
Celia	Basta el pesar;
	sosiega, por vida mía
Enrico	¿No te he dicho que no gusto
	que entren estos marquesotes
	todos guedejas, bigotes,
	adonde me dan disgusto.
	¿Qué provecho tienes de ellos?
	¿Qué te ofrecen, qué te dan
	éstos que contino están
	rizándose los cabellos?
	De peña, de roble o risco
	es al dar su condición:
	su bolsa hizo profesión
	en la orden de San Francisco.
	Pues, ¿para qué los admites?
	¿Para qué los das entrada?
	¿No te tengo yo avisada?
	Tú harás algo que me incites
	a cólera.

Line numbers: 530, 535, 540, 545, 550, 555, 560

---

529. Literally 'What is this? Oh, unhappy woman!' The case for
functional rather than directly verbal translation is very clear at
this point.

539. _Una punta le tiré_ means merely that Galván pinked his
opponent with the tip of his weapon; the image used in English leads
into the joke about fashionably padded clothing.

542. _peto_. Originally 'a breastplate'; by the 1620s it meant a
padded jerkin, worn both for fashion and for self-defence. After
about 1622 these garments came to be of exaggerated length; see

[Enrico and Galván pursue Octavio and Lisandro off stage.]

Celia	Oh heavens! What will he do?	529

Lidora   Oh, it's so funny!
just watch them running!

[Re-enter Enrico and Galván.]

Galván   I got him fair and square, I did!

Enrico   Cowards! Is that the best
they can show for themselves?

Celia   My love, what did you do?

Enrico   Nothing to speak of!
I managed one good blow
at the tall fellow; he'll carry a four-inch scar.

Lidora   You give your visitors a warm welcome!

Galván   I put an extra stitch   539
in the little one's jerkin
and out came all his stuffing.
He was well-padded, that one.   542

Enrico   Celia, I won't have it!
This happens every day.

Celia   Sweetheart, don't be angry;
be calm...

Enrico   How many times
must I tell you I won't have it?
- these smooth, long-haired gentry   547
coming in here to make trouble!
What do you ever get out of them?
What use are they for anything
but to stand around, patting their curls into place?
It's like getting blood from a stone.   554
They're professional have-nots;
you might as well fleece a hermit!
So why do you let them come?
Why give them houseroom?
I've warned you of this before.
One of these days you'll do something
to make me really angry.

Kennedy (1974: Guastavino), 229-32. If this one contained an arroba
of wool, it would have weighed almost two stone.

547.   marquesotes. See Kennedy (1974: Guastavino), 228. A
derisive term for the lindos who affected such fashions as the
peto, ringlets, and moustaches.

554-7. Literally 'Their character in giving is that of a rock,
oak, or crag; their purse has made its vows [sc. of perpetual
poverty] in the Franciscan Order.'

555. PK: el; HR: al.

Celia	Bueno está.
Enrico	Apártate.
Celia	Oye, mi bien,

porque sepas que hay también
alguno en éstos que da.   565
   Aqueste anillo y cadena
me dieron éstos.

Enrico	A ver.

La cadena he menester,
que me parece muy buena.

Celia	¿La cadena?
Enrico	Y el anillo 570

también me has de asegurar.

Lidora	Déjale algo a mi señora.
Enrico	Ella, ¿no sabrá pedillo?

   ¿Para qué lo pides tú?

Galván	Esta por hablar se muere. 575
Lidora	[Aparte] ¡Mal haya quien bien os quiere,

rufianes de Bercebú!

Celia	Todo es tuyo, vida mía;

y, pues yo tan tuya soy,
escúchame.

Enrico	Atento estoy. 580
Celia	Sólo pedirte querría

   que nos lleves esta tarde
a la Puerta de la Mar.

Enrico	El manto puedes tomar.
Celia	Yo haré que allá nos aguarde 585

   la merienda.

Enrico	Oyes, Galván:

ve a avisar luego al instante
a nuestro amigo Escalante,
a Cherinos y Roldán,
que voy con Celia.

Galván	Sí haré. 590
Enrico	Di que a la Puerta del Mar

nos vayan luego a esperar
con sus mozas.

Lidora	¡Bien a fe!
Galván	Ello habrá lindo bureo.

Mas que ha de haber cuchilladas.   595

---

566. <u>cadena</u>. Simply 'chain', but it is clearly meant to be an
object of value.

Celia	Very well.
Enrico	Now get out.
Celia	Listen, my love.
	They're not all wasted effort.
	These two, for instance, gave me
	this ring, and this gold chain. 566
Enrico	Hand them over.
	I want that chain – it looks a good one.
Celia	The chain?
Enrico	And the ring too.
Lidora	You might at least leave the mistress
	something for herself.
Enrico	She's a tongue, hasn't she?
	Why do you have to do the asking?
Galván	Because she can never keep her mouth shut,
	that's why.
Lidora	[Aside] Oh, these villains! 576
	God help us girls who love them!
Celia	It all belongs to you, my sweet,
	and so do I, so listen.
Enrico	I'm listening.
Celia	I only wanted to say:
	this afternoon, couldn't we all
	go out to the Harbour Gate?
Enrico	Why not? You can fetch your cloak...
Celia	And I can order food 586
	and wine for us to take.
Enrico	Galván! tell all the others
	– Fingers and Escalante and Roldán –
	I'm going out with Celia.
Galván	Right you are!
Enrico	Tell them to bring their girls;
	we'll meet by the Harbour Gate.
Lidora	That's more like it!
Galván	It should be good; 594
	with luck there'll be a fight.

576-7. Literally 'Bad luck to anyone who loves you well, you
ruffians of the Devil!' Bercebú for Belcebú, the name of the demon
Beelzebub.
586. merienda. Not, as commonly nowadays, a refreshment taken
around six in the evening, but the ingredients for a picnic.
594-5. bureo. A disreputable party. Vocabulary items like this
and turns of phrase like Ello habrá or Mas que mark Galván's
language as distinctively that of low life.

43

Celia	¿Quieres que vamos tapadas?
Enrico	No es eso lo que deseo.
	Descubiertas habéis de ir,
	porque quiero en este día
	que sepan que tú eres mía. 600
Celia	Como te podré servir,
	vamos.
Lidora	Tú eres inocente.
	¿Todas las joyas le has dado?
Celia	Todo está bien empleado
	en hombre que es tan valiente. 605
Galván	Mas que ¿no te acuerdas ya
	que te dijeron ayer,
	que una muerte habías de hacer?
Enrico	Cobrada y gastada está
	ya la mitad del dinero. 610
Galván	Pues, ¿para qué vas al mar?
Enrico	Después se podrá trazar,
	que ahora, Galván, no quiero.
	Anillo y cadena tengo,
	que me dio la tal señora; 615
	dineros sobran ahora.
Galván	Ya tus intentos prevengo.
Enrico	Viva alegre el desdichado,
	libre de cuidado y pena,
	que en gastando la cadena 620
	le daremos su recado.

Vanse y salen Paulo y Pedrisco de camino graciosamente.

Pedr.	Maravillado estoy de tal suceso.
Paulo	Secretos son de Dios.
Pedr.	¿De modo, padre,
	que el fin que ha de tener aqueste Enrico
	ha de tener también?

597-600. Enrico wants Celia to acknowledge his possession of her (thus, as he understands it, enhancing his honour) by a piece of shameless public conduct (thus degrading hers).

603. P: los; KR: las. 'All the jewels' must refer to the ring and the chain (see above, 11. 565-70).

607-8. Literally 'they told you yesterday that you had to do a killing', but clearly a promise has been made, and money paid over.

Celia	Should we wear our veils?
Enrico	No. 597
	Today I want you to show
	that you're mine.
Celia	For you I'd do anything.
	Lidora, we're going out.
Lidora	[To Celia] You must be out of your mind.
	That's the chain and the ring
	you've given away.
Celia	And why not
	for a man as brave as that?
Galván	Hey, wait! Remember you promised 607
	to do a killing today?
Enrico	That's right; they paid cash down,
	and I've spent half the advance.
Galván	Then you can't just... go out.
Enrico	We'll think about that later.
	Just for now, I don't feel
	like doing the job. Why should I?
	There's money enough and to spare
	– we've got the chain and the ring
	off Celia. 615
Galvan	I get your drift...
Enrico	Let the poor devil live
	as if he hadn't a care,
	and when our money runs out
	we'll settle his affair.

Exeunt Enrico and Galván.

SCENE THREE

Naples. By the Habour Gate. Enter Paulo and Pedrisco
dressed for a journey, the latter comically.

Pedr.	I still can't believe it.
Paulo	God's ways are secret.
Pedr.	So the end this Enrico
	comes to, you'll come to as well?

---

615.   la tal señora ('that lady') seems a casual and dismissive
way of referring to Celia. This would be in line with Enrico's
usual manner, but the phrase may have been chosen simply for the
rhyme.
  622-721. Metre: unrhymed hendecasyllables (relatively uncommon
in the comedia).

45

Paulo	Faltar no puede 625
	la palabra de Dios; el ángel suyo
	me dijo que si Enrico se condena
	me he de condenar, y si él se salva
	también me he de salvar.
Pedr.	Sin duda, padre,
	que es un santo varón aqueste Enrico. 630
Paulo	Eso mismo imagino.
Pedr.	Esta es la puerta
	que llaman de la Mar.
Paulo	Aquí me manda
	el ángel que le aguarde.
Pedr.	Aquí vivía
	un tabernero gordo, padre mío,
	adonde yo acudía muchas veces; 635
	y más allá, si acaso se le acuerda,
	vivía aquella moza rubia y alta
	que Archero de la Guarda parecía
	a quien él requebraba.
Paulo	¡Oh vil contrario!
	Livianos pensamientos me fatigan. 640
	¡Cuerpo flaco! Hermano, escuche.
Pedr.	Escucho.
Paulo	El contrario me tienta con memoria
	de los pasados gustos...
	<u>Echase en el suelo.</u>
Pedr.	Pues, ¿qué hace?
Paulo	En el suelo me arrojo desta suerte
	para que en él me pise: llegue, hermano, 645
	píseme muchas veces.
Pedr.	En buen hora,
	que soy muy obediente, padre mío.
	<u>Písale</u>.
	¿Písole bien?
Paulo	Sí, hermano.

---

631. Significantly, Paulo does not say 'So I believe' or 'So I hope', but 'So I imagine.' He has come to rely on fantasy, rather than on hope or faith.

638. The Archers of the Royal Guard, a hereditary corps, originally recruited by Charles V from among his Flemish subjects, were characteristically tall and fair-haired (Prieto, 167).

639–41. Pedrisco's worldly memories seem a mild enough stimulus to impure thoughts; nor is there evidence that such thoughts were ever Paulo's main problem. There is dramatic irony, then, in his outburst against the 'vile enemy' (the Devil), to whose non-fleshly

Paulo	That was the message the angel brought me, and who can doubt God's word? If Enrico is damned I am damned along with him; if Enrico is saved God will save me too.	
Pedr.	He must be very holy, this man Enrico, Father.	
Paulo	So my thought tells me.	631
Pedr.	Here we are at the harbour, and there's the Harbour Gate.	
Paulo	Just here the angel told me I must wait.	
Pedr.	Yes, I remember... somewhere round here a fat man kept a bar I used to go to, and his girl used to live over there. She had long, golden hair — a strapping lass she was, tall enough for a guardsman...	638
Paulo	Ah! temptation!	639
	The Devil vexes my frail body with thoughts of lust. Pedrisco, my brother...	
Pedr.	Father, what is it?	
Paulo	Satan has snared me with memories of the flesh... *He casts himself down upon the ground.*	643
Pedr.	Yes, but whatever are you at?	
Paulo	I cast myself down	644
	— oh tread me! oh abase me! tread me down! Why do you wait?	
Pedr.	Alright. (I'm only doing what I'm told, mind). Will this do Father?	
Paulo	Yes! trample my lusts!	

---

temptation he has so unthinkingly succumbed.

642-3. PR: _tiene..._ / _y_ con; KSD: _tienta..._ / _de los_. The latter is a little more specific.

643-4. Stage-direction. After l. 645 in P; sensibly relocated by R.

644-53. The trampling scene is based on a story of St Francis of Assisi, itself dramatized, says R, in Lope de Vega's _El serafín humano_. Paulo, of course, is far from sainthood, and further still from Franciscan humility.

Pedr.	¿No le duele?
Paulo	Pise, y no tenga pena.
Pedr.	¿Pena, padre?

¿Por qué razón he yo de tener pena?   650
Piso y repiso, padre de mi vida;
mas temo no reviente, padre mío.

Paulo   Píseme hermano.

Dan voces, deteniendo a Enrico.

Roldán	[Dentro] Deteneos, Enrico.
Enrico	[Dentro] Al mar he de arrojalle, vive el cielo.
Paulo	A Enrico oí nombrar.
Enrico	[Dentro] ¿Gente mendiga 655

ha de haber en el mundo?

Cher.	[Dentro] Deteneos.
Enrico	[Dentro] Podrásme detener en arrojándole.
Celia	[Dentro] ¿Dónde vas? Detente.
Enrico	[Dentro] No hay remedio.

Harta merced te hago pues te saco
de tan grande miseria.

Roldán   ¿Qué habéis hecho?   660

Salen todos.

Enrico   Llegóme a pedir un pobre una limosna;
dolióme el verle con tan gran miseria,
y porque no llegase a avergonzarse
otro desde hoy, cogíle yo en los brazos
y le arrojé en el mar.

Paulo	¡Delito inmenso! 665
Enrico	Ya no será más pobre, según pienso.
Pedr.	[Aparte] ¡Algún diablo limosna te pidiera!
Celia	¿Siempre has de ser crüel?

---

652.   Literally 'I'm afraid you might snuff it.' Reventar, 'to burst' is a vulgarism for 'to die'.

653.   This is presumably the moment (not otherwise indicated) when the trampling stops.

657-60.   It is unclear at what point the beggar is actually flung into the sea. It must be before l. 660 (literally 'What have you done?'). Celia's Detente (literally 'Stop!') in l. 658 sounds like a last-minute plea, perhaps already too late.

662.   miseria means both the fact of poverty and its physical symptoms, especially the state of being verminous. Hence the note of revulsion which the translation seeks to bring out more directly.

```
Pedr.      You'll get hurt!
Paulo                        Tread all the harder,
           and feel no pain for me.
Pedr.                            I'm not the one
           who's likely to.  Don't worry; I'll keep at it!
           But what's going to happen to you?              652
Paulo      Harder, brother, harder!
```
Voices and sounds of a scuffle are heard off stage.
```
Roldán     Stop, Enrico, stop!                             653
Enrico     God damn it! into the sea he's going!
Paulo      They said "Enrico"!
Enrico                         Beggars!
           the world is lousy with them!
Fingers    Let him go!
Enrico                  Are you the one to stop me?        657
           Over the edge with him!
Celia      Enrico!  Think what you're at!
Enrico     There, that's done with!
           He ought to thank me
           for putting him out of his pain!
Roldán     You've gone too far this time.
```
Enter Enrico, Roldán, Escalante, Fingers, Galván,
                Celia and Lidora.
```
Enrico     A beggar, whining for money!
           He stank of poverty — I couldn't face it.      662
           He won't make anyone else feel shame like that! 663
           — I threw him in the sea.
Paulo      Of all the wicked acts!
Enrico     He'll have no call to worry
           about money where he is now.
Pedr.      A hell of a fine thing                          667
           - asking for money from a man like you!
Celia      Why must you be so cruel?
```

663-4. P: <u>a vergonçarse / otro... cogíle en brazos</u>, a syllable
short in 1. 664; K: <u>a avergonçarse / a otro... cogíle yo en los</u>
<u>braços</u>; R: <u>a avergonzarse / a otro... cogíle en brazos</u>. R makes up
the line, amending from K, but retaining the same meaning as the
latter: 'and lest he should come to shame himself before another.'
But it is surely his own response, not the beggar's predicament,
which is likely to be uppermost in Enrico's mind. By amending 1.
664 from K's final phrase only, the meaning of P - 'lest anyone
else should be made ashamed' - can be preserved. For comment on
these lines as amended see Introduction, p. lxi.
     667. Literally 'Would that some devil had asked you for alms!'

49

Enrico	No me repliques,
	que haré contigo y los demás lo mismo.
Escal.	Dejemos eso agora, por tu vida. 670
	Sentémonos los dos, Enrico amigo.
Paulo	[A Pedrisco] A éste han llamado Enrico.
Pedr.	[A Paulo] Será otro;
	¿Querías tú que fuese este mal hombre
	que en vida está ya ardiendo en los infiernos?
	Aguardemos a ver en lo que para. 675
Enrico	Pues siéntense voarcedes, porque quiero
	haya conversación.
Escal.	Muy bien ha dicho.
Enrico	Siéntese Celia aquí.
Celia	Ya estoy sentada.
Escal.	Tú conmigo, Lidora.
Lidora	Lo mismo digo yo, seor Escalante. 680
Cher.	Siéntese aquí Roldán.
Roldán	Ya voy, Cherinos.
Pedr.	¡Mire qué buenas almas, Padre mío!
	Lléguese más, verá de lo que tratan.
Paulo	¿Que no viene mi Enrico?
Pedr.	Mire y calle,
	que somos pobres, y este desalmado 685
	no nos eche en la mar.
Enrico	Agora quiero
	que cuente cada uno de vuarcedes
	las hazañas que ha hecho en esta vida,
	quiero decir hazañas, latrocinios,
	cuchilladas, heridas, robos, muertes, 690
	salteamientos y cosas de este modo.
Escal.	Muy bien ha dicho Enrico.
Enrico	Y al que hubiere
	hecho mayores males, al momento
	una corona de laurel le pongan
	cantándole alabanzas y motetes. 695
Escal.	Soy contento.

---

683. P: verá lo; KR: verá de lo, correcting the length of the
line.
688. hazañas are 'heroic exploits'. Enrico both asserts and
perverts the values of worldly honour (cf. above, note on 11.
597–600).

Enrico	You shut your mouth, unless
	you want to go the same way
	- and any one else who argues.
Escal.	Oh, let it be, for God's sake.
	Enrico, let's sit down.
Paulo	[To Pedrisco] They called him Enrico.
Pedr.	It can't be the same one.
	How could it be a man like that?
	Why, he's as good as damned already!
	Let's stay and watch the way things go.
Enrico	Sit down, sit down; let's talk.
Escal.	That's right; do what he says.
Enrico	Celia by me.
Celia	Here I am, love.
Escal.	I'll have Lidora.
Lodora	Why, Escalante,
	that's my notion too.
Fingers	Sit over here, Roldán.
Roldán	Right you are, Fingers.
Pedr.	Just look at them, Father
	- they're a nice lot, I must say!
	Let's get a bit closer
	where we can hear them.
Paulo	But when
	will my Enrico come?
Pedr.	We'd best keep quiet. We're poor enough.
	If that one takes us for beggars,
	he'll think nothing of throwing us in the sea.
Enrico	Right, then, we'll have some stories.
	Let's all tell the tale
	of the best things we've done	688
	- robberies, I mean, knifings, woundings,
	burglaries, killings, hold-ups,
	and things like that.
Escal.	That's the stuff!
Enrico	And the one who's done most
	and worst wins the laurel,	693
	and we all make up songs to praise him.
Escal.	That suits me.

693-5. More literally 'let them crown him straightway with a laurel wreath, singing praises and verses about him.' Motete, normally a religious composition, is perhaps closer here to mote, a verse containing some personal allusion.

51

Enrico	Comience, seor Escalante.
Paulo	[Aparte] ¡Que esto sufre el Señor!
Pedr.	[A Paulo] Nada le espante.
Escal.	Yo digo ansí.
Pedr.	[Aparte] ¡Qué alegre y satisfecho!
Escal.	Veinte y cinco pobretes tengo muertos;
	seis casas he escalado y treinta heridas 700
	he dado con la chica.
Pedr.	[Aparte] ¡Quién te viera
	hacer en una horca cabriolas!
Enrico	Diga Cherinos.
Pedr.	[Aparte a Paulo] ¡Qué ruin nombre tiene!
	Cherinos: cosa poca.
Cher.	Yo comienzo.
	No he muerto a ningún hombre, pero he dado 705
	más de cien puñaladas.
Enrico	¿Y ninguna
	fue mortal?
Cher.	Amparóles la fortuna.
	De capas que he quitado en esta vida
	y he vendido a un ropero, está ya rico.
Enrico	¿Véndelas él?
Cher.	¿Pues no?
Enrico	¿No las conocen? 710
Cher.	Por quitarse de aquestas ocasiones,
	las convierte en ropillas y calzones.
Enrico	¿Habéis hecho otra cosa?
Cher.	No me acuerdo.
Pedr.	[A Paulo]
	Mas que le absuelve ahora el ladronazo.
Celia	Y tú, ¿qué has hecho, Enrico?
Enrico	Oigan voarcedes. 715
Escal.	Nadie cuente mentiras.

---

701. la chica. Escalante's 'smaller' weapon; the missing noun is perhaps espada ('sword') or navaja ('knife').
702-4. Cherinos. See above, note on characters, p. 4.
706. P: Ninguna; KR: Y ninguna, correcting the metre.
709. Literally the exchange reads: 'Does he sell them? / Well, wouldn't he?'
711-12. Literally 'To avoid these situations, he turns them into coats and breeches.' The ropilla, a jacket with elaborate sleeves, was worn over the doublet. The common 17th-century satirical motif of the dishonest tailor makes little impact today; hence the rather

```
Enrico                     Right, Escalante,
            you can begin.
Paulo                       God in Heaven!
            Can such things be?
Pedr.                              You've seen nothing yet.
Escal.      Here goes, then.
Pedri.                      Look at him
            - full of himself!
Escal.                            Murders:
            twenty-five, poor devils; break-ins, six;
            and razor-slashings: thirty.                    701
Pedr.       And may you swing for it, say I!
Enrico      Now, Fingers.                                   702
Pedr.                       Fingers! what a name!
            I ask you!
Fingers                 Off we go.
            I haven't what you'd call killed
            anyone, but I've knifed
            a hundred in my time.
Enrico      What? and none of them dead?
Fingers     They were lucky, that's all.
            Cloak-snatching's been my game.
            I sell them to a fence;
            he's a wealthy man today.
Enrico      What does he do with them?                      709
Fingers                               Sells them.
            What else?
Enrico      But aren't they recognized?
Fingers     Not when he's finished with them               711
            - take a look at your breeches!
Enrico      Anything else?
Fingers                      I can't remember
            anything else.
Pedr.                        Holy God!                      714
            He's giving him absolution!
Celia       Enrico, your turn now.
Enrico      I'm ready.
Escal.                   Tell the truth.
```

---

broader comic point in Chirinos' reply as translated.

    714.   Literally 'I'll be bound, the great thief's giving him absolution!' The previous question and answer resemble formulae from the confessional.

Enrico	¿Yo soy hombre

```
Enrico                          ¿Yo soy hombre
          que en mi vida las dije?
Galván                          Tal se entiende.
Pedr.     ¿No escucha, padre mío, estas razones?
Paulo     Estoy mirando a ver si viene Enrico.
Enrico    Haya, pues, atención.
Celia                           Nadie te impide.        720
Pedr.     ¡Mire a qué sermón atención pide!
Enrico    Yo nací mal inclinado
          como se ve en los efectos
          del discurso de mi vida
          que referiros pretendo.                       725
          Con regalos me crié
          en Nápoles, que ya pienso
          que conocéis a mi padre,
          que aunque no fué caballero
          ni de sangre generosa,                         730
          era muy rico; y yo entiendo
          que es la mayor calidad
          el tener en este tiempo.
          Crióme, al fin, como digo,
          entre regalos, haciendo                        735
          travesuras cuando niño,
          locuras cuando mancebo.
          Hurtaba a mi viejo padre,
          arcas y cofres abriendo,
          los vestidos que tenía                         740
          las joyas y los dineros.
```

716-7. The correct answer to Enrico's question is 'Yes'. We already know him as a breaker of contracts (ll. 607-10); we are soon to learn that he is a habitual perjurer and swindler (ll. 826-9). His honesty, such as it is at this stage, is a matter not of truth-telling, but of shamelessness.

718. Literally 'Are you not listening to these words?'

719. Cf. above, l. 684. The recurrence adds pathos to Paulo's situation.

720. P: Celio. An obvious error.

721. P: Mire; KR: Miren, correcting the metre. But to which group of people, rather than to Paulo alone, would Pedrisco speak from his place of concealment? Not to the ruffians, and not (unless at the cost of some loss of tension) to the audience either. It is tempting to reallocate the line to Celia, but there is no textual warrant for doing so.

Enricò	Did you ever hear anything else from me?	716
Galván	Can't say that I did.	
Pedr.	What do you think of them, Father, after all that?	718
Paulo	Hush! I'm still waiting to see my Enrico.	719
Enrico	Now quiet all round and listen.	
Celia	Who's interrupting?	
Pedr.	Let's see the kind of sermon this one preaches!	
Enrico	I was born wicked	722
	and that's the way it went	
	all my life long	
	- you'll hear the story now.	
	I had plenty as a boy	
	in Naples - where I think you know my father.	728
	He wasn't a gentleman;	729
	he had no noble blood,	
	but he had money, and these days	
	I think you'll find that counts for more.	
	Well, as I say, he brought me up,	
	and I had everything.	
	Always in trouble when I was small,	
	when I grew up, I kicked over the traces.	
	I took the old man's money,	738
	ransacked his private coffers,	
	his clothes, his jewels, his cash,	

722-1011. Metre: romance assonating in E-O. Initially apt for
Enrico's largely narrative speech.

722. mal inclinado. 'Inclination' and 'effects' were part of
the technical vocabulary used to describe the influence of the
stars on human character. Such language implies that Enrico
regards his own wickedness as predestined. But orthodox teaching
was that 'inclination' could be overborne by freewill.

728. Anareto's name, which will set the seal on Paulo's despair,
is not mentioned at this stage.

729-30. Because Paulo has not yet recognized Enrico, the
latter's statement that his father was not noble will further
postpone that recognition; once he has identified Enrico, the
information ought to cast some doubt on the supposed angel's message
(see above, l. 266).

738-41. Contrast the claims which Enrico will make in Act II
(below, ll. 1073-4).

Jugaba, y digo jugaba,
para que sepáis con esto
que de cuantos vicios hay
es el primer padre el juego.   745
Quedé pobre y sin hacienda
y como enseñado a hacerlo,
di en robar de casa en casa
cosas de pequeño precio.
Iba a jugar, y perdía;   750
mis vicios iban creciendo.
Di luego en acompañarme
con otros del arte mesmo:
escalamos siete casas,
dimos la muerte a sus dueños;   755
lo robado repartimos
para dar caudal al juego.
De cinco que éramos todos,
sólo los cuatro prendieron,
y nadie me descubrió   760
aunque les dieron tormento.
Pagaron en una plaza
su delito, y yo con esto,
de escarmentado, acogíme
a hacer a solas mis hechos.   765
Ibame todas las noches
solo a la casa del juego,
donde a su puerta aguardaba
a que saliesen de adentro.
Pedía con cortesía   770
el barato, y cuando ellos
iban a sacar qué darme,
sacaba yo el fuerte acero,
que riguroso escondía
en sus inocentes pechos,   775
y por fuerza me llevaba
lo que ganando perdieron.
Quitaba de noche capas:

---

747. P: y yo me he enseñado hazerlo; R: y yo me he enseñado a
hacerlo, both meaning 'and I have trained myself to do it [i.e. to
be without money].' H: y como enseñado a hacerlo ('and as someone
trained to do it') can be taken with either 'to gamble' or ' to
rob'. This last seems a plausible change: Enrico shows no sign of
being trained to bear poverty.

56

for gambling – notice that –
for gambling – that's the start
of all the crime there is.
I lost it all, of course,
and then – I'd gone so far –
I took to doing burglaries,
little jobs, small-time stuff.
Then back to the tables; I lost,
and got deeper into crime.
I took up with a crowd
of others in the same line.
We did seven break-ins
(killed the owners),
shared out the loot.
The croupiers got the lot.
There were five of us in the gang;
the police arrested four.
Nobody gave me away
– not even on the rack.
I saw them hanged in the square,
and I learned my lesson: 763
never go out on a job
unless you're on your own.
So every night I went
alone to the gambling club,
and I stood at the door, and I waited
for customers coming out.
Very politely, I asked them
"Could I have my usual commission?"   771
and while they fumbled for change
I whipped out my knife
and stabbed them before they knew it,
and off I went with the winnings
– so the winners were always the losers.
Cloak-snatching – I've done that too.

---

756. P: los robadores partimos makes little sense; HR: lo robado
repartimos.

763-4. Literally 'and I, at this, having taken warning, made it
my practice...' The sentence is so constructed that, for a moment,
it looks as if Enrico really has learned his lesson.

771. barato. Successful gamblers, by custom, distributed part
of their winnings to those looking on; this was the barato. In
practice it amounted to a protection-racket, and is so rendered
here.

tenía diversos hierros
para abrir cualquiera puerta   780
y hacerme capaz del dueño.
Las mujeres estafaba,
y no dándome el dinero,
visitaba una navaja
su rostro luego al momento.   785
Aquestas cosas hacía
el tiempo que fui mancebo;
pero escuchadme y sabréis,
siendo hombre, las que he hecho.
A treinta desventurados   790
yo solo y aqueste acero,
que es de la muerte ministro,
del mundo sacado habemos:
los diez muertos por mi gusto,
y los veinte me salieron,   795
una con otra, a doblón.
¿Diréis que es pequeño precio?
Es verdad; mas, voto a Dios,
que en faltándome el dinero,
que mate por un doblón   800
a cuántos me están oyendo.
Seis doncellas he forzado:
¡dichoso llamarme puedo,
pues seis he podido hallar
en este felice tiempo!   805
De una principal casada
me aficioné; ya resuelto,
habiendo entrado en su casa,
a ejecutar mi deseo,
dio voces, vino el marido,   810
y yo, enojado y resuelto,
llegué con él a los brazos,
y tanto en ellos le aprieto,
que perdió tierra; y apenas
en este punto le veo,   815
cuando de un balcón le arrojo,

786-9. Enrico's listeners, especially Paulo, may well feel that
they have the full measure of his depravity. Abruptly, they learn
that these things are merely _juvenilia_.
   796. P: _una con otra_, which, with _muerte_ understood, makes
sense; KR: _uno con otro_.

With my bunch of skeleton keys
I could open any door,
and overpower the owners.
I used to hold up women,
and if they wouldn't pay
I didn't stand on ceremony
- I razored their faces for them.
That's how I used to live   786
when I was a boy, but now
listen, and I'll tell you
what I've done since I was a man.
This knife and I between us
- it's a dangerous little customer -
have put below ground
no less than thirty men
- ten of them because I felt like it,
and for the other twenty
taken all round I got
roughly three dollars a time.   796
"Cheap at the price", you'd say.
That's true, but by Christ!
if I were short of the money,
I'd do it to you for the same.
I've raped six virgins - that's something:
to have found six nowadays!
Once, when I was struck
on some rich man's wife, and I'd gone
into the house, determined
to get what I wanted from her,
the bitch called out, and her husband
came into the room. I was mad!
I took a grip of him
and lifted him off the ground,
and once I'd got him like that
I ran to the open window

---

796. 'three dollars'. A doblón could be worth either two, four,
or eight gold escudos (see Bleiberg, I. 1152). The two-escudo
piece was worth about 24 reales (calculation based on Geoffrey
Parker, xiv). Using 'dollar' as a conventional equivalent for the
'piece of eight reales', we can derive a value of three dollars.

807-11. P has a comma after aficioné and a full stop after
deseo. CR revise these to a semicolon and a comma repectively.
Though R questions whether the lines are not corrupt, they appear
to make adequate, if clumsy, sense.

y en el suelo cayó muerto.
Dio voces la tal señora;
y yo, sacando el acero,
le metí cinco o seis veces   820
en el cristal de su pecho,
donde puertas de rubíes
en campos de cristal bellos
le dieron salida al alma
para que se fuese huyendo.   825
Por hacer mal solamente,
he jurado juramentos
falsos, fingiendo quimeras,
hecho máquinas, enredos.
Y a un sacerdote que quiso   830
reprehenderme con buen celo,
de un bofetón que le di,
cayó en tierra medio muerto.
Porque supe que encerrado
en casa de un pobre viejo   835
estaba un contrario mío,
a la casa puse fuego;
y sin poder remediallo
todos se quemaron dentro
y hasta dos niños hermanos   840
ceniza quedaron hechos.
No digo jamás palabra
si no es con juramento,
un pese o un por vida,
porque sé que ofendo al cielo.   845
En mi vida misa oí,
ni, estando en peligros ciertos
de morir, me he confesado,

822-3. P: _puestas... compas_; K: _puertas... compas_; HR: _puertas..._
campos: 'where gates of rubies in fair fields of crystal gave egress
to her soul, so that it might flee.' The rubies are blood, the
gates wounds, the crystal white flesh - elaborately _culto_ imagery.
See Introduction, p. lxxii.

826-9. Contrast Enrico's earlier insistence (ll. 716-7) on his
truthfulness.

835. Contrast this casual murder with his protestations in Act
II (ll. 1305 etc.) that he does not kill old men. Interestingly,
this implies that the inhibition is something which has grown on
him only recently.

838. The excuse is lame indeed, yet wholly plausible as a piece
of criminal doublethink.

and threw him out, and he died
where he fell. She began screaming.
I had my knife; I stabbed her
five or six times in the breasts.
Snow-white they were, and the blood ran down   822
like rubies over the slope,
and her life ran out with it too.
I've often perjured myself,   826
And set up frauds galore
just for the hell of it.
There was this priest who tried to tell me
I was leading a wicked life.
Christ! I hit him so hard
he was half dead when I'd finished.
Once, someone I was after
hid in a poor man's house
- an old man - I found out   835
and set the place on fire
and everyone inside
was burned - it couldn't be helped.   838
There were even a couple of children
- burned to ashes they were.
Whenever I speak I swear   842
- "By Christ!" or something like that -
because I know it's a sin.
I've never been to Mass.
I've never made my confession   847

842-5. Enrico's swearing poses inescapable - perhaps insoluble -
problems for the translator. The extreme register in English is
the obscene 'four-letter' series, but that, in the context of the
comedia, does not come across as supremely wicked; it merely seems
incongruously low. Enrico, indeed, is neither pure-minded nor
sexually virtuous (ll. 802-5), but what fuels his violent language
is, above all, his desire to 'offend Heaven' (l. 845). That in its
turn is close to the thematic core of the play. I have therefore
kept his swearing largely within the blasphemous range, highlighting
its violence and aggression by rhythmic and other effects.

844. P: un pese a (does not scan); K: un pésete o (metrically
sounder, but the phrase in question is pese a Dios); T: maldiciones
y por vidas (19th-century rather than 17th-century oaths); H: con
un pese o (ingenious and metrically correct)); R: un pese a o
(makes good the metre with four adjacent vowels and some hiatus).
None of the alternatives to P seems wholly convincing.

847-9. The refusal to confess will become an important issue in
Acts II and III.

ni invocado a Dios eterno.
No he dado limosna nunca,   850
aunque tuviese dineros:
antes persigo a los pobres,
como habéis visto el ejemplo.
No respeto a religiosos:
de sus iglesias y templos   855
seis cálices he robado
y diversos ornamentos
que sus altares adornan.
Ni a la justicia respeto:
mil veces me he resistido   860
y a sus ministros he muerto;
tanto que para prenderme
no tienen ya atrevimiento.
Y finalmente, yo estoy
preso por los ojos bellos   865
de Celia, que está presente;
todos la tienen respeto
por mí, que la adoro, y cuando
sé que la sobran dineros,
con lo que me da, aunque poco,   870
mi viejo padre sustento,
que ya le conoceréis
por el nombre de Anareto.
Cinco años ha que tullido
en una cama le tengo,   875
y tengo piedad con él
por estar pobre el buen viejo;
y como soy causa, al fin,
de ponelle en tal extremo,
por jugarle yo su hacienda   880
el tiempo que fui mancebo.

Todo es verdad lo que he dicho,
voto a Dios, y que no miento:
juzgad ahora vosotros
cuál merece mayor premio.   885

867–71. More confusion about honour (cf. ll. 598–600). Celia is
to be respected, but only because of Enrico (either because he can
enforce respect or because he is who he is). Her honour is seen as
derivative; only his is real. To live off her earnings, moreover,
is a curious form of 'worship', and a yet more curious topic for
boasting.

871–81. 'to maintain my father' introduces the real surprise of
Enrico's speech: that his relationship with Anareto actually

or begged for God's mercy, not even
when I was facing death.
Even when I've money
I never give for charity
- you've seen how I treat beggars.
I hate them! As for the Church,
what do I care for their shrines and their
                                        sacristies?
I've taken six chalices off them
besides the crosses and stuff
I stole off the altars.
The law? Don't make me laugh!
I couldn't count the times
I've got away, the men of theirs I've killed
- they know better than tangle with me.
And now at last I'm captured
by Celia here - you all know her,
and you respect her too   867
(or I'll know the reason why).
I worship lovely Celia
and when she's money in hand
I take what she gives me (which isn't much)
and use it to maintain my father.   871
He's old now, Anareto   873
- you've heard me mention his name -
and for the past five years
crippled and bedridden.
Well, I feel sorry for him;
he's been a good father
and he's little enough to show for it,
for I ran through his property
when I was young.
That's why he's destitute now.
And that's the God's truth, all of it,
and never a word of a lie.
Now you tell me which one of us
deserves the prize.

---

embodies a virtue. It is, admittedly, an isolated virtue - piedad
in the ancient, secular sense of Latin pietas ('filial obligation')
- and it remains anomalous, ineffectual, limited. Yet it already
involves some reparation - hardly repentance as yet - for earlier
crimes.
   873. Mention of Anareto at last enables Paulo to identify Enrico.
The enormity of this discovery blinds him to the much more startling
disclosure in which it is embedded.

```
Pedr.        [A Paulo]  Cierto, padre de mi vida,
             que con servicios tan buenos,
             que puede ir a pretender
             éste a la corte.
Escal.                    Confieso
             que tú el lauro has merecido.              890
Galván       Y yo confieso lo mesmo.
Cher.        Todos lo mismo decimos.
Celia        El laurel darte pretendo.
Enrico       Vivas, Celia, muchos años.
Celia        Toma, mi bien; y con esto               895
             pues que la merienda aguarda,
             nos vamos.
Galván                   Muy bien has hecho.
Celia        Digan todos: "¡Viva Enrico!"
Todos        ¡Viva el hijo de Anareto!
Enrico       Al punto todos nos vamos                900
             a holgarnos y entretenernos.
                              Vanse.
Paulo        Salid, lágrimas, salid;
             salid apriesa del pecho;
             no lo dejéis de vergüenza.
             ¡Qué lastimoso suceso!                  905
Pedr.        ¿Qué tiene, padre?
Paulo                        ¡Ay, hermano!
             Penas y desdichas tengo.
             Este mal hombre que he visto
             es Enrico.
Pedr.                  ¿Cómo es eso?
Paulo        Las señas que me dio el ángel           910
             son suyas.
Pedr.                   ¿Es cierto?
Paulo        Sí, hermano, porque me dijo
             que era hijo de Anareto,
             y aqueste también lo ha dicho.
Pedr.        Pues aqueste ya está ardiendo           915
             en los infiernos en vida.
```

887-9. Literally 'with such good services, this man can go and
petition at Court.' Pretendientes – petitioners for favours,
grants, and especially offices, would often attach a record of
services to their requests. Their numbers, assiduity, and anxiety
were much remarked; so was the lack of correlation between deserts
and rewards.

894. Literally 'Celia, may you live many years', but it is the
gesture of homage which matters.

Pedr.	Did you listen to him, Father?
	A man with his record 887
	ought to be in politics
	– they could use him.
Escal.	I've got to admit it;
	you win, Enrico.
Roldán	I second that.
Fingers	That's right.
Celia	The laurel wreath...
Enrico	Celia, I kneel to you. 894
Celia	And I crown you with it, sweet.
	The wine and food are waiting.
	Are we ready?
Galván	Bravo, Enrico!
Celia	Three cheers, then, for Enrico!
All	Enrico, son of Anareto! 899
Enrico	Let's eat, drink and be merry!
	Enrico and his companions leave the stage.
Paulo	Flow, my tears!
	Flow from my open heart!
	Why should I feel ashamed 904
	to weep for such a sight?
Pedr.	Father, what is it?
Paulo	Oh, my brother,
	if you only knew my trouble!
	That wicked man is Enrico himself.
Pedr.	It can't be true!
Paulo	The angel
	gave me a sign.
Pedr.	Are you sure?
Paulo	I know it; he told me
	to look for Anareto's son,
	and this man said
	his father's name was Anareto.
Pedr.	But that Enrico's burning in Hell
	already.

---

898. P: Enriq; K: Enrique. Both are wrong.

899. The repetition of Anareto's name reinforces Paulo's despair, and clarifies its cause for the slower members of Tirso's audience.

904. R finds an identical line in Calderón's El médico de su honra (II, 580), and suggests that it may derive from a song (or, less probably, from a proverbial expression).

916. P omits envidia, disrupting the metre; K (followed by R) supplies it.

Paulo	Eso sólo es lo que temo.
	El ángel de Dios me dijo
	que si éste se va al infierno,
	que al infierno tengo de ir,	920
	y al cielo si éste va al cielo.
	Pues al cielo, hermano mío,
	¿cómo ha de ir éste, si vemos
	tantas maldades en él,
	tantos robos manifiestos,	925
	crueldades y latrocinios,
	y tan viles pensamientos?
Pedr.	En eso, ¿quién pone duda?
	Tan cierto se irá al infierno
	como el despensero Judas.	930
Paulo	¡Gran Señor! ¡Señor eterno!
	¿Por qué me habéis castigado
	con castigo tan inmenso?
	Diez años y más, Señor,
	ha que vivo en el desierto	935
	comiendo yerbas amargas,
	salobres aguas bebiendo,
	sólo porque vos, Señor,
	juez piadoso, sabio, recto,
	perdonareis mis pecados.	940
	¡Cuán diferente lo veo!
	Al infierno tengo de ir.
	Ya me parece que siento
	que aquellas voraces llamas
	van abrasando mi cuerpo.	945
	¡Ay, qué rigor!
Pedr.	Ten paciencia.
Paulo	¿Qué paciencia, o sufrimiento
	ha de tener el que sabe
	que se ha de ir a los infiernos?
	Al infierno: centro oscuro	950
	donde ha de ser el tormento
	eterno y ha de durar
	lo que Dios durare. ¡Ah, cielo!
	¡Que nunca se ha de acabar!
	¡Que siempre han de estar ardiendo	955
	las almas! ¡Siempre! ¡Ay de mí!

Paulo	I know it.
	It is my only fear. God's angel told me
	that I should go to Hell if he did,
	and be saved if he were saved.
	But, brother, such a man as that!
	Wicked, cruel, a murderer
	many times over, a villain, a robber,
	evil in thought and deed
	– how can he ever be saved?
Pedr.	Small doubt of that; he's as sure of Hell
	as Judas Iscariot.
Paulo	My Lord and my God!
	Why have you punished me like this?
	Ten years and more, oh Lord!
	I have lived in the wilderness,
	eating bitter herbs,
	drinking brackish water – and why?
	So that you, oh Lord!
	holy and merciful judge of men,
	might forgive my sins.
	And now all that is changed
	and I must go to Hell!
	I can feel Hell's flames already
	devouring my body!
	How cruel, ah God! how cruel!
Pedr.	You must be patient, Father.
Paulo	Patient, you fool!
	How can a man be patient
	who knows that he is damned?
	Knowing he must be tortured
	in the dark heart of Hell
	forever and forever,
	as long as God himself
	exists. Don't you understand?
	Their torment never ends!
	Never. What shall I do?

Line numbers in right margin: 930 (at "as Judas Iscariot."); 953 (at "as long as God himself").

---

930. Judas Iscariot was the treasurer (despensero) of the Apostles and (in John 12: 6) a thief. At this stage Pedrisco does little more than agree with Paulo, as any commonsense view of Enrico must.

953-6. The violently disrupted rhythms offer a powerful image of Paulo's disturbed mind.

Pedr.	[Aparte] Sólo oírle me da miedo.	
	Padre, volvamos al monte.	
Paulo	Que allá volvamos pretendo;	
	pero no a hacer penitencia,	960
	pues que ya no es de provecho.	
	Dios me dijo que si aqueste	
	se iba al cielo, me iría al cielo,	
	y al profundo si al profundo.	
	Pues es ansí, seguir quiero	965
	su misma vida. Perdone	
	Dios aqueste atrevimiento:	
	si su fin he de tener,	
	tenga su vida y sus hechos,	
	que no es bien que yo en el mundo	970
	esté penitencia haciendo,	
	y que él viva en la ciudad	
	con gustos y con contentos,	
	y que a la muerte tengamos	
	un fin.	
Pedr.	Es discreto acuerdo;	975
	bien has dicho, padre mío.	
Paulo	En el monte hay bandoleros:	
	bandolero quiero ser,	
	porque así igualar pretendo	
	mi vida con la de Enrico,	980
	pues su mismo fin tenemos.	
	Tan malo tengo de ser	
	como él, y peor si puedo;	
	que pues ya los dos estamos	
	condenados al infierno,	985
	bien es que antes de ir allá	
	en el mundo nos venguemos.	
Pedr.	¡Ah, señor! (¿Quién tal pensara?)	
	Vamos, y déjate de eso,	

---

958. monte: 'essentially a rocky landscape with trees' (Oakley, 264, following Varey (1968), 48). In the play, as in reality, the hinterland of Naples is both mountainous and wooded.

966-7. The original is more specific than the translation here: 'God forgive this presumption.' Paulo is, indeed, presuming to act as a kind of one-man Providence, compelling the facts of his case to conform to his own notions of sense.

970-3. This is unconvincing: Paulo never displays even a normal appetite for worldly comforts, nor is he now going about the right way of getting more of them. See Introduction, p. lvii.

Pedr.   I'm scared
          when he talks like this.
          Father, let's take to the hills   958
          again.
Paulo   We will, Pedrisco,
          but not to do penance there
          - we shall get no good of that
          any more. God promised me
          if that man went to Heaven,
          I should go there too,
          and be damned if he were damned. So be it.
          I shall live as he has lived.
          God pardon me, but if I share his end)   966
          let me share his way of life.   )
          What sense does it make for me   970
          to do penance in this world,
          while he lives here in comfort
          in the city, and does as he likes?
          What sense does it make
          if, when we die, we shall both come
          to the same end?
Pedr.   There's something in that,
          Father.
Paulo   There are bandits in the hills.
          I'll be a bandit too.
          That's the best life, if I want   979
          to live like Enrico,
          since I must end as he will.
          I shall make myself as wicked
          as he is - worse, if possible
          for if the two of us
          are both condemned to Hell,
          we do well to get our revenge   987
          here and now.
Pedr.   Who would have thought it?
          But if you're set on this

---

987. The object of Paulo's revenge, as Enrico later recognizes
979-80. We are closer to Paulo's real motives here; cf. 11. 966,
969: 'I shall live as he has lived'; 'let me share his way of
life.' See also Introduction, p. lviii.
    981. P: su, ungrammatically; KR: un. But the confusion of first
and third persons is in line with Paulo's obsessive identification
with Enrico.
    987. The object of Paulo's revenge, as Enrico later recognizes
(11. 1970-1), is God.

	y de esos árboles altos	990
	los hábitos ahorquemos.
	Viste galán.
Paulo	Sí haré;
	y yo haré que tengan miedo
	a un hombre que, siendo justo,
	se ha condenado al infierno.	995
	¡Rayo del mundo he de ser!
Pedr.	¿Qué se ha de hacer de dineros?
Paulo	Yo los quitaré al demonio,
	si fuere cierto el traerlos.
Pedr.	Vamos, pues.
Paulo	Señor, perdona	1000
	si injustamente me vengo;
	tú me has condenado ya;
	tu palabra, es caso cierto
	que atrás no puede volver.
	pues, si es ansí, tener quiero	1005
	en el mundo buena vida,
	pues tan triste fin espero.
	Los pasos pienso seguir
	de Enrico.
Pedr.	Ya voy temiendo
	que he de ir contigo a las ancas
	cuando vayas al infierno.	1010

Fin de la primera jornada.

---

990.   'those trees'. Presumably the columns supporting the gallery at the rear of the stage.

993-6.   Literally 'And I will make them fear a man who, being just, has been condemned to Hell. I shall be the thunderbolt of the world.' For all its violence, Paulo's rage follows a logic of its own. The just man damned is a paradox, a monstrosity, and this ought to evoke fear. Paulo, by making himself truly monstruous, will ensure the proper reaction. He will be a portent, a natural disaster.

1000-4. Following the same logic, Paulo represents his rebellion as a kind of desperate conformity to God's will. See Introduction, p. lvii.

```
                let's leave our habits high
                in those trees.  You'd better dress          990
                like a gentleman.
Paulo                           I will.
                And I shall show the world                   993
                what a good man can do
                when he's damned.
                I shall destroy them all!
Pedr.           What shall we do for money?
Paulo           Why, steal it - from the Devil himself
                if he'll provide it.
Pedr.                           Let's be going.
Paulo           Lord, forgive me                             1000
                if my revenge is less than just.
                But you yourself have damned me
                already; your word is given
                and cannot be revoked.
                So be it, then; I'll make the best           1006
                of this world's goods, if in the next
                only pain awaits me.  I shall follow
                Enrico's footsteps.
Pedr.                           All that I mind              1009
                is that when you go down to Hell
                you'll drag me along behind.
```
                        END OF ACT ONE

   1006. buena vida. Again, it is hard to believe in Paulo's
appetite for a life of pleasure. Much more credible - and much
more perverse - is his more general commitment to a purely worldly
sense of what would make life 'good'. Cf. Enrico's use of hazañas
in ll. 688-91.
   1009-11. By a bold and effective stroke, this deeply serious Act
ends on a wry aside from the gracioso. But Pedrisco's remark itself
has serious implications. His naive fear of being borne off bodily
to Hell by Paulo is plainly absurd. Yet Paulo is allowing himself,
not much more sensibly, to be dragged in that direction by his
obsession with Enrico.

JORNADA SEGUNDA

Salen Enrico y Galván.

Enrico	¡Válgate el diablo, el juego!	
	¡Qué mal que me has tratado!	
Galván	Siempre eres desdichado.	
Enrico	¡Fuego en las manos, fuego!	1015
	¿Estáis descomulgadas?	
Galván	Echáronte a perder suertes trocadas.	
Enrico	Derechas, no las gano:	
	si las trueco, tampoco.	
Galván	El es un juego loco.	1020
Enrico	Esta derecha mano	
	me tiene destrüído:	
	noventa y nueve escudos he perdido.	
Galván	Pues, ¿para qué estás triste,	
	que nada te costaron?	1025
Enrico	¡Qué poco que duraron!	
	¿Viste tal cosa? ¿Viste	
	tal multitud de suertes?	
Galván	Con esa pesadumbre te diviertes	
	y no cuidas de nada;	1030
	y has de matar a Albano,	
	que de Laura el hermano	
	te tiene ya pagada	
	la mitad del dinero.	
Enrico	Sin blanca estoy; matar a Albano quiero.	1035
Galván	Y aquesta noche, Enrico,	

. . . .

Cherinos y Escalante...

1012-47. Metre: <u>lira</u>: stanzas of five seven-syllable lines and a final hendecasyllable, rhyming ABBACC.

1013. Literally 'How ill you've treated me!', but not addressed to Galván, or the latter would be less cool about the question of cheating.

1017. <u>suertes trocadas</u>. In games of chance, the losing cards or dice are the <u>azares</u>; the winning ones are the <u>suertes</u>. The complaint against a 'multitude of <u>suertes</u>' in l. 1028 suggests that, for Tirso, the latter term covered both kinds of luck. 'Loaded dice' here covers the immediate notion of 'luck exchanged'. But gaming and luck are more than side-issues in a work concerned with predestination and freewill; Paulo and Enrico 'exchange fortunes' in a much profounder sense (cf. below, ll. 2908, 3005).

ACT TWO

Scene one

Naples. Various places about the streets; also Anareto's
lodging.
Enter Enrico and Galván.

Enrico   Hell take the whole damned game!
        See how it's left me!   1013
Galván   You never had much luck.
Enrico   God blast these useless hands!
        Always out of touch!
Galván   The dice were loaded; how could you win?   1017
Enrico   I never can
        - not when I rig them; not by playing straight.
Galván   It's a fool's game anyway.
Enrico   This right hand will be my ruin
        - ninety-nine ducats gone!   1023
Galván   Why worry?
        They cost you little enough to get.
Enrico   And yet how soon they went!
        Did you ever see such a run
        of cards? Did you ever know worse?   1028
Galván   If you take it so hard
        you'll forget our main business
        - there's a killing to be done.
        Laura's brother wants
        Albano dead; he's paid
        half the price in advance.
Enrico   Now I've no money at all,
        I'll kill Albano.
Galván   There's more going on tonight;
        Fingers and Escalante...

1023. The gold _escudo_ (see above, note on 1. 796) was worth
slightly less than the _ducado_ (a unit of account), but 'ducat' is
used here as the more familiar term in English. Enrico, as he
retains his last coin, also retains his single virtue of _pietas_
after forfeiting all the others. There is a further analogy with
the parable of the Lost Sheep, important later in the play, and
hence with the operation of divine _piedad_ seeking out the sinner.

1028. It is not made clear in the original whether the game
which Enrico has been playing involves cards or dice. In the
translation I have assumed that it involves both.

1037. PR: _Escalante?_ An extra line is required here by both the
stanza and the sense; the latter can be made good by the change in
punctuation.

Enrico	A ayudallos me aplico:	
	¿No han de robar la casa	1040
	de Octavio el Genovés?	
Galván	Aqueso pasa.	
Enrico	Pues yo seré el primero	
	que suba a sus balcones;	
	en tales ocasiones	
	aventajarme quiero.	1045
	Ve y diles que aquí aguardo.	
Galván	Volando voy, que en todo eres gallardo.	

Vase.

Enrico	Pues mientras ellos se tardan,	
	y el manto lóbrego aguardan	
	que su remedio ha de ser,	1050
	quiero un viejo padre ver	
	que aquestas paredes guardan.	
	Cinco años ha que le tengo	
	en una cama tullido,	
	y tanto a estimarle vengo,	1055
	que, con andar tan perdido,	
	a mi costa le mantengo.	
	De lo que Celia me da,	
	o yo por fuerza le quito,	
	traigo lo que puedo acá,	1060
	y su vida solicito,	
	que acabando el curso va.	
	De lo que de noche puedo,	
	varias casas escalando,	
	robar con cuidado o miedo,	1065
	voy su sustento aumentando,	
	y a veces sin él me quedo.	
	Que esta virtud solamente	
	en mi vida destraída	
	conservo piadosamente,	1070
	que es deuda al padre debida	

1041. 'Octavio the Genoese' can be assumed to be rich, since banking was regarded as the typical Genoese occupation. Can we also assume that he is the same person as Lisandro's friend in Act I, and Laura's brother, named as Octavio in the casting of the present Act (ll. 1293 ff.)? If so, it adds an ironic gloss to his prudent moral advice in the earlier scene, and an extra twist to Enrico's treachery now. Both would be typically Tirsian subtleties.

1048-1328. Metre: quintillas, with an interpolated couplet at ll. 1178-9, and the unique rhyme-scheme ABAAB at 1300-4; see Williamsen (1970), 510.

Enrico	I know – a robbery
	at Octavio's house
	– that rich Genoese. 1041
Galván	That's right.
Enrico	Don't worry; I'll be there
	and over the balcony
	before them; for work like that
	I'm second to nobody.
	Tell then I'll wait for them here.
Galván	Game for anything, as ever!
	Right, I'll be going.

Exit Galván.

Enrico	Until they come
	and the night spreads its cloak
	to cover their deeds, I'll spend
	a little time with my father 1051
	who lives close by.
	He has spent the past five years
	paralysed in his bed,
	and he means so much to me,
	in spite of the life I live,
	that I pay for all his needs.
	From the money Celia gives me
	(or from what I can bully out of her)
	I keep all I can, and use it
	to cherish what little life
	is left him. If I get
	enough from a night's housebreaking
	(it takes nerve and skill to do it)
	I put it by to support him,
	even if I go without
	myself. It's my only virtue.
	I'm a criminal, a drifter,
	but I'll stick by that till the last. 1070
	It's what a son owes his father

1051-67. As May points out (see Introduction, p. lxi), Enrico's cherishing of Anareto is neither an ideal nor a fully adult relationship. The tell-tale phrase here is 'all I can' (l. 1060); it amounts, as we have seen, to one per cent.

1066. P: *sustentando*; R: *su sustento*.

1069. P: *virtud*; KR: *vida*.

1070. *piadosamente*. For the connotations of *piedad*, *piadoso* see above, note to ll. 870-81. The notion of mercy is present here, no doubt, but the more important meaning, which the translation keeps in view, is 'dutifully'. This is still a very residual virtue.

75

el serle el hijo obediente.
    En mi vida le ofendí,
ni pesadumbre le di:
en todo cuanto mandó   1075
obediente me halló
desde el día en que nací;
    que aquestas mis travesuras,
mocedades y locuras
nunca a saberlas llegó;   1080
que a saberlas, bien sé yo
que aunque mis entrañas duras,
    de peña, al blanco cristal
opuestas, fueron formadas
y mi corazón igual   1085
a las fieras encerradas
en riscos de pedernal,
    que las hubiera atajado;
pero siempre le he tenido
donde de nadie informado,   1090
ni un disgusto ha recibido
de tantos como he causado.
          Descúbrese su padre en una silla.
    Aquí está: quiérole ver.
Durmiendo está, al parecer.
Padre.

Anareto   ¡Mi Enrico querido!   1095
Enrico   Del descuido que he tenido
perdón espero tener
    de vos, padre de mis ojos.
¿Heme tardado?

Anareto   No, hijo.
Enrico   No os quisiera dar enojos.   1100
Anareto   En verte me regocijo.
Enrico   No el sol por celajes rojos
    saliendo a dar resplandor

1073-7. This is belied by ll. 738-41 above. It could mean only
that Enrico always obeyed any explicit orders which Anareto gave
him - a restricted sense which would still be, in May's terms,
'infantile'. It is likelier, though, that Enrico simply deceives
himself.

1078-9. The language of this (literally 'naughtiness, youthful
exploits, and follies') is mild indeed as a description of the
enormities of ll. 722-863. This speech has to be taken as
expressing Enrico's highly unreliable self-awareness - certainly
not as a trustworthy balance-sheet of his moral condition.

```
              - to be obedient.  I never offended him
              I never caused him pain.                              1073
              Whatever he told me to do,
              I did it, since I was born.
              He never got to know                                  1080
              of the trouble I was in                               1078
              when I was young, or my wild ways since.
              If he had, then I know for certain
              - though I've a heart as hard                         1083
              as stone itself, and tears
              run off it like water
              (more like a mountain beast's
              than a man's heart) - I'd put an end
              to all that.  But he knows nothing.
              I've always seen to that.
              Of all the disappointment that I've been to him
              he feels nothing at all.
                  He draws a curtain and discloses Anareto,
                            sleeping in a chair.
              Here he is; let me look at him...
              Asleep, I think...  Father...
Anareto       Enrico!
Enrico                   I should not have left you
              so long; forgive me, father.
              Am I late now?
Anareto                          No, my son.
Enrico        I would never want to distress you.
Anareto       To see you does me good.
Enrico        The sight of you, dear father,
              is more welcome to my eyes
```

1080. PK: _saberlo_; R: _saberlas_, to maintain the parallelism with
l. 1081. Objectively Enrico's claim is hard to credit: can Anareto,
alone in all Naples, not be aware of his son's reputation? The
point is, however, that it matters very much to Enrico to believe
this himself.

1083. P: _despeña el_; KR: _de peña al_. Literally 'Although my
hard bowels [of compassion] were shaped from rock, and stand
opposed to white crystal [i.e. water; in this instance, tears], and
[so is] my heart, like wild beasts surrounded with crags of
flint...' A good deal of remodelling seemed in order here.

1092-3. P: _Descubre_ (Enrico himself drawing back the curtain of
the recess in which Anareto lies); KR: _Descúbrese_ (which allows,
but does not require, his direct involvement). The actual cue is
Aquí está ('Here he is'), following.

```
                a la tiniebla mayor,
                que espera tan alto bien                          1105
                parece al día tan bien
                como vos a mí, señor.
                    Que vos para mí sois sol,
                y los rayos que arrojáis
                de ese divino arrebol                             1110
                son las canas con que honráis
                este reino.
Anareto                             Eres crisol
                    donde la virtud se apura.
Enrico          ¿Habéis comido?
Anareto                             Yo, no.
Enrico          ¿Hambre tendréis?
Anareto                             La ventura                    1115
                de mirarte me quitó
                la hambre.
Enrico                          No me asegura,
                    padre mío, esa razón,
                nacida de la afición
                tan grande que me tenéis;                         1120
                pero agora comeréis,
                que las dos pienso que son
                    de la tarde.  Ya la mesa
                os quiero, padre, poner.
Anareto         De tu cuidado me pesa.                            1125
Enrico          Todo eso y más ha de hacer
                el que obediencia profesa.
                    (Del dinero que jugué
                un escudo reservé
                para comprar qué comiese,                         1130
                porque aunque al juego le pese,
                no ha de faltar esta fe.)
                    Aquí traigo en el lenzuelo,
                padre mío, qué comáis.
                Estimad mi justo celo.                            1135
```

1105. P. etc.: <u>es para</u>; also R, commending H: <u>espera</u>. This last
yields a literal meaning: 'emerging through red clouds to give
splendour to the larger darkness that awaits so high a good.'

1108-12. More literally 'For you are the sun for me, and the
rays you cast from that divine glow are the white hairs with which
you honour this kingdom' - hinting, perhaps, at Anareto's later
role as a type of God the Father.

	than sunrise to the day,	1105
	colouring the dawn,	
	rolling back the dark.	
	Why, your white hairs	1108
	are like the sun's rays!	
	They shine over Naples,	
	bringing the city honour.	
Anareto	Your good heart	1112
	grows rarer, all the time.	
Enrico	Have you eaten yet?	
Anareto	Why, no.	
Enrico	You must be hungry, father.	
Anareto	I was until you came;	
	now I've forgotten.	
Enrico	Dear father, you love me too well.	
	I can't believe in that as a cure for hunger.	
	But you shall eat now;	
	it's long past the time for it.	1122
	Let me set the table for you.	
Anareto	You go to too much trouble.	
Enrico	All this and more	
	is what it means to be obedient.	
	[Aside] When I was playing dice	
	I set aside one ducat	
	to buy my father food	1130
	– the dice can do without it;	
	I won't neglect this duty!	
	[To Anareto] Here in this napkin	
	is food for you, father,	
	See how I care for you as I should.	

1112-13. Literally 'You are a crucible where virtue is refined'
– an odd compliment in which May, 152-3 discerns multiple ironies.
It seems to imply that Enrico's virtue, rather than actual, is
still in the making, and by an arduous process at that. Such
ironies transform the scene from an implausible moralistic tableau
into a thoughtful study of a flawed relationship.

1122-3. 'long past the time'. The original is more specific:
'two o' clock in the afternoon'. After barely five minutes more of
continuous action, Albano will observe (l. 1245) that the sun is
setting. A drastic instance of the comedia's non-naturalistic
foreshortening of time.

1130-4. Since the Act began there has been no time when Enrico
could have bought the food; the focus of Tirso's interest is the
relationship, not the literal narrative.

Anareto	Bendito, mi Dios, seáis
	en la tierra y en el cielo,
	pues que tal hijo me disteis
	cuando tullido me visteis,
	que mis pies y manos sea.	1140
Enrico	Comed, por que yo lo vea.
Anareto	Miembros cansados y tristes,
	ayudadme a levantar.
Enrico	Yo, padre, os quiero ayudar.
Anareto	Fuerza me infunden tus brazos.	1145
Enrico	Quisiera en estos abrazos
	la vida poderos dar.
	Y digo, padre, la vida,
	porque tanta enfermedad
	es ya muerte conocida.	1150
Anareto	La divina voluntad
	se cumpla.
Enrico	Ya la comida
	os espera. ¿Llegaré
	la mesa?
Anareto	No, hijo mío,
	que el sueño me vence.
Enrico	¿A fe?	1155
	Pues dormid.
Anareto	Dádome ha un frío
	muy grande.
Enrico	Yo os llegaré
	la ropa.
Anareto	No es menester.
Enrico	Dormid.
Anareto	Yo, Enrico, quisiera,
	por llegar siempre a temer	1160
	que en viéndote es la postrera
	vez que te tengo de ver,
	(porque aquesta enfermedad
	me trata con tal crueldad)
	que quisiera que tomaras	1165
	estado.
Enrico	¿En eso reparas?
	Cúmplase tu voluntad.
	Mañana pienso casarme.

1136-8. May, 153 comments that Anareto 'thanks neither God nor
Enrico for the food' which he does not, in fact, eat. The image of
son feeding father is a model of piedad, but one which is here
baulked of its completeness.

80

Anareto	God's name be praised	1136
	on earth as it is in Heaven	
	for giving me such a son	
	to be hands and feet for me	
	now I am old and crippled.	

Enrico   Let me see you eat.

Anareto   My limbs are tired and frail;
          I cannot lift myself.

Enrico   There; I will help you, father.

Anareto   Your arms give me new strength.

Enrico   I only wish that as I hold you
          I could give you life itself,
          because lying ill like this
          is a kind of death already.

Anareto   It is God's will; so be it.

Enrico   Your meal is ready now;
          shall I bring the table nearer?

Anareto   No, I would rather sleep.

Enrico   Then if you would, dear father,
          sleep.

Anareto   But I feel so cold.

Enrico   Let me draw the blankets
          closer about you.

Anareto   There's no need.

Enrico   Sleep, then.

Anareto   Enrico, listen: 1159
          each time I see you now
          I fear it may be the last time
          I shall ever see you...
          I am so ill these days
          and in such cruel pain...
          I want you to be married.

Enrico   Is that what troubles you?
          Just as you wish; I'll be married tomorrow.

1151-2. P: <u>voluntad / de Dios se cumpla</u> (too many syllables); K:
<u>voluntad / cumpla Dios</u> (metrically correct but still tautologous);
HR: <u>voluntad / se cumpla</u>. Enrico's protest is contrasted with
Anareto's resignation.

1159-66. The extended syntax in the original - perfectly natural
for an aged man collecting his thoughts - creates a certain suspense
as to what Anareto wants. The wish to see Enrico married is perhaps
something of an anti-climax, though its dramatic ironies are strong.
As May, 154 remarks, 'no one is ever told to settle down except by
someone who is sure he is unsettled.'

81

	[Aparte] (Quiero darle aqueste gusto, aunque finja.)	
Anareto	Será darme	1170
	la salud.	
Enrico	Hacer es justo	
	lo que tú puedes mandarme.	
Anareto	Moriré, Enrico, contento.	
Enrico	Darte gusto en todo intento,	
	por que veas de esta suerte	1175
	que por sólo obedecerte	
	me sujeto al casamiento.	
Anareto	Pues, Enrico, como viejo	
	te quiero dar un consejo.	
	No busques mujer hermosa,	1180
	porque es cosa peligrosa	
	ser en cárcel mal segura	
	alcaide de una hermosura	
	donde es la afrenta forzosa.	
	Está atento, Enrico.	
Enrico	Di.	1185
Anareto	Y nunca entienda de ti	
	que de su amor no te fías,	
	que viendo que desconfías,	
	todo lo ha de hacer ansí.	
	Con tu mismo ser la iguala;	1190
	ámala, sirve y regala;	
	con celos no la des pena,	
	que no hay mujer que sea buena	
	si ve que piensan que es mala.	
	No declares tu pasión	1195
	hasta llegar la ocasión,	
	y luego...	
	Duérmese.	
Enrico	Vencióle el sueño,	
	que es de los sentidos dueño,	
	al dar la mejor lición.	

1168-9. Stage-direction in KR, but not in P. Enrico's fantasy of total filial obedience is placed under immediate strain by this first practical test.

1181-4. Literally 'because it is a dangerous thing to be, in an insecure prison, the custodian of a beauty where some affront is certain.' The translation registers the central commonplace.

1186-9, 1191-4. Verbatim quotations from Lope de Vega, El remedio en la desdicha, ll. 692-9. The lines continue the flow of well-tried advice. But the injun tion never to doubt a wife's love

```
          [Aside] I must please him in this,           1168
          although it isn't true.
Anareto   The news will give me
          my health again.
Enrico                       Then I must do
          whatever you command.
Anareto   I shall die happy, Enrico.
Enrico    In all things I try to please you.
          You see? sinply because you wish it,
          I shall be married.
Anareto                       Then Enrico,
          let me give you an old man's advice.
          Don't marry for beauty, my son;
          a beautiful wife is dangerous.            1181
          What could be worse
          than to live defending a treasure
          you know you may lose
          at any moment. Enrico,
          are you listening?
Enrico                       Go on.
Anareto   And never let her think                    1186
          that you doubt her love for a moment;
          if she senses your mistrust
          she'll give you cause for it.
          Make her your second self.
          Love, serve and cherish her              1191
          - and beware of jealousy;
          no woman can be virtuous
          if she sees vice expected of her.
          Keep your love secret
          until the moment comes,
          and then, ah! then...
                       He falls asleep.
Enrico                       Sleep                    1197
          has mastered his senses
          just when the lesson
```

---

also points to what may well be Anareto's strategy in dealing with
his delinquent son. The latter's potential for good has to begin
with his father's trust in him - and, indeed, with God's trust in
him (see below, ll. 1535-40).

    1194. PK: <u>ven</u>; SDR: <u>ve</u>, confirmed by the Lopean original.

    1197-1202. This is finely in character - a blend of cynicism
(l. 1199 means virtually 'just when he was getting to the exciting
bit') and a genuine tenderness which continues even when Anareto is
no longer watching.

    1199. P: <u>a</u>; KR: <u>al</u>.

	Quiero la ropa llegalle	1200
	y de esta suerte dejalle	
	hasta que repose.	

<u>Cúbrele y sale Galván.</u>

Galván	Ya	
	todo prevenido está,	
	y mira que por la calle	
	viene Albano	1205
	a quien la muerte has de dar.	
Enrico	Pues ¿yo he de ser tirano?	
Galván	¿Cómo?	
Enrico	¿Yo le he de matar	
	por un interés liviano?	
Galván	¿Ya tienes temor?	
Enrico	Galván,	1210
	estos dos ojos que están	
	con este sueño cubiertos,	
	por mirar que están despiertos	
	aqueste temor me dan.	

No me atrevo, aunque mi nombre　　1215
tiene su altivo renombre
en las memorias escrito,
intentar tan gran delito
donde está durmiendo este hombre.

Galván	¿Quién es?	
Enrico	Un hombre eminente	1220
	a quien temo solamente	
	y en esta vida respeto,	
	que para el hijo discreto	
	es el padre muy valiente.	

Si conmigo le llevara　　1225
siempre, nunca yo intentara
los delitos que condeno,
pues fuera su vista el freno
que la ocasión me tirara.

Pero corre esa cortina,　　1230
que en no verle podrá ser,
pues mi valor afemina,
que rigor venga a tener
si ahora a piedad me inclina.

1224. <u>valiente</u> implies both physical courage and the domination over men and events which courage makes possible. 'Strength' seemed to do justice to the way in which Enrico here reinterprets, in terms of Anareto's moral authority, this crucial element in his

was coming to its point.
There; I'll cover him and so leave him.
May he rest well!

He draws the bedclothes over Anareto. As he does so,
Galván enters.

Galván   Everything's ready,
and look! Albano's coming
down the street.
It's him you have to kill.

Enrico   Am I to be so cruel?

Galván   What's that?

Enrico   Am I to kill him
merely for money?

Galván   Have you lost your nerve?

Enrico   Yes, and I'll tell you why.
Come here; do you see that man
sleeping? do you see his eyes?
Those eyes are watching me
and I dare not do it. Oh yes,
I know my reputation;
I know all I stand to lose,
but where that man lies sleeping
I dare do no murder.

Galván   What is he, then?

Enrico   One of the great; the only one
who ever made me afraid
– the only man I respect,
as every wise son knows
his father's strength.   1224
If he were always with me
I could not live as I do;
the sight of him would give me
pause when I was tempted.
But draw that curtain again.
Seeing him undermines my will
and makes me gentle; when he's hidden   1231
I can be my old self once more.

---

own scheme of values as a man of violent action.

1231. P: el no verla; K: en no verla; R: en no verle, giving the
literal sense 'for when I do not see him, it may be, since he
weakens my courage, that I will come to grow firm, if now he sways
me towards pity.' Enrico opts to rekindle his worldly valour, and
to step outside the domain in which Anareto has authority over
him. Drawing the curtain is the visible sign of this.

1234. P: aora piedad; KR: ahora a piedad.

Galván   Ya está cerrada.

Enrico   Galván,   1235
        ahora que no le veo,
        ni sus ojos luz me dan,
        matemos, si es tu deseo,
        cuantos en el mundo están.

Galván   Pues mira que viene Albano,   1240
        y que de Laura al hermano
        que le des muerte conviene.

Enrico   Pues él a buscarla viene,
        dale por muerto

Galván   Es llano.

Sale Albano, viejo, y pasa.

Albano   El sol a poniente va,   1245
        como va mi edad también,
        y con cuidado estará
        mi esposa.

Enrico   Brazo, detén.

Galván   ¿Qué aguardas, ya?

Enrico   Miro un hombre que es retrato   1250
        y viva imagen de aquél
        a quien siempre de honrar trato:
        pues di, si aquí soy cruel,
        ¿no seré a mi padre ingrato?

        Hoy de mis manos tiranas   1255
        por ser viejo, Albano, ganas
        la cortesía que esperas,
        que son piadosas terceras,
        aunque mudas, esas canas.

        Vete libre, que repara   1260
        mi honor, que así se declara,
        aunque a mi opinión no cuadre,
        que pensara que a mi padre
        mataba si te matara.

        ¡Ay, canas, las que aborrecen   1265
        . . . .
        pocos las ofenderán,
        pues tan seguras se van
        cuando enemigos se ofrecen.

1245-8. See Introduction, p. li.

1250-69. Drawing a curtain over Anareto's authority has not enabled Enrico to separate himself from it. Rather, it has become internalized in him; the sight of another old man not only inhibits him from violence but prompts him to use a hitherto unfamiliar

Galván	That's done.
Enrico	And now, Galván,
	away from the sight of his eyes,
	I'm ready to kill any number
	- the whole world if you like!
Galván	Here comes Albano now;
	you know that Laura's brother
	is counting on you to kill him.
'Enrico	Then if he's on his way,
	he's as good as dead.
Galván	There's nothing surer.

They leave Anareto's house. Albano, an old man, passes
across the stage.

Albano	The sun is almost set	1245
	- and my day too is nearly over -	
	my wife will be wondering	
	where I can be...	
Enrico	No; wait!	
Galván	What for? Why did you let him go?	
Enrico	He looked so like the other	1250
	- the man I do my best to honour.	
	Attacking him would be cruel;	
	it would be like wounding	
	my own father.	
	How could I treat him so?	
	Albano, you can go free.	
	My brutal hands will spare you	
	because you are old; your white hair	
	pleads for you better than any words.	
	I shall not harm you.	
	Whatever they say about me,	
	my honour tells me	
	that if I killed you it would be	
	like killing my father.	
	Why should white hairs bring distress?	1265
	If they're secure like this	
	against their enemies,	
	who dares attack them?	

---

moral language about his own actions.
  1265-9. A line is missing at l. 1266 to complete the quintilla.
The sense is reasonably plain, however: literally 'White hairs that
people hate... few will say a word against them, since they are so
safe when there are enemies about.'

Galván	¡Vive Dios, que no te entiendo!	1270
	Otro eres ya del que fuiste.	
Enrico	Poco mi valor ofendo.	
Galván	Darle la muerte pudiste.	
Enrico	No es eso lo que pretendo.	
	A nadie temí en mi vida;	1275
	varios delitos he hecho;	
	he sido fiera homicida,	
	y no hay maldad que en mi pecho	
	no tenga siempre acogida;	
	pero en llegando a mirar	1280
	las canas que supe honrar	
	porque en mi padre las vi,	
	todo el furor reprimí	
	y las procuré estimar.	
	Si yo supiera que Albano	1285
	era de tan larga edad,	
	nunca de Laura al hermano	
	prometiera tal crueldad.	
Galván	Respeto fue necio y vano.	
	El dinero que te dio,	1290
	por fuerza habrás de volver,	
	ya que Albano no murió.	
Enrico	Podrá ser.	
Galván	¿Qué es podrá ser?	
Enrico	Podrá ser, si quiero yo.	
Galván	El viene.	

Sale Octavio.

Octavio	A Albano encontré	1295
	vivo y sano como yo.	
Enrico	Yo lo creo.	
Octavio	Y no pensé	
	que la palabra que dio	
	de matarle vuesasté	
	no se cumpliera tan bien	1300
	como se cumplió la paga.	
	¿Esto es ser hombre de bien?	
Galván	Este busca que le den	
	un bofetón con la daga.	
Enrico	No mato a hombres viejos yo;	1305
	y si a voarcé le ofendió	

1276-9. More literally 'I have committed a whole series of crimes; I have been a murderous beast, and there is no wickedness that is not always welcome in my heart.' The translation seeks a

Galván	Don't understand a word; you've changed!
Enrico	It's not for want of courage.
Galván	You could have killed him, and you didn't...
Enrico	That's not the point!
	I never was afraid of anyone;
	you know my record: I've killed men. 1276
	I've done most things... wanted to do most things...
	but when I saw him then,
	white-haired, like my father;
	what could I do but choke back my anger
	and show respect, as I'd respected him
	before. If I'd only known
	that Albano was so old,
	I'd have told Laura's brother
	I wouldn't do it.
Galván	So what's the use of all that?
	You'll have to give back the money
	if Albano's still alive.
Enrico	I might. 1293
Galván	What do you mean,
	you "might"?
Enrico	I might if I want to.
Galván	Here he comes now.

Octavio enters.

Octavio	You, sir, gave me your word
	to kill him.
	You were paid promptly enough;
	I expected you to do it.
	Do you call this keeping your promise?
Galván	He's going the right way about it
	to get himself chibbed, this one. 1304
Enrico	I don't kill old men.
	If he's offended you, you kill him.

---

tone suitable to Enrico's state of mind, as he explores a contradiction within himself which is wholly new to him.

1293-4. Enrico reverts to the over-simplifying mode familiar to us from earlier scenes, and marked above all by the aggressive assertion of his own will (cf. above, ll. 514-5). This reversion to type produces a shift to a terser speech-style.

1299. P: metarle, corrected by R etc.

1304. un bofetón con la daga. In speaking of a bofetón (a slap with the open palm) from a dagger, Galván is being either facetious or colloquial. The translation borrows a criminal term for razor-slashing from the published work of the present (April 1986) Home Secretary; see also Partridge, 206.

           vaya y mátele al momento,
           que yo quedo muy contento
           con la paga que me dio.

Octavio   El dinero ha de volverme.   1310

Enrico   Váyase voarcé con Dios.
           No quiera enojado verme;
           que, ¡juro a Dios!...

Galván   Ya los dos
           riñen; el diablo no duerme.

Octavio   Mi dinero he de cobrar.   1315

Enrico   Pues yo no lo pienso dar.

Octavio   Eres un gallina.

Enrico   Mientes.
                  [Dale.]

Octavio   Muerto soy.

Enrico   Mucho lo sientes.

Galván   Hubiérase ido a acostar.

Enrico   A hombres como tú arrogantes   1320
           doy la muerte yo, no a viejos
        . . . .
           que con canas y consejos
           vencen ánimos gigantes.
           Y si quisieres probar
           lo que llego a sustentar,   1325
           pide a Dios, si él lo permite,
           que otra vez te resucite,
           y te volveré a matar.
           Dentro dice el Gobernador.

Gobern.   Prendedle, dadle la muerte.

Galván   Aquesto es malo.
           Más de cien hombres vienen a prenderte   1330
           con el Gobernador.

Enrico   Vengan seiscientos.
           Si me prenden, Galván, mi muerte es cierta;

    1307.   P: vaya y mátale, confusing third and second-person imperatives; R etc. correct this.

    1314. 'The Devil never sleeps' is a proverb. Enrico's intimations of good have an obvious bearing on the message given to Paulo; thus his relapse into aggression is very much in the Devil's interest. Galván speaks truer than he knows.

    1317. un gallina is a coward (from una gallina, 'a hen').

    1320-1. Enrico, trying to rationalize his rudimentary sense of

	I'm quite happy to keep	
	the money you gave me.	
Octavio	You'll give that money back!	
Enrico	Just go about your business	
	in peace; if you make me angry,	
	then, Jesus Christ! I'll...	
Galván	Fighting already!	
	The Devil never sleeps!	1314
Octavio	Give me back my money!	
Enrico	I don't intend to.	
Octavio	Coward!	1317
Enrico	Liar! Take that! [Stabs him.]	
Octavio	You've killed me.	
Enrico	Why, how you take it to heart!	
Galván	He'd have been better off	
	going home to bed.	
Enrico	Your kind	1320
	— the kind who show fight — are the ones	
	I kill, not old men.	
	Their white hairs, their wise words	1322
	could make any man afraid.	
	And if you're not convinced	
	now, you can ask God	
	to bring you to life again,	
	and I'll kill you twice over to prove it.	

The voice of the Governor of Naples is heard off stage.

Gov.	Take him, dead or alive!
Galván	This looks bad.
	Here's the Governor himself
	with a hundred men
	coming to take you.
Enrico	What do I care
	if he brings six times as many?
	They'll hang me for sure if they take me

---

responsibility, formulates it as a rule of conduct, established by his own will. The process, begun in l. 1305, is completed here, but the element of special pleading after the event is all too transparent.

1322. The memory of Anareto still dominates Enrico's thinking. Albano has not uttered any 'wise words' of advice (consejos); indeed, he may not even be a wholly admirable character. We are not told what Laura's brother has against him.

1329-70. Metre: unrhymed hendecasyllables.

	si me defiendo, puede hacer mi dicha	
	que no me maten, y que yo me escape;	
	y más quiero morir con honra y fama.	1335
	Aquí está Enrico: ¿no llegáis, cobardes?	

Galván   Cercado te han por todas partes.

Enrico   Cerquen
que, vive Dios, que tengo de arrojarme
por entre todos.

Galván   Yo tus pasos sigo.

Enrico   Pues haz cuenta que César va contigo.   1340

> Sale el Gobernador y mucha gente.
> y Enrico los mete a todos a cuchilladas.

Gobern. ¿Eres demonio?

Enrico   Soy un hombre solo
que huye de morir.

Gobern.   Pues date preso,
y yo te libraré.

Enrico   No pienso en eso.
Ansí habéis de prenderme.

Galván   Sois cobardes.

Gobern. ¡Ay de mí! Muerto soy.

Uno   ¡Gran desdicha!   1345
Mató al Gobernador. ¡Mala palabra!

> Retíralos y sale Enrico.

1333. The theme of Enrico's involvement with luck continues.
Luck has not served him too well recently (ll. 1027-8); it will soon
let him down again (l. 1787). The providence which operates beneath
the surface of worldly ill-fortune is another matter. Enrico has
not yet learned to trust that. But he does know how to trust.

1335. Literally 'to die with honour and fame'. In translation a
less explicit formula seemed more credible as speech.

1340. Literally 'Bear in mind that Caesar goes with you' - the
terms in which, in Plutarch's _Lives_, Julius Caesar reassured a
boatman, fearful of ferrying him across the Adriatic in a storm.
Not a readily recognized allusion now, and thus replaced in

```
                but if I resist my luck might hold.            1333
                I might escape, or at least
                die fighting.  This way, you cowards!          1335
                Come and meet Enrico!
Galván          But you'll be surrounded...
Enrico                              So?
                I can cut a way through them
                - by God I can!
Galván                          I'm with you.
Enrico          I'll fight like Caesar!                        1340
                No-one can touch us.
```

The Governor enters, with a great following. Enrico attacks
them all with his knife.

```
Gov.            Are you a devil?                               1341
Enrico                          Only a man
                who doesn't fancy dying.
Gov.            Give yourself up
                and I'll stand surety...
Enrico                                  Forget it!
                This is the only way you'll take me!
Galván          The cowards won't fight.                       1344
Gov.            Help me! I'm hurt...
Soldier                         He's dead!
                The Governor's dead!  My God                   1346
                he's killed the Governor!
```

The troops withdraw, carrying the Governor's body.
Enrico and Galván escape.

---

translation by something much more general.

    1341-2. In other moods of truculence or defiance, Enrico declares that he is the Devil (above, ll. 495-6; below, l. 1715). Here, in extremis, he tells the truth.

    1344-7. P gives inadequate stage-directions. Galván's taunt of cowardice suggests that the Governor's troops rely on their display of superior force, and that only Enrico shows fight. Having stabbed the Governor, he must surely make his escape at once, to return by another entrance after the soldiers have carried away their dead commander.

Enrico	Y aunque la tierra sus entrañas abra,
	y en ella me sepulte es imposible
	que me pueda escapar; tú, mar soberbio,
	en tu centro me esconde; con la espada 1350
	entre los dientes tengo de arrojarme.
	Tened misericordia de mi alma,
	Señor inmenso, que aunque soy tan malo,
	no dejo de tener conocimiento
	de vuestra santa fe. Pero ¿qué hago? 1355
	¿Al mar quiero arrojarme cuando dejo
	triste, afligido, un miserable viejo?
	Al padre de mi vida volver quiero,
	y llevarle conmigo; a ser Eneas
	del viejo Anquises.
Galván	[Dentro] ¿Dónde vas? Detente. 1360
Enrico	Seguidme por aquí.
Galván	Guarda tu vida.
Enrico	Perdonad, padre de mis ojos,
	el no poder llevaros en mis brazos,
	aunque en el alma bien sé yo que os llevo.
	Sígueme tú, Galván.
Galván	Yo ya te sigo. 1365
Enrico	Por tierra no podemos escaparnos.
Galván	Pues arrójome al mar.
Enrico	Su centro airado
	sea sepulcro mío. ¡Ay, padre amado!
	¡Cuánto siento el dejaros!
Galván	Ven conmigo.
Enrico	Cobarde soy, Galván, si no te sigo. 1370
	[Vase.]

1346. **¡Mala palabra!** It seems scarcely credible that this phrase
('bad word') should function as a 17th-century equivalent of
'Expletive deleted'. 'Grave news' might be nearer the mark.

1348. P: _sepultè_, nonsensically; KR: _sepulte_.

1351. PKR: _en la boca_; SDT: _entre los dientes_ - a more precise
image than 'in my mouth'; also metrically sounder, though its
textual tradition is the weaker of the two.

1353-5. This is Enrico's first expression of any religious
sentiment; he has not reacted like this to any previous crisis
(above, ll. 847-9). The immediate result, significantly, is an
access of concern for Anareto.

1358-60. R (p. 3) envisages Enrico as moving towards the
curtained recess in which he has left Anareto, then rushing off
through another exit to hurl himself into the sea. Aeneas rescuing
his father Anchises from the sack of Troy was a traditional figure
of _pietas_.

1360-1. P marks Enrico's final line at 1361 with _Dentro_

Scene two

Naples. The sea coast. Enter Enrico.

Enrico   There's no escape from this;
         not now. If the earth should open
         and swallow me up, they'd still find me.
         The sea's my only hope.
         If I take my sword in my teeth
         and dive in... Have mercy on my soul,   1353
         great God! I may be evil
         but I know enough of your faith
         to ask for that. Yet how can I
         plunge into the sea, and leave
         that poor old man to mourn
         for me? No, I'll go back to my father   1358
         as Aeneas turned back for his.
         He shall go with me.

Galván   [Off stage] Where are you off to? Stop!

Enrico   This way, Galván.

Galván   [Off stage]   Save your life!

Enrico   Father, forgive me!
         I cannot bear you in my arms.
         I shall carry you in my heart, I know.
         We'll go together, Galván.

Galván   [Off stage]   Which way?

Enrico   There's no escape by land.

Galván   [Off stage] Into the sea, then.

Enrico   May I find my rest   1367
         in its angry waters. Oh, my father!
         how can I bear to leave you?

Galván   [Off stage]   Here I go!

Enrico   No weakness now. Galván! I'm coming!

He rushes off.

('within'), naming no speaker. R, following this, has Enrico
re-enter before l. 1362. But it seems distracting to take him off
stage for barely a line – the more so if he plunges behind Anareto's
curtain at one instant determined to play Aeneas, only to emerge a
moment later apologizing. By contrast, it makes very good sense to
have Galván deliver all his lines off stage.

1367-8.   Literally 'May its angry centre be my grave.' The
underlying paradox of peace in the midst of storm is registered in
the translation. But notions of baptism and of 'dying to live
again' are not too far away (see Introduction, p. lii). These
loosely symbolic allusions, however, are not organized in any kind
of allegory: Enrico will come out of the water (ll. 1685-6) in no
greatly improved spiritual state.

1370-1.   No stage-direction in P; KR: _Vanse_, but if Galván is off
stage already, a singular is needed.

95

Band.1	A ti solo, Paulo fuerte, pues que ya todos te damos palabra de obedecerte, que sentencies esperamos estos tres a vida o muerte.	1375
Paulo	¿Dejáronos ya el dinero?	
Pedr.	Ni una blanca nos han dado.	
Paulo	Pues, ¿qué aguardas, majadero?	
Pedr.	Habémoselo quitado.	
Paulo	¿Que ellos no lo dieron? Quiero sentenciar a todos tres.	1380
Pedr.	Ya esperamos ver lo que es..	
Los tres	Ten con nosotros piedad.	
Paulo	De ese roble los colgad.	
Los tres	¡Gran señor!	
Pedr.	Moved los pies, que seréis fruta extremada, en esta selva apartada, de todas aves rapantes.	1385
Paulo	De esta crueldad no te espantes.	
Pedr.	Ya no me espanto de nada. Porque verte ayer, señor, ayunar con tal fervor, y en la oración ocupado, en tu Dios arrebatado,	1390
	pedirle ánimo y fervor para proseguir tu vida en tan grande penitencia y en esta selva escondida verte hoy con tanta violencia,	1395
	capitán de forajida gente, matar pasajeros tras robarles los dineros, ¿qué más se puede esperar? Ya no me pienso espantar.	1400

1371-1470. Metre: quintillas.

1371-3. For the non-naturalistic chronology of Paulo's rise to bandit chief see Introduction, p. lii.

1377. 'a cent'. The blanca, as its name implies, was originally a silver coin. By Tirso's day the term was mostly used for low-denomination copper coinage.

1383, 1385. In early editions these lines are variously distributed among the captives. R's solution, followed here, is

Scene three

In the woods, not far from Naples.

Enter Paulo, dressed as a bandit, other Bandits bringing
three Prisoners, and Pedrisco in comic bandit costume.

Bdt.1	Paulo, you're our chief!	1371
	We've all sworn to obey you.	
	It's for you to decide	
	whether they live or die.	
Paulo	Did they hand over their money?	
Pedr.	Didn't give us a cent.	1377
Paulo	Then string them up, you fool!	
Pedr.	We'd taken it off them first.	
Paulo	You mean they didn't	
	hand it over? Very well!	
	This is my verdict...	
Pedr.	Wait for it; here it comes.	
Pris.	Mercy! ah, mercy!	
Paulo	Hang them all three from that oak!	
Pris.	Master! we beg you...	
Pedr.	Get moving!	
	You'll make a nice crop of fruit	
	for the birds to peck at	
	here in the wild woods.	
Paulo	Does my cruelty surprise you?	1389
Pedr.	Nothing surprises me.	
	It seems only yesterday,	
	there you were, master, fasting	
	and praying away like mad	
	– all wrapped up in your God;	
	begging to him for strength	
	to keep on living like that;	
	doing penance all the time.	
	And look at you now – in the woods,	
	the head of a regular gang	
	of cut-throats, robbing travellers,	
	and killing them off – just like that!	
	What more do you want? I'm not	
	surprised by anything now,	
	nor likely to be.	

the one which allows the widest discretion to producers.

1389.   Literally 'Don't be alarmed...' Pedrisco's reply points
the obvious contrast between Paulo's former life and his present
activities.   But thoughtful spectators will sense another reason
for alarm: the implications which Paulo's conduct as judge will
have for a story which is going to be about Paulo under judgment.

97

Paulo	Los hechos fieros	1405
	de Enrico imitar pretendo,	
	y aun le quisiera exceder.	
	Perdone Dios si le ofendo,	
	que si uno el fin ha de ser	
	esto es justo y yo me entiendo.	1410
Pedr.	Así al otro le decían	
	que la escalera rodaba	
	otros que rodar le veían.	
Paulo	¿Y a mí que a Dios adoraba,	
	y por santo me tenían	1415
	en este circunvecino	
	monte, el globo cristalino	
	rompiendo el ángel veloz,	
	me obligase con su voz	
	a dejar tan buen camino	1420
	dándome el premio tan malo?	
	Pues hoy verá el cielo en mí	
	si en las maldades no igualo	
	a Enrico.	
Pedr.	¡Triste de ti!	
Paulo	Fuego por la vista exhalo.	1425
	Hoy, fieras, que en horizontes	
	y en napolitanos montes	
	hacéis dulce habitación	
	veréis que mi corazón	
	vence a soberbios Faetontes.	1430
	Hoy, árboles, que plumajes	
	sois de la tierra, o salvajes,	
	por lo verde que os vestís,	
	el huésped que recibís	
	os hará varios ultrajes.	1435

1408-10. Cf. above, ll. 966-7, 1000-4, and notes thereon.

1411-13. PR: Y si al otro, and the whole sentence framed as a question. But the reference is clearly to a widely-known joke: el otro is a common term for the protagonist of such stories; Reynolds (1956), 13-14 identifies a source in the jest-book of Juan de Arguijo (1619). From this viewpoint, the suggestion of C: Así al otro makes good sense: 'That's what people used to say...'

1417-18. Literally 'breaking the crystalline sphere'. An angel descending to earth would pass through the caelum cristallinum, which separated Paradise from the other heavenly spheres (see the diagram in Yates, 111).

1425. Literally 'I breathe out fire through my eyes.' If it is to convince at all, the ultra-violence of this speech requires

```
Paulo                          It's Enrico.
            I'm trying to live like him
            – or worse than him, if I can.
            May God forgive me my crimes,                    1408
            but if my end is the same,
            how else should I live?  I know what I'm doing.
Pedr.       That's what they said about the man              1411
            who fell downstairs.
            "He knows what he's doing", they said.
Paulo       The hours I spent in prayer!
            (They used to call me a saint!)
            It was in these very woods,
            quite near... and then the angel
            came down from heaven and destroyed it all.       1417
            His message made me do it!
            That was why I left
            the path of virtue: was I to get
            such an evil reward?  Very well!
            Then Heaven will have to learn
            that I can do as much harm
            as Enrico – and more.
Pedr.                          Poor man!
Paulo       My head is all aflame!                           1425
            Now all you wild beasts,
            housing here, in the thick of the wood,
            see what my heart can do
            – it is so wild, so proud.                        1429
            Now, you green trees, untamed,                    1431
            feathering the earth, you'll find
            a guest has come among you
            with ugly deeds in mind.
```

---

fairly radical handling in translation.

1429-30. The translation suppresses the mythological allusion:
'that my heart surpasses proud Phaethons'. Phaethon, son of the
sun-god, took over his father's chariot for a day, but could not
control the fiery steeds, and was destroyed by a thunderbolt from
Zeus. His associations are with fire, presumption, and destruction.

1431-5. Literally 'Trees who are the earth's plumage (or savages,
because dressed in green), the guest whom you receive will inflict
several outrages on you.' The notion of savages receiving atrocious
treatment from an alien visitor is arresting in a 17th-century
Spanish context. Can it be a distant echo of the tradition of Las
Casas? The playwright, after all, had spent two years in Santo
Domingo.

```
               Más que la naturaleza
          he de hacer por cobrar fama,
          pues para mayor grandeza
          he de dar a cada rama
          cada día una cabeza.                              1440
               Vosotros dais, por ser graves,
          frutos al hombre süaves;
          mas yo con tales racimos
          pienso dar frutos opimos
          a las voladores aves.                             1445
               En verano y en invierno
          será vuestro fruto eterno;
          y si pudiera hacer más,
          más hiciera.
Pedr.                    Tú te vas
          gallardamente al infierno.                        1450
Paulo      Ve y cuélgalos al momento
          de un roble.
Pedr.                   Voy como el viento.
Hombre 1   ¡Señor!
Paulo              No me repliquéis
          si acaso ver no queréis
          el castigo más violento.                          1455
Pedr.      Venid los tres.
Hombre 2                    ¡Ay de mí!
Pedr.      Yo he de ser verdugo aquí,
          pues a mi dicha le plugo,
          para enseñar al verdugo
          cuando me ahorquen a mí.                          1460
                     Vase con los tres.
Paulo      Enrico, si de esta suerte
          yo tengo de acompañarte,
          y si te has de condenar,
          contigo me has de llevar,
          que nunca pienso dejarte.                         1465
               Palabra de ángel fue,
```

1436-49. For the anti-natural implications of these lines see Introduction, p. lxxii.

1443. P: <u>razones</u>, nonsensically; KR: <u>racimos</u> ('clusters', as of grapes). The translation shifts the disturbingly physical effects of <u>süaves</u>, <u>racimos</u>, <u>opimos</u> to other lexical items: 'glut', 'swell', 'ripen'.

1460-1. P: <u>Vase</u>; R adds <u>con los tres</u>. In fact, those who leave must be Pedrisco, the three prisoners, and an escort of at least a couple of other bandits.

```
                I'll make a name for myself                          1436
                with ugly, unnatural deeds,
                and to my greater glory
                I'll set a head a day
                on every branch.
                You yield soft fruits;
                I'll glut the birds of the air
                with such a crop as never                             1443
                was fruited here before.
                Let them swell and ripen here,
                in season and out of season,
                an ever-living harvest
                of manfruit.  If I knew
                how to do more, I'd do it.
Pedr.           You're certainly going to Hell
                handsomely.
Paulo                          Hang them, I say,
                from the oak tree.
Pedr.                              I'm on my way.
Pris.1  Master! I beg...
Paulo                          Not a word!
                unless you want to suffer
                something worse.
Pedr.                          Get going!
Pris.2                                      Mercy!
Pedr.           I've got the hangman's job.
                Still, I suppose there's hope:
                when they come to get me,
                at least I can show them the ropes.
                     Exit Pedrisco with Prisoners.
Paulo           Enrico, if this is the way
                to be with you, so be it.
                If it leads to damnation, so be it.
                You can take me with you.
                I'll never leave you.                                 1465
                The angel gave his word.
```

1465. 'I'll never leave you.' The climax so far of Paulo's
identification with Enrico (cf. above, ll. 1406, 1423). The release
of pent-up emotional commitment is all the more striking because
ll. 1461-5 are, for the first time, actually addressed to Enrico.

1466. PR: de ángel, requiring vowel-hiatus; K: del ángel,
metrically straightforward. But P's reading sets the angel's word
in an especially reliable category, like palabra de amigo, palabra
de caballero.

	tu camino seguiré; pues cuando Dios, juez eterno, nos condenare al infierno, ya habremos hecho por qué.	1470

Cantan dentro.

Músicos	No desconfíe ninguno, aunque grande pecador, de aquella misericordia de que más se precia Dios.	
Paulo	¿Qué voz es ésta que suena?	1475
Band.2	La gran multitud, señor, de esos robles nos impide ver dónde viene la voz.	
Músicos	Con firme arrepentimiento de no ofender al Señor, llegue el pecador humilde, que Dios le dará perdón.	1480
Paulo	Subid los dos por el monte, y ved si es algún pastor el que canta este romance.	1485
Band.2	A verlo vamos los dos.	

[Vanse los dos.]

Músicos	Su Majestad soberana da voces al pecador por que le llegue a pedir lo que a ninguno negó.	1490

Sale por el monte un Pastorcillo tejiendo
una corona de flores.

Paulo	Baja, pastorcillo; que ya estaba, vive Dios, confuso con tus razones, admirado con tu voz. ¿Quién te enseñó ese romance, que le escucho con temor, pues parece que en ti habla mi propia imaginación?	1495

1470. PK: auemos; STR: habremos.

1471-1616. Metre: romance, assonating in O. This ballad-metre is appropriate for the Shepherd's song, whose form is then continued in the spoken dialogue. The translation gives the song a stanzaic character, loosely related to George Herbert's The Elixir.

1490-1. 'in the wood', coupled with Paulo's 'come down', implies that the Shepherd appears in the gallery above the main stage. This

102

```
           I'll follow wherever you lead,
           and when God comes to judge us
           and sends us both to Hell,
           we'll know we've given him cause.
                      A song within.
Singers        Let no man then despair                        1471
               or fear to meet his fate,
               since to the chief of sinners
               God's mercy is so great.
Paulo      What was that voice?  Who was singing?
Bdt.2      We couldn't tell where it came from, master.
           The trees grow so thick up there.
Singers        To all men who repent
               and vow to sin no more,
               though they be chief of sinners
               God's mercy still is sure.
Paulo      Climb up and see who it is.
           It must be some shepherd singing.
Bdt.2      We'll both go and find out.
                      [Exeunt both Bandits.]
Singers        The sinner by God's grace
               finds words to shape his cries
               and beg of him that mercy
               which he to none denies.                       1490
           Above, in the wood, a young Shepherd appears,
                  weaving a crown of flowers.
Paulo      Little shepherd, come down,
           and tell me who you are.
           The words of your song are strange,
           stranger still the air.
           Where did you learn those words, that tune
           that speak the secrets of my mind                  1497
           yet fill me with fear?
```

---

would make Paulo's efforts to detain him by force (ll. 1614-16)
appear especially futile, and an apt visual symbol, as R observes,
of the equally vain attempt to seize his own salvation.

1497-8. PK: _falta... imaginación_; SDT: _habla... indignación_:
both, in their different ways, nonsensical. Preferable to either
is HR: _habla... imaginación_. The imagination has played all too
large a part in Paulo's response to the Devil (cf. also l. 631).
Yet imagination can respond to divine promptings too, and so become
a force for good. This is one of the themes of Tirso's _La república
al revés_, which deals with the Iconoclast controversy in
9th-century Byzantium.

Pastor.	Este romance que he dicho,	
	Dios, señor, me le enseñó;	1500
	o la iglesia, su esposa,	
	a quien en la tierra dio	
	poder suyo.	
Paulo	Bien dijiste.	
Pastor.	Advierte que creo en Dios	
	a pies juntillas, y sé,	1505
	aunque rústico pastor,	
	todos los diez mandamientos,	
	preceptos que Dios nos dio.	
Paulo	¿Y Dios ha de perdonar	
	a un hombre que le ofendió	1510
	con obras y con palabras	
	y pensamientos?	
Pastor.	¿Pues no?	
	Aunque sus ofensas sean	
	más que átomos del sol,	
	y que estrellas tiene el cielo,	1515
	y rayos la luna dio,	
	y peces el mar salado	
	en sus cóncavos guardó.	
	Esta es su misericordia;	
	que con decirle al Señor:	1520
	"Pequé, pequé, muchas veces",	
	le recibe al pecador	
	en sus amorosos brazos;	
	que en fin hace como Dios.	
	Porque si no fuera aquesto,	1525
	cuando a los hombres crió,	
	no los criara sujetos	
	a su frágil condición.	
	Porque si Dios, sumo bien,	
	de nada al hombre formó	1530
	para ofrecerle su gloria,	

1499. Question and answer regarding a supernatural song also
form the subject of one of the most famous of Spanish ballads - the
Romance del Conde Arnaldos (Durán, I, 153, no. 286). The singer's
response there is, on the face of it, different: 'I only tell this
song to those who go with me.' Yet in another sense, this is the
heart of the matter in El condenado too.

1501. If the Shepherd has learned his song directly from God, he
is probably a supernatural being; if from the Church, he is a mortal
shepherd, though an unusually well-informed one. The use of o not y
- 'or', rather than 'and' - preserves this ambiguity.

Shep.	The Lord in Heaven taught me,	1499
	or holy Church, his bride	1501
	who holds His power on earth.	
Paulo	That's true.	
Shep.	And you must understand	
	that I believe with all my heart,	
	and, though a shepherd, know	
	the holy laws of God.	
Paulo	Then tell me: can God forgive	
	a man who has sinned against him	
	in deed and word and thought?	
Shep.	Why yes! whatever his crimes	1512
	– let them be numberless	
	as atoms in the sun,	
	stars in the night sky, moonbeams at full moon,	
	fish in the hollow seas –	
	such is God's mercy,	
	the man needs only to say	
	"Forgive me, Lord, for I have sinned"	1521
	and be forgiven straightaway	
	and gathered in God's arms,	
	for God will still be God.	
	If it were otherwise,	
	would he have made man	
	frail as man is?	
	God made man out of nothing	
	to have a share in his glory.	
	What credit to God to have made him	
	imperfect, and left it at that?	

1512 P6. Compared with the way in which Calderón would have presen   a major doctrinal statement of this sort, the Shepherd's homily appears unstructured. Yet it has its own simple but adequate coherence. After a short affirmation of belief in God's mercy (ll. 1512-24), two kinds of ground for that belief are explored: the nature of God and the nature of man (ll. 1525-55). The central section of the homily expounds the doctrines of incarnation and atonement, through which these two are reconciled (ll. 1556-72); a series of examples of divine forgiveness follows (ll. 1573-96). The method is that of religious humanism rather than scholastic logic; the speech now reads the more persuasively on that account.

1521. Literally 'I have sinned many times.' Though early punctuation does not make this clear, 'many times' must refer to the sinning, not the admission of guilt.

no fuera ningún blasón
en su majestad divina
dalle aquella imperfección.
Diole Dios libre albedrío,   1535
y fragilidad le dio
al cuerpo y al alma; luego,
dio potestad con acción
de pedir misericordia,
que a ninguno le negó.   1540
De modo que, si en pecando
el hombre, el justo rigor
procediera contra él,
fuera el número menor
de los que en el sacro alcázar   1545
están contemplando a Dios.
La fragilidad del cuerpo
es grande, que en una acción,
en un mirar solamente
con deshonesta afición,   1550
se ofende a Dios; de ese modo,
porque este triste ofensor,
con la imperfección que tuvo,
le ofende una vez o dos,
¿se había de condenar?   1555
No, señor, aqueso no;
que es Dios misericordioso,
y estima al más pecador,
porque todos igualmente
le costaron el sudor   1560
que sabéis, y aquella sangre
que liberal derramó,
haciendo un mar a su cuerpo,
que amoroso dividió
en cinco sangrientos ríos;   1565
que su espíritu formó
nueve meses en el vientre
de aquélla que mereció
ser virgen cuando fue madre
y el claro oriente del sol   1570
que como clara vidriera,

1537. P: <u>al cuerpo, y al alma, luego</u>; R: <u>al cuerpo; y al alma,
luego</u> (meaning that the body is frail but the soul is capable of
asking for mercy). H: <u>al cuerpo y al alma; luego</u> best reflects
Paulo's actual frailties, which are at least as much of the soul as

No; he gave man free will
and frailty of body and soul,
but, at the same time, gave him
power to act and ask
for the mercy he never refuses.
Think, after all, if whenever
man sinned, God's justice took him
and never spared him, who
would be left to share, in Heaven,
the glories of God's house
and the splendours of his face.
Our bodies are frail indeed;
with a single act, or a look
whose thought is unchaste, we might
offend against God — and so,
suppose some wretched sinner
(imperfect, as men are)
offends him once, or twice,
is he to be damned for that?
Not for a minute! No!
for God is merciful,
and he can see the worth
in the very worst of sinners.
For all men, equally,
he sweated — this you know —   1561
for all he shed his blood
in generosity
and the five streams of his wounds
flowed in a single sea
of compassion. It was for this
his spirit knew nine months' shaping
in his virgin mother's womb,
like the sun that shines through glass   1570

---

of the body.
    1561-5. Literally 'and that blood which he generously shed,
making his body a sea, which he lovingly divided in five rivers
flowing with blood.' The five wounds of Christ were heraldically
familiar from the royal arms of Portugal, about whose origins Tirso
was later to write a play, Las quinas de Portugal.
    1565. P: rayos; KSDTR: ríos.
    1570-2. The sun shining through glass was a traditional figure
for the Virgin Birth. R quotes an example from the 15th-century
poet Fray Iñigo de Mendoza. The origins apparently lie in an
Advent homily attributed to St Augustine (Davies, 377).

sin que la rompiese, entró.
Y si os guiáis por ejemplo,
decid: ¿no fue pecador
Pedro, y mereció después   1575
ser de las almas pastor?
Mateo, su coronista,
¿no fue también su ofensor?
y luego ¿no fue su apóstol,
y tan gran cargo le dió?   1580
¿No fue pecador Francisco?
Luego, ¿no le perdonó
y a modo de honrosa empresa,
en su cuerpo le imprimió
aquellas llagas divinas   1585
que le dieron tanto honor,
dignándole de tener
tan excelente blasón?
¿La pública pecadora,
Palestina no llamó   1590
Magdalena, y fue santa
por su santa conversión?
Mil ejemplos os dijera
a estar despacio, señor,
mas mi ganado me aguarda,   1595
y ha mucho que ausente estoy.

Paulo   Tente, pastor, no te vayas.

Pastor.   No puedo tenerme, no,
que ando por aquestos valles
recogiendo con amor
una ovejuela perdida   1600
que del rebaño huyó,
y esta corona que veis
hacerme con tanto amor
es para ella, si parece,
porque hacérmela mandó   1605
el Mayoral que la estima
del modo que le costó.

1575-6. St Peter denied Christ at the time of his arrest
(Matthew 26: 69-75), but was afterwards given the charge 'Feed my
sheep' (John 21: 15-17).

1577-80. St Matthew, once a tax-collector, then called to be an
apostle (Matthew 9: 9-13; Luke 5: 27.-30); traditionally identified
as Matthew the evangelist. The Loa sacramental in Tirso's Deleitar
aprovechando describes him as Christ's 'secretary' (Lois Vázquez,

108

```
                    – entering, yet not breaking.
                    Do you want examples?  Listen.
                    Wasn't Peter a sinner too
                    – Peter, the keeper of souls?                    1575
                    And Matthew, who wrote his story                 1577
                    – hadn't he sinned against him,
                    but was chosen to be an apostle
                    and do him such great service?
                    Was Francis not a sinner?                        1581
                    And wasn't Francis forgiven?
                    And didn't he come to bear
                    as a badge of his salvation
                    those same five wounds as his master?
                    What man had greater honour?
                    And Mary Magdalene – think:                      1589
                    "a woman that was a sinner"
                    they called her.  But she was converted
                    and became a saint.  If only
                    I had time, I could go on for ever.
                    But my sheep are waiting for me.
                    I have been away too long.
Paulo               Stay, little shepherd; don't go.
Shep.               I can stay no longer; no,
                    I must search the valleys through
                    for a single lost ewe-lamb                       1601
                    who left the fold and ran away.
                    And I weave this crown of flowers
                    lovingly, with my own hands,
                    to honour our returning stray.
                    So the Master of our flock
                    – he who paid the price for her;
```

---

125). The poem's three New Testament instances of repentance and
forgiveness are, as here, Peter, Matthew, and Mary Magdalen.

1581-8. St Francis of Assisi, converted after a misspent youth,
eventually came to bear the stigmata, the marks of Christ's wounds.
For the use of blasón in this context cf. the note on ll. 1561-5.
Tirso may well have imagined Paulo in his earlier life as
consciously, if obtusely, imitating this saint (cf. above, note on
ll. 644-53).

1589-92. The story in Luke 7: 36-50 of the 'woman which was a
sinner' is traditionally associated with St Mary Magdalen. In the
Loa (Lois Vázquez, 125) her previous condition is described in
identical terms: pública pecadora.

1601. The allusion to the parable of the Lost Sheep (Matthew 18:
12-14; Luke 15: 4-7) is clear.

El que a Dios tiene ofendido,
pídale perdón a Dios,   1610
porque es señor tan piadoso
que a ninguno le negó.

Paulo   Aguarda, pastor.

Pastor.   No puedo.

Paulo   Por fuerza te tendré yo.

Pastor.   Será detenerme a mí   1615
parar en su curso al sol.

                         [Vase.]

Paulo   Este pastor me ha avisado
en su forma peregrina,
no humana sino divina,
que tengo a Dios enojado   1620
por haber desconfiado
de su piedad, claro está,
y con ejemplos me da
a entender piadosamente
que el hombre que se arrepiente   1625
perdón en Dios hallará.
    Pues si Enrico es pecador,
¿no puede también hallar
perdón? Ya vengo a pensar
que ha sido grande mi error.   1630
Mas, ¿cómo dará el Señor
perdón a quien tiene nombre,
¡ay de mí!, del más mal hombre
que en este mundo ha nacido?
Pastor, que de mí has huído,   1635
no te espantes que me asombre.
    Si él tuviera algún intento
de tal vez arrepentirse,
lo que por engaño siento

1609-12.   The translation remodels these lines as an additional
verse of the Shepherd's song, whose meanings and rhythms the
original also echoes at this point.
    1615-16.   'the sun'. Anareto and the Shepherd – both of them
figures of persons of the Trinity – are both compared to the sun
(cf. above, ll. 1102-12). These references interact with other
light-imagery – for example, with Paulo's Phaethon-like presumption
(ll. 1429-30).
    1616-17.   No stage-direction in P. For the manner of Paulo's
attempt to detain the Shepherd see above, note to ll. 1490-1.
    1617-46.   Metre: décimas (paired quintillas). Cf. Lope de Vega,

```
              he who knows her worth - commands.
              And he that God offends                              1609
              to God should make his plea,
              whose mercy is to none denied
              and is forever free.
Paulo         Wait, shepherd, wait!
Shep.                             I cannot wait.
Paulo         I'll keep you here by force!
Shep.         You cannot hold me.  Could you make          1615
              the sun stop in its course?
                   [The Shepherd disappears again.]
Paulo         This shepherd is more than mortal
              - he brings a warning from God
              that I have angered him                      1620
              by doubting his grace.  Of course!
              that was why he came: to show me,
              by giving examples of mercy,
              that any man who repents
              is sure of God's forgiveness.
              Enrico may be a sinner
              but does that mean that he
              can never be forgiven?
              I must have been wrong - so wrong!
              And yet, how can the Lord
              forgive a man who must be
              - for everybody says so -
              the worst man in the world?
              Oh, it's no use!  Oh, shepherd!
              Why did you run away?
              Do you wonder I don't understand
              what to make of it all?
              If he only showed some spark                 1637
              of repentance - only the thought -
              then I would know that my fears
```

Arte nuevo de hacer comedias (Sánchez Escribano and Porqueras Mayo, 162): 'décimas are a good metre for complaints.'

1620. 'I have angered him.' Typically, Paulo registers the Shepherd's message first as an expression of God's wrath, and only secondarily as holding out any hope of forgiveness.

1631. P: mrs, nonsensically; KR: mas.

1637-41. The most coherent of the several literal meanings which these lines will bear would run: 'If he had any intention of perhaps repenting, then what I mistakenly suffer might well be resisted, and I would live happy'.

	bien pudiera resistirse,	1640
	y yo viviera contento.	
	¿Por qué, pastor, queréis vos	
	. . . .	
	que halle su remedio medio?	
	Alma, ya no hay más remedio	1645
	que el condenarnos los dos.	
	Sale Pedrisco.	
Pedr.	Escucha, Paulo, y sabrás,	
	aunque de ello ajeno estás	
	y lo atribuyas a engaño,	
	el suceso más extraño	1650
	que tú habrás visto jamás.	
	En esa verde ribera,	
	de tantas fieras aprisco,	
	donde el cristal reverbera,	
	cuando el afligido risco	1655
	su tremendo golpe espera,	
	después de dejar colgados	
	aquellos tres desdichados,	
	estábamos Celio y yo,	
	cuando una voz que se oyó	1660
	nos dejó medio turbados.	
	"Que me ahogo", dijo y vimos	
	cuando la vista tendimos	
	. . . .	
	. . . .	1665
	. . . .	
	como en el mar hay tormenta,	
	y está de sangre cubierta,	
	para anegallos bramaba.	
	Ya en las estrellas los clava,	1670
	ya en su centro los avienta,	
	en los cristales no helados	
	las dos cabezas se veían	
	de aquestos dos desdichados,	
	y las olas parecían	1675
	ser tablas de degollados.	
	Llegaron al fin, mostrando	

1647-1701. Metre: quintillas.

1652-6. Literally 'On that green shore, the enclosure of so many wild beasts, where the crystal [water] glitters, as the stricken crag awaits its tremendous blow.' Pleasingly descriptive, but not particularly apt for Pedrisco, these lines have to be greatly

were follies, and stand up to them,
and live in peace again.
How can the shepherd suppose
there's any cure for Enrico?
Or any answer but this:
both of us must be damned.

Enter Pedrisco.

Pedr. Wait till you hear this, Paulo!
- you weren't there - you won't know what to think!
It's the strangest thing you ever saw
in your life! Celio and I
had strung up those three poor prisoners.
We thought we'd take a walk
down by the shore; there's plenty of game   1652
and you can watch the waves
hammering away at the cliffs.
Well, when we'd got down there
we heard someone shouting
"Help me, I'm drowning!" So we took a look.
There were two of them out there,   1664
swimming for all they were worth.
There was a heavy sea running,
tossing them high and plunging them deep,
and patches of blood on the water,
and they were pretty far gone.
You could only see the heads of them
bobbing above the waves,   1672
for all the world like two poor criminals
stuck up on a plank somewhere   1676
as a horrible warning.
They never gave up, though,

---

simplified for him to speak them credibly in English.

1660. P: <u>vez</u>; KR: <u>voz</u>.

1664-6. Several lines are missing here; they must at least establish the presence of the two swimmers.

1668. P: <u>cubierta</u>; HR: <u>sedienta</u>. The rhyme in P is defective, but if the two men are being buffeted by waves on a rocky coast, it makes sense to think that the water might be 'covered' with blood.

1672. Literally 'in the unfrozen crystals' - meaning, as usual, water.

1676. <u>tablas de degollados</u> were boards on which the heads of decapitated criminals were displayed. Audiences would have recognized this as a likely fate awaiting Enrico and Galván - and, if it came to that, Paulo and Pedrisco too.

	el valor que significo,	
	mas, por no estarte cansando,	
	has de saber que es Enrico	1680
	el uno.	
Paulo	Estoilo dudando.	
Pedr.	No lo dudes, pues yo llego	
	a decirlo, y no estoy ciego.	
Paulo	¿Vístele tú?	
Pedr.	Vile yo.	
Paulo	¿Qué hizo al salir?	
Pedr.	Echó	1685
	un por vida y un reniego.	
	¡Mira qué gracias le daba	
	a Dios que ansí le libraba!	
Paulo	¡Y dirá ahora el pastor	
	que le ha de dar el Señor	1690
	perdón! el juicio me acaba.	
	Mas poco puedo perder,	
	pues aquí le llego a ver,	
	en proballe la intención.	
Pedr.	Ya le trae tu escuadrón.	1695
Paulo	Pues oye lo que has de hacer.	

<u>Sacan a Enrico y a Galván atados y mojados</u>.

Enrico	¿Dónde me lleváis ansí?	
Band.1	El capitán está aquí,	
	que la respuesta os dará.	
Paulo	[<u>A Pedrisco</u>] Haz esto.	
Pedr.	Todo se hará.	1700

<u>Vase Paulo</u>.

Band.1	Pues ¿vase el capitán?	
Pedr.	Sí.	
	¿Dónde iban vuesas mercedes,	
	que en tan gran peligro dieron	

1681. Paulo's mistrust is in the first instance a neutral quality, neither good nor bad; it becomes a fault only when misapplied. Here, for example, it is perfectly reasonable: Enrico's arrival really is an extraordinary event.

1686. <u>por vida de</u> ('by the life of...'); <u>reniego de</u> ('I renounce...') were common formulae in 17th-century swearing.

1691. 'It's absurd.' More literally 'It's beyond my judgment.' How Enrico is to be forgiven is at this stage not merely beyond Paulo's judgment, but beyond that of any spectator. Where Paulo goes wrong is in thinking that, if he cannot comprehend it, the thing cannot happen.

1694. P etc.: <u>el</u>; HR: <u>en</u>. On 'trying / to find what's in his

	and in the end they made it,	
	and – anyway, this is the point:	
	one of them's Enrico.	
Paulo	No!	
	I don't believe it.	1681
Pedr.	You'd better	
	believe it; I'm telling you,	
	and I'm not blind.	
Paulo	You saw him?	
Pedr.	With these eyes.	
Paulo	What did he do when he landed?	
Pedr.	Swore till the air was blue.	1686
	There's all the thanks that God	
	gets for saving his life.	
Paulo	How can that shepherd pretend	
	that God would ever forgive	
	a man like that? It's absurd.	1691
	and yet I've nothing to lose,	
	now that he's here, by trying	
	to find what's in his mind.	1694
Pedr.	The lads are bringing him in.	
Paulo	Listen, then: this is what	1696
	you have to do...	

They converse apart. The Bandits bring in Enrico and Galván,
                wet from the sea and bound.

Enrico	Where are you taking me?	
Bdt.1	You can ask the captain that.	
	He'll tell you soon enough.	
Paulo	[To Pedrisco] You understand?	
Pedr.	I'll do it.	

Exit Paulo.

Bdt.1	What's wrong with the captain?	
	Isn't he stopping?	
Pedr.	No.	
	Now, gentlemen, perhaps	
	you'd be good enough to tell me	
	where you were going; you ought to know

---

mind' see Introduction, p. lviii.

1696-1700. The audience do not overhear Paulo's whispered
instructions; the suspense and surprise in the ensuing scenes are
thereby enhanced.

1700-1. PK: Vase after os dará; SD: after haz esto; R: after
todo se hará, and clarifying that it is Paulo who leaves the stage.

1702-77. Metre: romance assonating in E-O.

	como es caminar por agua?	
	¿No responden?	
Enrico	Al infierno.	1705
Pedr.	Pues ¿quién le mete en cansarse	
	cuando hay diablos tan ligeros	
	que le llevarán de balde?	
Enrico	Por agradecerles menos.	
Pedr.	Habla voarcé muy bien	1710
	y habla muy a lo discreto	
	en no agradecer al diablo	
	cosa que haga en su provecho.	
	¿Cómo se llama voarcé?	
Enrico	Llámome el diablo.	
Pedr.	Y por eso	1715
	se quiso arrojar al mar	
	para remojar el fuego.	
	¿De dónde es?	
Enrico	Si de cansado	
	de reñir con agua y viento	
	no arrojara al mar la espada,	1720
	yo os respondiera bien presto	
	a vuestras necias preguntas	
	con los filos de su acero.	
Pedr.	Oye, hidalgo, no se atufe	
	ni nos eche tantos retos,	1725
	que juro a Dios, si me enojo,	
	que le barrene ese cuerpo	
	más de setecientas veces,	
	sin las que en su nacimiento	
	barrenó naturaleza.	1730
	Y ha de advertir que está preso,	
	y que si es valiente, yo	
	soy valiente como un Héctor,	
	y que si él ha hecho muertes	
	sepa que también yo he muerto	1735
	muchas hambres y candiles	
	y muchas pulgas a tiento.	

1705. 'To Hell.' This is true enough, though Enrico makes the reply merely out of truculence.
1715. Literally 'I am called the Devil' (cf. ll. 495-6).
1729. P: que su; KR: que en su.
1733. Literally 'I am brave as Hector, but the mock-modest idiom substituted in the translation seemed to fit Pedrisco's tone.

```
                it's dangerous walking on water.
                Well, where were you going?
Enrico                                  To Hell.                  1705
Pedr.     You might have saved yourselves trouble
          and left it to the devils
          to get you there for free.
Enrico    I wouldn't be beholden
          even to them!
Pedr.                   That's good!
          I can see you're nobody's fool.
          There's no call to thank the Devil
          - he's in it for what he can get!
          What's your name?
Enrico                     Satan.                                 1715
Pedr.                          So
          that's why you jumped in the water
          - to cool off a bit.  And where
          do you come from?
Enrico                      See here:
          if I hadn't had to drop
          my sword when I was swimming
          or risk going down in the storm,
          I'd give you the kind of answer
          that'd stop your damn fool questions!
Pedr.     You want to watch yourself,
          my fine young gentleman,
          and listen to me for a change!
          Don't think you can frighten me
          because once I lose my temper,
          by God, I'll put a few hundred
          holes in your belly (not counting
          the ones that are there by nature)!
          You're our prisoner; don't you forget it.
          You might be brave as they come,
          but I'm pretty brave myself                             1733
          and if it comes to killing,
          well I've killed a few - thirsts - in my time;  1735
          I've snuffed out plenty - of candles -
          and croaked the odd dozen - fleas.
```

1735-7. More literally 'know that I too have killed many hungers
and candles, and many fleas, located by touch.' For the _gracioso_'s
comic hunger see ll. 77 ff. The translation prefers 'killing a
thirst', as more of a live idiom in English, to 'killing hunger'.

117

	Y si es ladrón, soy ladrón,	
	y soy el demonio mesmo,	
	y, ¡por vida!...	
Band.1	Bueno está.	
Enrico	¿Esto sufro y no me vengo?	1740
Pedr.	Ahora ha de quedar atado	
	a un árbol.	
Enrico	No me defiendo:	
	haced de mí vuestro gusto.	
Pedr.	Y él también.	
Galván	De esta vez muero.	1745
Pedr.	Si son como vuestra cara,	
	vos tenéis bellacos hechos.	
	Ea, llegaldos a atar,	
	que el capitán gusta de ello.	
	Llegad al árbol.	

Átalos.

Enrico	¿Que ansí	1750
	me quiera tratar el cielo?	
Pedr.	Llegad vos.	
Galván	¡Tened piedad!	
Pedr.	Vendarles los ojos quiero	
	con las ligas a los dos.	
Galván	¿Viose tan extraño aprieto?	1755
	Mire vuesarced que yo	
	vivo de su oficio mesmo	
	y que soy ladrón también.	
Pedr.	Ahorra razón aquesto	
	de trabajo a la justicia,	1760
	y al verdugo de contento.	
Band.1	Ya están vendados y atados.	
Pedr.	Las flechas y arcos tomemos,	

1739. ¡por vida! See above, note on l. 1686. Pedrisco is about to utter some major oath.

1742-3. Such shifts from aggression to apathy are very much a part of Enrico's character; there will be several more in the prison scene (ll. 2209-11; 2365-74).

1746-7. Literally 'If they are like your face, you have rascally deeds [sc. to your credit].' The interplay between Pedrisco and Galván is marked by the use of the vos form (second person plural), employed between near-equals. By contrast, Pedrisco has addressed Enrico with the polite third-person, even when provoking him.

1753. PK: vendarlos; SD: vendarle; R: vendarles, the correct

```
          And if you're a thief, I'm another
          - in fact I'm the very Devil -
          so you can get...                                    1739
Bdt.1                     Steady, Pedrisco.
          Don't overdo it now.
Enrico                        Christ!
          Do I have to stand for this?
Pedr.     Yes, 'cause we're going to tie you
          against that tree.
Enrico                        Go ahead.                        1742
          I can't be bothered to struggle.
Pedr.     And the other one.
Galván                        This is where Galván
          gets his.
Pedr.              Look at the face on him!                    1746
          I'll bet he's got a record!
          Tie them tightly, lads!
          You know how the captain likes it.
          Tightly, against the tree.
                   The prisoners are tied to trees.
Enrico    So this is the luck I get!
Pedr.     You next!
Galván              Go easy, can't you?
Pedr.     Now blindfold them.
Galván                         Oh no!
          That's going a bit too far!
          Look, friend, I'm in the trade myself.               1756
          I'm a thief too, back home.
Pedr.     Fine! We can save the law a job,
          and put the hangman out of work.
Bdt.1     All bound and blindfolded.
Pedr.     Now fetch out the crossbows.                         1763
```

---

grammatical choice.

1756. Galván, taking no chances with Pedrisco, addresses him with the relatively civil _vuesarced_; only when free again does he risk _tú_ (below, ll. 2034-5). The English version opts for another kind of ingratiation: 'Look, friend...' On Pedrisco's reply see Introduction, p. xxxiv.

1759-61. P: _Ahorra razón_; KSDR: _Ahorrará con_, but P is surely intelligible: 'This saves a reason for work as far as the law is concerned, and for pleasure as far as the hangman is concerned.'

1763. _arcos_ means merely 'bows', but these are crossbows; see also l. 1774: _jara_ ('a crossbow-bolt'), and the stage-direction at ll. 1850-1.

	y dos docenas, no más,	
	clavemos en cada cuerpo.	1765
Band.1	Vamos.	
Pedr.	[Aparte] Aquesto es fingido:	
	nadie los ofenda.	
Band.1	[Aparte] Creo que el capitán los conoce.	
Pedr.	[Aparte] Vamos, y ansí los dejemos.	

[Vanse.]

Galván	Ya se van a asaetarnos.	1770
Enrico	Pues no por aqueso pienso	
	mostrar flaqueza ninguna.	
Galván	Ya me parece que siento	
	una jara en estas tripas.	
Enrico	Vénguese en mí el justo cielo,	1775
	que quisiera arrepentirme,	
	y cuando quiero no puedo.	

Sale Paulo, de ermitaño, con cruz y rosario.

Paulo	[Aparte] Con esta traza he querido	
	probar si este hombre se acuerda	
	de Dios, a quien ha ofendido.	1780
Enrico	¡Que un hombre la vida pierda	
	de nadie visto ni oído!	
Galván	Cada mosquito que pasa	
	me parece que es saeta.	
Enrico	El corazón se me abrasa,	1785
	que mi fuerza esté sujeta.	
	¡Ah fortuna, en todo escasa!	
Paulo	Alabado sea el Señor.	
Enrico	Sea por siempre alabado.	
Paulo	Sabed con vuestro valor	1790
	llevar este golpe airado	
	de fortuna.	
Enrico	¡Gran rigor!	
	¿Quién sois vos, que ansí me habláis?	
Paulo	Un monje que este desierto,	
	donde la muerte esperáis,	1795
	habita.	

1766-9. Early texts give no indication that these are asides, but they very clearly are.

1775-7. There may be something in the notion that Enrico here demonstrates 'sufficient' grace (i.e. the desire to repent), but not 'efficacious' grace (the ability to do so). Yet his incapacity is, as Maurel (1971), 544 wisely remarks, 'légitimée par la nécessité dramatique'. Enrique's intimations of truth are still only sporadic, like his acceptance here of divine justice.

	A couple of dozen shots apiece
	ought to finish them off a treat.
Bdt.1	Right you are.
Pedr.	[Aside] It's all a game, remember.
	No one's to touch them mind.
Bdt.1	[Aside] I reckon the captain knows them.
Pedr.	[Aside] Now we leave them like that.
	[Exeunt Pedrisco and the Bandits.]
Galván	They've gone for their weapons.
	When they get back, they'll kill us.
Enrico	Alright, they're going to kill us.
	They'll never make me weaken, though.
Galván	You speak for yourself! I can feel
	my guts full of arrows already.
Enrico	Heaven can do its worst to me. 1775
	That's fair enough; I should repent.
	I want to but I can't.

Enter Paulo as a hermit, with cross and rosary.

Paulo	[Aside] In this disguise I'll test him, 1778
	and see if he remembers
	the God he offended.
Enrico	To die like this
	with no one to see or hear!
Galván	Each time a fly goes past
	I think it's an arrow.
Enrico	Hell's fire! It makes me mad
	to be bound and helpless like this.
	Oh, Lady Luck's a mean bitch to the last!
Paulo	The Lord's name be praised!
Enrico	Amen to that, say I.
Paulo	Lift up your courage, and resist
	Fortune's shrewd blow.
Enrico	A cruel blow indeed.
	But who might you be?
Paulo	A hermit
	who dwells in this wilderness
	where you await your death.

1778-1906. Metre: quintillas.

1778-80. The aside ensures that slower-witted spectators will recognize Paulo and understand his plan.

1787. PK: a fortuna... escasa, with which R concurs, eliminating the comma after sujeta in the previous line, to give as the literal meaning 'that my strength should be subject to fortune, grudging in everything.' ST: ¡Ah fortuna... escasa! seems more aptly truculent, and is followed in the translation here.

Enrico	¡Bueno, por cierto!	
	Y ahora, ¿qué nos mandáis?	
Paulo	A los que al roble os ataron	
	y a mataros se apartaron,	
	supliqué con humildad	1800
	que ya que con tal crueldad	
	de daros muerte trataron,	
	que me dejasen llegar	
	a hablaros.	
Enrico	¿Para qué?	
Paulo	Por si os queréis confesar,	1805
	pues seguís de Dios la fe.	
Enrico	Pues bien se puede tornar,	
	padre, o lo que es.	
Paulo	¿Qué decís?	
	¿No sois cristiano?	
Enrico	Sí soy.	
Paulo	No lo sois, pues no admitís	1810
	el último bien que os doy.	
	¿Por qué no lo recibís?	
Enrico	Porque no quiero.	
Paulo	[Aparte] (¡Ay de mí!	
	Esto mismo presumí.)	
	¿No veis que os han de matar	1815
	ahora?	
Enrico	¿Quiere callar,	
	hermano, y dejarme aquí?	
	Si esos señores ladrones	
	me dieren muerte, aquí estoy.	
Paulo	[Aparte] ¡En qué grandes confusiones	1820
	tengo el alma!	
Enrico	Yo no doy	
	a nadie satisfacciones.	
Paulo	A Dios, sí.	
Enrico	Si Dios ya sabe	
	que soy tan gran pecador,	
	¿para qué?	
Paulo	¡Delito grave!	1825

1808. Enrico cannot see Paulo, and may be uncertain, in spite of
ll. 1794-6, as to what his precise status is. But the audience,
who know what Paulo is doing, may well doubt whether he now has any
right to be called 'father'.
1810-13. There are several ironies here. If Enrico is not a

122

Enrico	Well, that's encouraging!
	What do you want with us?
Paulo	I met the band of men
	who tied you to the oak,
	going to fetch their weapons.
	They plan a cruel death for you.
	I begged them, first,
	to put off their evil purpose
	and let me speak with you awhile.
Enrico	And what's the good of that?
Paulo	You're Christians, I suppose.
	You would want to make your confession.
Enrico	Forget it, Father,
	or whatever you call yourself.	1808
	You might as well go back.
Paulo	What are you saying?
	Are you not a Christian after all?
Enrico	I am.
Paulo	You can't be	1810
	or how could you refuse
	this last good gift at my hands?
	Why not accept it?
Enrico	Because I don't want to.
Paulo	[Aside] Just as I feared!
	Listen, those men are coming back,
	and when they come, they'll kill you.
Enrico	Brother,
	let me alone, and save your breath.
	They can kill me and welcome.
	They know where they can find me.
Paulo	[Aside] What am I to make of this?	1820
Enrico	And I'll give satisfaction to no man.
Paulo	But to God you must.
Enrico	Why should I
	if God already knows
	the kind of sinner I am?
Paulo	Oh, what an error!

Christian because he refuses Paulo's offer of confession, Paulo,
rejecting divine mercy, is not a Christian either. Paulo's attempt
is a 'last good' as much for him as for Enrico; yet it is only
debatably a 'good' at all.

  1820–1. More literally 'In what great confusions I find my soul!'
A clear case for 'functional' translation.

	Para que su sacro amor	
	de darle perdón acabe.	
Enrico	Padre, lo que nunca he hecho,	
	tampoco he de hacer ahora.	
Paulo	Duro peñasco es su pecho.	1830
Enrico	Galván, ¿qué hará la señora	
	Celia?	
Galván	Puesto en tanto estrecho,	
	¿quién se ha de acordar de nada?	
Paulo	No se acuerde de esas cosas.	
Enrico	Padre mío, ya me enfada.	1835
Paulo	¿Estas palabras piadosas	
	le ofenden?	
Enrico	Cosa es cansada,	
	pues si no estuviera atado,	
	ya yo le hubiera arrojado	
	de una coz dentro del mar.	1840
Paulo	Mire que le han de matar.	
Enrico	Ya estoy de aguardar cansado.	
Galván	Padre, confiéseme a mí,	
	que ya pienso que estoy muerto.	
Enrico	Quite esta liga de aquí,	1845
	padre.	
Paulo	Sí haré, por cierto.	

Quítales las vendas.

Enrico	Gracias a Dios que ya vi.	
Galván	Y a mí también.	
Paulo	En buen hora,	
	y vuelvan la vista ahora	
	a los que a matarlos vienen.	1850

Salen los bandoleros con escopetas y ballestas.

Enrico	Pues, ¿para qué se detienen?
Pedr.	Pues que ya su fin no ignora,
	digo, ¿por qué no confiesa?
Enrico	No me quiero confesar.

1828–9.   'what I've never done / I'll not do now.'   This has been, from the beginning, the form of Enrico's self-assertion (cf. above, ll. 514–15; 716–17; 1320–1).

1831–3.   In a deliberate snub Enrico turns away from Paulo to talk about the most worldly of his worldly involvements.   Galván, however, is in no state to match this coolness.

1838–40.   Aubrun (1957), 148–9 suggests that these lines would have chimed with popular resentment against 'parasites sermonneurs'.

	So that his blessèd love	
	may work your forgiveness.	
Enrico	Father, what I've never done	1828
	I'll not do now.	
Paulo	His heart's like flint.	
Enrico	Galván, what's Celia up to	1831
	do you suppose?	
Galván	How the hell should I know	
	at a time like this?	
Paulo	Forget these worldly thoughts.	
Enrico	Father, you know, I'm beginning	
	to find you a bore.	
Paulo	Can it be	
	that my pious words offend you?	
Enrico	It can; I'm sick of them	
	and you. If I weren't tied up	1838
	I'd have kicked you over the clifftop	
	before now.	
Paulo	Remember, death is near you.	
Enrico	Let it come! I'm tired of waiting.	
Galván	Why not confess me, Father?	1843
	I reckon I'm dead already.	
Enrico	Get this damned blindfold off me,	
	Father.	
Paulo	Indeed I will!	
	He takes the blindfold off him.	
Enrico	Thank God I can see again!	
Galván	Take mine off too.	1848
Paulo	[Doing so] And welcome!	
	Now you can feast your eyes	
	on the men who are coming to kill you.	

Enter the bandits and Pedrisco armed with crossbows and guns.

Enrico	Still waiting? What is it this time?
Pedr.	Well, now you know what's coming,
	what I say is: why not make your confession?
Enrico	Because I don't choose to.

1843. 'Why not confess me...' Though this is further comic cowardice on Galván's part, it would still be Paulo's role as a genuine religious to take the request seriously and to respond to it. That he fails to do either removes his last shred of credibility.

1848. Despite the placing of the original stage-direction, it is clear that Galván's blindfold is not removed until after también.

Pedr.	Celio, el pecho le atraviesa.	1855
Paulo	Dejad que le vuelva a hablar.	
	Desesperación es ésa.	
Pedr.	Ea, llegalde a matar.	
Paulo	Deteneos: (¡triste pena!)	

Pedr.   Celio, el pecho le atraviesa.   1855
Paulo   Dejad que le vuelva a hablar.
        Desesperación es ésa.
Pedr.   Ea, llegalde a matar.
Paulo   Deteneos: (¡triste pena!)

        . . . .
        porque si éste se condena,   1860
        me queda más que dudar.
Enrico   Cobardes sois; ¿no llegáis,
        y puerta a mi pecho abrís?
Pedr.   De esta vez no os detengáis.
Paulo   Aguardad, que si le herís,   1865
        más confuso me dejáis.
          Mira que eres pecador,
        hijo.
Enrico   Y del mundo el mayor;
        ya lo sé.
Paulo   Tu bien espero.
        Confiésate a Dios.
Enrico   No quiero,   1870
        cansado predicador.
Paulo   Pues salga del pecho mío,
        si no dilatado río,
        de lágrimas tanta copia
        que se anegue el alma propia,   1875
        pues ya de Dios desconfío.
          Dejad descubrir, sayal,
        mi cuerpo, pues está mal,
        según siente el corazón,

1855–6; 1858–9; 1864–5. These repeatedly countermanded orders
add very considerably to the suspense. It is impossible to tell
whether Enrico and Galván will survive, or what Paulo will do next.
    1857. P: esta; KSDR: esa, restoring the rhyme. Ironically Paulo
accuses Enrico of a fault (desesperación) which is closely akin to
his own desconfianza; cf. below, l. 1969.
    1859. The stanza lacks a line, whose content might conceivably
make the interpretation of l. 1861 a little easier.
    1861. PKR: me queda más que dudar, which might mean 'more matter
for doubt' or, as translated, 'something more [i.e. worse] than
doubt', or might indicate an enhanced, though unwelcome, degree of
certainty. The sentence might be punctuated either as a statement
or as a question. SDT: no queda más que esperar is simpler, and
arguably less interesting.

Pedr.	Celio,	1855

Pedr.   Celio,   1855
          shoot him!
Paulo   Wait!
          Let me talk to him again.
          You are dying in despair.   1857
Pedr.   Take aim...   1858
Paulo   Wait, I say!
          If he <u>is</u> damned it leaves me
          in doubt, and worse than doubt.
Enrico   Cowards! What's holding you back?
          Why don't you finish the job?
Pedr.   This time we'll finish it. Now...   1864
Paulo   Wait! If you wound him
          how shall I know what to think?
          My son, remember
          you have been a sinner.
Enrico   The greatest in the world,
          I know.
Paulo   I only seek your good.
          Make your confession.
Enrico   I will not.
          Preacher, you bore me.
Paulo   Then let the tears   1872
          flow from my stricken heart
          in rivers deep enough
          to drown my soul,
          now I no longer trust in God.
          Then strip this robe   1877
          from my sinful body,
          for my heart knows

1872-1901. This speech is in a sense Paulo's last word - hence
much of its pathos. But it is not Tirso's last word, either
theologically or dramatically. In translation its sustained poetic
intensity seemed to call for a stronger stanzaic pattern than
usual. Within each quintilla, however, much reshaping has been
done.
     1872-5. Literally 'Let there issue from my breast, if not a
broad river, a flow of tears sufficient to drown the very soul'.
The 'if not...' formula, common in 17th-century Spanish poetry,
will not transfer readily to English.
     1877-8. PKDTR: Dejad descubrir; S: dejad de subir; H: dejad de
cubrir is a good deal more sensible than the latter, but P's
reading will do: 'Habit, let my body go uncovered'.

```
        una rica guarnición                            1880
        sobre tan falso cristal.
          En mis torpezas resbalo,
        y a la culebra me igualo;
        mas mi parecer condeno,
        porque yo desecho el bueno,                     1885
        mas ella desecha el malo.
          Mi adverso fin no resisto,
        pues mi desventura he visto,
        y da claro testimonio
        el vestirme de demonio                          1890
        y el desnudarme de Cristo.
        Colgad ese saco ahí
        para que diga, (¡ay de mí!),
        "en tal puesto me colgó
        Paulo, que no mereció                           1895
        la gloria que encierro en mí."
          Dadme la daga y la espada;
        esa cruz podéis tomar;
        ya no hay esperanza en nada,
        pues no me sé aprovechar                         1900
        de aquella sangre sagrada.
          Desataldos.
```

[Desatan a Enrico y a Galván.]

Enrico   Ya lo estoy,
         y lo que no he visto creo.

1880-1.   The religious habit, which the audience can see as a
coarse cloth garment, is described as a rich setting for a jewel –
except that Paulo no longer regards the person inside it (himself)
as having any worth. Yet in God's sight this cannot be true, since
Christ, by his atonement, gave all men value. Thus the ser /
parecer contrast ('being and seeming') is exploited in two ways:
Paulo is wiser (about the habit) than the audience's own eyes; but
the audience, if it has listened to the Shepherd (ll. 1558-60), is
wiser about Paulo than he is himself.

1884.   mi parecer condeno, literally interpreted, is a neat
example of Tirso's serious wit. Most obviously it means 'I condemn
my thought', and Paulo goes on to explain why his comparison with
the snake is not an apt one. On another level the meaning is 'I
condemn my appearance', and this is the effect when Paulo, unlike
the snake, reveals a disreputable garb (his bandit costume) under
his good outer habit. For further implications of the snake image
see Introduction, p. xliii-xlix.

1891-2.   Paulo has begun to remove his habit at l. 1877; he does
so painfully and clumsily (l. 1882). His difficulties, like King
Lear's 'Pray you, undo this button', add a good deal to the dramatic

```
                  it is too good to house                          1880
                  so base a thing.
                  How clumsily
                  my hands move to their work,
                  as a snake shuffles off its skin!
                  Yet snakes at least                              1884
                  change worse for better;
                  I slough off goodness, wear my sin.
                  Knowing my fate,
                  I here embrace my certain ill.
                  Witness this change:
                  see how I put off Christ                         1891
                  to wear the Devil.
                  And hang my vestments here.
                  Let them proclaim:
                  "Here Paulo left us, who could not deserve       1895
                  the glory we contain."
                  Give me my sword and dagger now,
                  and take this cross.
                  The holy blood shed here is powerless.           1899
                  I have forgotten how
                  to reach it, and all hope is loss.
                  Untie them.
                              [They do so.]
Enrico                        They have already freed us.
                  I never saw so strange a thing                   1903
                  - yet I believe it.
```

and emotional tension. The stage-direction <u>Quítase el sayal</u> ('He
takes off his habit') at this point seems oddly located; it is not
in P, and R supplies it only with some doubts.

1895. Pathetically – and ominously – Paulo believes that he
needed to 'deserve' his vocation as a hermit. There was a time
when he claimed not to think so (cf. above, ll. 33–5), but from an
early stage, reliance on his own merits has seriously confused his
approach to grace (cf. ll. 193–8; 934–40).

1899–1901. Literally 'There is no longer hope in anything, for I
do not know how to avail myself of that sacred blood.' With
Paulo's <u>no sé</u> here contrast Enrico's <u>no puedo</u> (above, ll. 1776–7).
Enrico 'cannot' repent; he requires to be moved to do it, but we
know that he is capable of being moved. Paulo 'does not know how';
he needs to be taught, and he is not very teachable.

1903. PKCR: <u>lo que no he visto creo</u>; SDTH: <u>lo que he visto no</u>
<u>creo</u> ('what I have seen I do not believe'). But P makes sense in
context, and carries relevant echoes of Christ's reproof to St
Thomas: 'blessed are they that have not seen, and yet have
believed' (John 20: 29).

Galván	Gracias a los cielos doy.	
[Enrico]	Saber la verdad deseo.	1905
Paulo	¡Qué desdichado que soy!	
	¡Ah, Enrico, nunca nacieras!	
	Nunca tu madre te echara	
	donde gozando la luz	
	fuiste de mis males causa;	1910
	o pluguiera a Dios que ya	
	que infundido el cuerpo y alma,	
	saliste a luz, en sus brazos	
	te diera la muerte un ama,	
	un león te deshiciera,	1915
	una osa despedazara	
	tus tiernos miembros entonces,	
	o cayeras en tu casa	
	del más altivo balcón,	
	primero que a mi esperanza	1920
	hubieras cortado el hilo.	
Enrico	Esta novedad me espanta.	
Paulo	Yo soy Paulo, un ermitaño,	
	que dejé mi amada patria	
	de poco más de quince años,	1925
	y en esta oscura montaña	
	otros diez serví al Señor.	
Enrico	¡Qué ventura!	
Paulo	¡Qué desgracia!	
	Un ángel rompiendo nubes	
	y cortinas de oro y plata,	1930
	preguntándole yo a Dios	
	qué fin tendría: "Repara",	
	me dijo, "ve a la ciudad	

1905 ff. Distribution of speakers in P: l. 1905 (with preceding line) to Galván, l. 1906 to Paulo, ll. 1907–21 to Enrico, l. 1922 to Enrico; in KSD: l. 1905 to Galván, l. 1906 to Enrico, ll. 1907–21 to Paulo, l. 1922 to Enrico. The reallocation by R, followed here, seems the most sensible.

1906–21. R describes this speech as 'one of the weakest in the play'. It has its faults: the parallel between ama, león, and osa reads oddly, and the whole thing has a general air of hysteria. Yet it expresses well enough the pain, depression, and anger which are all that Paulo, having surrendered his last hopes, can feel.

1907–2050. Metre: romance assonating in A–A.

1921. PKS: huviera; DR: hubieras. THe second person seems the obvious reading: 'before you had cut off the thread of my hope'.

Galván	Thank your stars
	we're free, that's all.
Enrico	What has it been about,
	all this? Tell me the truth.
Paulo	Oh, all my happiness lost! 1906

Galván   Thank your stars
           we're free, that's all.

Enrico   What has it been about,
           all this? Tell me the truth.

Paulo   Oh, all my happiness lost!   1906
           Enrico! Why were you born?
           Why did your mother bring you
           to life to destroy my life?
           Or, once living, why in God's name
           couldn't your nurse have smothered you
           lying in her arms, or a lion or a bear
           made away with you, torn you to pieces,
           young as you were?
           Couldn't you have fallen
           from the highest window of your house?
           Why did you have to live
           to bring my hopes to an end?

Enrico   You fill me with wonder.   Explain.

Paulo   Enrico, my name is Paulo.
           When I was fifteen, or a little older,   1925
           I left the home that I loved
           and in these wooded hills
           I spent ten years of my life
           in God's service, as a hermit.

Enrico   What happiness!   1928

Paulo   What evil fortune!
           One day, I was praying to God
           to know what my end would be,
           and an angel came down, through clouds
           and veils of gold and silver.
           He told me: "Go to the city;
           there you will see Enrico..."

1925. 'fifteen or a little older'. Paulo is thirty now (above, l. 193), and has been a hermit for ten years (ll. 108 etc.), beginning, presumably, about the age of twenty. Of the five-year gap which this leaves he tells Enrico nothing; later we learn that he has been a soldier (ll. 2816-7). This elaboration of an implied biography reflects the depth in which Tirso has imagined him.

1928. A most surprising comment, coming from Enrico. The line would make some sense as a rather confused attempt to say something which Paulo might find apt. Or perhaps it should be delivered ironically - 'Bully for you!' But we should not read too much piety into it.

```
             y verás a Enrico" (¡ay alma!)
             "hijo del noble Anareto,                        1935
             que en Nápoles tiene fama.
             Advierte bien en sus hechos,
             y contempla en sus palabras,
             que si Enrico al cielo fuere,
             el cielo también te aguarda;                     1940
             y si al infierno, al infierno".
             Yo entonces imaginaba
             que era algún santo este Enrico,
             pero los deseos se engañan.
             Fui allá, vite luego al punto,                   1945
             y de tu boca y por fama
             supe que eras el peor hombre
             que en todo el mundo se halla.
             Y ansí, por tener tu fin,
             quitéme el saco, y las armas                     1950
             tomé, y el cargo me dieron
             de esta forajida escuadra.
             Quise probar tu intención
             por saber si te acordabas
             de Dios en tan fiero trance;                     1955
             pero salióme muy vana.
             Volví a desnudarme aquí,
             como viste, dando al alma
             nuevas tan tristes, pues ya
             la tiene Dios condenada.                         1960
Enrico       Las palabras que Dios dice
             por un ángel son palabras,
             Paulo amigo, en que se encierran
             cosas que el hombre no alcanza.
```

1935. 'the noble Anareto'. It is interesting that Paulo recalls this palpably equivocal detail, and odd that Enrico does not correct it (except that it would be clumsy to have him interrupt again).

1961–2014. Little in Enrico's previous portrayal has prepared us for his positive response now. The real preparation comes from Paulo's extraordinary behaviour; the test of plausibility here is whether his conduct could have affected Enrico in the way which this speech reflects. In these terms, his response, while not predictable, is still convincing – largely because the speech contains so much of the old Enrico.

1961–4. In the Spanish text, the parenthesis, the repetition,

```
              (Oh, the pain
              that message brought me!)
              "...Enrico, noble Anareto's son.              1935
              He is well-known in Naples.
              Watch carefully how he acts;
              take note of all that he says,
              for if he goes to Heaven
              then you will go there too,
              and to Hell if he goes to Hell."
              I thought then that Enrico
              must be some great saint.
              Ah! how our wishes deceive us!
              I went, and I found you at once,
              and learned, from your own mouth
              and from your reputation,
              that you were the worst man in the world.
              And I was to share your end!
              So I laid aside my habits,
              got myself weapons,
              and soon became the leader
              of this band of brigands.
              I sought to know your mind
              -- to know if, in your last straits,
              you remembered God.
              Much good it did me!
              So again, as you saw just now,
              I stripped off my vestments, and gave
              my soul this last sad message:
              God has damned it already.
Enrico        Paulo, my friend, if God                     1961-3
              sent anyone word by an angel,
              wouldn't the words be the kind
              to carry some hidden meaning                  1964
              that men alone couldn't reach?
```

---

and the embedded relative clauses create a potent impression that
Enrico – not one of nature's abstract thinkers – is painstakingly
working out just what it is that he does think.

    1963. 'Paulo, my friend'. Contrast his former contempt:
'Father, or whatever you call yourself' (l. 1808).

    1964. Enrico stumbles across a truth which has evaded Paulo. He
is, even so, only half right: this message was not from God. Yet
if Paulo had taken it less unreflectingly, he would have suffered
less.

```
No dejara yo la vida                              1965
que seguías, pues fue causa
de que quizá te condenes
el atreverte a dejarla.
Desesperación ha sido
lo que has hecho, y aun venganza                  1970
de la palabra de Dios,
y una oposición tirana
a su inefable poder;
y en ver que no desenvaina
la espada de su justicia                          1975
contra el rigor de tu causa,
veo que tu salvación
desea; mas, ¿qué no alcanza
aquella piedad divina,
blasón de que más se alaba?                       1980
Yo soy el hombre más malo
que naturaleza humana
en el mundo ha producido:
el que nunca habló palabra
sin juramento; el que a tantos                    1985
hombres dio muertes tiranas;
el que nunca confesó
sus culpas, aunque son tantas;
el que jamás se acordó
de Dios y su Madre Santa;                         1990
ni aun ahora lo hiciera,
con ver puestas las espadas
a mi valeroso pecho;
mas siempre tengo esperanza
en que tengo de salvarme,                         1995
```

1965-8. 'I wouldn't have left...' Enrico, as we already know
from ll. 1828-9, sets a value on not changing his fixed course.

1969. 'despair' returns the accusation of l. 1857 above.

1970-3. 'a sort of revenge' is close to the truth about Paulo
(cf. above, l. 987). But it also describes an attitude well within
Enrico's compass, as Anareto will later remind him (ll. 2482-91).

1974. PK: el; SR: en.

1974-8. Again the Spanish syntax embodies Enrico's groping
towards a conclusion, repeating forms of ver ('to see'), and
postponing the all-important verb desea ('he wants'). The eventual
assertion of a religious hope is made that much more credible.

1980. P: acaba, not very meaningfully; KR: alaba: 'To what does
that divine mercy not extend - the blazon in which he takes most

```
I wouldn't have left the life                    1965
you were living; after all, that
might be the very reason
which meant that you were damned.
It seems like an act of despair                  1969
to me - a sort of revenge                        1970
for the message you had from God.
It's setting yourself up
against his almighty power.
And seeing he hasn't brought down                1974
the full weight of his justice
to crush you for it, I think
he wants you to be saved.
I think he must - and he can,
for he delights in mercy                         1980
above all things.  Look at me.
Now I'm the worst man on God's earth:
my every second word's                           1984
a blasphemy; I've murdered
more men than I care to remember;
I've never made my confession
- though - Hell! - I've enough to confess.
I've never given a thought
to God or his lady mother;
I wouldn't do it now
with the sword at my throat.                      1992
But I do still have hope                          1994
that I will be saved.
```

---

pride?' **Blasón** invokes the motif of Christ's five wounds, expounded
in the Shepherd's homily above (ll. 1561-5; 1586-8).

1984, 1985, 1978, 1989. Literally 'he who never spoke a word
without swearing... he who... he who... he who...' The repeated
third-person relatives would hardly be credible as spoken English.

1992-3. Literally 'though I see the swords set against my doughty
breast.' The translation opts for a more compact, though still
dramatic phrase.

1994-2000. As a statement of beliefs which Enrico is supposed to
have held throughout his career of plunder, rape, and murder, this
simply does not make sense; it is even contradicted by ll. 1989-90,
just before. The lines are only credible if we envisage Enrico,
confronted by Paulo's strange story, as being forced to think
seriously about these matters for the first time - as having to ask
himself, in an exploratory way, what assumptions enable him to live.
One can believe in some such process of self-discovery, but not in
a piety which has been there all the time.

```
                puesto que no va fundada
                mi esperanza en obras mías
                sino en saber que se humana
                Dios con el más pecador,
                y con su piedad se salva.                    2000
                Pero ya, Paulo, que has hecho
                ese desatino, traza
                de que alegres y contentos
                los dos en esta montaña
                pasemos alegre vida                          2005
                mientras la vida se acaba.
                Un fin ha de ser el nuestro:
                si fuere nuestra desgracia
                el carecer de la gloria
                que Dios al bueno señala,                    2010
                mal de muchos gozo es;
                pero tengo confianza
                en su piedad, que siempre
                vence a su justicia sacra.
Paulo           Consoládome has un poco                      2015
Galván          Cosa es, por Dios, que me espanta.
Paulo           Vamos donde descanséis.
Enrico          [Aparte]  (¡Ay, padre de mis entrañas!)
                Una joya, Paulo amigo,
                en la ciudad olvidada                        2020
                se me queda; y aunque temo
                el rigor que me amenaza
                si allá vuelvo, he de ir por ella,
                pereciendo en la demanda.
```

1996-7. Literally 'Although [or 'since'; <u>puesto que</u> will bear
either meaning] my hope is not based on works of my own'. The
language here seemed too specifically theological to come naturally
to Enrico in modern English.

1998. P etc.: <u>sino saber</u>; HR: <u>sino en saber</u>.

1998. <u>se humana</u> implies 'shows human feeling', 'is humane', but
there is also a link with 'God becoming man' in the Incarnation.
English 'kind' has a long history of etymological aptness in this
context; cf. Davlin, 5-17.

2001-6. By an abrupt transition – as if embarrassed by what he
has found himself saying – Enrico returns to more familiar ground:
the pursuit of pleasure (<u>alegre vida</u>) in this world. On the
implications of his proposal to Paulo see Introduction, p. lxiii.

2011. Literally 'The misfortune of many is a pleasure', i.e.
company in misery makes the trouble more bearable. This is not
much of a consolation for being damned, but Enrico – as he at once
makes clear – cannot believe that he will be damned. The phrase

```
        It's nothing to do with things              1996
        I've done, or haven't done.
        It's just that I know that God
        is kind to the worst of sinners.             1998
        His mercy is what saves us.
        But, Paulo, seeing you've done               2001
        this damn fool thing already,
        cheer up; we'll stick together,
        and have as good a time
        as we can, out here in the wilds.
        We'll make a life of it
        - what life we've got left.
        We're going the same way, it seems.
        If the worst comes to the worst
        and neither makes it to Heaven,
        at least two's company.                       2011
        But I'll still put my trust                   2012
        in God's mercy; it's stronger
        even than his justice.
Paulo   You comfort me a little.
Galván  It's uncanny, all this; that's what it is!
Paulo   Come and rest awhile.
Enrico  [Aside] But what will become of my father?
        Listen, Paulo, my friend:
        when I fled from Naples,
        I left a precious jewel                       2019
        behind me; if I'm caught there
        it's the end, but I must go back and get it,
        if I die in the attempt.
```

---

is, as R notes, proverbial (Correas, 529).

   2012-14. Enrico's attitude has two components. One is the naive conviction, not far removed from his gambler's trust in luck, that God will see him through. The other, more positive factor is his notion of what God is like. Its key term, repeated three times here (ll. 1979, 2000, 2013), is piedad - the reciprocal form of that relationship of loving obligation which he has sought, in typically inadequate fashion, with his own father. Significantly, his thoughts now turn (l. 2018) to Anareto.

   2019-20. 'a precious jewel'. Primarily, this means Anareto. But there are other overtones: the fate of Enrico's soul, and his accesss to the kingdom of Heaven (the 'pearl of great price' of Matthew 13: 46) also depend on his return to Naples.

   2023. PR: si allá muero ('if I die there') makes l. 2024 ('though I perish in the quest') tautologous. SDT: si allá vuelvo yields a more constructive meaning: 'though I fear the severity which threatens me if I go back there, I will go, though I perish...'

	Un soldado de los tuyos	2025
	irá conmigo.	
Paulo	Pues vaya	
	Pedrisco, que es animoso.	
Pedr.	Por Dios, que ya me espantaba	
	que no encontraba conmigo.	
Paulo	Dalde la mejor espada	2030
	a Enrico, y en esas yeguas	
	que al ligero viento igualan	
	os pondréis allá en dos horas.	
Galván	Yo me quedo en la montaña	
	a hacer tu oficio.	
Pedr.	Yo voy	2035
	donde paguen mis espaldas	
	los delitos que tú has hecho.	
Enrico	Adiós, amigo.	
Paulo	Ya basta	
	el nombre para abrazarte.	
Enrico	Aunque malo, confianza	2040
	tengo en Dios.	
Paulo	Yo no la tengo	
	cuando son mis culpas tantas;	
	muy desconfiado soy.	
Enrico	Aquesa desconfianza	
	te tiene de condenar.	2045
Paulo	Ya lo estoy, no importa nada.	
	¡Ah, Enrico, nunca nacieras!	
Enrico	Es verdad; mas la esperanza	
	que tengo en Dios, ha de hacer	
	que haya piedad de mi causa.	2050

[Fin de la segunda jornada.]

2031-3. Literally 'On these mares which equal the swift wind, you will be there in two hours.' For the problems raised by 'two hours' see Introduction, p. lii.

2034-7. More literally 'I'm staying on to do your work... I'm going where my back will pay for the crimes you've committed.' The pun made possible by English 'job' underlines this parodic version of the 'fortunes exchanged' motif.

2038-9. Literally 'The name is already enough [for me] to embrace you.' A verbal cue in lieu of a stage-direction.

2043. muy desconfiado soy. 'I am very mistrustful' - not the description of a mood (as it would be if the verb used were estoy) but a statement of Paulo's inherent character.

	Send one of your men with me.	
Paulo	Pedrisco can go.	
	He's a brave fellow.	
Pedr.	I was scared out of my mind	
	he'd never ask me!	
Paulo	Give Enrico our best sword	
	and two of our fastest horses.	2031
	In a couple of hours's hard riding	
	you can be in Naples.	
Galván	I'll stop here in the woods	2034
	and do your job.	
Pedr.	Where I'm going	
	they'll make me take the rap	
	for all the jobs you've done.	
Enrico	Goodbye, my friend.	
Paulo	Dear friend!	2038
	[They embrace.]	
Enrico	Wicked I may be, but I still	
	have trust in God.	
Paulo	I've none;	
	I have been so great a sinner.	
	I despair of trust in anything.	2043
Enrico	It's that despair will damn you.	2044
Paulo	I am damned already.	
	What does it matter? Oh, Enrico!	
	Better you had never been born!	
Enrico	Better indeed, but my hope in God	2049
	will win his mercy yet!	2050

END OF ACT TWO

2044-50. A neat chiasmus to end the Act: Paulo, first as seen by
Enrico, then as seen by himself; Enrico, first as seen by Paulo,
and then from his own viewpoint.

2049-50. Again, Enrico relies on God's _piedad_, but he naively
assumes that his irrational hope will somehow work upon that
quality to save him. This is not quite how things turn out;
rather, God's pity will work upon Enrico, using the opportunity
afforded by his hope.

2050.   Enrico speaks of _mi causa_, using the word for a legal
'case'. The reference heightens the irony of the scene with which
Act III will open, with Enrico in gaol and his 'case' - in purely
worldly terms - about as unpromising as it could possibly be.

<u>Salen Pedrisco y Enrico en la cárcel, presos</u>.

Pedr.   ¡Buenos estamos los dos!
Enrico   ¿Qué diablos estás llorando?
Pedr.   ¿Qué diablos he de llorar?
            ¿No puedo yo lamentar
            pecados que estoy pagando   2055
              sin culpa?
Enrico   ¿Hay vida como ésta?
Pedr.   ¡Cuerpo de Dios con la vida!
Enrico   ¿Fáltate aquí la comida?
            ¿No tienes la mesa puesta
            a todas horas?
Pedr.   ¿Qué importa   2060
            que la mesa llegue a ver,
            si no hay nada que comer?
Enrico   De necedades acorta.
Pedr.   Alarga tú de comida.
Enrico   ¿No sufrirás como yo?   2065
Pedr.   Que pague aquél que pecó,
            es sentencia conocida;
              pero yo que no pequé,
            ¿por qué tengo de pagar?
Enrico   Pedrisco, ¿quieres callar?   2070
Pedr.   Enrico, yo callaré;
              pero la hambre hará
            que hable el que muerto se vio,
            o que calle aquél que habló
            más que un correo.
Enrico   ¿Que ya   2075
              piensas que no has de salir
            de la cárcel?
Pedr.   Error fue.
            Desde el día que aquí entré,
            he llegado a presumir

2051-2147. Metre: <u>redondillas</u>, with l. 2051 standing in
isolation from the first of these stanzas.
    2051. The temptation to translate <u>¡Buenos estamos los dos!</u> as
'Another fine mess you've gotten us into!' was strong, and perhaps
ought not to have been resisted. The actors of <u>gracioso</u> roles were
the popular comedians of their day.
    2063-4. More literally 'Cut short your follies... You extend our

ACT THREE
Scene One
Naples. A prison cell.
Pedrisco and Enrico are discovered in chains.

Pedr.	Look at the pair of us now!	2051
	I ask you!	
Enrico	What the hell	
	are you snivelling about?	
Pedr.	What the hell does it look like?	
	I'm weeping for all the crimes	
	I'm charged with – specially since	
	I didn't do them.	
Enrico	What's wrong with this for a life?	
Pedr.	Sod this for a life, I say!	
Enrico	Still moaning about your food?	
	Mealtimes are regular here	
	you've got to admit.	
Pedr.	So what?	
	Mealtimes without any meals	
	are a lot of no use.	
Enrico	Let's have	2063
	less griping!	
Pedr.	Let's have more grub!	
Enrico	Can't you put up with it, like me?	
Pedr.	You've done wrong; you pay for it	
	– that's the way it should be.	
	But I've done nothing.	
	Why should I pay for it too?	
Enrico	Oh, shut your mouth, Pedrisco!	
Pedr.	I'll shut it, Enrico, but hunger	2072
	will open it fast enough	
	if I'm too far gone to move	
	– or shut me up for good, of course.	
Enrico	So now you don't believe	
	we'll ever be out of here?	
Pedr.	Oh, I believe it alright!	
	Since we first got into this prison	

---

food-supply.' The pun on <u>acortar</u> / <u>alargar</u> is replaced in
translation by an alliterative echo.
  2072-5. Literally 'But hunger will make a dead man speak, and
will silence one who spoke more than a courier.' <u>Correo</u> was
criminal slang for an informer (Prieto, 212), which may be
Pedrisco's meaning. Couriers were, in any event, the bearers of
news, and may have had the reputation of being indiscreet about
confidential messages (cf. Wardropper (1970), 489).

141

```
                que hemos de salir los dos...                    2080
Enrico     Pues, ¿de qué estamos turbados?
Pedr.      Para ser ajusticiados,
           si no lo remedia Dios.
Enrico        No hayas miedo.
Pedr.                            Bueno está;
           pero teme el corazón                                  2085
           que hemos de danzar sin son.
Enrico     Mejor la suerte lo hará.
                        Salen Celia y Lidora.
Celia         No quisiera que las dos,
           aunque a nadie tengo miedo,
           fuéramos juntas.
Lidora                      Bien puedo,                           2090
           pues soy criada, ir con vos.
Enrico        Quedo, que Celia es aquesta.
Pedr.      ¿Quién?
Enrico             Quien más que a sí me adora,
           mi remedio llega ahora.
Pedr.      Bravamente me molesta                                 2095
              la hambre.
Enrico                    ¿Tienes acaso
           en qué echar todo el dinero
           que ahora de Celia espero?
Pedr.      Con toda la hambre que paso,
              me he acordado, vive Dios,                          2100
           de un talego que aquí tengo.
                        Saca un talego.
Enrico     Pequeño es.
```

2080-3. The point of the original is made by the pause after Pedrisco's 'we'd be leaving together...' Enrico takes him up wrongly on this, but the essential caveat follows: '...to go to our execution, unless God supplies a remedy.' The translation deliberately broadens this effect a little.

2086. danzar sin son – 'dance without music'; that is, on the end of a rope.

2087. As in much of Act II, Enrico's confidence is focussed in a primitive, pre-religious way on luck.

2087-8. Celia and Lidora are perhaps envisaged as entering on the level of the backstage gallery and looking down, as visitors, into the gaol. This would make for some amusing by-play with the bag in which Pedrisco tries to catch the hoped-for money (l. 2119).

2088-91. Literally Celia says that she does not want the two of them to go in together. It may be that she wants to go in alone.

```
                I've known we'd be leaving together...         2080
Enrico          Then what are we worrying for?
Pedr.           I'll tell you what's worrying me:
                if God doesn't think of something quick
                we're both of us for the drop.
Enrico          Don't you believe it!
Pedr.                             Oh yes?
                I can just see the two of us
                dangling out there in the breeze.             2086
Enrico          Our luck will hold; you'll see!               2087
                     Enter Celia and Lidora.
Celia           I'm not frightened of anyone,                 2088
                naturally, but I'd prefer
                not to go in with you, Lidora.
Lidora          As I'm your servant, madam,
                I can always go in with you,
                can't I?
Enrico                   Listen!  That's Celia's voice.
Pedr.           And who's she?
Enrico                         She's a woman
                who loves me more than her soul.
                Help must be on its way.
Pedr.           I hope it is!  I'm hellish hungry!
Enrico          She'll have brought me money;                 2097
                I need somewhere to put it.
                Pedrisco, do we have a bag?
Pedr.           It just so happens                            2099
                - the thought of food put it out of my mind -
                that I've got one somewhere... Here!
                     He pulls out a small sack.
Enrico          It's not very big.
```

But the disclaimer 'although I'm not frightened' (l. 2089) makes it
seem likelier that she wants to send her servant ahead. Lidora's
reply would then be a tart reminder that, unlike Celia, she does
not have a choice.

2093. PKR: más que así ('more than this' - accompanied, R thinks,
by some illustrative gesture); H: más que a sí seems more natural.

2097. That Enrico hopes for money from Celia is consistent with
their old relationship. He no doubt plans to use it to bribe his
way out of prison - something which casts a very Tirsian scepticism
over the panoply of human justice displayed in this Act.

2099-2101. Literally 'Despite all the hunger I'm suffering, I've
remembered... a bag'. The term used can be either masculine or
feminine in form; in modern usage at least, talego would mean
something rather smaller than talega.

```
Pedr.                    A pensar vengo
                que estamos locos los dos:
                tú en pedirle, en darle yo.
Enrico    ¡Celia hermosa de mi vida!                      2105
Celia        [Aparte] ¡Ay de mí! Yo soy perdida.
             Enrico es el que llamó.
                Señor Enrico.
Pedr.                           ¿Señor?
             No es buena tanta crïanza.
Enrico    Ya no tenía esperanza,                          2110
          Celia, de tan gran favor.
Celia        ¿Cómo estás?
Enrico                       Bueno,
          . . . . . . . . . . . . . . . . . . . .
          y ahora mejor, pues ven
          a costa de mil suspiros
             mis ojos los tuyos graves.                   2115
Celia     Yo os quiero dar...
Pedr.                          ¡Linda cosa!
          ¡Oh! ¡Qué mujer tan hermosa!
          ¡Qué palabras tan süaves!
             Alto, prevengo el talego.
          Pienso que no han de caber.                     2120
Enrico    Celia, quisiera saber
          . . . . . . . . . . . . . .
          . . . . . . . . . . . . . .
          qué me das.
Pedr.                     Tu dicha es llana.
Celia     Las nuevas de que mañana
          a ajusticiaros saldrán.
Pedr.        El talego está ya lleno;                     2125
          otro he menester buscar.
Enrico    ¿Que aquesto llegue a escuchar?
          Celia, escucha.
Pedr.                       Aquesto es bueno.
Celia        Ya estoy casada.
Enrico                          ¿Casada?
          ¡Vive Dios!
Pedr.                    Tente.
Enrico                           ¿Qué aguardo?            2130
          ¿Con quién, Celia?
```

  2112.   PR: ¿Cómo estás?... Bueno; KSD: ¿Cómo os va?... Para
serviros / siempre, Celia, me irá bien. P does not rhyme, and

```
Pedr.                              I think we're both
                daft: you for asking,
                and me for giving it you.
Enrico          Celia, my darling!
Celia           [Aside]                 Whatever shall I do?
                He's here - Enrico!  Did you call, sir?
Pedr.           "Sir" - I don't like the sound of that.
                It's too polite by half.
Enrico          Celia, I never looked for
                such kindness as this from you...
Celia           Are you quite well?
Enrico                              Quite well,
                and better now for seeing,
                after such sufferings,
                your true concern for me.
Celia           I bring you...
Pedr.                           Marvellous!
                Wonderful!  What a lovely woman!
                It's a pleasure to listen to her.
                Hold on!  Here's the bag.
                I hope it's big enough.
Enrico          Celia, what have you brought me?
Pedr.           Oh, your luck's in; I know it!                2122
Celia           I bring you news that tomorrow morning
                they'll take you out to be hanged.
Pedr.           That's burst the bag!
                We're going to need another.
Enrico          You can't mean it!  Celia, listen!...
Pedr.           "Listen"!  That's a good one, that is!
Celia           I'm married now, Enrico.
Enrico                                  Married!
                Christ!  I'll...
Pedr.                           Steady!
Enrico                                      Let me alone!
                Who is it, Celia?
```

---

omits a line; the other texts patch the stanza adequately, but the
tone of Enrico's reply ('To serve you, Celia, it will always go well
with me') seems unacceptably wheedling.
    2121-2. The rhyme-scheme (but not the sense) implies two missing
lines here.
    2122. Literally 'Your luck is plain'- perhaps with unconscious
irony on Pedrisco's part, for Enrico's luck is about to fall very
flat indeed.

Celia	Con Lisardo,
	¡y estoy muy bien empleada!
Enrico	Mataréle.
Celia	Dejaos de eso,
	y poneos bien con Dios.

. . . .

Lidora	Vamos, Celia.	
Enrico	Pierdo el seso.	2135
	Celia, mira.	
Celia	Estoy de prisa.	
Pedr.	Por Dios, que estoy por reirme.	
Celia	Ya sé que queréis decirme	
	que se os diga alguna misa.	
	Yo lo haré; quedad con Dios.	2140
Enrico	¡Quién rompiera aquestas rejas!	
Lidora	No escuches, Celia, más quejas;	
	vámonos de aquí las dos.	
Enrico	¡Que esto sufro!	
Pedr.	¿Hay tal crueldad?	
	¡Lo que pesa este talego!	2145
Celia	¡Qué braveza!	
	<u>Vanse</u>.	
Enrico	Yo estoy ciego.	
	¿Hay tan grande libertad?	
Pedr.	Yo no entiendo la moneda	
	que hay en aqueste talego,	
	que, vive Dios, que no pesa	2150
	una paja.	
Enrico	¡Santos cielos!	
	¡Que aquestas afrentas sufra!	

2131. If <u>Lisardo</u> were not confirmed by the rhyme with <u>aguardo</u>, there would be a powerful case for reading <u>Lisandro</u>, the name of Celia's foppish admirer from Act I; see Kennedy (1974: <u>Guastavino</u>), 227n.

2134. 'make your peace with God'. Like the offer of a Mass for Enrico's soul, this advice comes unconvincingly from the worldly Celia. It will be repeated with increasing urgency: by prison guards and officials, by Franciscan friars, by Pedrisco, and with conclusive force by Anareto. Enrico rejects all these appeals but the last. In strict reciprocity, the message ought to become harder to recognize with each rejection, but that is not how Tirso sees grace as working.

2145. Literally 'What a lot this bag weighs!' Whether wryly, as

Celia	It's Lisardo	2131
	and I find it suits me very well.	
Enrico	I'll kill him.	
Celia	Forget all that	
	and make your peace with God.	2134
Lidora	Celia, we must be going.	
Enrico	I shall go mad! Celia, listen...	
Celia	I don't have time.	
Pedr.	It's enough	
	to make you laugh; it really is.	
Celia	I understand; you meant to ask me	
	to have a Mass said for your soul.	
	Of course I will, darling! God bless you!	
Enrico	I'll tear these bars apart!	
Lidora	Don't listen, Celia; we've heard enough.	
	It's time we went now.	
Enrico	Christ!	
	do I have to suffer this?	
Pedr.	How callous can you get?	
	Might as well stuff this bag	2145
	now, I suppose...	
Celia	Isn't he <u>fierce</u>?	2146

Exeunt Celia and Lidora.

Enrico	I am blind with anger!	
	That whore! See how she treats me!	2147
Pedr.	Here, there's something wrong	
	with the money in this bag	
	- it doesn't weigh anything.	
Enrico	Jesus! To think	
	I have to sit here and take it!	2152

---

in Spanish, or punningly, as in the translation, the line has to express Pedrisco's rueful awareness that Enrico's hopes have collapsed.

2146. Celia's final words define both the shallow sensationalism of her present feelings about Enrico and the nature of the glamour that he once held for her.

2147. <u>libertad</u>, besides referring to Celia's cavalier treatment of him, carries overtones of sexual looseness.

2148-2225. Metre: <u>romance</u> assonating in E-O. Cf. the same verse-form used for Enrico at his worst in ll. 722 ff. and 1702 ff.

2152. Enrico's typical reaction when crossed (cf. ll. 1740, 2127) is to grow furious that he, of all people, should have to suffer such things - an attitude rooted in his self-image as someone who gets his way by sheer force of will (ll. 514-5).

	¿Cómo no rompo estos hierros?	
	¿Cómo estas rejas no arranco?	
Pedr.	Detente.	
Enrico	Déjame, necio.	2155
	¡Vive Dios, que he de rompellas	
	y he de castigar mis celos!	
Pedr.	Los porteros vienen.	
Enrico	Vengan.	

<u>Sale un portero</u>.

Port.	¿Ha perdido acaso el seso	
	el homicida ladrón?	2160
Enrico	Moriré si no me vengo.	
	De mi cadena haré espada.	
Pedr.	Que te detengas te ruego.	
Port.	Asilde, matalde, muera.	
Enrico	Hoy veréis, infames presos,	2165
	de los celos el poder	
	en desesperados pechos.	
Port.	Un eslabón me alcanzó	
	y dio conmigo en el suelo.	
Enrico	¿Por qué, cobardes, huís?	2170
Pedr.	Un portero deja muerto.	
(<u>Dentro</u>)	Matalde.	
Enrico	¿Qué es matar?	
	A falta de noble acero	
	no es mala aquesta cadena	
	con que mis agravios vengo.	2175
	¿Para qué de mí huís?	
Pedr.	Al alboroto y estruendo	
	se ha levantado el alcaide.	

<u>Salen el alcaide y gente, y asen a Enrico</u>.

2153-4. R notes the strong alliterative effect: 'the snarl of the caged beast'.

2157. Literally 'punish my jealousy', but what Enrico seeks to punish is the cause of his jealousy, i.e. Celia.

2162. Literally 'I'll make a sword of my chain', that is, 'I will use it as a weapon.' The prisoners would seem to be manacled (perhaps shackled too) but with some limited freedom of movement.

2165. In the original, Enrico addresses these lines to <u>infames presos</u> ('infamous prisoners'), from which H concluded that there must be other prisoners on stage. Neither the stage-directions (such as they are) nor the original cast-list confirm this. But Enrico and Pedrisco are clearly imagined as being held in the

	Why can't I smash these fetters?	2153
	Why can't I rip out these bars?	
Pedr.	Cool down!	
Enrico	Let me be, you fool!	
	By Christ, I <u>will</u> break free	
	and pay her out, the bitch!	2157
Pedr.	The guards are coming.	
Enrico	Let them come!	

Enter First Guard.

1st.G.	That one who's in for murder	
	- has he gone mad or something?	
Enrico	I'll pay her out if it kills me.	
	I'll beat her brains out with this chain!	2162
Pedr.	For God's sake, Enrico, cool down!	
1st.G.	Hold him! Stop him! Dead or alive!	
Enrico	I'll show this whole damned prison	2165
	what jealousy can do	
	when a man's desperate.	
1st.G.	He caught me with the chain...	
	I'm done for.	2169
Enrico	Cowardly bastards!	2170
	Why don't you come and get me?	
Pedr.	He's killed that guard for certain.	
Voices	[<u>Off stage</u>] Get in there and kill him!	
Enrico	Killed?... What's killing?	
	They took away my sword,	
	but this chain's good enough	
	to get even with them. Come on!	
	Come in and get me!	
Pedr.	With all this noise and riot,	
	the prison Governor's come	
	to see what it's about.	

<u>Enter the Prison Governor and Guards, who overpower Enrico.</u>

'common gaol', where others might be present. Celia's visit, for
example, seems to be prompted by curiosity to see whatever
prisoners there are; she certainly does not expect to find Enrico
(above, ll. 2106-7).
    2169. Literally 'and knocked me to the ground'; the line is
virtually a stage-direction.
    2170. <u>cobardes</u>, in a context of 17th-century honour, was a more
demeaning insult than the literal 'cowards', and is so translated.
The line implies that other guards have entered the cell and are
now retreating in the face of Enrico's fury. No stage-direction
confirms this, however.

149

Alc.	¡Hola! Teneos. ¿Qué es esto?	
Port.2	Ha muerto aquese ladrón	2180
	a Fidelio.	
Alc.	Vive el cielo,	
	que a no saber que mañana	
	dando público escarmiento	
	has de morir ahorcado,	
	que hiciera en tu aleve pecho	2185
	mil bocas con esta daga.	
Enrico	¡Que esto sufro, Dios eterno!	
	¿Que mal me traten ansí?	
	Fuego por los ojos vierto.	
	No pienses, alcaide infame,	2190
	que te tengo algún respeto	
	por el oficio que tienes,	
	sino porque más no puedo.	
	Que a poder, ¡ah cielo airado!,	
	entre mis brazos soberbios	2195
	te hiciera dos mil pedazos,	
	y despedazado el cuerpo,	
	me le comiera a bocados,	
	y que no quedara pienso	
	satisfecho de mi agravio.	2200
Alc.	Mañana a las diez veremos	
	si es más valiente un verdugo	
	que todos vuestros aceros.	
	Otra cadena le echad.	
Enrico	Eso sí, vengan más hierros,	2205
	que de hierros no se escapa	
	hombre que tantos ha hecho.	
Alc.	Metelde en un calabozo.	

2180. ladrón, like cobarde, carried a highly specific imputation of dishonour.

2181. The name Fidelio for a prison guard provokes all manner of speculation. There are no other resemblances, though, with Beethoven's libretto, and no credible channel of influence suggests itself.

2185-6. Literally 'I would make a thousand mouths [i.e. openings] in your treacherous breast.'

2187-9. The literal meaning – 'Eternal God, do I suffer this? That they should treat me as badly as this? I pour out fire through my eyes' – matters less here than Enrico's working-up of his feelings to their appalling climax at ll. 2196-8. Cf. also note to l. 2152.

```
Pr.Gov.   Stay where you are!  What happened?
2nd. G.   The bastard killed Fidelio, sir.              2180-1
Pr.Gov.   God!  If I didn't know
          they were hanging you tomorrow
          to make a public example,
          I'd cut your vile heart out                     2185
          here and now, with my own dagger.
Enrico    How dare you?  Christ almighty!                 2187
          How dare you treat me like this?
          My brain will melt with rage!
          Don't think I've any respect                    2190
          for your stinking uniform
          - it's just that I can't get at you.
          Because if I could, do you know what I'd do?
          I'd crush you with my bare hands;
          I'd break you into pieces
          - thousands of pieces - and when I had,
          I'd eat them, raw, one at a time,                2198
          and even then I'd not be satisfied,
          after the things you've done to me.
Pr.Gov.   Tomorrow at ten we shall see
          whether the public hangman
          can face you down.
          Put another chain on him.
Enrico    Another chain! that's right.                    2205
          Weighed down by so many crimes,
          they weigh me down with chains.
Pr.Gov.   Put him in one of the dungeons.                 2208
```

2190-2. Enrico's forceful but still abstract language - 'Do not think, infamous governor, that I have any respect for the office you hold' - demands a more concrete treatment in English.

2198. Literally 'I would eat it up in mouthfuls.' Here, by contrast, the effect is shockingly physical; 'raw' in English does the work of bocados in the original.

2205-7. hierros ('irons' or 'chains') was pronounced identically with yerros ('errors' or 'crimes'). Enrico suggests that he has earned the former by committing so many of the latter. The pun is among the most hackneyed in the 17th-century repertoire, and goes well with Enrico's collapse into weary resignation.

2208. Enrico is to be transferred from the common area of the gaol to an individual cell. In production this might be represented initially by the curtained recess at the back of the stage. But the direction after l. 2225 makes it clear that the dungeon scene itself is not meant to be played in that limited area.

Enrico	Aquese sí es justo premio,	
	que hombre de Dios enemigo,	2210
	no es justo que mire al cielo.	
Pedr.	¡Pobre y desdichado Enrico!	
Port.	Más desdichado es el muerto	
	que el cadenazo cruël	
	le echó en la tierra los sesos.	2215

[Llévanle.]

Pedr.	Ya quieren dar la comida.	
(Dentro)	Vayan llegando, mancebos,	
	por la comida.	
Pedr.	En buen hora,	
	porque mañana sospecho	
	que han de añudarme el tragar,	2220
	y será acertado medio	
	que lleve la alforja hecha	
	para que allá convidemos	
	a los demonios magnates	
	a la entrada del infierno.	2225

Vase, y sale Enrico.

2212-16. The textual problems here concern (a) the point at which the Governor's party, with Enrico and the dead gaoler, leave the cell, and (b) the allocation to speakers of ll. 2212-16.

(a) After l. 2211, P has no stage-direction; K has Llévanle ('They take him out') and then omits ll. 2212-5. Thus the party might, as R thinks, leave before l. 2212. But this would leave no clue as to when the Second Guard, still involved in the dialogue at this point, ought to make his exit. The alternative, preferred here, is to place Llévanle at ll.2215-6.

152

Enrico	Right again, it seems.
	I've been God's enemy;
	why should I ever see the light?
Pedr.	Poor fellow! Poor Enrico! 2212
2nd.G.	Try being sorry for <u>him</u>
	stretched out dead with his brains on the floor.
	Poor Enrico! Murdering bastard!
	[<u>Exeunt Prison Governor, guards and Enrico</u>.]
Pedr.	Must be a mealtime soon...
Voices	[<u>Off stage</u>] Get your plates! Food's coming!
Pedr.	About time too.
	Tomorrow I reckon I might
	find swallowing harder work.
	Still, it's not a bad notion
	to get a good load on board
	for the trip I'm taking.
	If I've any to spare, when we get to Hell
	I can always hand it around
	– it'll give the top devils a treat. 2224-5

Exit Pedrisco.

(b) R follows early editions in giving l. 2212 to the Guard and
ll. 2213-15 to Pedrisco, assigning l. 2216 to the Guard again. Yet
if the Guard has already left – as, on either view of (a), he must
have done – this last line must surely belong to Pedrisco. (This
also removes the oddity of having two official announcements made
of the impending mealtime.) It follows that the allocation of the
two previous speeches also needs to be reversed (as in H).

For the lines of interpretation which these changes make possible
see Introduction, p. xlvi.

2221. PR: <u>miedo</u>; KSDTH: <u>medio</u> ('probably right', says R).

2224. <u>los demonios magnates</u>; that is, the really important
devils.

Enrico	En lóbrega confusión,	
	ya, valiente Enrico, os veis;	
	pero nunca desmayéis;	
	tened fuerte corazón,	
	porque aquesta es la ocasión	2230
	en que tenéis de mostrar	
	el valor que os ha de dar	
	nombre altivo, ilustre fama.	
	Mirad.	
(Dentro)	¿Enrico?	
Enrico	¿Quién llama?	
	Esta voz me hace temblar.	2235
	Los cabellos erizados	
	pronostican mi temor;	
	mas, ¿dónde está mi valor?	
	¿Dónde mis hechos pasados?	
(Dentro)	¿Enrico?	
Enrico	Muchos cuidados	2240
	siente el alma. ¡Cielo santo!	
	¿Cúya es voz que tal espanto	
	infunde en el alma mía?	
(Dentro)	¿Enrico?	
Enrico	A llamar porfía.	
	De mi flaqueza me espanto.	2245
	A esta parte la voz suena	
	que tanto temor me da;	
	¿si es algún preso que está	
	amarrado a la cadena?	
	Vive Dios, que me da pena.	2250
	Sale el Demonio, y no le ve.	

2225-6. Pedrisco shuffles off in his chains; such movement was possible within the common gaol. Cf. the call Vayan llegando, ('Come nearer') at l. 2217. Enrico then enters, more heavily chained (see above, l. 2204). According to the conventions of 17th-century staging, this would signal a change of location to the inner cell or dungeon where Enrico is now confined; cf. for a similar effect, ll. 406-7 and note.

2226-2311. Metre: décimas, with interpolated romance (assonating in O) for the celestial singers at ll. 2285-8 and 2299-2302. McClelland, 60-1, 156-9 comments illuminatingly on the whole of this scene.

2226. The lóbrega confusión (literally 'gloomy confusion') is that of Enrico's mind, as well as of his dark cell. It is important for the scene which follows that comedia performances took place in

Scene two
A dungeon in the same prison.
Enrico enters, alone and in chains.

Enrico	Well, Enrico, for all your courage,
	this is how it ends
	— in darkness, stupidly. But take heart
	be strong, never give up.
	Now's the time to prove
	the stuff you're made of. Now
	you can make yourself a name
	that will last forever.
	Remember that.
Devil	[Within] Enrico?
Enrico	Who was that? I'm suddenly afraid.
	That voice chills my very flesh.
	Where is my courage? Where
	is all the bravery I used to show?
Devil	[Within] Enrico?
Enrico	Again it comes,
	and troubles my soul. Dear God!
	Who has the power to make me
	feel fear like this?
Devil	[Within] Enrico?
Enrico	Calling me still!
	Why am I so unmanned?
	It came from over there...
	Some prisoner, perhaps, in chains?
	My God, I feel sorry for him...

2226

2230

2236

2248

The Devil appears, but Enrico does not see him.

---

daylight. Thus, while Enrico cannot be certain of what he sees, the audience is meant to see everything. On this issue generally see Varey (1977: AmH), 14–16.

2230–3. Enrico's old values of physical courage and worldly reputation, invoked here, will not last him long; by ll. 2238–9 he is asking what has become of them.

2236–7. The literal meaning – 'My hair, standing on end, foretells my fear' – is translated here into an equally conventional, but perhaps less obtrusive symptom.

2248–50. This spontaneous compassion for one who shares his plight recalls Enrico's response to Paulo at the end of Act II. It is still rudimentary, and applied to the Devil it involves dangers which the latter is quick to exploit (ll. 2277–8). Yet it is, as far as it goes, encouraging.

Demon.	Tu desgracia lastimosa	
	. . . .	
	siento.	
Enrico	¡Qué confuso abismo!	
	No me conozco a mí mismo	
	y el corazón no reposa.	
	Las alas está batiendo	2255
	con impulso de temor;	
	Enrico, ¿éste es el valor...?	
	Otra vez se oye el estruendo.	
Demon.	Librarte, Enrico, pretendo.	
Enrico	¿Cómo te puedo creer,	2260
	voz, si no llego a saber	
	quién eres y adónde estás?	
Demon.	Pues agora me verás.	
Enrico	Ya no te quisiera ver.	
Demon.	No temas.	
Enrico	Un sudor frío	2265
	por mis venas se derrama.	
Demon.	Hoy cobrarás nueva fama.	
Enrico	Poco de mis fuerzas fío:	
	no te acerques.	
Demon.	Desvarío	
	es el temer la ocasión.	2270
Enrico	Sosiégate, corazón.	
Demon.	¿Ves aquel postigo?	
Enrico	Sí.	
Demon.	Pues salte por él, y ansí	
	no estarás en la prisión.	
Enrico	¿Quién eres?	
Demon.	Salte al momento	2275
	y no preguntes quién soy,	
	que yo también preso estoy,	
	y que te libres intento.	

2258. 'thunders' – perhaps a clue to how the Devil's voice should sound. That in turn would give the audience a hint not to trust what the voice says. But it is no more than a hint – like the fact that, at l. 2272, the spectators can see no door in the wall. Neither Enrico nor the audience has any definitive guidance as to which of his prompters is diabolical and which divine; see Introduction, p. lxiv-lxv.

2263-4. P: no stage-direction; KSDR: <u>Descúbrese</u>, which need only mean that he throws back his cloak. Yet perhaps he should not do even that. Enrico, after all, refers to him throughout as 'the shadow', which suggests that he never gets a clear view of his

Devil	Unhappy Enrico!
	Your plight is wretched indeed.
Enrico	I feel utterly lost!
	I hardly know myself.
	My heart beats and beats in fear.
	Where is your courage, Enrico?
	Now the voice thunders again... 2258
Devil	Enrico,
	I come to set you free.
Enrico	How can I believe that?
	I don't know who you are
	or where you are.
Devil	In a little while 2263
	you shall see me.
Enrico	I'm not sure that I want to.
Devil	Don't be afraid.
Enrico	A cold sweat
	creeps through my veins.
Devil	Today you can make your name 2267
	famous.
Enrico	I hardly trust
	my own strength. Keep your distance!
Devil	How foolish you are to fear
	luck when it comes your way! 2271
Enrico	I'll keep as calm as I can.
Devil	You see that door in the wall?
Enrico	Why, yes.
Devil	One step outside,
	one bold step, and you're free.
Enrico	Who are you?
Devil	Make your move now,
	and never ask who I am.
	I am a prisoner too, 2277
	and I want you to have your freedom.

---

visitor. The translation leaves this possibility open, and
enhances the Devil's ambiguity by insinuating a perverse echo of
John 16: 16.

2267, 2271, 2277. 'make your name' recalls Enrico's own
aspiration in l. 2233; 'luck' addresses itself to his gambler's
instinct; 'I am a prisoner too' appeals to the fellow-feeling which
he displays in ll. 2248-50. The Devil works with elements that are
already there in Enrico's personality, turning to account even his
victim's spiritual growing-points.

2277-8. The Devil equivocates: he is indeed a prisoner (being
damned), but does not, in any true sense, desire Enrico's liberty.
Cf. also Introduction, p. lv.

Enrico	¿Qué me dices, pensamiento?	
	¿Libraréme? Claro está.	2280
	Aliento el temor me da	
	de la muerte que me aguarda.	
	Voime. Mas ¿quién me acobarda?	
	Mas otra voz suena ya.	

Cantan dentro.

Músicos	Detén el paso violento:	2285
	mira que te está mejor	
	que de la prisión librarte	
	el estarte en la prisión.	
Enrico	Al revés me ha aconsejado	
	la voz que en el aire he oído,	2290
	pues mi paso ha detenido,	
	si tú le has acelerado.	
	Que me está bien he escuchado	
	el estar en la prisión.	
Demon.	Esa, Enrico, es ilusión	2295
	que te representa el miedo.	
Enrico	Yo he de morir si quedo:	
	quiérome ir; tienes razón.	
Músicos	Detente, engañado Enrico;	
	no huyas de la prisión,	2300
	pues morirás si salieres,	
	y si te estuvieres, no.	
Enrico	Que si salgo he de morir,	
	y si quedo viviré,	
	dice la voz que escuché.	2305
Demon.	¿Que al fin no te quieres ir?	
	. . . .	
Enrico	Quedarme es mucho mejor.	
Demon.	Atribúyelo a temor;	
	pero, pues tan ciego estás,	

2281-2. Enrico's reactions are confused, but not self-deceiving; he recognizes his desire to escape as having more to do with fear than with valour, but regards his hesitation too as a piece of cowardice.

2285. The song is attributed to Músicos, but Enrico speaks consistently of a single 'voice'. No doubt it had an instrumental accompaniment.

2285-8. More literally 'Stay your rash steps; consider that it is better for you, rather than escaping from prison, to remain in prison.' The stanza is devoid of lyricism (and is possibly meant to be so), but the metre and assonance are precisely those of the

158

Enrico	What should I make of it all?	
	Should I escape? Of course	
	I must escape, for fear	2281
	of the death that's in store for me.	
	I will go. And yet I dare not.	
	And now there's another voice...	
	A song within.	
Singers	Better to bear captivity	2285
	in patience here than rashly flee.	
Enrico	The voice in the air gave me	
	a different message.	
	It told me to stay here,	
	while you urge me to go.	
	The voice said it was better so.	
Devil	Such voices are illusory,	
	Enrico. They are bred of fear.	
Enrico	And yet, if I stay here, I die.	
	What you say is true; I must escape.	
Singers	Rather than die a fugitive	2299
	endure these bonds, and you shall live.	
	Better to bear captivity	
	in patience here than rashly flee.	
Enrico	I shall be killed if I escape,	
	but if I stay I shall live.	
	So the voice told me.	
Devil	Then you won't go after all?	
Enrico	It's better for me to stay here.	
Devil	I'd put that down to lack of courage.	2308
	But since you are such a fool,	

Shepherd's song in Act II. I have been unable to preserve this
effect in translation; perhaps a producer might contrive some
resemblance in the music.

2295. PKS: _Enrique_; DR: _Enrico_.

2299–2302. The literal sense is 'Stop, deceived Enrico; do not
flee from prison, for you will die if you go out, and not if you
stay where you are.' The lines refer to Enrico's spiritual life or
death, but he fails to understand this. He heeds the voice because
it promises him life, and his sense of betrayal when the
death-sentence is read to him is total (below, ll. 2368–74).

2308. _temor_ ('fear'). The Devil is once again appealing to
Enrico's notion of his own bravery. But Enrico has already realized
(ll. 2236–8, 2257, 2281–2) how inadequate a support this is.

	quédate preso y verás	2310
	cómo te ha estado peor.	
	Vase.	
Enrico	Desapareció la sombra,	
	y confuso me dejó.	
	¿No es éste el portillo? No.	
	Este prodigio me asombra.	2315
	¿Estaba ciego yo, o vi	
	en la pared un portillo?	
	Pero yo me maravillo	
	del gran temor que hay en mí.	
	¿No puedo salirme yo?	2320
	Sí: bien me puedo salir.	
	Pues, ¿cómo? ¿Que he de morir?	
	La voz me atemorizó.	
	Algún gran daño se infiere	
	de lo turbado que estoy.	2325
	No importa: ya estoy aquí	
	para el mal que me viniere.	
	Sale el alcaide con la sentencia.	
Alc.	Yo solo tengo de entrar;	
	los demás pueden quedarse.	
	Enrico.	
Enrico	¿Qué mandáis?	2330
Alc.	En los rigurosos trances	
	se echa de ver el valor:	
	ahora podréis mostrarle.	
	Estad atento.	
Enrico	Decid.	
Alc.	[Aparte] Aun no ha mudado el semblante.	2335
	En el pleito que es entre partes, de la una el	

2312-27. Metre: redondillas. The metrical separateness of this short speech throws it into relief as a summing-up of Enrico's experiences so far; the inherent balance of the redondilla form underwrites his continuing uncertainties.

2323. 'The voice made me afraid.' Does Enrico mean the Devil's voice, which certainly perturbed him (ll. 2242-3), or the other voice, which warned him that escape would mean death (ll. 2301-2)? He may not even know the answer himself; this is very much the speech of a man in two minds.

2328-2446. Metre: romance assonating in A-E, with prose for the death-sentence at ll. 2336-50.

2328-9. The guards' reluctance to enter Enrico's cell - readily understandable after what he has done to their colleague - enables

```
                  stay here in your chains... You'll soon see
                  how little good it does you.
                              Exit the Devil.                        2312
Enrico       The shadow has gone,
                  and left me in confusion.
                  Wasn't there a door, there in the wall?
                  No, nothing... I don't understand.
                  Was I blind, or did I really see
                  a door just there?  What is there in that
                  to make me so frightened?
                  Couldn't I still escape?
                  Of course I could!  And yet,
                  if it means that I have to die...
                  The voice made me afraid.                          2323
                  This turmoil of feelings
                  promises me no good, I fear.
                  Still, here I am, and I'll bear
                  the worst that's coming to me.
       Enter the Prison Governor with the sentence of death.
Pr.Gov.      I'll go in alone.                                       2328
                  The rest can stay outside.
                  Enrico...
Enrico                     What is it now?
Pr.Gov.      There are some occasions                               2331
                  that are true tests of a man's courage.
                  This is one of them.
                  Listen to me.
Enrico                     Go on.
Pr.Gov.      [Aside] He doesn't turn a hair!                        2335
                  [He reads].    "In the case of His Majesty's       2336
```

Tirso to present a fine, taut scene of man-to-man defiance between
Enrico and the Governor.
    2331-3. Disconcertingly, the Governor addresses himself first to
Enrico's sense of his own valour and reputation. This recalls the
latter's unsuccessful attempts to steel himself (ll. 2230-3), and
even some aspects (ll. 2267, 2308) of the Devil's strategy of
temptation. This failure of human justice to transcend worldly
limitations is typical of Tirso's moral vision; compare the
inadequacy of royal justice in El burlador de Sevilla to cope with
Don Juan.
    2335. Literally 'He has not altered his countenance.'
    2336-50. Various liberties (some of them noted below) have been
taken with this passage to reproduce in English its authentic air
of legal documentation.

promotor fiscal de su Majestad,   ausente,   y   de
la otra,   reo acusado,   Enrico,   por los delitos
que tiene en el proceso,   por ser matador,   faci-
noroso,   incorregible y otras cosas.   Vista,   etc.,
fallamos,   que le debemos de condenar,   y conden-
amos,   a que sea sacado de la cárcel donde está,
con soga a la garganta   y pregoneros delante que
digan su delito,   y sea llevado a la plaza pública,   donde estará una horca   de tres palos   alta
del suelo,   en la cual sea ahorcado naturalmente;
y ninguna persona   sea osada   a quitalle de ella
sin nuestra licencia y mandado.

    Y por esta sentencia definitiva juzgando,   ansí
lo pronunciamos y mandamos,   etc.   2350

Enrico	¿Que aquesto escuchando estoy?
Alc.	¿Qué dices?

Enrico   Mira, ignorante,
que eres opuesto muy flaco
a mis brazos arrogantes;
que si no, yo te hiciera...   2355

Alc.   Nada puede remediarse
con arrogancias, Enrico;
lo que aquí es más importante
es poneros bien con Dios.

Enrico ¿Y vienes a predicarme,   2360
con leerme la sentencia?
Vive Dios, canalla infame,
que he de dar fin con vosotros.

Alc.   El demonio que te aguarde.

                   <u>Vase</u>.

2337. <u>promotor fiscal... ausente</u>. The king's chief prosecuting
official might well have been absent from Naples, one of the
Spanish Crown's more peripheral possessions.

2339-40. <u>facinoroso</u> - 'a habitual criminal', or more specifically
'a highway robber'. It seemed aptest here to refer to Enrico's
actual crimes in slightly more detail.

2340. <u>incorregible</u>. Being 'incorrigible' is not in itself an
offence in English (or Scots) law, but the implication that Enrico
is beyond hope in terms of the law is thematically important.
'Offences... too numerous to be mentioned' conveys something of
this.

2345-6. <u>una horca de tres palos alta del suelo</u>. The <u>tres palos</u>
might be the three pieces of timber used to construct the gallows,
but it would be odd for the sentence to specify this. Taken with
<u>alta del suelo</u> ('high above the ground'), the phrase seems likelier

	Procurator Fiscal in this his kingdom of	2337
	Naples, against the accused, Enrico, duly	
	indicted and found guilty of divers crimes	
	of murder, armed robbery, assault and sundry	
	other charges too numerous to mention, etc.	2339

Our sentence is that he be condemned to 2340
death, and we hereby condemn him to be taken
from his place of imprisonment with the rope
about his neck, and the public criers going
before him to proclaim his crimes, and to be
brought in this manner to the principal
square of this city of Naples, where there
shall be erected a gallows, raised very high 2345
above the ground, and thereon to be hanged
by the neck until he be dead. And let none
dare remove his body therefrom without our
express licence and command. Given under our 2349
hand and seal, this day, etc., etc.

Enrico   You dare to tell me that!
Pr.Gov.   What do you mean — "dare"?
Enrico   Don't play the fool with me!
          If you were a man worth fighting,
          and not the thing you are,
          I'd...
Pr.Gov.   Bluster won't help you now,
          Enrico. All that matters
          is to make your peace with God.
Enrico   Christ! Are you going to preach at me
          after reading that thing?
          You creeping bastard, I'll kill you!
          So help me, I will!
Pr.Gov.   Very well then;
          I leave you — to the Devil.
                    Exit Prison Governor.

---

to be a measurement, but I am unable to find any such meaning for
palo.
    2349-50. A more familiar concluding formula in English here
replaces the literal 'And delivering judgment by this definitive
sentence, we pronounce and order it thus'. A hint of sentencia
definitiva is preserved by introducing 'found guilty' into the
preamble above.
    2360. P: pedricarme, but the hint of rusticity which this
spelling involves would be quite out of character here.
    2363. P: he dar; KSDR: he de dar.

Enrico	Ya estoy sentenciado a muerte;	2365
	ya mi vida miserable	
	tiene de plazo dos horas.	
	Voz que mi daño causaste,	
	¿no dijiste que mi vida,	
	si me quedaba en la cárcel,	2370
	sería cierta? ¡Triste suerte!	
	Con razón debo culparte,	
	pues en esta cárcel muero	
	cuando pudiera librarme.	

<u>Sale un portero</u>.

Port.	Dos padres de San Francisco	2375
	están para confesarte	
	aguardando afuera.	
Enrico	¡Bueno!	
	¡Por Dios, que es gentil donaire!	
	Digan que se vuelvan luego	
	a su convento los frailes,	2380
	si no es que quieran saber	
	a lo que estos hierros saben.	
Port.	Advierte que has de morir.	
Enrico	Moriré sin confesarme,	
	que no ha de pagar ninguno	2385
	las penas que yo pasare.	
Port.	¿Qué más hiciera un gentil?	
Enrico	Esto que he dicho baste;	
	que, por Dios, si me amohino,	
	que ha de llevar las señales	2390
	de la cadena en el cuerpo.	
Port.	No aguardo más.	

<u>Vase</u>.

2365-74. Throughout these scenes, Enrico is defiantly aggressive when approached by others, but lapses into depressive meditation when left to himself. Such abrupt contrasts of mood come naturally to him; cf. above, ll. 1285-1313; 1740-3; 2187-2211. Nor do his musings bring him any closer to repentance; if anything, they tend the other way. But his 'worked up' criminal personality is all the time being separated out from his confused and vulnerable inner self. This break-up of a once assured identity will give Anareto's appeal its fullest impact. For Tirso this would have illustrated how grace turns even human imperfections to its own good purpose. It also reflects a sound psychological understanding on his own part.

2372-4. The first of three erroneous conclusions: that the voice

Enrico	Condemned to death...	2365
	that leaves me... let's say two hours	
	– all I have left to live.	
	Oh, voice, voice, why did I listen to you?	
	Didn't you tell me my life	
	would be safe if I stayed in prison?	
	Well, you've certainly something to answer for:	2372
	here I am, dying in prison,	
	when I might have escaped.	

Enter a Guard.

Guard	There's two Franciscan friars	2375
	waiting outside to confess you.	
Enrico	They must be joking! Look:	
	you tell them to go back	
	where they came from. This cell	
	might not be healthy for them.	
	I can still use my chains.	2381
Guard	But you're going to your death.	
Enrico	So I'll die without confession.	
	I'll face my punishment	2385
	without help from anyone.	
Guard	You talk like a heathen.	
Enrico	I've told you; now take notice.	
	If you get me on the raw,	
	by God, I'll beat it into you!	
	Remember the chain!	
Guard	I'm off!	

Exit Guard.

---

which he has just heeded has deceived him.

2375. The series of Franciscan references in El condenado (cf.
above, ll. 644-53, 1581-8) is not easily accounted for. The
Franciscans seem to have played no major part in the controversy
over grace and freewill. But it is perhaps relevant that in that
debate the harshest positions – those, that is, most opposed to the
general tendency of Tirso's play – were defended by their age-old
rivals of the Dominican Order.

2381-2. More literally 'if they do not want to experience a
taste of these chains'. A pun on the two senses of saber: 'to
taste of' and 'to know'.

2385-6. Less reflective by nature than Paulo, Enrico can be more
reliable in his view of his own motives. This demand to be
unchallenged as the central figure in his own story accords with
much of his other conduct, and is singled out for reproof by
Anareto (below, ll. 2480-1).

Enrico	Muy bien hace.

Enrico
        Muy bien hace.
¿Qué cuenta daré yo a Dios
de mi vida, ya que el trance
último llega de mí?   2395
¿Yo tengo de confesarme?
Parece que es necedad:
¿Quién podrá ahora acordarse
de tantos pecados viejos?
¿Qué memoria habrá que baste   2400
a recorrer las ofensas
que a Dios he hecho? Más vale
no tratar de aquestas cosas.
Dios es piadoso y es grande;
su misericordia alabo;   2405
con ella podré salvarme.

                    Sale Pedrisco.

Pedr.
Advierte que has de morir
y que ya aquestos dos padres
están de aguardar cansados.

Enrico
¿Pues he dicho yo que aguarden?   2410

Pedr.
¿No crees en Dios?

Enrico
               Juro a Cristo
que pienso que he de enojarme,
y que en los padres y en ti
he de vengar mis pesares.
Demonios, ¿qué me queréis?   2415

Pedr.
Antes pienso que son ángeles
los que esto a decirte vienen.

Enrico
No acabes de amohinarme,
que, por Dios, que de una coz
te eche fuera de la cárcel.   2420

Pedr.
Yo te agradezco el cuidado.

Enrico
Vete fuera y no me canses.

Pedr.
Tú te vas, Enrico mío,
al infierno como un padre.

                     Vase.

2395. PR: último llega de mí; K: último llegado ha; SD: último ha llegado ya. The later editions rather gratuitously tidy up Enrico's painful clumsiness of expression.

2405-6. Literally 'I praise his pity; with it, I shall be able to be saved.' Here is Enrico's second error: his turning away from repentance. He has barely advanced from the instinctual optimism of ll. 1994-2000, and the time for that attitude is rapidly running out.

2415-6. When Enrico distinguished correctly between the

Enrico	Best thing you can do – run away!
	But what shall I do, now the end
	is so near. What account shall I give
	to God? Should I confess?
	No, that would be stupid.
	I couldn't remember half the sins
	I've committed, the things I've done
	against the laws of God. Better forget it.
	Why bother with things like that?
	God is merciful and great.
	In his vast charity	2405
	I can still be saved.

Enter Pedrisco.

Pedr.	You're going to your death
	any moment, Enrico, and those two friars
	won't wait forever.
Enrico	Did I ask them to wait?
Pedr.	Don't you believe in God?
Enrico	I warn you – don't try my patience
	too far. I swear to Christ
	if you do, you'll suffer for it
	– you and those two damned friars.
	Devils, all of you! What do you want with me? 2415
Pedr.	Angels, I'd call them.
	Think of the message they bring.
Enrico	Oh go to Hell and leave me alone,
	or I'll kick your backside so hard
	you'll go straight out through the wall.
Pedr.	Thanks very much; don't mind if I do!
Enrico	Go away, Pedrisco; you bore me.	2422
Pedr.	Enrico, old friend, you're taking
	the royal road to Hell.	2424

Exit Pedrisco.

---

promptings of good and evil, it was 'without understanding how'
(McClelland, 158). He has now lapsed into a confusion of values in
which the two terms are inverted.

2422.   Perhaps because of Pedrisco's genuinely funny reply,
Enrico is milder in dismissing him than in driving out other
visitors.   This is a well-imagined touch of characterization,
rather than a sign of readiness to repent.

2424.   como un padre. Literally 'like a father' (or 'a
patriarch', or perhaps 'a priest'). Besides these more obvious
meanings, un padre could be a brothel-keeper; see Reynolds (1975),
505-8. One suspects, though, that Tirso's audiences would have had
little difficulty with the notion of someone 'going to Hell like
one of the clergy' – that is, by a privileged route.

Enrico	Voz, que por mi mal te oí	2425
	en esa región del aire,	
	¿fuiste de algún enemigo	
	que así pretendió vengarse?	
	¿No dijiste que a mi vida	
	la importaba de la cárcel	2430
	no hacer ausencia? Pues di,	
	¿cómo quieren ya sacarme	
	a ajusticiar? Falsa fuiste;	
	pero yo también cobarde,	
	pues que me pude salir	2435
	y no dar venganza a nadie.	
	Sombra triste, que piadosa	
	la verdad me aconsejaste,	
	vuelve otra vez, y verás	
	cómo con pecho arrogante	2440
	salgo a tu tremenda voz	
	de tantas oscuridades.	
	Gente suena; ya sin duda	
	se acerca mi fin.	

<u>Salen el padre de Enrico y un portero.</u>

Port.	Hablalde:	
	podrá ser que vuestras canas	2445
	muevan tan duro diamante.	
Anareto	Enrico, querido hijo,	
	puesto que en verte me aflijo	
	de tantos hierros cargado,	
	ver que pagues tu pecado	2450
	me da sumo regocijo.	
	¡Venturoso del que acá	
	pagando sus culpas va	
	con firme arrepentimiento;	
	que es pintado este tormento	2455

2425–42. The inversion of values is complete: the voice is identified as an 'enemy' (l. 2427), the traditional term for the Devil; the shadow is linked with 'pity', a central notion in any apprehension Enrico has of God (l. 2437, and cf. above, ll. 1979, 2000, 2013). Intellectually, Enrico could not be more wrong than he is at this moment.

2437–42. Enrico's last and most dangerous error. Though his instinct still identifies the shadow as 'sad' and its voice as 'terrible', he invokes the Devil, and promises to obey him. The offer of salvation arising from Anareto's entrance owes as little to Enrico's immediate intentions, or to his intellectual convictions

Enrico	Voice in the air, why did I listen to you?	2425
	Were you some enemy	
	taking his revenge?	

Enrico   Voice in the air, why did I listen to you?   2425
        Were you some enemy
        taking his revenge?
        You told me, if I valued my life,
        to stay here in prison. Yet now
        they're taking me out to be hanged.
        You were a liar, but I was a coward.
        I could have made my escape
        and outwitted them all.
        And you, you strange, sad shadow   2437
        who took pity on me
        and told me the truth, come back,
        and see how eagerly,
        urged on by your terrible voice,
        I rush to escape from this darkness.
        But now more people are coming.
        This must be the end.

                <u>Enter a Guard, with Anareto.</u>

Guard   Speak with him.
        It may be your white hairs
        will move even his hard heart.   2446

Anareto Enrico, dear son,
        it grieves me to find you
        in such a place, in chains,
        and yet I can rejoice
        to know that you are paying
        the price of your sins.
        Happy the man who can pay
        in this world for his wickedness,
        and show true penitence
        – for this world's torments are as nothing   2455

(cf. the previous note) as it does to his works. On all these counts he is as undeserving as Paulo. For related theological issues see Introduction, p. xli.

2446. Literally 'so hard a diamond'. This metaphor for Enrico's heart spans the notions of hardness and great worth. It makes sense to assume that the Guard withdraws at this point, leaving father and son alone for their scene together; see ll. 2480-1, below.

2447–2531. Metre: <u>quintillas</u>.

2455–6. Modern audiences may find it chilling that Anareto is happy to see his son suffer now to avoid Hell hereafter. Yet this must also be taken with what follows in the next few lines: Anareto's willingness to suffer pain himself for his son's sake.

	si se compara al de allá!	
	La cama, Enrico, dejé,	
	y arrimado a este bordón	
	por quien me sustento en pie,	
	vengo en aquesta ocasión.	2460
Enrico	¡Ay, padre!	
Anareto	No sé,	
	Enrico, si aquese nombre	
	será razón que me cuadre	
	aunque mi rigor te asombre.	
Enrico	Eso, ¿es palabra de padre?	2465
Anareto	No es bien que padre me nombre	
	un hijo que no cree en Dios.	
Enrico	Padre mío, ¿eso decís?	
Anareto	No sois ya mi hijo vos,	
	pues que mi ley no seguís;	2470
	solos estamos los dos.	
Enrico	No os entiendo.	
Anareto	Enrico, Enrico,	
	a reprehenderos me aplico	
	vuestro loco pensamiento,	
	siendo la muerte instrumento	2475
	que tan cierto os pronostico.	
	Hoy os han de ajusticiar,	
	y no os queréis confesar.	
	¡Buena cristiandad, por Dios!	
	pues el mal es para vos,	2480
	y para vos el pesar.	
	Aqueso es tomar venganza	
	de Dios; el poder alcanza	
	del empíreo cielo eterno.	

2465. Question-mark omitted in P; there in K etc., R.

2466-7. The resonance of these lines is deepened by Anareto's dual identity as a loving human parent and a type of God the Father. Enrico's failure of 'belief' is a ground for human reproach, but it is also seen as cutting him off from God's fatherhood.

2470. ley has two meanings: 'law' and 'religion'. Both are active here. Enrico has infringed both the law of God and the human Anareto's moral code; his rejection of religion cuts him off from fellowship with his earthly parent, and from reconciliation with God. Tirso perhaps had in mind the words of the Prodigal Son: 'Father, I have sinned against Heaven and in thy sight, and am no more worthy to be called thy son' (Luke 15: 21).

	compared with those of Hell.	
	I left my bed, Enrico,	
	and leaning on this pilgrim's staff,	
	made my way here for this	
	— to see you.	
Enrico	Oh father, father!	
Anareto	Should you give me that name, I wonder?	
	(Do you think that I speak harshly?)	
Enrico	Can a father say that to his son?	
Anareto	No son should call me "father"	2466
	who does not believe in God.	
Enrico	Father, how can you say that?	
Anareto	You are no longer my son	
	if you do not keep my law.	2470
	The two of us are alone.	2471
Enrico	I do not understand you.	
Anareto	Oh Enrico!	
	I must reproach you now	
	for your wild thoughts,	
	with death so near you	2475
	and so certain to come.	
	This very day they are to hang you,	
	and still you refuse confession!	
	A fine kind of Christianity!	
	All the evil must fall on you!	2480
	The sorrow must all be yours!	
	You're taking revenge on God	2482
	attacking his heavenly power.	

2471. This line will bear a double sense: that father and son
are radically estranged by Enrico's obduracy, or that they now
stand face to face, confronting one another more directly than ever
before.

2475. Literally 'death being the instrument' (sc. 'of my
rebuke').

2480-1. These lines could mean that Enrico will come off worst
as a result of his defiance (broadly the sense of ll. 2487-96
below), or that he is at fault in trying to take upon himself the
full weight of his own sins (cf. above, ll. 2385-6). There is some
support for the latter in l. 2479: 'A fine kind of Christianity!'

2482-3; 2487-8. 'taking revenge on God'. This is what Paulo has
sought to do (l. 987); cf. Enrico's reproach to him (ll. 1970-3).

```
              Enrico, ved que hay infierno          2485
              para tan larga esperanza.
                 Es el quererte vengar
              de esa suerte, pelear
              con un monte o una roca,
              pues cuando el brazo le toca          2490
              es para el brazo el pesar.
                 Es con dañoso desvelo,
              presumiendo darle enojos,
              escupir el hombre al cielo,
              pues que le cae en los ojos            2495
              lo mismo que arroja al cielo.
                 Hoy has de morir: advierte
              que ya está echada la suerte;
              confiesa a Dios tus pecados,
              y ansí, siendo perdonados,             2500
              será vida lo que es muerte.
                 Si quieres mi hijo ser,
              lo que te digo has de hacer;
              si no (de pesar me aflijo),
              ni te has de llamar mi hijo           2505
              ni yo te he de conocer.
Enrico           Bueno está, padre querido,
              que más el alma ha sentido,
              (buen testigo de ello es Dios),
              el pesar que tenéis vos,               2510
              que el mal que espero afligido.
                 Confieso, padre, que erré;
              pero yo confesaré
              mis pecados, y después
              besaré a todos los pies                2515
              para mostraros mi fe.
```

2485-6. Literally 'there is a Hell for so long deferred a hope'.
Here it is the difference between the two protagonists which is to
the fore.   Enrico is persistently hopeful, but hope without
repentance assumes the other meaning of esperanza, i.e. 'waiting'.
(For the parallel with Don Juan see Introduction, p.   lxiii .)
Enrico cannot keep his spiritual options open forever.   But Paulo's
theologically and etymologically opposite des-esperación (l. 1969)
would foreclose them from the outset.   Cf. the passage from Blosius
quoted by Maurel (1971), 520-1.

2494.   P (the only text to supply ll. 2477-96) omits this line; H
reconstructs.   The meaning required - 'for a man to spit at Heaven'
- is clear enough.

2498.   Literally 'the die is cast', but the translation, avoiding
the homophony with 'you must die', loses the oblique reference to

```
              Do understand, Enrico,
              if you put this off too long                    2485
              you are courting damnation.
              Trying to take revenge                          2487
              like that is senseless.
              You might as well attack
              a mountain or a rock
              with your bare fists
              – it won't be the rock that gets hurt.
              It's as if a man, inspired
              by malice against Heaven,
              craned his neck upwards
              to spit in its face
              – it falls back in his eyes.
              Today you must die; there's no argument;
              that's all over; you have to accept it.          2498
              Confess your sins to God
              and God will pardon them,
              and your death will be your life.
              If you want to be my son
              you must do what I tell you.
              If not (though the words choke me),              2504
              you cannot be called my son,
              and I cast you off from henceforth.
Enrico        Dear father, do not be troubled.                 2507
              My soul has been more touched
              (as God is my witness)
              by the sorrows you feel
              than by all my fears
              of the death which awaits me.
              Father, I acknowledge that I have done wrong,
              but I shall confess my sins
              and I shall humble myself                        2515
              before you and others
              in proof of my faith.
```

Enrico's trust in luck.
  2504-6. Literally 'If not (I am afflicted with sorrow), you shall neither be called my son, nor shall I know you.'
  2507-11. Taken in its dramatic context, Enrico's penitence ought not to appear as an arbitrary volte face, or as a merely formal surrender to his father's authority. It is, first and foremost, a reaction to his father's grief – that is, to Anareto's love.
  2515. Literally 'I shall kiss the feet of everyone' – the traditional gesture of submission, which Enrico offers not only to Anareto, but to all those he has wronged.

	Basta que vos lo mandéis,	
	padre mío de mis ojos.	
Anareto	Pues ya mi hijo seréis.	
Enrico	No os quisiera dar enojos.	2520
Anareto	Vamos porque os conféseis.	
Enrico	¡Oh, cuánto siento el dejaros!	
Anareto	¡Oh, cuánto siento el perderos!	
Enrico	¡Ay, ojos! Espejos claros,	
	antes hermosos luceros,	2525
	pero ya de luz avaros.	
Anareto	Vamos, hijo.	
Enrico	A morir voy;	
	todo el valor he perdido.	
Anareto	Sin juicio y sin alma estoy.	
Enrico	Aguardad, padre querido.	2530
Anareto	¡Qué desdichado que soy!	
Enrico	Señor piadoso y eterno,	
	que en vuestro alcázar pisáis	
	cándidos montes de estrellas,	
	mi petición escuchad.	2535
	Yo he sido el hombre más malo	
	que la luz llegó a alcanzar	
	de este mundo, el que os ha hecho	
	más que arenas tiene el mar	
	ofensas, mas, Señor mío,	2540
	mayor es vuestra piedad.	
	Vos, por redimir el mundo	
	por el pecado de Adán,	
	en una cruz os pusisteis:	
	pues merezca yo alcanzar	2545
	una gota solamente	
	de aquella sangre rëal.	
	Vos, Aurora de los cielos,	
	vos, Virgen bella, que estáis	

2524-6. Simplified in translation from 'Clear mirrors, formerly
beautiful morning-stars, but now niggardly of light.' Either
Enrico's eyes – which, having learned to reflect the truth, will
soon be deprived of light – or Anareto's eyes, now dimmed by sorrow
as well as by old age. The earlier link between Anareto and images
of light (ll. 1102-12) supports the latter reading, but here all the
poetic resonances of this highly-charged language are surely in
play.
2528. Enrico's courage – the ground of his self-projection, and
even of that secular honour which the Prison Governor commended to

174

	It is enough, dear father,	
	that you command it.	
Anareto	Then you are once again my son.	
Enrico	I would not grieve you for the world.	
Anareto	Come with me, and make your confession.	
Enrico	It breaks my heart to leave you.	
Anareto	It breaks my heart to lose you.	
Enrico	Oh eyes! once bright as stars,	2524
	how little light you have left!	
Anareto	Come now.	
Enrico	I am going to my death	
	with all my courage gone.	2528
Anareto	I cannot think or speak.	
Enrico	Wait, dear father.	
Anareto	Oh my son, my son!	
Enrico	Merciful, eternal God,	
	enthroned on high above the stars	2533
	in glory, hear my prayer.	
	I have been the worst of men	2536
	- the worst this world ever knew.	
	My crimes against you, oh God,	
	have been more than the sands of the sea.	2539
	But your mercy, Lord, is greater yet.	
	You suffered death on the cross	
	to redeem the world	
	from the sin of Adam.	
	Oh, grant me one drop	
	of the noble blood you shed there!	
	And you, pure light of dawn,	
	celestial Virgin whom angels attend,	

---

him, has been stripped from him at the last.

2532-87. Metre: romance assonating in A. Initially the new metre functions as a formal marker for Enrico's prayer.

2533-4. Literally 'who, in your castle, tread shining hills of stars'. For Heaven as castle cf. above, l. 187; the echo of Paulo's very different address to God is characteristic of the play's close-knit poetic texture.

2536-7. Enrico has described himself in these terms before, going on, there as here, to reflect on God's mercy (ll. 1981-3, 1998-2000).

2539-40. This stock image for an imponderably great number is one which the Shepherd, in his sermon to Paulo, did not use (cf. ll. 1513-18). Yet the two passages are clearly linked: what is happening here bears out the truth of the Shepherd's claims.

	de paraninfos cercada,	2550
	y siempre amparo os llamáis	
	de todos los pecadores,	
	yo lo soy, por mí rogad.	
	Decilde que se acuerde	
	a su Sacra Majestad	2555
	de cuando en aqueste mundo	
	empezó a peregrinar.	
	Acordalde los trabajos	
	que pasó en él por salvar	
	los que inocentes pagaron	2560
	por ajena voluntad.	
	Decilde que yo quisiera,	
	cuando comencé a gozar	
	entendimiento y razón,	
	pasar mil muertes y más	2565
	antes que haberle ofendido.	
Anareto	Adentro dan priesa.	
Enrico	Gran Señor, ¡misericordia!	
	No puedo deciros más.	
Anareto	(¡Que esto llegue a ver un padre!)	2570
Enrico	[Aparte] La enigma he entendido ya	
	de la voz y de la sombra:	
	la voz era angelical,	
	y la sombra era el demonio.	
Anareto	Vamos, hijo.	
Enrico	¿Quién oirá	2575
	ese nombre que no haga	
	de sus dos ojos un mar?	
	No os apartéis, padre mío,	
	hasta que hayan de expirar	
	mis ojos.	

2553. The last, least self-dramatizing, and most truthful of
Enrico's self-definitions: no longer 'the Devil' (ll. 495-6), 'the
worst man in the world' (ll. 1981-3), or even 'a man who doesn't
fancy dying' (ll. 1341-2), but simply 'I am a sinner.'

2560-1. Literally 'those who, innocent, paid by another's
will'. R observes that it seems strange to regard sinners, even
saved ones, as 'innocent', and that T prefers a more orthodox
formula. Enrico, however, is not expounding theology; he is
expressing his deepest feelings. These include the conviction
(voiced at ll. 2562-6) that his sins are things which, had he come
to grace earlier, he would not have done. 'Innocent' seems to
convey the same belief about other sinners, condemned initially by
the choice made by Adam ('another's will').

```
                perpetual help of every sinner,
                I am a sinner; pray for me.                        2553
                Entreat the Lord in majesty
                to think how once he too began
                his pilgrimage in this world.
                Recall all that he suffered here
                to save all those who paid                         2560
                their unconsenting share
                in man's old choice.
                Tell him, oh tell him,
                that once I knew reason and wisdom,                2563
                I would rather have faced death in all its shapes
                than given him offence.
Anareto         They are coming for us now.
Enrico          Lord have mercy upon me!
                It is the only thing
                that I can say to you.
Anareto         What sights for a father's eyes!                   2570
Enrico          [To himself] Now I understand                      2571
                why the voice was at odds with the shadow.
                The voice was from God,
                but the shadow was the Devil.
Anareto         Come, my son.
Enrico                          "My son" – who can hear
                himself given that name
                and not shed tears?                                2576
                Stay by me, father
                until it's all over.
```

2563-4. PKSDR: comencé; H: comienzo; C: comience. It is true that Enrico's enlightenment is a very recent thing. But the narrative tense (literally 'when I began to enjoy understanding and reason') is surely right for a convert who believes that the real story of his life begins with his conversion. The logic of Tirso's lines, once again, is a logic of character.

2570. Literally 'That a father should come to see this!' Though not exclusively his (Lisandro uses it at ll. 520-1), this type of formula is characteristic of Enrico (cf. ll. 2127, 2152, 2351). Anareto's use of it now seems to underline their kinship at this poignant moment.

2571-3. Enrico in his state of grace can read with full understanding the signs to which he responded so uncertainly before.

2576-7, 2582. Literally 'and not make of his two eyes a sea'; 'he is a sea of mercy'. The first use of the image refers to tears, the second to immensity. The notion of pity links the two. The sea image also has its place in the play's overall design (cf. Enrico's escape in Act II; above, note on ll. 1367-8).

Anareto	No hayas miedo.	2580
	Dios te dé favor.	
Enrico	Sí hará,	

que es mar de misericordia,
aunque yo voy muerto ya.

Anareto   Ten valor.

Enrico   En Dios confío.
Vamos, padre, donde están   2585
los que han de quitarme el ser
que vos me pudisteis dar.
                 Vanse y sale Paulo.

Paulo   Cansado de correr vengo
por este monte intrincado;
atrás la gente he dejado   2590
que a ajena costa mantengo.
    Al pie de este sauce verde
quiero un poco descansar,
por ver si acaso el pesar
de mi memoria se pierde.   2595
    Tú, fuente, que murmurando
vas entre guijas corriendo,
en tu fugitivo estruendo
plantas y aves alegrando,
    dame algún contento ahora,   2600
infunde al alma alegría
con esa corriente fría
y con esa voz sonora.
    Lisonjeros pajarillos,
que no entendidos cantáis,   2605
y holgazanes gorjeáis
entre juncos y tomillos,
    dad con picos sonorosos
y con acentos süaves

2582-4.   P punctuates as here.   R revises this by inserting a
full stop after <u>misericordia</u>, and making <u>Aunque yo voy muerto ya...</u>
<u>en Dios confío</u> into a single sentence, interrupted by Anareto.   But
it makes good sense to follow P in contrasting that dependence on
his own courage which even Anareto still urges upon Enrico with his
new-found and total trust in God.

2587.   T adds a clumsy little coda, with Enrico kneeling to be
blessed and declaring that he dies with a quiet mind.   No doubt
this was felt to be edifying in 1824; it has little to do with the

Anareto	Do not fear; I am with you.
	God be with you too.
Enrico	So he will be,
	for his mercy is boundless,	2582
	though I am dead already.
Anareto	Have courage.
Enrico	I have trust in God.
	Come, father; you gave me my being;
	let us go together to meet
	the men who will take it from me.	2587

Exeunt Anareto and Enrico.

Scene three
A clearing in the woods. Enter Paulo.

Paulo	I am tired of walking	2588
	the tangled paths of this wood.
	I have left my men behind
	- the men I maintain
	at the cost of those we rob! -
	and come to rest awhile
	under this green willow,
	and perhaps break free
	of the sorrow that haunts my mind.
	Swift-flowing spring,
	delighting birds and flowers
	as you chatter across the stones,
	give me, too, some delight.
	Set my heart at ease,
	with your cool waters
	and your murmuring voice.
	Little songbirds,
	innocent flatterers,
	untaught musicians, idlers
	among reed-beds and wild thyme,
	cheer my sad spirits
	with your melodies;
	with your gentle voices

---

imaginative depth at which Tirso's creativity works.
  2588-2615. Metre: <u>redondillas</u>.
  2588-9. <u>correr</u>. Not used here in its primary sense of 'to run', but rather with the meaning 'go through', often applied to vicissitudes or difficulties. The 'tangled wood' (<u>monte intrincado</u>) is, in one aspect, an inner landscape, representing Paulo's confused thoughts. For further implications of the natural description see Introduction, p. lxxii.

                    gloria a mis pesares graves   2610
                    y sucesos lastimosos.
                       En este verde tapete
                    jironado de cristal,
                    quiero divertir mi mal
                    que mi triste fin promete.   2615
              Echase a dormir y sale el Pastor con la corona,
                               deshaciéndola.

Pastor.   Selvas intrincadas,
                 verdes alamedas,
                 a quien de esperanzas
                 adorna Amaltea,
                 fuentes que corréis   2620
                 murmurando apriesa
                 por menudas guijas,
                 por blandas arenas,
                 ya vuelvo otra vez
                 a mirar la selva,   2625
                 a pisar los valles
                 que tanto me cuestan.
                 Yo soy el Pastor
                 que en vuestras riberas
                 guardé un tiempo alegre   2630
                 cándidas ovejas.
                 Sus blancos vellones
                 entre verdes felpas
                 jirones de plata
                 a los ojos eran.   2635
                 Era yo envidiado,
                 por ser guarda buena,
                 de muchos zagales
                 que ocupan la selva,
                 y mi Mayoral,   2640
                 que en ajena tierra
                 vive, me tenía
                 voluntad inmensa,
                 porque le llevaba,
                 cuando quería verlas,   2645
                 las ovejas blancas
                 como nieve en pellas.

_____

    2616-2777.   Metre: endechas: six-syllable lines (a traditional
form for lamentations) assonating in E-A.

                               180

```
                 help me rise above my cares.
                 On this green ground
                 beside this glittering stream,
                 at peace for a moment,
                 I can forget my end.
```
He lies down to sleep, and the Shepherd enters, with the
                 floral crown which he is now unmaking.

Shep.   Tangled forests, green glades,   2616
                 the colour of hope;
                 fresh springs, running over
                 firm pebbles, fine sand
                 - I am here once again
                 to look on the woodlands
                 and wander the valleys
                 that cost me such pain.
                 I am that shepherd
                 who once ranged your hillsides,
                 happily watching
                 his innocent sheep
                 - whiter than silver
                 the gleam of their fleeces,
                 scattered like jewels
                 over the green.
                 Once I was envied
                 as the best watchman
                 of all my companions
                 at work in the wood.
                 My master, who dwells
                 in a far-distant country,
                 loved me and praised me.
                 Whenever he wanted
                 his flocks led before him,
                 mine were the fairest
                 - their fleeces like snow.

2616-9. Literally 'Tangled forests, green poplar groves, whom
Amalthea adorns with hopes'. In Greek myth the she-goat Amalthea
suckled the infant Zeus. With her attribute, the Horn of Plenty,
she stood allegorically for nature's fruitfulness. The
constellation representing her with her kids appeared in the
spring, and was therefore linked with the renewal of greenery.
Green was the colour of hope. The reference, obscure to a modern
ear, and even incongruous, given the Shepherd's strongly Christian
associations (though this would have worried a 17th-century public
less), is dropped from the translation.

                              181

```
              Pero desde el día
              que una, la más buena,
              huyó del rebaño,                          2650
              lágrimas me anegan.
              Mis contentos todos
              convertí en tristezas,
              mis placeres vivos
              en memorias muertas.                      2655
              Cantaba en los valles
              canciones y letras,
              mas ya en triste llanto
              funestas endechas.
              Por tenerla amor,                         2660
              en esta floresta
              aquesta guirnalda
              comencé a tejerla.
              Mas no la gozó,
              que engañada y necia                      2665
              dejó quien la amaba
              con mayor firmeza.
              Y pues no la quiso,
              fuerza es que ya vuelva,
              por venganza justa,                       2670
              hoy a deshacerla.
Paulo         Pastor, que otra vez
              te vi en esta sierra,
              si no muy alegre,
              no con tal tristeza,                      2675
              el verte me admira.
Pastor.       ¡Ay, perdida oveja!
              ¡De qué gloria huyes,
              y a qué mal te allegas!
Paulo         ¿No es esa guirnalda                      2680
              la que en las florestas
              entonces tejías
              con gran diligencia?
Pastor.       Esta misma es;
              mas la oveja necia                        2685
              no quiere volver
              al bien que le espera,
              y ansí la deshago.
```

2669-71. The symbolism of unmaking the garland speaks for
itself, as does that of the Shepherd's complaint generally. The

```
              But the fairest of all, now,
              the favourite, has left me
              and fled from the sheepfold,
              and I am all tears.
              In sorrow I wander
              where once I was happy.
              My joys have the life
              of cold memories – no more.
              And the songs that I sang
              in the days of my gladness
              are changed to sad music.
              My lost lamb – I loved her,
              and here in this forest
              I wove her this garland,
              but she never knew,
              and fickle and foolish,
              she left me, despising
              a love that was faithful.
              So now I unmake it.                          2669
              She would never have wanted it.
              She was untrue.
Paulo         Shepherd, I've seen you
              before in these mountains,
              not happy, it's true,
              but not grieving as now.
              How strangely you've altered!
Shep.         Oh little lost lamb!
              what glory you run from,
              to run to what peril!
Paulo         Is this the same garland
              you wove then, so carefully?
Shep.         It is, but the stray
              is foolish and stubborn.
              She will not return
              to the good that awaits her.
              So now I unmake it.
```

---

tone here is uncompromising: literally 'I must now unmake it again in just retribution.' Yet the keynote is not vengeance; rather, it is a necessary reciprocity. The moment is, like Anareto's rejection of Enrico's sonship, still part of a call to repentance. More truly chilling is the note of cool curiosity in Paulo's reply.

2686. PR: no quiere; SDT: no quiso ('she would not'), making the refusal past and irrevocable. But the whole point of the scene is that this is not so.

Paulo	Si acaso volviera,
	zagalejo amigo, 2690
	¿no la recibieras?
Pastor.	Enojado estoy,
	mas la gran clemencia
	de mi Mayoral
	dice que aunque vuelvan, 2695
	si antes fueron blancas,
	al rebaño negras,
	que las dé mis brazos
	y, sin extrañeza,
	requiebros las diga 2700
	y palabras tiernas.
Paulo	Pues es superior
	fuerza es que obedezcas.
Pastor.	Yo obedeceré;
	pero no quiere ella 2705
	volver a mis voces,
	en sus vicios ciega.
	Ya de aquestos montes
	en las altas peñas
	la llamé con silbos 2710
	y avisé con señas.
	Ya por los jarales,
	por incultas selvas,
	la anduve a buscar:
	¡qué de ello me cuesta! 2715
	Ya traigo las plantas
	de jaras diversas
	y agudos espinos
	rotas y sangrientas.
	No puedo hacer más. 2720
Paulo	En lágrimas tiernas
	baña el Pastorcillo
	las mejillas bellas.
	Pues te desconoce,
	olvídate de ella 2725
	y no llores más.

2703. Paulo, following the distorted view of God which he has long held (cf. above, l. 163), interprets the Shepherd's relation to his master, and to the latter's saving intention, as part of a pattern of power and compulsion.

Paulo	If she should come back,
	shepherd-boy – tell me:
	would you still welcome her?
Shep.	She made me angry.
	But my great master
	has infinite mercy,
	and if they return,
	though their fleeces, once white,
	are blackened and fouled,
	I must welcome all strays
	to my arms without coldness,
	and speak comfort to them
	and kind words of love.
Paulo	Your master's your master.
	You have to obey him.

Paulo   If she should come back,
        shepherd-boy – tell me:
        would you still welcome her?
Shep.   She made me angry.
        But my great master
        has infinite mercy,
        and if they return,
        though their fleeces, once white,
        are blackened and fouled,
        I must welcome all strays
        to my arms without coldness,
        and speak comfort to them
        and kind words of love.
Paulo   Your master's your master.
        You have to obey him.   2703
Shep.   So I will, but the stray
        no longer heeds me.
        Blind in her folly
        she wanders at will.
        High in the rocks
        and the crags of these mountains,
        I called and I whistled
        to bid her come home.
        Down in the thickets,   2712
        the bushes and briars,
        I struggled to seek her
        – the pain that it cost me!
        The soles of my feet
        are all bloodied and broken
        with the print of the barbs
        and the thorns that I trod.
        What more can I do?
Paulo   (The shepherd is weeping,
        poor fellow!) Why, nothing,   2724
        since she has rejected you;
        only forget her
        and dry your tears.

2712-19. For comment on the implicit identification of the Shepherd with Jesus Christ, see Introduction, p. lxx.

2724-6. Paulo accepts the strictly rational reciprocity which informs one part (ll. 2669-71) of the Shepherd's utterances. But he rejects every other element in them, including those very regrets which keep any hope for the lost creature alive.

```
Pastor.   Que lo haga es fuerza.
          Volved, bellas flores,
          a cubrir la tierra,
          pues que no fue digna                    2730
          de vuestra belleza.
          Veamos si allá
          con la tierra nueva
          la pondrán guirnalda
          tan rica y tan bella.                     2735
          Quedaos, montes míos,
          desiertos y selvas,
          a Dios, porque voy
          con la triste nueva
          a mi Mayoral,                             2740
          y cuando lo sepa
          (aunque ya lo sabe)
          sentirá su mengua,
          no la ofensa suya,
          aunque es tanta ofensa.                   2745
          Lleno voy a verle
          de miedo y vergüenza:
          lo que ha de decirme
          fuerza es que lo sienta.
          Diráme: "Zagal,                           2750
          ¿ansí las ovejas
          que yo os encomiendo
          guardáis?"  ¡Triste pena!
          Yo responderé...
          No hallaré respuesta,                     2755
          si no es que mi llanto
          la respuesta sea.
                        Vase.
```

2727. The Spanish is delicately ambiguous: is the Shepherd
compelled to forget the lost sheep, or to shed tears? In the
play's poetic logic – at one, here, with its theology – he must do
both. The ambiguity is sacrificed in the translation, though both
elements are present in the speech which follows.

2732-5. A possible alternative reading would be 'Let us see if
there, in the new country [i.e. the territory into which the sinful
soul has strayed], they will put a garland on her so rich and so
fair.' This amounts to asking whether the rewards of sin can make
up for the loss of salvation. Con la tierra nueva – 'with' rather
than 'in' the new land – reads oddly in such a context, but the

```
Shep.      Then so I must.                                    2727
           Go back, lovely flowers,
           to cover the earth.
           My lamb could not deserve
           beauty like yours.
           In this new ground, perhaps,                       2732
           you will bloom again
           to make her a garland
           as rich, as rare.
           My woods and lonely hills,
           I leave you now.
           Farewell, for I must bring
           this sad news to my master.
           And when he knows it                                2741
           (though he knows it already),
           he will feel the loss,
           not the offence
           (though the offence is grave).
           I am ashamed and afraid
           to come before him.
           I know what he will say.
           His words will go to my heart.
           He will say: "Lad,
           is this the way you keep
           the sheep I give you?"
           Alas, what shall I answer?                          2754
           There is nothing to answer,
           unless my tears are the answer.
                        Exit the Shepherd.
```

---

early editions are unanimous on this point. More tellingly, the question as applied to Paulo would be pointless even in a worldly sense: he has got no reward whatever from his sin, but lives in the acutest misery. The translation, therefore, construes the _tierra nueva_ as the 'new ground' where the flowers now fall, and makes the flowers themselves the subject of _la pondrán guirnalda_ ('will make her a garland'). This would link the notion of a persisting, if residual, hope with the theme (above, ll. 2616-19) of natural renewal.

2741-4. The Shepherd's master is clearly identified as God: he has supernatural knowledge and a divine compassion.

2754-7. In the most obvious allegorical reading, the Shepherd plays the part of a subordinate. Yet he also represents the Good Shepherd himself, giving these lines an especially important resonance. See Introduction, pp. lxx-lxxi.

Paulo	La historia parece	
	de mi vida aquesta.	
	De este Pastorcillo	2760
	no sé lo que sienta;	
	que tales palabras	
	fuerza es que prometan	
	oscuras enigmas.	
	Mas, ¿qué luz es ésta	2765
	que a la luz del sol	
	sus rayos se afrentan?	
	Música celeste	
	en los aires suena,	
	y, a lo que diviso,	2770
	dos ángeles llevan	
	una alma gloriosa	
	a la excelsa esfera.	
	¡Dichosa mil veces,	
	alma, pues hoy llegas	2775
	donde tus trabajos	
	fin alegre tengan!	

Con la música suben dos ángeles al alma de Enrico por una
apariencia y prosigue Paulo:

	Grutas y plantas agrestes,	
	a quien el hielo corrompe,	
	¿no veis como el cielo rompe	2780
	ya sus cortinas celestes?	
	Ya rompiendo densas nubes	
	y esos transparentes velos,	
	alma, a gozar de los cielos	
	feliz y gloriosa subes.	2785
	Ya vas a gozar la palma	
	que la ventura te ofrece:	

2758-64. Intellectually, Paulo knows what to think of the
Shepherd's story. But he cannot respond to it on any other level;
instead, he drifts into speculation on possible hidden meanings.
This is perhaps a natural reaction if he has just awoken,
bewildered, from a dream. Yet it is strangely contrasted with his
over-responsiveness to his original dream, and to the Devil's
message in Act I. In any event, the further vision of Enrico saved
ought to put him on the right track now. It does not.

2777-8. This stage-direction might well begin to take effect a
few lines earlier – perhaps at l. 2770, where Paulo starts to
describe his vision. For comment on this tableau see Introduction,
p. xlv.

Paulo	This story is so like my own.	2758

Paulo   This story is so like my own.   2758
What am I to make of this shepherd?
His words must carry in them
some deep and complex mystery.
But where does that light come from,
suddenly brighter than the sun?
Heavenly music filling the air!
and now a vision
— two angels, bearing a soul in glory
up to the heights of Heaven.
Oh, happy, happy soul, to go
where all your labours
will find their joyful end!   2777

Music. A picture is seen of two angels, bearing to heaven the soul of Enrico.

Woodlands and caves   2778
that feel the grip of earthly frosts,
see how the heavens
rend all their veils apart.
And through those cloudy canopies,
to live in glory in the skies,
the soul triumphant takes its rise.
Oh happy soul, reap the reward   2786
your fortune has reserved.

2778-2837. Metre: redondillas.

2778. The change to a new metre is another possible cue for Paulo's awakening. But in that case we have to determine whether he sees the vision of the ascending soul while asleep or while awake. If the former, ll. 2782-5, which describe the withdrawal of the apariencia, become a puzzle, for Paulo is certainly awake when he delivers these lines. How can the vision persist until then? If the latter, what is it that the still sleeping Paulo has described already at ll. 2770-3? It seems better to have him wake up beforehand – perhaps at l. 2758, as suggested.

2786-8. The sight of Enrico saved – or, indeed, of any soul saved – ought to carry a message of hope for Paulo. In fact it only reminds him of his belief that he is cut off from salvation. This is reinforced by two contradictory, but equally misleading attitudes, both widely diffused throughout the text of El condenado: the strenuous moralism which sees salvation as a question of personal deserving (merecer), and the passive fatalism which attributes it to luck (ventura).

| | ¡triste del que no merece | |
| | lo que tú mereces, alma! | |

Sale Galván.

Galván	Advierte, Paulo famoso,	2790
	que por el monte ha bajado	
	un escuadrón concertado	
	de gente y armas copioso,	
	que viene sólo a prendernos.	
	Si no pretendes morir,	2795
	solamente, Paulo, huir	
	es lo que puede valernos.	
Paulo	¿Escuadrón viene?	
Galván	Esto es cierto:	
	ya se divisa la hilera	
	con su caja y su bandera.	2800
	No escapas de preso o muerto	
	si aguardas.	
Paulo	¿Quién la ha traído?	
Galván	Villanos, si no me engaño,	
	como hacemos tanto daño	
	en este monte escondido,	2805
	de aldeas circunvecinas	
	se han juntado.	
Paulo	Pues matallos.	
Galván	¿Que te animas a esperallos?	
Paulo	Mal quién es Paulo imaginas.	
Galván	Nuestros peligros son llanos.	2810
Paulo	Sí, pero advierte también	
	que basta un hombre de bien	
	para cuatro mil villanos.	
Galván	Ya tocan. ¿No los oyes?	
Paulo	Cierra,	
	y no receles el daño,	2815
	que antes que fuese ermitaño	
	supe también qué era guerra.	

[<u>Vanse</u>.]

2814. <u>Cierra</u>. The word of command for an attack, as in
<u>¡Santiago y cierra España!</u>, reputedly the battle-cry of medieval
warriors against the Moors.

2816-7. We might never have suspected this of Paulo, yet it is
wholly consistent with his violent temper, his yet more violent
imagination, and his rapid rise to success as a bandit chief.

2817-8. By 11. 2821-2 Galván is off stage. Some plausible way
of getting him there is needed. It would be strange if, following

<pre>
              Pity the man who cannot earn
              what such a soul deserved.
                   The vision disappears. Enter Galván.
Galván   Paulo, be quick, they're coming!
              A whole army of men
              marching through the wood
              in good order, and well-equipped.
              It's for us that they're coming.
              Stay here if you'd rather get killed,
              but if we want to live, Paulo,
              we'd better run for it.
Paulo   An army, you say?
Galván   That's right.
              Look down there, and you'll see them
              marching along with drums and banners.
              They'll take you prisoner or kill you
              if you stay here, for sure!
Paulo   Who brought them?
Galván   It was the peasants, I reckon
              (we've made too many raids
              from our hideout here).
              Three or four villages got together
              and...
Paulo   Kill them then!
Galván   You mean you're stopping to put up a fight?
Paulo   You don't know who Paulo is yet, do you?
Galván   I know we're in trouble, that's all.
Paulo   Yes, we're in trouble, but just remember:
              one real man is worth
              four thousand of these peasants.
Galván   There's the drum! Don't you hear it?
Paulo   Strike home and never heed the danger!   2814
              I was a soldier before I was a hermit   2816
              and I know something of war.   2817
                   Exeunt Paulo and Galván.
</pre>

Paulo's stirring exhortation, his henchman were to rush off and
leave him; presumably, then, the two leave together. There follows
a rapid sequence of stage-fights: first Paulo and then Galván
contending with the peasants. The stage-direction at this point is
remodelled accordingly. The original (PR) called for the entry of
'all the peasants who can, armed, and a Judge.' A cast of fifteen
- the minimum, with doubling, for a production of El condenado -
ought to be able to manage three or four peasants here, and the
same number at ll. 2821-2.

**Salen los labradores que pudieren, con armas
[peleando con Paulo], y un Juez.**

Juez   Hoy pagaréis las maldades
que en este monte habéis hecho.

Paulo   En ira se abrasa el pecho.   2820
Soy Enrico en las crueldades.

**Entralos acuchillando y sale Galván por otra puerta
huyendo, y tras él muchos villanos.**

Vill.1   Ea, ladrones, rendíos.

Galván Mejor nos está el morir;
mas yo presumo hüir,
que para eso tengo bríos.   2825

Vanse y dice dentro Paulo:

Paulo   Con las flechas me acosáis,
y con ventaja reñís:
más de doscientos venís
para veinte que buscáis.

Juez   Por el monte va corriendo.   2830

Baje Paulo por el monte rodando, lleno de sangre.

Paulo   Ya no bastan pies ni manos;
muerte me han dado villanos;
de mi cobardía me ofendo.
Volveré a darles la muerte;
pero no puedo. ¡Ay de mí!   2835
El cielo a quien ofendí
se venga de aquesta suerte.

Sale Pedrisco.

Pedr.   Como en las culpas de Enrico
no me hallaron culpado,
luego que públicamente   2840
los jueces le ajusticiaron,
me echaron la puerta afuera,
y vengo al monte. ¿Qué aguardo?

2821. Paulo's identification with Enrico is complete, and almost entirely perverse. It is achieved through cruelty, yet cruelty, even in his worst days, was never all that there was to Enrico. By now, of course, he has ceased to be anything like what Paulo supposes him to be.

2830. There is no indication that the Judge's voice is heard off stage, but that is where he has to be.

2830-1. Paulo - behind the scenes just long enough to be made to look suitably blood-boltered - now falls from the backstage gallery (as R thinks, down a staircase leading onto the stage).

2836-7. These lines do not express repentance; they simply state

In the woods; a little later.
Enter Paulo, fighting with many armed Peasants, led by a
Judge.

Judge   The time has come to pay
           for all your acts of banditry.
Paulo   My blood is up; burning with fury,
           in cruelty I am Enrico!   2821

He drives them out, still fighting. From the other side
enter Galván, pursued by many Peasants.

Peasant Thieves! Give yourselves up!
Galván   We'd be better off dead...
           but I'll chance it and run.
           I reckon I've strength to make it.

Galván and his pursuers go off fighting. Paulo's voice is
heard off stage.

Paulo   A near miss that time! Keep trying!
           You've the advantage of us
           - sending two hundred men
           to bring in twenty!
Judge   [Off stage]
           He's getting away through the wood.   2830

Paulo falls onto the stage, as if he had rolled downhill
through the wood. He is covered in blood.

Paulo   Neither hands nor feet
           will help me now; I'm done for.
           Killed by peasants! I despise myself!
           What a cowardly end! But I'll come back
           and kill them again... I can't do it.
           No, this is Heaven's revenge   2836
           for my crimes against God.

Enter Pedrisco.

Pedr.   When they condemned Enrico
           they found me "not guilty",
           and as soon as they'd hanged him
           they turned me loose again.
           So I came back to the woods.

---

how Paulo sees events as working. He expects Heaven to avenge
itself because he believes in a vengeful God. It may even have
been a part of his purpose to justify such vengeance (cf. above,
ll. 1000-4). In fact, what Providence sends him at this point is
Pedrisco, bringing human compassion and the news that Enrico, after
all, is saved - a last clue to hope.
   2838-3006. Metre: romance assonating in A-O. Appropriate for
the narrative passages at ll. 2838-51, 2867-84, and 2945-74.

	¿Qué miro? La selva y monte	
	anda todo alborotado.	2845
	Allí dos villanos corren,	
	las espadas en las manos.	
	Allí va herido Fineo,	
	y allí huye Celio, y Fabio,	
	y aquí, que es grande ventura,	2850
	tendido está el fuerte Paulo.	
Paulo	¿Volvéis, villanos, volvéis?	
	La espada tengo en la mano;	
	no estoy muerto, vivo estoy,	
	aunque ya de aliento falto.	2855
Pedr.	Pedrisco soy, Paulo mío.	
Paulo	Pedrisco, llega a mis brazos.	
Pedr.	¿Cómo estás ansí?	
Paulo	¡Ay de mí!	
	Muerte me han dado villanos,	
	pero ya que estoy muriendo,	2860
	saber de ti, amigo, aguardo:	
	¿qué hay del suceso de Enrico?	
Pedr.	En la plaza le ahorcaron	
	de Nápoles.	
Paulo	Pues ansí,	
	¿quién duda que condenado	2865
	estará al infierno ya?	
Pedr.	Mira lo que dices, Paulo;	
	que murió cristianamente,	
	confesado y comulgado,	
	y abrazado con un Cristo,	2870
	en cuya vista enclavados	
	los ojos, pidió perdón	
	y misericordia, dando	
	tierno llanto a sus mejillas	
	y a los presentes espanto.	2875
	Fuera de aqueso, en muriendo,	
	resonó en los aires claros	
	una música divina,	

2848–9. _Fineo... Celio... Fabio_. We learn nothing more about these members of Paulo's gang (Celio has been mentioned briefly at ll. 1659, 1855), but the invented names enhance the sense of a life extending beyond the confines of the play. For a similarly 'novelistic' effect cf. above, ll. 1925, 2816–7.

2850. _ventura_ in this context means 'ill fortune' and is rendered with this in mind.

```
          But... wait a minute.
          There's something wrong here.
          What's all that disturbance?
          What are those peasants doing
          with swords in their hands?
          They've got Fineo                          2848
          wounded down there - and there's Celio and Fabio,
          running for their lives.  And who's here?
          - my God!  Would you credit it?            2850
          It's Paulo, Paulo himself
          and I think he's dead.
Paulo     So you've come back!  Well, you peasants,
          you see I can still hold a sword.
          You haven't killed me yet; I'm alive.
          I can still... just... breathe...
Pedr.     Paulo, old friend, it's Pedrisco.          2856
Paulo     Pedrisco, how glad I am
          to see you!
Pedr.                  How did this happen?
Paulo     I am ashamed to tell you.
          I let myself be killed by peasants.
          But since I am dying, tell me, friend,
          what happened to Enrico?
Pedr.     They hanged him in the square at Naples.
Paulo     Of course, of course...                    2864
          And now his soul will be damned
          in Hell forever.
Pedr.     Watch what you're saying, Paulo.
          He died like a Christian:
          confessed; made his communion;
          knelt and embraced the cross,
          and fixing his eyes on Our Lord,
          begged for his pardon and pity
          with tears pouring down his cheeks.
          Everyone was amazed.
          And that wasn't all - when he died,
          people heard heavenly music
```

2856. Pedrisco addresses Paulo in terms of tender familiarity,
hardly conceivable in their former relationship.
   2864. **Pues ansí** is first a reaction complete in itself - 'So
that's how it is' - and then a preliminary to Paulo's full response
- 'If that's how it is, who can doubt...?'

	y para mayor milagro	
	y evidencia más notoria	2880
	dos paraninfos al lado	
	se vieron patentemente,	
	que llevaban entre ambos	
	el alma de Enrico al cielo.	
Paulo	¿A Enrico, el hombre más malo	2885
	que crió naturaleza?	
Pedr.	¿De aquesto te espantas, Paulo,	
	cuando es tan piadoso Dios?	
Paulo	Pedrisco, eso ha sido engaño:	
	otra alma fue la que vieron,	2890
	no la de Enrico.	
Pedr.	¡Dios santo,	
	reducilde vos!	
Paulo	Yo muero.	
Pedr.	Mira que Enrico gozando	
	está de Dios; pide a Dios	
	perdón.	
Paulo	¿Cómo ha de darlo	2895
	a un hombre que le ha ofendido	
	como yo?	
Pedr.	¿Qué estás dudando?	
	¿No perdonó a Enrico?	
Paulo	Dios es piadoso...	
Pedr.	Es muy claro.	
Paulo	Pero no con tales hombres.	2900
	Ya muero; llega tus brazos.	
Pedr.	Procura tener su fin.	
Paulo	Esa palabra me ha dado	
	Dios: si Enrico se salvó,	
	también yo salvarme aguardo.	2905

Muere.

2879–80. Literally 'a greater miracle and a more noteworthy proof'. The miracle is proof, essentially, of God's will and power to save Enrico – or Paulo. To reinforce the latter point, the details in Pedrisco's tale – the music, the two angels – are identical with those of Paulo's vision in ll. 2768–73.

2887–91. Pedrisco's cry of reducilde (literally 'break him down!') is understandable. But to 'reduce' Paulo is just what God will not do; he carries, inescapably, the burden of his own freewill.

196

	high up in the air; and another miracle	2879
	- still greater - they saw a vision:	
	two angels, bearing his soul	
	to Heaven between them.	
Paulo	Enrico! The worst man ever!	
	That monster!	
Pedr.	Why should you wonder at it,	2887
	when God is so merciful?	
Paulo	Pedrisco, you must have been wrong!	
	It was some other soul they saw,	
	not Enrico's.	
Pedr.	Oh, dear God!	
	Convince him, quickly.	
Paulo	I am dying.	
Pedr.	Listen: Enrico's in Heaven now;	
	and you must pray to God for pardon.	
Paulo	And how could God forgive	
	a man who has offended him	
	as I have done?	
Pedr.	How can you doubt it?	
	Didn't he spare Enrico?	
Paulo	God is merciful...	2899
Pedr.	Of course!	
Paulo	But never to such men.	
	I am dying; hold me, Pedrisco.	
Pedr.	Try to end as he did.	
Paulo	God gave me that promise:	2903
	if Enrico was saved,	
	I will be saved; I've a right to expect it.	

Paulo dies.

2899. 'God is merciful' - the same phrase that Enrico used
(above, l. 2404), while still uncertain whether he should repent.
Paulo's state of mind is not too far from Enrico's in that earlier
speech. But he turns away from the reflection at once: 'never to
such men...' Men like Enrico, men like himself - Paulo knows the
rules. He should do, for tragically, he himself has made them; his
moralism locks him firmly into his fatalism.
2903-5. In no sense are these last lines a turning away from
despair. Assent to the proposition that he must be saved because
Enrico is saved does not liberate Paulo from the mechanistic view
of fatality, the moralistic calculus, or the notion of God as
merciless which have dogged him from the beginning. See also
Introduction, p. lx.

Pedr.	Lleno el cuerpo de lanzadas,	
	quedó muerto el desdichado.	
	Las suertes fueron trocadas:	
	Enrico, con ser tan malo,	
	se salvó, y éste al infierno	2910
	se fue por desconfiado.	
	Cubriré el cuerpo infeliz,	
	cortando a estos sauces ramos.	
	Mas, ¿qué gente es la que viene?	

<u>Salen los villanos</u>.

Juez	Si el capitán se ha escapado,	2915
	poca diligencia ha sido.	
Vill.1	Yo lo vi caer rodando,	
	pasado de mil saetas,	
	de los altivos peñascos.	
Juez	Un hombre está aquí.	2920
Pedr.	¡Ay, Pedrisco desdichado!	
	Esta vez te dan carena.	
Vill.2	Este es criado de Paulo	
	y cómplice en sus delitos.	
Galván	Tú mientes como villano,	2925
	que sólo lo fui de Enrico,	
	que de Dios está gozando.	
Pedr.	Y yo, Galván...	
	...Galvanito hermano,	
	no me descubras aquí,	2930
	por amor de Dios.	
Juez	Si acaso	
	me dices dónde se esconde	
	el capitán que buscamos,	
	yo te daré libertad.	
	Habla.	
Pedr.	Buscarle es en vano	2935
	cuando es muerto.	
Juez	¿Cómo muerto?	
Pedr.	De varias flechas y dardos	
	pasado le hallé, señor,	
	con la muerte agonizando	
	en aqueste mismo sitio.	2940

2906. <u>lanzadas</u>. Lances were not mentioned as part of the peasants' weaponry, and would, in any case, be little use for fighting in the woods. Translated, therefore, simply as 'wounds'.

2908. Literally 'Their fates were interchanged.' Cf. l. 1017.

2912. PR: <u>Cubran</u> - 'let them cover' - but only Pedrisco is there to do it. H: <u>cubriré</u> seems well-found. No doubt Pedrisco hides

```
Pedr.    He had so many wounds                          2906
         he could live no longer, poor Paulo!
         See how their luck turned out!                 2908
         Who could have expected this?
         Enrico, though he was so wicked,
         is saved, and Paulo goes
         to Hell, damned for despair.
         I'll cover his poor body                        2912
         with boughs from these willows.
         But now someone's coming...
```
Enter the Peasants and Judge, with Galván as their prisoner.

```
Judge    If the captain has escaped
         all our work was in vain.
Peasant  I saw him roll down the hillside
         with hundreds of arrows in him,
         shot from the cliffs up above.
Judge    There's someone hidden in those trees.
Pedr.    Here it comes, Pedrisco;
         you'll get the treatment this time!
Peasant  This fellow was Paulo's helper
         and right-hand man in all his crimes.
Galván   You're a liar; you ought to know
         I only served Enrico
         - and Enrico is with God.                       2927
Pedr.    And so did I, Galván.
         [Aside, to Galván] And for God's sake, old friend,
         don't give me away!
         - you wouldn't do that, now, would you?
Judge    If you will tell me where
         your captain is hiding,
         you shall go free. Now, talk.
Pedr.    [Emerging] There's no point in looking for him;
         he's dead.
Judge                  Dead? How?
Pedr.    Wounded with many arrows
         - that's how I found him, sir,
         in the last throes of his agony,
         here, on this very spot.
```

---

the body behind the curtains of the rear-of-stage recess. For
comment on el cuerpo infeliz see Introduction, p. lxvii.
   2926. PK: Enrique; SR: Enrico.
   2927. How, in any case, can Galván know this? See Introduction,
p. lii.

199

Juez	Y ¿dónde está el cuerpo?
Pedr.	Entre aquestos ramos
	le metí. Mas, ¿qué visión
	es causa de tanto espanto?

<u>Descúbrese fuego y Paulo lleno de llamas.</u>

Paulo	Si a Paulo buscando vais,	2945
	bien podéis ya ver a Paulo,	
	ceñido el cuerpo de fuego	
	y de culebras cercado.	
	No doy la culpa a ninguno	
	de los tormentos que paso:	2950
	sólo a mí me doy la culpa,	
	pues fui causa de mi daño.	
	Pedí a Dios que me dijese	
	el fin que tendría en llegando	
	de mi vida el postrer día;	2955
	ofendíle, caso es llano;	
	y como la ofensa vio	
	de las almas el contrario,	
	incitóme con querer	
	perseguirme con engaños.	2960
	Forma de un ángel tomó	
	y engañóme; que a ser sabio,	
	con su engaño me salvara;	
	pero fui desconfiado	
	de la gran piedad de Dios,	2965
	que hoy a su juicio llegando,	
	me dijo: "Baja, maldito	
	de mi Padre, al centro airado	
	de los oscuros abismos,	
	adonde has de estar penando."	2970

2943-4. Spoken in the original by Pedrisco: 'But what vision is
the cause of such great astonishment?' In the translation the
function of these two lines is transposed to the opening of Paulo's
speech.

2944-5. Pedrisco draws back the curtain to reveal Paulo in
torment. The 'flames' may have been conventional representations
in coloured paper, but the fire could have been simulated by some
special effect from below the stage (cf. note to ll. 2974-5).

2947-8. Tirso and his audiences shared a literal belief in these
physical horrors of damnation. Their verbal and visual presence
may be disconcerting to a public which does not. But other aspects
of Paulo's speech still convince: its unremitting self-reproach
seems the logical outcome of his utterly ruined life.

| Judge | Where is he, then? |
| Pedr. | It was among these branches |

```
Judge      Where is he, then?
Pedr.                     It was among these branches
           that I laid his body.                         2943
           A fire appears and in it Paulo wreathed in flames.
Paulo                          Why stare?                 2944
           Why be amazed?  If you seek Paulo,
           here he is - can you not see him? -
           his body ringed with flames                   2947
           and gripped by fiery serpents.
           I can blame no one for it
           - this torture which I bear -
           none but myself, for I brought it all about.
           I prayed to God to tell me
           what end I should have when I came
           to the last day of my life.
           That was a sin; the case is clear,            2956
           and, as the enemy of man
           was quick to see the sin committed,
           he it was who drove me on,
           pursuing me with his deceits.
           He took on the guise of an angel
           and tried to trick me; had I been wiser,      2962
           his very stratagem might have led me
           to my salvation.  But I despaired             2964
           of God's abundant mercy.
           And now, when I come to his judgment,
           this is his word for me: "Depart,you cursed,  2967
           into everlasting darkness,
           to be punished in the abyss."
```

2956. The offence lay in the demand for a 'natural certainty' of salvation; see Introduction, p. xl.

2962-3. con su engaño might mean 'despite his deceit', or possibly 'through his deceit'. Either would be apt. Paulo, if wise, could have seen through the Devil's message. But by taking Enrico as an extreme example of the kind of man God's mercy could still reach, he could have been strengthened in his faith.

2964-5. Paulo's fault, it must be stressed again, does not consist in failing to assent to some obligatory proposition about God; it is a failure of trust. As a result of that failure, he can only believe in a God who rejects him.

2967-70. The words of the curse are loosely modelled on Matthew 25: 41 which, in its fuller context, is a condemnation for lack of charity. It is no coincidence that there has been little of that in Paulo's religion.

	¡Malditos mis padres sean	
	mil veces, pues me engendraron!	
	¡Y yo también sea maldito,	
	pues que fui desconfiado!	
	Húndese por el tablado y sale fuego.	
Juez	Misterios son del Señor.	2975
Galván	¡Pobre y desdichado Paulo!	
Pedr.	¡Y venturoso de Enrico,	
	que de Dios está gozando!	
Juez	Porque toméis escarmiento,	
	no pretendo castigaros;	2980
	libertad doy a los dos.	
Pedr.	Vivas infinitos años,	
	hermano Galván, pues ya	
	de ésta nos hemos librado,	
	¿qué piensas hacer desde hoy?	2985
Galván	Desde hoy pienso ser un santo.	
Pedr.	Mirando estoy con los ojos	
	que no haréis muchos milagros.	
Galván	Esperanza en Dios.	
Pedr.	Amigo,	
	quien fuere desconfiado,	2990
	mire el ejemplo presente,	
	no más.	
Juez	A Nápoles vamos	
	a contar este suceso.	
Pedr.	Y porque éste es tan arduo	
	y difícil de creer,	2995
	siendo verdadero el caso,	
	vaya el que fuere curioso	
	(porque sin ser escribano	
	dé fe de ello) a Belarmino;	
	y si no, más dilatado	3000
	en la Vida de los Padres	

2971-2. This curse is Paulo's only direct mention of his parents; contrast Enrico's bond with Anareto.

2974-5. The effect of Paulo's disappearance was probably worked with a trapdoor (Shergold, 229).

2975-8. The survivors react to these portents according to their not very impressive capacities: the Judge and Galván with the most bathetic of platitudes; Pedrisco with the rather smugly pious phrase previously used by Galván to ward off his own punishment (above, ll. 2926-7).

2985-91. For comment on these exchanges see Introduction,

```
            A curse upon my father,                          2971
            and my mother, that she bore me!
            And a curse upon my own head too,
            mistrustful and despairing!                      2974
        He is plunged out of sight as the flames rise up.
Judge       God's ways are strange.                          2975
Galván      Poor, unhappy Paulo!
Pedr.       And happy Enrico
            who is now with God!
Judge       You'll learn your lesson from this.
            Why should I try to punish you?
            Both of you can go free.
Pedr.       Congratulations, Galván
            - we're both well out of that!
            What'll you do with yourself                     2985
            from now on?
Galván                      As of today,
            I reckon I'll become a saint.
Pedr.       The way I see it,
            you aren't going to do many miracles.
Galván      You've got to trust in God.
Pedr.                               That's true, friend.
            Anyone who doesn't
            should look at what's just happened.
Judge       On to Naples, then,
            - let's go and tell our story.
Pedr.       It's a hard one to believe                       2994
            - though the tale's quite true.
            If you want witnesses
            (though, not being magistrates,                  2998
            you might not), you can look it up
            in Bellarmine's book, or in                      2999
            the great Lives of the Fathers
```

---

p. lxviii.

2994-3006. For the transformation of Pedrisco in this final
speech see Introduction, p. lxvii.

2998-9. Literally 'so that, without being a notary, he may
provide sworn testimony of it'. It is not clear whether 'he' is
Bellarmine or, as seems more likely, the curious spectator who
wants chapter and verse. The essential element, in either case, is
the ironic rejection of legalism - a concern very much in line with
the play's major themes.

2999-3002. For these references see Introduction, p. xxxviii-ix
The sources are far from easy to find, as Tirso, one suspects, knew
very well.

podrá fácilmente hallarlo.
Y con aquesto da fin
a **El mayor desconfiado**,
y pena y gloria trocadas.   3005
El cielo os guarde mil años.

Fin

3004. It was customary for a <u>comedia</u> to end with a reference to
its own title (which, as in the present case, may not be precisely
in the form by which the play is generally known). Here we have
title and subtitle, the latter highlighting the play's double
construction, through the 'fortunes exchanged' motif.

3006. The conventional ending might also request applause, or
pardon for the author's faults. But the ending of <u>El condenado</u>
involves the damnation of a human soul, which is arguably no matter

```
(that gives the longer version)
- you'll find it easily, I'm sure.
And now our play is ended
of the man DAMNED FOR DESPAIR                    3004
or GLORY AND PUNISHMENT
EXCHANGED.   And so, farewell.
God grant you all long life!                     3006
```

The End

---

for applause. As for the issue of forgiveness, that has been
explored on a more serious level altogether. Pedrisco, then,
salutes the audience in words which, still within the tradition,
avoid these formulae. They also carry a certain ambiguity: 'May
Heaven keep you for a thousand years.' Everyone desires long life;
everyone needs to be protected by Heaven. But, given the human
fallibility displayed in what has gone before, the wish remains
enigmatic. The audience still have their own salvation to work out.